The Icarus Parallel

~

W. M. Pearson

Heron's Wing

Heron's Wing Press
Williamsburg, VA

Heron's Wing Press is a creative collaborative of small press authors whose mission is, "writers helping writers." If you would like more information, a media event with an author, or reproduction information please go to www.heronswing.com

~

*For their unending support and enthusiasm for the
realization of this project, this book is lovingly
dedicated to Barbra Amerson and Rebecca Hill.*

*A special acknowledgement, too, for the
inspiration provided by the people of Crete.*

Chapter 1

Their war began before any of them could remember. They were unwelcome and unwanted in their own country. Under French rule since the time of Napoleon, Algeria now seemed controlled by sadists and madmen. For over five generations the colons sucked the life from their country, taken the best for themselves and left the natives the dregs. The colonials, the hated pied-noirs, now held the power of life and death over them.

Crowded into the confining limits of the putrid cell, the men sat hunched and silent, heads drawn down between their shoulders like turtles. Those with eyes open stared at the filthy floor. They did not trust themselves to look at one another, afraid of what they might see, terrified of what others might see in their faces. Some screwed their eyes tightly shut. One tried in vain to stuff clenched fists into his ears to shut out the noise. The youngest, a boy no more than 14 or 15, pressed his mouth tightly against his arm to muffle breathless sobs he could not stifle.

The screams began hours before from somewhere below. At first they were high like a woman's, bouncing and reverberating from the dank stone walls. Now the tortured vocal cords, although scarcely able to produce more than sibilant animal grunts and squeaks, still conveyed terror, extreme pain and the limits of endurance. The voice surrounded the men, squeezed them, penetrating like the point of an ice pick, painfully plucking at nerves already raw.

It would be only a matter of time until their turn came to take the place of the man below. Those familiar with their captor's interrogation procedures knew the exquisite pain that would be inflicted upon their defenseless bodies. Death seemed the only limiting factor. They remembered electric shocks to the genitals, ears and temples, as well as the soaped necks of the champagne bottles they were forced to sit upon until they felt they were being torn apart. They cringed anew at the thought of hanging naked from hooks in the ceiling, being beaten until they lost consciousness. Revived by buckets of icy water, the questions and beatings always began anew.

On a routine sweep through the souks of Oran in November 1961, a group of paramilitary pied-noirs, led by a man named Bonisseur, found them purely by accident. One of Bonisseur's men literally fell into their hiding place. There were eight of them, most already known to the OAS. The identity of their leader, the most sought after of them all, was unknown to the Frenchmen. Perhaps most fortunate of all for the prisoners, the pied-noirs were unaware the man they sought so diligently was among their captives. Vicious interrogations provided the torturers with his name, but none knew where he might be found. Only after the French forced one of the prisoners to drink a bottle of beer, then shot him in the stomach, did they get the information they sought. The wounded terrorist screamed for hours in agony before finally giving his captors the information they sought. A promise of medical assistance, of an end to his misery, was the key to persuading him to babble all he knew, including the name and description of their leader, who they would find among those in the holding cell.

His reward ended the pain. One little pill, one little lead pill placed behind the ear put an immediate end to his suffering. Those taken with him, shut up in a holding cell one floor above, listened to him scream until the end. They knew what was next.

Jean Paul Bonisseur, present through most of the interrogation, watched from a chair in the background. As soon as the identity of Belkacem ben Boulaid was known Bonisseur gave the nod that ended the session. He ordered the four others in the room to remove the body and fetch ben Boulaid. While his men busied themselves carrying out his orders, Bonisseur left to retrieve a fresh pack of Gauloise Caporals from his office two floors above.

Exactly what happened in the interim remained a mystery. All four of his men were armed. Two attended to the body while the other two went to the holding cell to pick out ben Boulaid. In a desperate bid for freedom the occupants attacked the armed guards when they entered the holding cell. One of the guns was torn from the grasp of a soldier and turned on its owner, killing him instantly. The cell was so small and crowded that the remaining guard could not maneuver sufficiently to protect himself as he was overcome by wiry arms and grasping hands. He succeeded in shooting two of them before he went down. The five remaining prisoners, now armed with two machine pistols, spilled into the narrow hallway, eager to make good their escape.

The guards moving the body heard the first burst of firing. When the shooting continued, they ran toward the noise, their arms at the ready. A bloody shoot-out in the hallway ensued and both of the remaining guards were killed, as well as two more prisoners. A third was badly wounded and left unconscious where he fell. The two remaining prisoners, now well-armed, took to their heels. In their frantic rush to escape they discovered a back stairway leading to the floor above and an unguarded exit. From there they effected their escape and disappeared among the general populace.

Bonisseur heard the firing and shouts and descended the nearest staircase at a run. By the time he arrived, however, it was over. All that remained were his four dead comrades, the two dead terrorists and their wounded companion. The wounded man almost lost an arm from a fusillade and was shot in the neck. He remained unconscious, bleeding to death ten minutes later.

It was confirmed that one of the escapees was Belkacem ben Boulaid, for he was positively identified two weeks later in the mountainous region of Kabylia. Until the end of the war in 1962 he avoided capture. Rather than participating in the celebrations following Algeria's independence, he seemed to disappear from the face of the earth.

Chapter 2

Amid the low scrub and boulders the growls and clanking of the ancient bulldozer broke the stillness. Clouds of dust billowed, bloomed, then settled again, as if the earth itself were an immense magnet. The thorny brush was bisected by a beige scar the width of the dozer's blade. The machine provided the only movement, as it created a road where none existed before.

The south coast of Crete, noted for its lack of roads, was sparsely populated. The few villages that existed were separated by miles of wasteland and were mostly accessible only by narrow tortuous trails incised into the mountains rising above the Plain of Messara.

In spite of its inaccessibility, this area was not devoid of inhabitants. Upon piles of dirt and boulders pushed up by the bulldozer a dozen peasants perched. The men shaded their eyes with their hands to relieve the hammering rays of the sun. Two women, their heads and the lower halves of their faces wrapped in dark shawls, their eyes barely visible with the stark contrast from sunlight to shadow, sat apart from the men. Like birds of prey they watched attentively, not realizing the opening of Pandora's Box awaited them.

Attention riveted upon the bulldozer and its operator, there was no discussion among the group. The driver concentrating upon the task at hand, took no apparent notice of his audience. Actually, he was very aware of them. He sat atop this roaring antique while other ground-bound mortals could merely look on in awe and wonder. With practiced nonchalance he maneuvered his steed forward and back, a cigarette dangling from the corner of his mouth. With unexpected suddenness the earth opened up and the nose of the bulldozer dropped. As one, the peasants sprang to their feet. The monster slammed into reverse and, with motor roaring, backed out of the hole. On level ground once more, he quickly shut off the engine. Before the motor issued its final rumble he snatched the cigarette and threw it aside, leapt from his seat to the treads, and then to the ground.

The silence was broken only by the soft southerly wind which soughed through the brush. As one, the group of spectators advanced to stand behind the operator. Moving cautiously, they leaned forward trying to see into the opening. One of the men, Zakari, moved forward, intent upon discovering the cause of the cave-in. In his haste he stubbed his toe and pitched head-first into the darkness.

From above someone shouted a warning. "Prosoxi!" Look out! But it came too late. Anxiously, they crowded around the opening, faintly perceiving him in the shadows below, on his hands and knees in the dirt, unmoving. Their concern for him was answered by a soft Greek oath, whispered in seeming disbelief.

"Panagia."

Then louder, "PANAGIA!"

The group from above spilled into the dark shadows and stopped momentarily by Zakari's side. Their eyes were slow to adjust to the low light, but as their vision improved their mouths fell open in breathless amazement. They stood on a floor of packed earth in an almost-round chamber. Pottery of all sizes and shapes lay scattered in total disarray, leaving barely enough room to walk. Along one curved wall ran a stone shelf. Among the pottery were various vessels and statues of bronze or obsidian, although two of the statues were of terra cotta. The terra cotta figures depicted bare-breasted women wearing skirts that flared gently from the waist, cut in such a manner that, even though the skirts reached the ground, the feet and ankles were exposed.

A match pulled from a shirt pocket and struck against a stone that formed part of the wall flared, piercing the gloom. Its light reflected briefly from something yellow and metallic on the floor among the jumble of pottery. Still on his hands and knees, Zakari was the only one to notice the flash virtually in front of his face, his body shielding the glint from the match's flame from the view of the others. With a trembling hand he reached out to brush dirt and broken pottery shards from the area before him. He barely suppressed a gasp of surprise, for lying before him was the statue of a youth. Instinctively he grasped and pulled it between his knees, immediately aware of its weight in relation to its size. One word drove all other thoughts from his mind: Xrisos! Gold!

Scrabbling frantically, he stuffed it into the waistband of his pants. Although not bulky in size, its weight was remarkable. As he pushed himself to his feet he pulled his short-waisted jacket close around his middle, hiding the bulge caused by the statue.

Everyone talked at the same time, each expressing his own thoughts. Everyone except Zakari, who continued to hug his jacket close to his stomach. As unobtrusively as possible he backed out of the hole. Once in the sunlight he looked quickly around to ensure he was alone. Satisfied to see no one he left the scar of the road and melted into the scrub. As far as he knew no one saw him leave or take the statue, but he could take no chances. He headed for the mountains that rose immediately from the narrow coastal plain.

The others, including the driver, slowly emerged and stood around the bulldozer. Everyone was convinced that this was a tomb, probably Minoan. The driver's only choice was to find the nearest phone and call the Director of the Archaeological Museum in Iraklion. He knew that any finds such as this were jealously claimed by the state. Those that failed to report them were liable to spend time in prison.

Leaving the peasants still talking among themselves he began the hot, dusty walk to retrieve his small truck. The nearest phone was in the village of Akoumia, another fifteen kilometers distance. As the crow flew, Iraklion was but a little more than 60 kilometers away, but the road was a convoluted snake winding over the mountains into the Plain of Messara, and then over more mountains, before it finally reached the walled city of Iraklion itself. It would be several hours before someone from the museum would return.

Dusk lay soft on the land, rendering the harsh surroundings in pastels when the silence was again broken by the roar of motors. A Land Rover, following the small truck of the bulldozer driver, raised an angry cloud of dust as their vehicles bounced toward the silhouette of the bulldozer standing among the scrub. Both vehicles skidded to a halt and all four doors of the Land Rover opened simultaneously, disgorging five men dressed in business suits. The driver stood respectfully aside to allow the shortest of the men to advance towards the opening. It was immediately evident who was in charge. Four of the newcomers stood slightly behind a short, wiry, mustachioed and balding individual. Flipping on a powerful electric torch, the director entered the tomb. His light played over the ceiling and the rough walls, swinging back and forth. When the beam dropped to the floor, however, its movement became frantic. It probed every corner, but all that remained were a few shards of broken pottery. The clay jars, ceremonial vessels and statues were no longer there. The tomb was empty.

Chapter 3

St. John Wood Martin, one of the original agents of the Office of Strategic Services in World War II, was personally recruited in January 1942, direct from his position in a distinguished Boston law firm, by General William "Wild Bill" Donovan. Martin, "The Saint," as he was known by his peers since Harvard Law School in the early 30's, was recognized as a whiz kid. He attacked his studies and subsequent caseload with the same selfless zeal with which he attacked opposing rugby teams in blood-letting scrums for the Crimson. In addition to his athletic abilities and bulldog tenacity, he was endowed with unusual language and analytical skills. All of these attributes he passed on to his son, Carter, born the summer prior to the Japanese attack on Pearl Harbor.

While many of his peers perished at the hands of various organizations dedicated to the Axis cause, St. John Martin survived. Throughout the war he served with distinction, operating behind enemy lines on numerous occasions in the Balkans, Italy and Egypt.

At the end of September 1945, less than ten days after the end of the war, President Harry S. Truman issued an executive order disbanding the Office of Strategic Services, stating that he wanted no part of what he called a "peacetime Gestapo." Martin returned to the same law firm from which he was snatched three and a half years earlier. He applied himself to a steadily increasing caseload, but in spite of all outward appearances, he was not happy being "back in the traces," as the senior partner like to put it. He missed the scent of danger and secretly longed to return to intelligence. By mid-August 1946 he confided to his wife his desire to again serve his country in a role that at once satisfied his patriotic and intellectual bents and provided the adrenaline rush upon which he thrived.

Periodically his path crossed those of some of his old wartime comrades. Over drinks at a club on tree-lined Commonwealth Avenue, frequented by men of a certain age and class, they spoke in subdued tones of the new agency. Some of the veterans, men he knew during the free-wheeling days of the war, enjoyed considerable influence in Washington and urged him to join them.

A phone call from a man from the Cairo days finally convinced St. John he would never again be happy slogging through corporate law cases. They wanted him, his expertise and his dedication. A place awaited him in an American embassy in a country viewed as being vital to the interests of the U.S. It would be like a homecoming.

St. John's father was the product of formative years spent with his family in the U.S. diplomatic corps as a career diplomatic officer. Most of his assignments were as Charge d'Affaires to this embassy or that. He observed first-hand how often politically socially inept men were appointed to represent the United States abroad, the appointment the result of either huge contributions to a Presidential election campaign, or cronyism. Rarely if ever could one of these appointees even speak the language of the country in which he found himself and simply served as a figurehead in the embassy. All the real work was undertaken by the professional diplomats. A strict disciplinarian, he saw to it that his son received the best of educations.

The standards instilled into St. John Martin by his own father carried over to Carter's education. Once he established a residence, his family joined him overseas. At that point the elder Martin undertook the task of the preparation and education of his own son. His first assignment in 1946 was as Liaison Officer in the American Embassy in Teheran. When his family arrived in the Iranian capital in October 1946, he ensured Carter's assimilation of local language and culture by placing him in a type of Iranian day school for sons of the privileged. By the first grade he was as fluent in Farsi as any of his native-born playmates. When they departed Teheran in June of 1948 he was completely bi-lingual.

St. John's next assignment was to Athens, this time as Agency Chief of Station. In Athens the process was repeated. Most of Carter's companions that summer were again sons of members of the government and, by the time school started in September, he was competent enough to understand, grasp and respond intelligently in Demotic Greek to most scholastic situations. To ensure that he maintained his proficiency in Farsi, his father saw to it that twice a month he spent the day with the sons of the Iranian ambassador.

By 1951 St. John was put in charge of the coordination of all Northern European intelligence activities and posted to Brussels. Once there, the 10 year old Carter was enrolled in a Jesuit academy. Although traditional Episcopalian, his father believed the education provided by such an environment superior to any other in the world and fully espoused the rigid discipline insisted upon by the Brothers. From 1951 until 1958 Carter attended the school for nine months each year. During all holidays and for the first month of the summer he traveled with his family throughout Europe and the Middle East. The remaining two months he was sent back to the U.S. to live with his uncle's family.

St. John believed that as an American, his son should be fully aware of his own country and family's roots. This also gave him the opportunity to perfect his English, which at times seemed to escape him. During his time in Colorado he hunted, fished, hiked, learned mountain climbing with his cousins and acquainted himself with his native country. Through the expertise of his uncle, an instructor in a training program that turned out Commandos for the American Army during the Second World War, he also became accomplished in more than one discipline of self-defense.

By the time he was ready to enter college in 1959 he was a seasoned traveler, self-confident and self-reliant. At his father's urging he matriculated at Georgetown University, where he majored in International Affairs and International Law. Many of his friends and classmates were the sons and daughters of the foreign diplomatic corps assigned to their country's embassies in Washington. Some were childhood classmates with whom he attended schools in Iran, Greece and Belgium. In spite of his blond hair, piercing blue eyes, trim yet muscular physique and All American good looks, his fluency in languages other than English and his choice of companions often caused him to be mistaken for one of the foreign students. He was fun-loving and gregarious on one level, while on another he could be intense and highly competitive.

Through prodigious efforts, including summer school classes, he graduated with honors in three and a half years. Upon graduation he felt fully prepared to take the next logical and expected step: into the intelligence agency that was his father's home since before Carter could even remember. Fortunately, he expected no less of himself.

Six months prior to graduation he interviewed with an officer in the Career Training Program. Follow-up interviews with other officers from the program, including one by the program director himself, delved into his background, interests, language abilities and interests in foreign affairs. Two weeks later he was scheduled for three days of testing. He cut classes for two of the three days and reported ready for whatever might be in store for him. Tests ran the gamut from physical and psychological exams to exhaustive written tests designed to discern aptitude, vocation and personality. At the completion of the three days Carter returned to school and immersed himself in his studies while awaiting the results of the security clearance check that was initiated more than two months before.

Notification of his having received his security clearance came the week he received his undergraduate degree from Georgetown. He was requested by the agency to report for what would be one of a series of polygraph tests. Carter viewed the interrogation by the operator of the polygraph as being exhaustive and intrusive, as well as embarrassing and demeaning. He experienced little consolation when told by the testing official that all employees of the agency, including the director, were tested periodically while in service. A week later he received word that his clearance was in order.

In late December 1962, following his graduation two weeks earlier, he flew back to Washington, D.C. from a ski trip in Jackson Hole ready to begin work. His first assignment was really no assignment at all, for he found himself back in school. Termed "the indoctrination period," his group spent a month familiarizing themselves with communism and foreign policy of the Soviet Union. Lectures and reading assignments concentrated on the Soviets and the party concept and gave new recruits ideas of what they might expect to encounter. They eventually learned how the Russian threat is countered by the government and the agency.

At the conclusion of this period, Carter was assigned to the Cyprus desk under the aegis of the Near East Division. Like most of the others in his group, he hoped for assignment in covert operations, but took the news with equanimity.

In early February 1963, he accompanied his mother to National Airport to see his father, stationed in Washington since the previous year, off to New York and Beirut. His mother chided her husband for leaving Washington, even if for only three months. St. John's philosophy, however, reflected that of his old boss. "Washington is our home now, but my place is in the field. In order to be of help to my group, to understand their situations and problems, I must see and experience them first hand."

Two months later the phone on Carter's desk at the Agency buzzed. He was asked to step into the office of his superior, a man known to Carter for years and who worked for St. John on numerous occasions. With sympathetic gentleness he was advised of his father's death.

While in the Lebanese coastal city of Sidon he was brutally murdered. A man driving a Vespa motor scooter simply pulled alongside the elder Martin's car in slow traffic and an accomplice riding behind him sprayed the interior with machine gun fire. Before speeding away and losing themselves in traffic, the driver of the Vespa pulled the pin on a hand grenade with his teeth and dropped it through the open window. In addition to killing St. John, both the driver and bodyguard, native Lebanese, were slain. Fedayeen, ostensibly out of Jordan, claimed responsibility for the act by placing calls to the largest and most widely read Beirut newspapers that same afternoon.

Within The Agency nothing was known of the group claiming responsibility. Files were searched and researched and The Agency's massive computers were queried. Telexes clattered endlessly to little avail. Christian sources in Beirut, as well as agents in Amman, were contacted and asked to provide identification. Three days later Palestinian Alliance, a small Fedayeen group, was positively identified.

They were strongly suspected to originally be out of Syria. Disaffected by the seeming lethargy and inability of the main organization to achieve the Ba'athist Party's stated goal of the assassination of Jordan's King Hussein and the reincorporation of the Kingdom of Jordan back into Greater Syria, a renegade splinter faction decided to strike on their own initiative. Palestinian Alliance took its first serious step into international terrorism.

The group was reportedly comprised of young radicals under the informal leadership of one Belkacem Ben Boulaid. Heretofore they involved themselves in nothing more serious than loosely organized and poorly planned operations. They made forays into Israel, always from Jordan, trying to discredit the Jordanians and push Israel into reprisals on the Hashemite Kingdom, all designed to eventually bring the little king down. Ben Boulaid was at first thought to be Lebanese, although some said he came from Libya or Syria. The Agency's sources in the Middle East finally identified him as Algerian, where his unorthodox and savage methods while working with the FNL, the National Liberation Front in Algeria, proved highly successful against the French colonial pied-noirs. The French employed every tactic they knew to bring him to bay, but in every instance but one he eluded them. When independence was achieved he still remained at large. Never a public figure or symbol of the Front, he was nevertheless regarded by his peers and adversaries alike as an astute tactician and ferocious fighter. Following the ouster of the pied-noirs from Algeria he simply dropped from sight. There were no known photographs of him and no one knew where to find someone who could describe him by more than his reputation.

Try as they might, no one could find any justification, real or imagined, for the fatal attack on St. John Martin. There was never any hard indication his attackers knew his identity when they assassinated him. Apparently their logic lead them to believe he was someone important because of his chauffeured car and body guard. His appearance would fool no one into thinking he was Middle-eastern. The conclusive assumption was that the deed was perpetrated merely for its impact in the Arab world. If this was the goal of Palestinian Alliance, they succeeded beyond all expectations. The assassination was trumpeted by radio and newspapers and the group was acclaimed throughout the Mideast, entirely out of proportion to the actual impact of their act, as having struck a resounding blow for the Palestinian cause. Once the international press identified St. John Martin, the Arab press linked him to the U.S. intelligence community and accused him of working directly with the Jews.

Carter's sorrow, shock and anger at the news were quickly internalized. His years of education with the Jesuits taught him self-control and the acceptance of the inevitability of such things as death. He realized that in this line of work there was always the chance of losing one's life. Through the years his father found himself in more than one life threatening situation. Carter found it ironic that his father should die this close to retirement age and should have been able to enjoy the fruits of his long years of service. As far as he knew, this trip was nothing more than an innocuous inspection tour. But then, Carter did not know the real reasons behind St. John's going to Lebanon, and would probably never be privy to the details.

When he shared the news to his mother her eyes filled with tears and her lips and chin quivered, but the set of her head and shoulders and the straightness of her spine never relaxed. She, too, through the decades of living with St. John, came to accept certain things as inevitable. She knew danger was omnipresent in his line of work, knew of some of his close calls during the war years. Her first words after Carter told her of the tragedy were simple and direct.

"I can only be thankful for our many years together. He was a good and dedicated man, Carter: a man with principle, a man with firm convictions. He was a good husband and a loving father. He was so proud when you came into The Agency. It's up to you now. I know people have certain expectations of you because you are your father's son. Don't let them - or him - down."

His mother's words warmed him. He vowed to her that he would do all he could to carry on as his father wished. To himself he vowed he would do everything possible to avenge his father's death.

Three days after the deadly attack a plane bearing a spartan, flag-draped casket landed at Andrews Air Force Base. The next day, a Friday, St. John Wood Martin was buried in a simple ceremony next to the graves of his parents in a small private cemetery in Connecticut. Carter spent the weekend at his parent's estate, helping his mother greet those who came to express their condolences and making sure everything was in order. The following Tuesday he returned to his desk.

Dispersal of information in the intelligence community is based on need to know. He never did discover the real reasons for his father's presence in Lebanon. Even discreet enquiries were met with a polite silence or a raised eyebrow. He was never told The Agency knew who was behind his assassination, nor was the name Palestinian Alliance spoken in his presence. He turned his energies to his job, which at that time consisted of analyzing information collected from various sources on the internecine squabbles between the Turks on one side of Cyprus and the Greeks under the leadership of Archbishop Makarios on the other. Through his grasp of Greek he was invaluable in the translation of intercepted communications and reports from Greek agents on the island itself. He worked with Turkish linguists and analysts whose job it was to watch and analyze the other side of the situation. As tensions grew, Carter and his colleagues spent increasingly long hours at their desks.

Because of its strategic placement in the eastern end of the Mediterranean, Cyprus became the crossroads where one was liable to encounter all manner of intrigue. Some sorties against Israel were suspected to have originated from the shores of the island. For Carter, the activity on Cyprus represented a microcosm of the entire Mideastern situation. By helping to monitor the movement of men and materiel passing through the region, both openly and clandestinely, and using his native intelligence and intuition to collate that information with reports from collateral sources, he became adept at recognizing potential trouble with a remarkable degree of accuracy. His concise and insightful reports soon brought him to the attention of those for whom he worked.

In scanning his daily workload of communications traffic one afternoon several weeks later, his attention was drawn to an item buried in a stack of messages. A seemingly offhand remark concerning the arrival of "friends" from near Damascus was buried amongst reports of shipping movements between Cypriot and Lebanese ports. Carter was frustrated because much of the communications was badly garbled. His first inclination was that the "friends" were perhaps Palestinian. He studied the most badly garbled section of the message intently and was rewarded by being able to decipher what he took to be a name, Abu Bekr. He knew the leaders of the Palestinian movement all took noms de guerre, many of which began with Abu this or that. In the extensive reference library available to him Carter found mention of Abu Bekr, first caliph of the Muslim Empire, who ruled from 632 until his death in 634. The father-in-law of the prophet Muhammad, he made Islam a political and military force throughout Arabia. With this discovery Carter's excitement grew.

The mention of a group, possibly Fedayeen, en route to Cyprus was highly noteworthy. He was aware of pro-Palestinian sentiments in Athens and among the communities on the Greek side of the Green Line separating the belligerents on Cyprus. From his Greek friends with whom he spoke occasionally, and the Athenian dailies he scanned for noteworthy news items, he knew the government in Athens was not at all averse to receiving Palestinian representatives. Papandreou's government openly expressed support for their cause.

Carter brought the item to the attention of the chief of the Mideastern desk, who passed the information on to his superiors. The only indication he might be on the track of something important was when he was asked to pay special attention to any further indications of activity of this sort. When he asked if the name Abu Bekr denoted any special importance to anyone he was told he would be advised should they find out anything. In the meantime he was to look carefully for any further mention of "friends."

For the next two weeks he sifted through reams of intercepted communications, hoping to find something, anything, but his efforts were fruitless. At the beginning of the third week two small paragraphs in a weekly intelligence summary told of an abortive seaborne raid on the coast of Israel by a small group of terrorists. The Israelis intercepted them shortly after they landed in rubber dinghies near Netanya. It was assumed they were dropped into the waters of the Mediterranean several miles off the Israeli coast by a larger boat, such as one of the myriad tramp steamers that plied the waters of the inland sea. Of the seven individuals in the raid six were killed shortly after reaching the beach and the seventh was wounded and captured following a brief exchange of fire. In the dinghies were an assortment of explosive devices and each terrorist was heavily armed. It was assumed they planned the raid on the coastal town itself. No mention was made of their affiliation other than the fact that they were referred to in the report as 'suspected' Palestinians. Carter's first assumption was that these were probably the "friends" mentioned in the intercepted message.

Over the subsequent months he occasionally read other reports of raids upon Israel's coast, some successful. These usually appeared in the weekly intelligence summaries, although periodic news reports sometimes appeared either in the New York Times or the Washington Post. It was evident the Fedayeen were not yet ready to concede defeat and give up their infiltration and assault tactics.

On a hot, muggy day in early June he was directed to report to a conference room on the floor above his office. Finding the room empty, he entered and took a chair along one side of a table in the center of the room. There was nothing to indicate the reason for his requested presence. He sat alone for a quarter of an hour listening to the whisper of the air conditioning. A door-sized section of seemingly blank wall opened inward and a man of medium height and wearing glasses entered. He seemed harried and preoccupied and, at first, did not acknowledge Carter. Carter tried to place his face, but could not recall having seen him before. The newcomer briskly approached the far side of the highly polished table and placed two files and his brief case onto its surface. Only then did he turn to Carter.

"Mr. Martin. How do you do?"

Carter pushed his chair back from the table and stood immediately. "Fine, sir, thank you."

The man reached across the table and offered his hand. "Thank you for meeting with me today. I'm sorry I'm a little late.

My name is Nicholas Ware. I'm the Special Assistant to Mr.
Delaney, Chief of the Near East Section. Normally he would
meet with you himself, but his presence was required elsewhere
and he asked me to stand in for him. He and your father worked
closely for a number of years. Incidentally, I was very sorry to
hear about your father. A fine man, I must say."

Carter thanked Ware, but continued to wonder what was
behind his summons.

"Please sit down. I trust you won't mind if I call you
Carter?"

Carter nodded his acquiescence and they both took seats.
Ware picked up the top folder in front of him, upon which was
prominently stamped TOP SECRET. He opened it to reveal
sheets of paper Carter instantly recognized as message intercept
forms with which he worked every day. The top sheet contained
several items circled in red and brief notations handwritten in the
margin. He picked up the first, studied it a moment and laid it
aside. Beneath it were more forms, all with notations in red or
blue pencil. He then opened the second folder, also stamped TOP
SECRET, but this time the words EYES ONLY followed the
classification. The file was slim and contained but one
typewritten page. Even before Ware looked up he began to
speak.

"Carter, I hear from various sources that your work with
us is exemplary. You seem to have a nose for finding the
unobtrusive yet important details, which, believe it or not, is a
talent extremely difficult to teach. Your bringing Abu Bekr to
our attention was nothing short of a stroke of luck. The fact that
you have neither seen nor heard further mention of him is not to
be construed as a failure. Unknown to you, we have our
operatives in Syria and Lebanon, as well as in Cyprus, trying to
turn up anything at all on him. What we wanted was positive
identification, something we could hang our hat on. Needless to
say, it hasn't been easy, but our efforts have provided positive
results."

With the mention of Abu Bekr Carter's attention became
focused on Ware's every word.

"You may be interested to know that we have identified
Abu Bekr. He is the brains behind a Palestinian group, actually a

group of renegades, a splinter group, known as "Palestinian Alliance."

Carter's expression did not change, for the name was meaningless to him. He continued to sit back in his chair with his elbows resting on its arms, his hands clasped across his stomach. One thought did occur to him and he leaned forward while Ware looked at the report in front of him.

"The Palestinian Alliance. Were they the ones who went to Cyprus, the ones mentioned in the message some time ago? Were they also the ones who tried the raid on Netanya and were intercepted by the Israelis? A couple of weeks after the mention of Abu Bekr in the message, I read of a failed attack on that coastal city by some Palestinians. Were they the same group?"

"All indications point to them. We've received only vague confirmation from the Israelis, but we think they are the same."

"Was Abu Bekr with them by any chance when they were intercepted?"

"We don't think so. As a matter of fact, we're almost positive he didn't participate beyond the planning stage. Also, his name has been brought up since then as being present at a meeting in the Beka'a Valley. I don't recall the exact place, but I believe it was one of the secret training camps."

It was obvious to Carter from what Ware was telling him that this Abu Bekr was more than just another terrorist. He felt a momentary flush of pride in being recognized as the one to bring him to The Agency's attention, but before he could further congratulate himself Ware's monotone recitation of known facts brought Carter back to the present.

"There are strong indications from some of our sources - and the Israelis corroborate this - that some of the Alliance's activities are being moved out of Cyprus to another location in the Mediterranean. As you may be aware, the Greek government has always been somewhat supportive of the Palestinian cause. We have reason to believe they may be planning to set up shop in Crete."

"Crete?"

"The island of Crete is not at all out of the question. Its Eastern end, like much of the rest of it, is sparsely populated.

There are many areas where a group of men could lose themselves. Outside of differences in language, Palestinians would not stand out from the indigenous population, so there would be no problem with their blending in with their surroundings. They could operate out of such an area with relative safety. Although Crete's not so far from the center of conflict, it's just remote enough that activity could be carried on there that would not be right under the eyes of the Mossad. At least that's believed to be their reasoning."

The discussion interested Carter, but he still wondered how this meeting would concern him. He was impatient to see where Ware was going with this and knew they did not call a relative newcomer in merely for a casual chat. He looked at the older man expectantly. What came next was like a thunderbolt to Carter.

"Israeli intelligence is certain Palestinian Alliance is moving at least part of its operation to Crete. Undoubtedly Abu Bekr will be overseeing and coordinating activity. There's already one Mossad agent working out of the town of Ieraperta on the southeastern coast. They feel certain this is the general area where the Fedayeen will be operating. It behooves us to put a man on the island, as well. Carter, in going over your files and performance reports we've come to the conclusion that you're the person we need on site."

Carter sat for a moment in stunned silence. When he found his tongue all he could do was blurt out, "Me!? I have no field experience at all, Mr. Ware. I'm flattered, of course, that you would consider me, but I can't help wonder why."

Ware gave Carter a tight grin before he responded.

"That's a fair question. There are times when we don't necessarily need someone with years of Agency experience to take on a job such as this one. What we do need is someone to play a role and it just so happens there are several of us who feel this particular assignment will fit right in with your background - fluency in Greek and French for one thing. Also, you look like the type of person you will be required to portray. We want you to attempt to recruit an agent. If you are successful you will be working with the only person we've been able to identify who knows the target by more than reputation. The man I'm talking about is a pied-noir from Oran. He fought against Abu Bekr in Algeria when Bekr was known only as Belkacem Ben Boulaid, and we believe he can identify him by sight. He was with the 10th Paratroop Division in Algiers. Abu Bekr was in the 10th's clutches for a short time in late '61. Somehow he escaped, but the man we hope you'll be able to recruit for us, Jean Paul Bonisseur, knows our target.

"Basically, you will establish a persona, that of a young, inexperienced American, one who speaks only English and is out of the U.S. for the first time. You won't be totally alone in this endeavor, but it will appear so. We anticipate your willingness to work with us on this project."

Carter could only nod his head in mute assent as his mind raced to take in everything he was hearing. He could not believe he was being asked to assume such a position of responsibility and the uncertainty left him totally ill at ease. There were a thousand questions he wanted to ask, should ask, but could not find the words.

Ware continued, "Your mission will be to identify Bekr with the assistance of our Franco-Algerian friend, obtain positive identification and simply let us know that he is, in fact, on Crete. It's all very simple when you think about it. There will be some special training involved, and for this you will be sent to Peary for a period of instruction.

"I've just given you the rudiments of this operation, for only after you accept - if you accept - will we begin to get into the specifics. Time is of the essence, however, and we need an answer by tomorrow. If you accept the assignment any questions you have, and I'm sure you will have many, will be answered in detail."

Ware pushed his chair from the table, stood up and gathered the files and returned them to his briefcase. Lost in thought, Carter sat and looked at his hands clutched tightly in his lap to keep them from trembling. When he finally realized that Ware was standing on the far side of the table he quickly pushed his chair back and rose to his feet. Ware waited a moment, a bemused look on his face, and then extended his hand. "Nice to meet you, Martin. I look forward to talking to you tomorrow." With these final words he strode from the room.

Carter immediately fell back into his chair, deep in thought. Once again, the only sound to be heard was the soft whisper of the air conditioning. His first reaction to the meeting was to question his abilities. What if he failed? What if he embarrassed himself and the Agency? His thoughts drifted to his father and he wished he were here to advise him. From the stories his father told him after the war and the books he read on the exploits and accomplishments of the OSS, this was just the type of operation St. John Martin and others like him, countless men and women in wartime Europe and the Mideast, were often given. They received an assignment, a minimal amount of training by today's standards, and ultimately left to their own devices. If they found themselves in difficulty, and they often did, they normally could not count on receiving any backing from the organization. He felt sure he could count on The Agency. Most OSS operatives were no older or more experienced than he and much less well-trained. He recalled his mother's admonishment to make his father proud of him. He was being offered an opportunity to do just that.

Carter slept little that night. His nerves were drawn tight as bowstrings and he could not keep the wheels from turning in his mind every time he thought of the step they were asking him to take. In spite of lack of sleep he arose at five o'clock with the adrenaline still pumping. As he did six mornings each week, he slipped on running shoes and shorts and jogged five miles through the humid Washington dawn. When he finished his run he drank a cup of hot tea while perusing the Washington Post, showered and shaved, then dressed for work. After a light breakfast in a coffee shop not far from his apartment he headed in to work. He was excited and nervous, anxious to tell them of his decision.

By 9:30, unable to concentrate any longer upon the day's workload in front of him, he picked up his phone and dialed an internal line. A feminine voice with a lilting Southern accent responded almost immediately. He identified himself and asked for Mr. Ware. Within moments the connection was made.

"This is Ware."

"Good morning, Mr. Ware. This is Carter Martin." He took a deep breath. "I've given a great deal of thought to our meeting yesterday and was just calling to tell you I accept."

With barely a pause Ware responded. "Thank you, Martin. We thought you would. O.K., I'll get back with you this afternoon." Without another word he rang off.

Carter eased the receiver back onto its cradle, stretched his legs under his desk, clasped his hands behind his head and leaned back in his chair. A smile tugged at the corners of his mouth.

Chapter 4

Sweat poured from Zakari as he struggled up the rock strewn path, his breath coming in short painful gasps. As he hurried along he threw furtive glances back over his shoulder to see if he was being followed. Periodically he stopped, seemed to sniff the air, his nostrils flaring, looking carefully around to see if there was anyone observing him. The short respites allowed him to catch his breath, but he felt far from refreshed. His heart pounded and the rasping roar of his breathing made it seem as if he breathed through his ears. Still, he hugged his arms around his middle, feeling the solid bulge weighing him down more and more. His arms ached from supporting the small but heavy statue and his mind raced. At this moment his greatest concern was being seen.

Cretan peasants were adept at suddenly appearing out of the rocks or brush. It was as if the gods suddenly turned a rock into a man. One instant there was no one and the next moment, with no sound, someone would appear. Zakari knew.

Out hunting rabbits one day above the Plain of Messara he chanced upon two men digging with shovel and pick amid the traces of a foundation and wall. A ragged jacket, upon which were scattered two oil lamps and several fragments of pottery, lay on the ground. He immediately forgot about rabbits and crouched down to watch. He set his shotgun against a boulder and quietly reached inside his shoulder bag. Among the shotgun shells his fingers found a small package. He pulled it from the bag and opened it, careful not to make any noise. Inside was a fistful of dark olives with wrinkled skins and a piece of paximadi, the hard dry bread made from ground chickpeas. Should he become thirsty he knew there was a small spring nearby.

In 1942, during the Second World War, when the Germans sent in paratroopers to invade their island, he retreated to the caves in the high mountains with the men and a few women who made up the resistance movement. Although barely a teenager, he was allowed to join the inner circle of the resistance in his district. Employed several times as a courier, the leaders felt his youth would place him above suspicion should he be stopped by the Germans. During that time he traversed this rugged terrain, often at night, with only stars to light his way. His young legs and sturdy physique carried him successfully from the peaks to the valleys and back again time after time. He was no less at home now.

He watched the men for almost an hour. During that time he saw them discover several more fragments. He marked the spot in his mind before he crept away without either man's having been aware of his presence. Later he returned and dug in the same area, but the two men either destroyed everything left in the resistant earth with their primitive methods, or they already removed anything that might represent possible value.

Zakari finally reached his property after dark. A faint pink glow remained in the west, but it cast little light. Although his house was dark he wanted to reassure himself he was really alone. The only sound to be heard was the soft bleating of his milk goat and the sleepy stirrings of his few chickens roosting in the lower branches of an olive tree.

Zakari removed the statue from the front of his trousers and cached it inside the trunk of one of his ancient, gnarled olive trees. Walking toward the house he picked up a stout olive branch he kept as a staff and pushed open his front door. Staff at the ready, he found some stick matches, struck one and held it aloft to cast as much light as possible in the one room house. All that greeted him were wavering shadows, but they were shadows with which he was familiar.

Reassured now, his breathing returned to normal. His heart, too, ceased hammering from the exertion of his climb from the road construction site. There would be nothing to worry about from the other peasants who watched the bulldozer with him. He was positive no one saw him take the statue. Besides, given the opportunity they, too, would spirit away as much as they could carry.

The bulldozer operator was from another part of the island and Zakari knew the man did not know him. This knowledge was reassuring, for the police would eventually become involved and would question the inhabitants of that part of the island, looking for anyone who might possess any information concerning either the missing contents of the tomb or the names of any of those present that day.

He lit a small kerosene lantern and took a rough cloth bag from a corner of the room. He returned to the olive tree, set the lantern on the ground, removed the statue from the bole and stuffed it into the bag. Staying in the shadows as much as possible, he walked away from the light and into the boulders surrounding his one and a half hectares of land.

Mostly limestone, Crete is renowned for the caves, which honeycomb the island. Zakari's property was no exception and he soon found a hole in the rock into which he placed the statue concealed in the cloth bag. He looked around, marked the spot, then returned to his lantern.

He was anxious to examine this statue more closely. He was sure it was gold, but tomorrow morning would be soon enough. Now he was stooped from fatigue. He could not chance having his new-found treasure in his house and he was sure no one else could find his hiding place.

"Avrio," he thought to himself. Tomorrow. Tonight he would have a large glass of homemade red wine, a hunk of bread, and fall into bed.

Chapter 5

The wheels turned rapidly within The Agency and within little more than a week Carter was notified of his reporting date at "The Farm." He arranged to ride with three other men also slated for special training. As they rode through rural Virginia they speculated upon their upcoming training and of what it would consist. Stories abounded, but no one seemed to know any specifics. Each expounded his theory of what lay ahead, but no one seemed able to come up with any concrete idea of what awaited them. Carter found himself simply looking out the window of the moving car as the countryside and small towns rolled by. He envisioned what his assignment would concern. It seemed to require no great feats on his part and appeared to be cut and dried. He was anxious to get started and felt no qualms about the upcoming training period. In fact, he looked forward to whatever they might throw at him. He knew he was prepared physically and did not dwell on the mental aspects.

Upon arrival they were assigned quarters and the first evening were given the obligatory welcome speech by the Base Chief. This was followed by the Security Officer's do's and don'ts. Any thought of time away from the training area, although not forbidden, was discouraged. Their time would be well-filled by training sessions, night study and exercises. By the time they went to their quarters that night they suspected they would see little of the outside over the next few months.

Training was hard work and Carter was glad he stayed in condition with running, skiing and mountain climbing. In addition to the physical conditioning program, he and the others in his class were immersed in the martial arts. Carter was no novice, but the things he now learned were of a more practical and earnest nature, including how to disarm, cripple or, if necessary, kill an opponent.

His major interest, however, was in the classes designed to teach them how to run either single agents or networks. On this subject he was always digging to discover more and more information. In practical exercises he learned the methods required to convince the Algerian Bonisseur, to work with him to identify Abu Bekr. To Carter this was all much more than theory. He was not interested in learning the methods of penetrating an organization, for Ware assured him he would not be required to do so. On the other hand, methods of finding Abu Bekr and the subsequent surveillance of him and his group were vital to the success of his projected mission. Carter could see where these lessons would be immensely useful to him. With this realization he strove to perfect his techniques.

Due to the primitiveness of the location on Crete where he would most probably find the Fedayeen Carter was certain Bekr would have no phone to tap. The possibility the Arabs would even have such a method of communication was remote. Likewise, he was certain the man would not be receiving any mail. The most likely communications would be by radio or courier and radio intercept techniques could be of prime importance. Because of the political situation, he was reasonably convinced he would not be able to count on any assistance from Greek officials. Once Bonisseur was found and recruited it would be the two of them working in tandem. He threw himself into the practical exercises, taking great satisfaction at the completion of each exercise.

The first week of August he was called from classes and directed to board one of the aircraft that dropped into the training facility from time to time. He knew they were scheduled to be there for at least two more months for more specialized training and the honing of skills. Dumbstruck by the suddenness of the move, he searched his mind for any reason he might be dropped from the program, but could find none.

Upon deplaning at Andrews Air Force Base, he was met by an Air Force captain who handed him an envelope then turned and walked away. Carter strolled a short distance from the plane before he tore it open. Inside was a memorandum directing him to report to Ware's office at nine o'clock the following morning. Still puzzled, Carter picked up his baggage and took a cab to his apartment.

Ware greeted him with scarcely more visible enthusiasm than at their first meeting in June. After a perfunctory series of questions concerning his training he opened a file in front of him, then scanned the contents for a moment before raising his eyes to look at Carter over the tops of his half-lensed glasses.

"Well, Martin, it looks as if you did yourself proud." Inwardly Carter heaved a great sigh of relief, but his only outward response was a barely perceptible nod. "I expect you're anxious to get on with whatever is in store for you. Quite frankly, we need for you to be in the field."

This time Carter's response was more emphatic, for since June he often visualized the moment when contact might be made with Abu Bekr. He felt he was ready as he would ever be for whatever they might ask of him and his only wish was to prove himself. He was not prepared, however, for Ware's next statement.

"As far as anyone is concerned, today is your last day with The Agency. In a nutshell, you have decided you made a mistake by coming with us and handed in your resignation."

Carter sat forward in his chair, startled and unsure of where this conversation was leading. "Resignation!?"

"Yes, your resignation. We want it to appear as if you came to this decision on your own. Here's the scenario: you have come to realize intelligence is not the field for you. In six days you'll be on an airplane for Greece, another young, unemployed, footloose American. This is the '60's. There are young people all around who are doing that very thing. They, like you, feel an overpowering need to get away, find themselves. It's not so unusual. You graduated from the university not so long ago and feel a need to get out, get away, far from your home and family. You're striking out on your own. You speak only English, although you did take French in High school and Spanish in college. Like most Americans, however, you are basically monolingual.

"The next four days will be spent briefing you on all the information we have on Bonisseur. You'll need to commit this to memory. You will not, however, return here. When you walk out these doors today you will indicate to whoever necessary that you never intend to return."

Ware reached across the desk and passed a business card to Carter. "Any contact during the next four days will be at this address in McLean. It's a residential neighborhood and you'll meet with a gentleman named Dennis Maddry. He's the one who'll give you all the particulars. Under no circumstances will you call The Agency or this office. Any questions you may have should be addressed to Maddry, and then only in person or from a pay phone. Incidentally, his line is secure.

"At the end of the four days Maddry will give you a ticket for Greece. The fifth day, which is Saturday, you'll fly to New York and leave from Kennedy on a TWA flight through Rome to Athens. From there an Olympic Airways flight will take you to Iraklion. Between flights in Athens you'll have several hours. Maddry will give you the name of your contact there and you are to place a call to him as soon as you arrive. Do you have any questions?"

Carter thought for a moment before he responded. "There is one problem. What do I tell my mother?"

"Yes, well, we've thought about that and it's been decided it will be best if you tell her nothing more than the official story. I've never met her, but I understand she's a remarkable woman. Of course, she'll be concerned that you've left us and probably surprised to discover you'll be leaving for Europe. We feel sure you can handle the situation."

Carter merely nodded. He knew the news would not only surprise his mother, but would probably hurt her. The additional news that he would be leaving for Europe in the immediate future would come as a shock. He realized he would just break it to her as gently as possible and deal with the consequences of her reaction.

"Well, if you have no further questions at this time, I need your signature on your letter of resignation. Those with whom you worked in your section have been told this morning of your decision and your desk has been permanently assigned to the person who took over for you when you left for Peary."

Carter heard the door of Ware's office open behind him while he signed the letter, but he did not turn around. Ware looked past him and nodded before speaking.

"That should do it then. This gentleman will take you down on one of the private elevators. Good luck to you, Carter."

He stood to shake Ware's hand and then turned without another word and followed his escort out of the office.

That night he called his mother to tell her he was back and made arrangements to eat dinner with her on Sunday night. Over coffee following dinner he told her of his decision to leave The Agency and go to Greece. He thought she took the revelation remarkably well, only asking him why he came to this decision. As logically as possible he told her of his realization he was not cut out for intelligence work and was planning to take some time to find himself. As far as he could see, he would be able to do that in Greece. He was surprised when she expressed agreement.

"Why not? You have a number of friends in Athens and you do know the language. Besides, it will give you the time to...how do they put it these days...find yourself?"

When he left that night she hugged him tightly and sent him upon his way with a litany of motherly concerns and advice.

During the next four days he was briefed by Maddry and put his affairs in order. As he did not plan to be gone for an extended period of time he decided to merely close his apartment and gave a key to a friend, asking that she look in periodically. Those that questioned his sudden decision to chuck it all were given the prearranged cover story. All seemed to accept it at face value and on Friday night several of his friends gave him a bon voyage party at a restaurant in Georgetown.

Courtney Corcoran, Coco to her close friends, was a young woman he dated several times while still at the university and who was now the aide to a fast-rising young senator. They returned to his apartment where they spent the night together. They awoke about eleven, took a shower together, soaped each other's bodies thoroughly, and made love one final time under the stinging spray. By three they were on their way to National Airport in Coco's car, arriving just in time for him to check in for his 4:37 flight. She pulled to a stop at the entrance to the terminal and Carter jumped from the car. He jerked his luggage from the trunk, kissed her quickly, told her he would call her as soon as he came back to town and disappeared through the glass doors.

He arrived in New York with almost five hours to kill until his flight would depart Kennedy. After checking his bags at the ticket counter he found a spot away from the bustle of the other travelers and pulled a dog-eared paperback from his shoulder bag.

The book, Henry Miller's The Colossus of Maroussi, was more than just a travelogue of Miller's voyage to Greece in the late 30's. It contained a captivating account of Crete. He reread of Athens and the sights and people of mainland Greece. Most of the archaeological sites Carter knew well. The chapters on Crete itself were written just recently enough that he was sure many of the people and places would be much as they were when the author visited them in the late 30's prior to World War II.

The hours rolled by quickly now as he devoured the work, visualizing the land that awaited him. So immersed was he in the prose that at times he actually seemed to become a part of the story, not just an observer. With Miller he strolled the stones of Knossos and Phaistos, marveled at the legacy of the Minoans and champed at the bit to meet their descendants, the modern day Cretans. It came as a surprise when he finally realized his flight was being called. He marked his place and picked up his hand luggage before heading eagerly for the concourse.

Once the plane took off he returned to his reading, but before long his eyes closed and the book fell from his lap. The next thing he knew the stewardess was touching him on the arm to ask if he would like some breakfast. To his astonishment he could see the sun shining brightly on the clouds and the blue waters of the Atlantic far below them. By the time he finished breakfast and several cups of coffee, the flight was descending and the cabin crew made preparations for landing at Rome Fumincino.

The view as they landed was far from interesting. The airport was nowhere near Rome and was a modern steel and glass monstrosity that squatted in the middle of concrete runways and ramps. Despite the hour of his body clock, he found a bar inside the terminal and saluted his arrival in Rome with a Campari and soda. More than anything he was drinking to being once more in Europe.

The miles from Rome to Athens flew by and before long the nose of the plane dipped perceptibly as they began their descent into Athens. Carter watched avidly from the window, eager to see any landmark familiar to him. They were still over the blue waters of the Mediterranean and other than an occasional island or the wake of a ship, he saw nothing he recognized. It was not until they were on final approach, skimming above the beaches of Glyfada, seeming to barely miss the rooftops and the dome and cross of a Greek Orthodox church that he finally knew he was almost home. It amused him that he still thought of Athens as home, but several years' absence did not diminish his feeling of belonging. Good memories of the city and friends made his return that much more poignant... he regretted he would not be able to call or spend time with them. Only one call to make and that he must do as soon as he was through customs.

A screech of tires and the thud of the landing gear sent shudders through the metal capsule that brought him once more like a magic carpet to this land that through centuries nurtured and refined civilization. Here, below his feet was the birthplace of great men, from Aristotle to Zeno. The Alpha and the Omega. Carter smiled inwardly. The pure, strong early afternoon sunlight brilliantly illuminated the city around him. Everything was as he remembered and he thrilled anew with the wonder of it.

The excitement of his fellow passengers was transmitted to him as they descended en masse from the plane. Family members and friends waved excited welcomes from the observation deck of the terminal. Their enthusiasm made Carter want to wave in return. Everyone scurried through the heat waves shimmering off the tarmac into the relative coolness of the interior.

After the formalities of customs he left the main terminal and headed for the smaller one, the hub for all domestic flights. He quickly checked in at the Olympic Airways counter, confirmed that his flight for Crete would not be leaving for another four hours and went in search of a telephone.

In a corner of the passenger waiting area he found a fly blown compartment containing a working telephone, closed the door behind him and dug in his pockets for his address book. Encoded in ciphers only he would understand was the number given to him by Maddry at their final meeting. From his pants pocket he took a handful of Greek coins, chose one and inserted it into the slot. He dialed the number and waited, listening to a series of mechanical clanks and clunks, silence, and then the strange buzz of the phone ringing on the other end. After two rings the receiver was lifted.

"Matejowsky."

Carter was finally in contact with his control, Glen Matejowsky. This was the man to whom he would send his reports. Their conversation was short, business-like and to the point. He was given an address of a pension, a bed and breakfast, near the port in Iraklion, where he could obtain room and board for as long as he liked. Should he wish to obtain lodging elsewhere after a few days that would be up to him, but with the Daskaloyanni family he would be centrally located.

One last item was a number in the port city of Chania. If he needed anything at all, or possessed information that needed to be acted upon immediately, he was to call that number. The contact was called Horiatis. Carter smiled to himself. This was obviously an alias, for Horiatis meant "The Villager." As soon as Carter located Bonisseur and made contact with him, regardless of the results, he was to advise Chania without delay.

Under no circumstances was Carter to telephone Athens. No one knew how many ears could be listening between Crete and the mainland. Soviet intelligence ships regularly plied the waters of the Mediterranean gleaning all manner of information. Any hint of activity on the island would certainly be passed to whoever was supporting the Fedayeen. There must be absolutely no chance his mission be compromised. Carter assured Matejowsky of his complete understanding and compliance before hanging up.

With time on his hands, he wandered outside and then headed for the bar in the terminal. As he sipped an Ouzo he thought again of what lay ahead. From two tables away voices intruded upon his reverie and brought him back to the present. Two men, one American and the other English, sat in earnest discussion. Carter soon began to eavesdrop attentively.

Although not arguing, their conversation was intense. He soon realized their subject was archaeology. At first he thought they were talking about the Golden Age of Greece, an era Carter knew something about. They, however, were more interested in another age, an earlier era, for names such as Marinatos, Thera,

Santorini, Minoans, Knossos and a cataclysm of some sort were at the very heart of the discussion.

Carter knew of Knossos, site of the Minoan palace of the great King Minos close to Iraklion, partially excavated and reconstructed after a fashion around the turn of the century by the Englishman, Sir Arthur Evans. Santorini he knew was an island northwest of Crete. The two men talked of an eruption on Santorini, one that virtually destroyed the island and all its inhabitants. Their theory of a gigantic fireball and tsunami rolling across the Mediterranean to devastate the Minoans on Crete held Carter enthralled. Someone named Galanopoulos was trying to tie the volcanic activity into the Biblical plagues in Egypt, which lay only 450 miles to the southeast. Additionally, this Galanopoulos believed the collapse of Thera following the eruption, and the waters rushing to fill the void, caused dramatic lowering of sea level on all eastern Mediterranean shores. The result of this, he expostulated, led to the temporary formation of a land bridge, not in the Red Sea, but in an area known in modern times as the Sea of Reeds. It was across this land bridge the Jews passed to escape from Egypt with Moses leading them. The waters racing back towards land in the form of a gigantic tidal wave caught the pursuing Egyptians and swept them away. The major disagreement seemed to be only when and how many eruptions occurred.

With an announcement over the public address system, the two men rose to leave. Carter wanted to follow them and hear more of their theories. Their conversation raised so many questions in his mind about the history of the region and the demise of the Minoans. Their arguments sounded plausible to him, so very logical. He watched with regret as they exited the bar.

With time remaining before his own flight left, he wandered around the terminal and ended up in the gift shop. On racks with the magazines and periodicals were several books on Greece. He picked up several and thumbed through them. In one he found numerous pictures and texts on Crete, all designed for the casual tourist. In spite of this it contained far more up-to-date material than was available to him in the libraries in D.C. He paid for his purchases and walked back to the waiting room where he studied the information until his flight was at last announced ready for boarding. Even after he took his seat on the plane, he continued to look at the photographs of the major sites. He marveled at the beauty of the artifacts displayed in the archaeological museum in Iraklion. He imagined the thrill of digging up such wonders.

The flight from Athens lasted little more than an hour and before he knew it they began their descent. He looked out his window and saw the stark beauty of the mountainous island rising from the incredibly blue water of the sea. As the aircraft made its final approach it flew parallel to the north coast. Slightly below them stretched miles and miles of deserted beaches. Not far inland were small villages surrounded by orchards of what he imagined to be olive trees. He was soon able to pick out individuals here and there on the ground working in their fields. In each field windmills with white cloth sails turned under the late afternoon sun. With surprising suddenness, they skimmed over a rocky cliff and almost immediately the wheels touched the runway.

As soon as he stepped onto the tarmac Carter experienced an unexpected rush of elation. He closed his eyes and took a deep breath, inhaling the dust and residual heat of the late August day. If he thought his arrival in Athens was a homecoming, there was even more kinship here. The feeling of recognition and welcome was strong. With a slight shrug of his shoulders he opened his eyes once more and turned to walk across the two lane coastal road to the terminal.

Chapter 6

Zakari awoke with a start. Motes of dust floated across narrow rays of sunlight shining through the cracks of his shutters. They sailed gently out of the deep shadows of the room, across the stilettos of light, and back into the gloom. Through the fog of sleep that still engulfed him Zakari could hear the clucking and cackling of his hens and the crowing of his one rooster. Each morning they fluttered down from their perches in the olive trees with the first light of day to begin their incessant scratching and pecking in the dirt surrounding the house. From further away came the plaintive bleating of his one katsika, his milk goat. Since he descended the mountain the day before she was confined to her remained enclosure. Now she was hungry and wanted to be milked. The thought of a sauce pan of boiled goat's milk with sugar made Zakari's mouth water. With nothing substantial to eat since before noon yesterday, his empty stomach ached. He lay fully clothed in his rumpled, foul smelling bed, still wearing the sweaty clothes in which he fell asleep the night before. He idly wondered what awakened him so suddenly. Certainly not the normal morning sounds of his animals. Not even his hunger could have dragged him so suddenly from his seemingly drugged sleep. What could it have been?

"Kyrie Zakari!"

The sound of his name being called shocked him like a bolt of electricity. He sat straight up in bed, his heart tripping in his chest, his breath suddenly coming in strained rasps. Cold clamminess gripped his body and fear wrapped him its stifling grip.

"Kyrie Zakari! Ela 'do!" Come here!

Zakari slipped silently from his bed and walked gingerly across the dirt floor. When he put his eye close to a crack between the boards of the closed shutters sunlight knifing through the cracks between the boards traced patterns of light across his stubbled face. It shone upon the film of sweat and mixture of earth and body oils that covered his face, highlighting his sun-wrinkled skin with its deep creases like striations chiseled into granite. It also revealed the fear in his eyes.

He peered carefully, but intently, through the small aperture, searching to the limits of the view it offered. He saw nothing and quickly moved to another crack, where he scanned the area leading up to the front of his house. He could still see nothing. Finally he moved to the door and searched there too, but could still see no one.

"Zakari, ela oxo!" Come out!

It was then that Zakari recognized the voice. He heaved a sigh of relief, feeling fear instantly replaced by resentment over his being disturbed. In exasperation he threw back the wooden latch on his door and pulled it open. The sudden onslaught of bright morning sunshine blinded him, causing him to rub his eyes vigorously, trying to wipe away the stabbing pain. When he could once more open his eyes without discomfort, he put his hand above his eyebrows, shading his face, and searched for the source of the voice.

"Kalimera!" Good morning.

And then Zakari found him. Just beyond the olive trees, near the two gigantic boulders marking the entrance to the path stood Barba Yorgi, Old George, Yorgos Pseramanolis, The Bull, the old man of the mountains. His broad but stooped shoulders supported his massive head with its lion's mane of white hair and full white beard. Hands, now gnarled with age, but still strong as steel, gripped a thick staff of olive wood. Barba Yorgi sometimes used it as a walking stick to help him negotiate the rocky, uneven paths that crisscrossed the mountains. Other times he used it as a weapon. His dexterity and speed with the staff was known to all the inhabitants of the region.

Two years earlier, as he walked along the side of a road, a car approached from behind. He moved over almost into the ditch then turned to watch until it was safely past him. The woman in the passenger's side gesticulated and pointed in his direction. The driver applied the brakes and stopped just beyond where Barba Yorgi stood, engulfing both the old man and the car in a cloud of choking dust. The woman stuck her head out the window, looked back at the old man, then turned to the driver and shoved a 35 mm camera into his hands. The door on the driver's side opened and a man got out. Barba Yorgi watched with steely eyes as he approached.

"Photographia, photographia." Photograph, photograph. Obviously, he found the old man to be photogenic and his wife insisted he take some snapshots of "local color" to add to their summer vacation album.

Barba Yorgi neither moved nor said a word. He watched the red-faced, overweight man come towards him, noticed the pale blue eyes and the light colored hair beginning to show traces of gray at the temples. What he noticed most of all were the lederhosen, knee socks and sturdy walking shoes. The man approached within arm's length of him before Barba Yorgi, without changing expression, addressed him.

"Yermanos eisai?" Are you German?

The man looked puzzled. "Was?" What?

"Deuts? Bist du Deuts?" asked Barba Yorgi, this time in a heavily accented German, using the familiar form of the verb.

The German tourist ignored the intended insult, threw back his head and laughingly replied, "Yawohl, ich bin Deutch. Darf ich...?"

But he never finished his question. With blinding speed, the butt of Barba Yorgi's staff came up from the ground, neatly knocking the camera from between the German's fat hands. As it rose through the air it disintegrated into bits of plastic and glass. The roll of film burst from the inside, unrolling like a celluloid serpent as it flew through the air and fluttered to the ground some distance away.

The momentary look of surprise and outrage on the man's face was replaced by a look of fear. He saw the staff descending and his mouth dropped open and his eyes gaped. With a dull thud and a sharp crack the staff landed squarely on his left shoulder. His shrill scream of pain was quickly joined by the excited shouts of his wife. The German turned, his shoulder sagging painfully and unnaturally, and made his way as quickly as possible to the passenger side of the car. His wife left the door open and scooted over under the steering wheel. Before the injured man could slam the door the car began to move, spitting dust and gravel from beneath the spinning wheels.

They were not fast enough, however. Barba Yorgi followed closely behind. As the car began to pull away he took one last swing with his staff. The rear window shattered, spraying the occupants with a shower of glass. Through the broken window came the clearly audible sound of the man's screams and guttural curses. His wife fought the steering wheel, frantic with fear, struggling to bring the car under control as it careened from one side of the road to the other.

In the middle of the road, legs akimbo, brandishing his staff at the retreating car, stood Barba Yorgi. "Malakka!!" he shouted at the rapidly disappearing vehicle. Then, holding his staff with both hands in front of him, he threw back his head and roared with laughter. Decidedly satisfied with himself, he gave a shrug of approval, left the road and melted into the olive grove.

Sustaining a badly broken shoulder, the tourist reported the attack to the authorities in Chania. He and his wife told police of being viciously attacked by a wild man for no reason at all. The police conducted an inquiry, questioned people living in the immediate area, but each person questioned professed ignorance of the incident. As for the old man, no one seemed to know who he might be. At least that was the story the police got from those they questioned. Thanks to the efficiency of the mountain grapevine, everyone knew about the incident hours before the arrival of the police. In their opinion Barba Yorgi's actions repaid a small measure of the treatment he and other Cretans experienced at the hands of the German occupation forces during World War II. Secretly they applauded him, revered him, and bought him rounds of raki in the villages where he turned up from time to time.

He now stood outside Zakari's house. Why was he here? What did he want? Curious, Zakari motioned the old man to approach. He leaned heavily on his staff, his movements appearing labored. When he raised his head Zakari noticed the light in the expressionless brown eyes. These were not the eyes of an old man. Rather, they took in everything. Zakari felt as if he were being measured. Remembering his manners, he asked the old man if he would like something to drink.

"Kafes," replied Barba Yorgi. Coffee. "Varigliko." Lots of sugar.

Zakari motioned for him to sit on the bench against the front wall of his house and went inside to prepare the Turkish coffee that is a staple of every Greek household. He took the long handled copper cooker down from the nail on the wall, filled it with enough water for two cups, spooned in the heaping measures of coffee and sugar, lit the one gas burner with a wooden match and held the cooker over the flame. The mixture soon began to boil and when the foam reached the very top of the cooker, threatening to spill out and down its sides, he extinguished the flame. Carrying two small cups, each filled to the brim, he went back outside and handed one to the old man.

"Efcharisto, pedimou," he muttered. Thank you, my child.

Taking the steaming mixture from Zakari, he brought it immediately to his lips and slurped noisily at the foam. A smile of contentment and satisfaction turned up the corners of his mouth under his drooping mustache and he swiped at the droplets of the brown liquid that clung to it with the back of his hand. He heaved a huge sigh, leaned back against the rough exterior of the house and pulled a box of cigarettes from the sash around his waist. He lifted the lid of the box and offered one to Zakari. From his sash he also fished a box of matches, struck one against the stones of the side of the house and lit both cigarettes. Barba Yorgi took a puff, inhaled deeply, placed his small cup on the heavy material of his pantaloons and closed his eyes. They did not talk for several minute, the quiet broken only by the occasional sounds of slurping coffee and the exhalation of cigarette smoke.

The old man's very presence bothered Zakari deeply. His passing this way was the first time in over a year. Why should he appear on his doorstep today? Studying him, he noted the collar on the soiled white shirt, ripped and resewn with black thread in huge, clumsy stitches. Usually sticking out of the top of Barba Yorgi's vest could be seen a transistor radio in a brown imitation leather cover, the old man's proudest possession. Zakari could not recall having heard it play, did not even know if it contained batteries. It was simply a part of his attire and he was never without it. For whatever reason it was not in its usual place this day. Zakari did not comment on its absence.

When he finished, Barba Yorgi tilted his head back, upended the cup over his open mouth and let the sweet slurry of dark powdered grounds slide onto his extended tongue. When the last drop fell he placed the cup on the bench beside him, turned to Zakari and began to speak of the weather, the prospect of winter rains, the olive crop and the widow in the next village. Nothing of substance. Banalities. Thinking that his visitor just happened to be in the area and dropped by to pass the time of day, Zakari began to relax. Little by little he lowered his defenses and allowed himself to be lulled into a sense of calm. Barely listening now, his responses to the old man's monologue were grunts and monosyllables. His mind began to drift, like the smoke from their cigarettes on the gentle morning breeze.

"Did you hear about the discovery down on the new road?" asked Barba Yorgi.

The question shocked Zakari, but he forced himself to respond with feigned indifference. "Discovery? What discovery?"

"The new road along the coast. You know the one. Yesterday the bulldozer fell into a hole as it worked. Burial place of some sort. Minoan, they say. Full of pottery and other antikas. The driver called the museum in Candia, but by the time the director and some of his men got back all of the things there were gone. Just some pieces of broken pottery lying on the ground was all that was left."

"I'll wager the director was upset," stated Zakari noncommittally, wondering where this discussion was going.

I hear he called the police and the Archaeological Commission in Athens. They think maybe this tomb was important. The driver told them of some of the things he saw with his own eyes: some of the things that disappeared. Police are questioning people in the nearest villages to see if they know anything about it. I hear they've even offered money to anyone who can tell them anything that'll lead them to the things which were taken."

"You mean paid informers?"

"Well, Zakaraki, it wouldn't be the first time they've tried this. It works, too, sometimes." The old man's use of the affectionate diminutive form of Zakari's name made him even more wary.

"How much are they offering?"

"Five thousand drachmas. The authorities think the things in the tomb were very important. Did I tell you they are all gone? Somebody took everything!"

As nonchalantly as possible, Zakari posed the question: "Who do they think took them?"

"Oh, you know, there are always people watching when any sort of construction or excavation is going on. The driver says there were several men and two women watching him until he made his discovery. They were still there when he left to find a telephone, but were gone when he came back. That's when they discovered the director's 'treasure' was nowhere to be found." Barba Yorgi chuckled, a deep rumbling sound, and turned to face Zakari. "He says one man fell in the hole right after it was discovered. As soon as the others arrived he jumped up and ran away from the place. He ran bent over, as if hurt in pain. Ran into the brush in the direction of the mountains."

"Any idea who it was?" asked Zakari.

"The driver didn't know him. He thinks he recognized one person who was there, but he's not sure."

Zakari chewed on this bit of information. If even one of the people was identified the police would use any measure available to force him to reveal the names of the others who were there. Their methods were well-known and they would not hesitate to employ them, particularly if the tomb was as important as Barba Yorgi said.

"Who's the man the driver thinks he recognized?" asked Zakari.

"He thinks his name is Mitzos. Mitzos something...diaolo!...what was the name he said? My mind's not as good as it used to be. I sometimes have trouble remembering things. What...oh, now I remember! Detorakis. Mitzos Detorakis. You know him? Lives in Plakias with his aunt, the widow Marika."

Zakari's blood turned to ice. No, not Detorakis, he thought to himself. That weakling! If the police just threaten him with even a little bit of pain he'll tell everything. What am I going to do?

"The police went to his aunt's house to question him. Funny thing. His aunt hasn't seen him since last evening. He left late. Said he couldn't sleep and wanted to go walk. Hasn't returned since. The police are asking everyone if they've seen him. Seems to have vanished. No one's seen him."

Struggling to bring his emotions under control, Zakari stood up and walked a few paces away from the old man on the bench. He stood looking through the olive trees, his mind fixed on the hole in the rocks where his statue lay hidden. He wondered about Detorakis. He must find him, tell him he would kill him if he said anything to the police. Tell him anything to make him keep his mouth shut.

Hearing movement behind him, he turned to see the old man pushing himself up from the bench with the aid of his staff. Finally erect, he faced Zakari and held out his hand.

"Thank you for your hospitality. Fevgo." I must be on my way.

Zakari wished him well. "Kalo taxidi, Kyrie Yorgos."

The old man walked a number of paces and then stopped. Slowly turning, he studied Zakari's face for a moment.

"A great treasure they say, Zakaraki, one that could make a poor man very rich. Take care." Then he turned and continued towards the path between the boulders.

"Xeri!!," Zakari's mind screamed. He knows!!

Chapter 7

The light of late afternoon/early dusk bathed the rocky crags to the south with an almost unearthly pastel glow as Carter strode toward the terminal building. The sun, just slipping behind the peaks to the northwest, transformed the sea from the cerulean blue he remarked with awe on the flight from Athens to a sheet of polished copper.

To get to the terminal he first needed to cross a two lane road. Below the crest of the hill to his left came the deep throated roar of a motor and he paused on the side of the road and glanced in that direction expecting to see a truck appear. From the rapidly increasing level of sound he estimated whatever sort of vehicle was coming seemed to be traveling fast. Like a jack popping out of its box, a canary yellow convertible with top down crested the hill hardly more than a hundred meters away. There were still people crossing the road in both directions and the driver shifted into a lower gear and leaned on his horn. At the sound of the horn pedestrians glanced quickly to their left then scattered like chickens. Still traveling at an excessive speed, the car pulled abreast of Carter and then accelerated once more. From his appearance Carter surmised the driver was Greek. In front, seated next to him was a deeply tanned blonde woman and in the back two more attractive young women and a young man, all of whom appeared to be northern Europeans.

Someone's found the good life, Carter thought and smiled.

A man standing beside him muttered something in Greek and Carter glanced in his direction. The man glared after the yellow car, the muscles of his jaw standing out rigidly as he clenched his teeth. His final gesture before hurrying across the road was to throw up his hand, palm outward and fingers spread apart, toward the car and its occupants.

Carter recognized the explicit insult in the gesture and wondered what caused such a strong reaction. It was one of the first signals of its type he learned as a young boy in school in Athens. Like boys everywhere, he and his friends knew it was not a nice thing to do. Knowing this, they used it liberally.

He continued into the terminal and located a telephone, put a coin into the slot, dialed the four numbers he embedded in his memory and waited for it to ring at the other end. It was answered almost immediately by a woman.

"Empros?"

In English he began to tell her who he was and why he was calling. In the middle of his first sentence she interrupted him and Carter stopped.

"Prepi na perimente. Excuse, please. Wait moment. Wait moment."

This was followed by the sound of the receiver being laid carefully on a solid surface and muffled voices in the background. The receiver was soon picked up again, this time by a man.

"Hallo, this is Daskoloyanni. Can I help?"

"Yes," responded Carter, "My name is Carter Martin. I've just arrived in Iraklion and I'm looking for a place to stay temporarily. Someone I met in Athens gave me your number and said I should call you upon arrival."

"Mr. Martin, you say. Someone suggested you stay at our pension? Yes, Mr. Martin, you are welcome. Of course we have room for you. Where you now?"

Carter explained he was at the airport and asked how he should get to Iraklion.

"Take bus to Eleftherios Square. You get off there. Right after bus enter city walls it make first stop at square. My son Nikos wait for you. He is 14 years old. Wear white shirt and shorts. What you wear?"

Carter told him how he was dressed. "I have a briefcase and a large leather valise. His name is Nikos?"

"Nai, uh, yes. Nikos. My son. You look for him."

Fine, Mr. Daskaloyanni. Thank you. I look forward to meeting you."

Carter replaced the receiver and went to retrieve his luggage. From there he found a bus with 'Iraklio' on its destination marquee, boarded and found an empty seat. Shortly afterwards the bus pulled away from the airport and before long the walls of the city loomed ahead of them. The road made a sharp turn to the right as it reached the wall and climbed parallel to it. Two hundred meters further on it reached the top and turned left, where it stopped in Eleftherios Square.

Among the trees, along the sidewalks, in the middle of the streets and along the top of the wall, strolled what must have been most of the population of Iraklion. The buildings surrounding the square, hotels and restaurants, all with groups of tables lining the wide street around the tree-filled island. Every table was full. Waiters hurried here and there, carrying trays of drinks and platters of food from which mouthwatering aromas arose. The few cars on the streets were almost totally blocked by groups of strollers, many of whom walked arm in arm taking their evening volta, the ritual evening promenade.

Carter stepped from the bus onto the sidewalk, salivating almost uncontrollably at the sight and smell of the food. The old aromas remembered from childhood: rosemary, thyme and the many other herbs and spices the Greeks used in their cooking assailed him.

"Mr. Martin?"

Carter turned at the sound of the voice calling his name. A slim youngster of about fourteen wearing kaki shorts and a short-sleeved white shirt stood in the evening gloom.

"Yes. Are you Nikos?"

"Nai. Give me your bag. I carry." He took the bag and motioned for Carter to follow him. They walked across the street and entered a narrow alley between a hotel and another building. The way sloped downward and soon Nikos turned into a gate in a high wall. Carter followed him into the yard.

On the steps of the veranda was a tall, older gentleman, leaning against the pillar supporting the roof. He smoked a cigarette held in a four inch black holder with a brass or copper band at the end. As Carter approached he stepped down into the yard.

"Hallo, Mr. Martin. I am Daskaloyanni."

"Carter Martin. Nice to meet you."

"Car-tear. Car-tear. You are American, no? I call you Car-tear. Come in. Leave bag on veranda." Mr. Daskaloyanni spoke rapidly in Greek to Nikos, who nodded, took Carter's bag and descended the steps with it.

"Come, Car-tear," said Daskaloyanni and entered the house, holding the door open for Carter.

Standing in the entry hall stood an attractive, dark haired woman wearing a black dress. Her smile lit up the entrance as Daskaloyanni introduced her as his wife, Rania.

Carter took her proffered hand, finding it warm and dry. She was several years younger than her husband. Her mouth was generous and her eyes enormous and dark. Her only words were, "Allo, Meester Marteen." As soon as he began to speak to her Daskaloyanni interrupted him, telling him she spoke only French and German. Carter almost slipped into French, but at the last moment caught himself. In spite of her obvious lack of understanding she seemed to comprehend his pleasure at meeting her and her smile radiated warmth.

The Daskaloyanni's ushered him into their living room, with its windows overlooking the harbor. Daskaloyanni asked him for his passport and gave him a short form printed in Greek, English, French and German to fill out. He explained the cost per day and the fact that a continental breakfast would be served each morning at 7:30.

Nikos came back into the room and stood at the door. His father turned to Carter. "Car-tear, your room ready now. Are you tired? You want take shower? Follow Nikos. He show you the way."

Carter thanked the whole family and followed the boy, who led him along the front of the house and up a set of stone stairs to the top floor. They passed through a door into a passageway with five doors along its length. At the last one Nikos paused and opened it, motioning for Carter to follow.

It was a small room with a washstand on one wall, a bed against the other, and a window overlooking the lights of the harbor. He thanked Nikos for his help, closed the door after the boy left, undressed quickly and, taking a towel, went down the hall to the bathroom, where he luxuriated under a lukewarm shower. The water sluiced away the grime of his journey and much of his fatigue.

After brushing his teeth, Carter returned to his room, where he put on a pair of shorts and a tee shirt. Barefooted, he left his room and took the door out onto the flat roof with its two foot high parapet. A blast of sound rolled up from the direction of the sea and he turned in the direction of the harbor. Leaning over the parapet, he could make out a ship pulling away from the dock, its lights twinkling brilliantly against the darkness. He watched it slowly traverse the harbor, passing in front of the ancient Venetian fortress and then slip between the lights marking the entrance to the harbor. As the ship sailed away to the north it left a trail of phosphorescence behind it. Carter was hypnotized and watched until he could no longer distinguish between the lights of the ship and the stars which descended to the horizon.

Utter fatigue finally claimed him. He made his way back to the room, stripped off his shirt and shorts and fell naked into bed. He fell asleep immediately, his tired body caressed by the sea breezes wafting through the window.

After what seemed only moments he partially opened one eye and saw it was daylight. The room was cloaked in soft shadows. He opened his other eye slightly, groaning as he struggled to remember where he was. The bed felt strange and the room was certainly not familiar. Raising up on one elbow he looked through bleary eyes at his surroundings. When his sleepy gaze passed over his open suitcase and clothes memory flooded back. With no idea of the time the sweetness of the August morning and the muted sounds coming from the direction of the harbor made him believe it was still early. He pulled on his shorts and walked out of his room to the rooftop. The sun, not long out of the sea, was barely beginning to heat the air. In the harbor fishing boats chugged out past the protective sea wall to the deeper waters beyond. The sea itself sparkled in the morning sun, the surface riffled occasionally by a slight breeze. Gentle swells marked the only motion of the Mediterranean. Its color was even more brilliant than he remembered from the day before.

Voices from below caught his attention and he crossed the terrace to the parapet overlooking the front yard. Nikos, dressed as the night before, stood with a basket of fresh bread on his arm. Mrs. Daskaloyanni was standing on the veranda, out of Carter's sight, talking to her son. When Carter called down a good morning Nikos looked up, smiled and waved...

Mrs. Daskaloyanni stepped from under the verandah's overhang, shading her eyes from the morning sun, and smiled up at Carter. "Kalimera."

He parroted her greeting, "Kalimera," which provoked a delightful, throaty laugh from the attractive lady.

"Good! Good! Speak ellinika now. You speak Greek!" She touched all five of her fingertips together, pointed them in the direction of her mouth and said, "Fagito. Fagito. Ela na tromai." She then waved for him to come down.

Carter looked at Nikos and shrugged, pretending not to understand.

"She say, 'time to eat.' Come down and we have, how you say, breakfast. Come eat breakfast. Na tromai."

Mrs. Daskaloyanni shaded her eyes once more from the morning sun as she looked up at Carter. Her smile was brilliant. "Nai. Eat. Come eat." She laughed again then mounted the steps and disappeared into the house.

"I'm coming right now," he said to Nikos, and returned to his room. He splashed cold water on his face and lathered it quickly with shaving cream from an aerosol can in his dop kit. The blade dragged painfully across barely-soaked whiskers, but he was ravenous and the promise of food made his stomach growl in anticipation. From his bag he pulled an old, long-sleeved blue Levi work shirt almost threadbare from years of wear, stepped into a pair of deck shoes and headed downstairs.

A couple who were apparently guests of the pension were already seated. Carter introduced himself and they responded in lilting, accented English. They introduced themselves as Arne and Pia Larsen and asked Carter if he was newly arrived. When he responded he was, they told him they were concluding a week of vacation. Unfortunately, they were on their last day and would leave by boat that night to begin their return to Denmark. They were celebrating their honeymoon in Greece and rhapsodized about the sea and their visit to the villages in the mountains. They visited as many of the archaeological sites as their limited time would allow. Both were tanned a deep bronze, with blonde hair that contrasted beautifully with their golden complexions.

Mrs. Daskaloyanni entered the room with a large pot of steaming coffee on a tray. Setting it down in the middle of the table, she announced, "Café. Du café pour tout le monde!"

While everyone ate they talked of all the wonderful sights seen and done. When questioned about his reason for coming to Crete, Carter gave them an abbreviated version of his story. Pia and Arne told him how jealous they were that their short adventure was ending as his was beginning. They envied him his freedom. When asked what they planned for their last day, they replied they were going to the beach and invited Carter to join them. Carter readily agreed, to which Pia commented with finality, "Good! As soon as breakfast is over we will take our bathing clothes and show you where we find the bus."

Carter wolfed down the rest of his bread, butter and marmalade, dunked the remaining crust in his coffee then popped it into his mouth. When Arne and Pia left the table to get ready, he poured himself another half cup. This is the way life should be, he thought to himself, luxuriating in the feeling of freedom. He saw Mrs. Daskaloyanni busy in the kitchen, her back to him. Unobserved, he admired her slim back and legs and her thick, shiny dark hair.

Arne's calling him brought him from his musings. He left the table, thanked Mrs. Daskaloyanni for breakfast and joined the couple at the gate. They made their way up the street toward the square, where they boarded a waiting bus. Carter noticed the men walking down the aisle cast openly appraising glances at Pia. He could not blame them, for she was a true beauty.

A mile and a half beyond the airport the bus stopped. Across the road could be seen the cabanas and open air restaurant of the beach. A number of people frolicked in the surf, which was less calm than earlier in the morning. The weather was considerably warmer than when he rolled out of bed earlier and Carter unbuttoned his shirt and pulled it off as they walked.

He watched as Pia and Arne both wrapped towels around themselves and changed out of their clothes into swimming suits. This was common on European beaches but Carter never tired of the women's dexterity. Emulating Arne, Carter wrapped his towel around his waist and dropped his shorts and underwear. As he bent over to pick up his swimming suit his towel suddenly fell from his waist, leaving him naked. Pia's laughter rang out as he struggled to wrap the towel around himself once more and put his suit on at the same time.

"Don't worry," said Pia. "This is Europe. No one pays any attention. If this were Denmark you could walk the beach all day long with no clothes on and no one would notice. You Americans with your complexes and phobias about the body! You need to learn to relax."

"Come. Run to the water," called Arne, as he turned seaward. Arne and Pia, each took one of his hands, pulling him towards the gentle surf. When they neared the surf line they released his hands and all three plunged into the shallow water. Carter came up spouting and licking his lips. For the first time in years he tasted the salty waters of the Mediterranean. He floated with ease, the water's natural buoyancy bobbing him to the surface. Pia popped up next to him and quickly found her footing in the sand. When she stood the water came only to mid-thigh.

And what thighs they are, he thought to himself. She was magnificent. Her bikini was tiny. Her stomach was flat and her breasts were small but perfectly formed. Carter envied Arne, who stroked away from the shore.

They spent the rest of the morning on the beach, ate lunch in the beach-side restaurant in the shade of the palm frond roof. Being careful not to overdo his first day in the sun, after lunch he remained in the shade, people-watching and reading.

When in mid-afternoon they returned, their bodies were glowing from the sun and sticky and itchy from the layer of salt covering them. He felt sorry for Arne and Pia, for they would leave this wonderful land and return to the far north. Once back home their tans would quickly fade, leaving only memories and slides as souvenirs of their honeymoon under the sun.

That night they dined at a restaurant located in Fountain Square, across from the Knossos Restaurant. After dinner they returned to the pension and he helped them carry their luggage to the port, where they would take the inter-island ferry, Keftiu. When it came time for them to board, Arne pumped Carter's hand warmly and Pia hugged him, then kissed him on both cheeks. "If you are ever in Aalborg, please come see us. You will always be welcome," said Arne.

"If you come back to Crete next year, I should still be here. Write me in care of the pension. I plan to rent a house, but I'll let the Daskaloyanni's know where I am and how to get in touch with me. I look forward to seeing you again. Have a safe trip."

He watched as they mounted the gangplank and found spots at the crowded rail on the second deck. They waved as lines were cast off and the ship began to move away from the dock. It was not until the ship turned for its run across the harbor and out into the open sea that he finally lost sight of them.

The combination of the day's sun, the wine with dinner and jet lag all weighed heavily on him. He trudged back to the pension, stuck his head into the house to speak to the Daskaloyanni's and then headed for his room. Before going to bed he jumped into the shower, wrote a brief card to his mother and then turned out the light. As soon as he lay down he was asleep.

Chapter 8

Carter awoke the next morning feeling completely refreshed. He rushed to shower and shave, returned to his room, where he dressed in haste and then descended to breakfast. He ate ravenously, consuming a whole crusty baguette, numerous pats of butter, half a jar of marmalade and cup after cup of coffee. Finally sated, he pushed his chair back from the table, patted his stomach and stared in spite of himself at the two couples shuffled into the room. They were burnt such a painful red that Carter imagined he could see waves of heat and wisps of smoke rising from their tortured bodies.

Both couples were from Chester, located near Liverpool. In their mid-50's, they had saved all year for their traditional summer holiday, 'a fortnight among the swarthy Mediterranean types.' Sheila and Clive Atwell resembled Jack Spratt and his wife. Regis and Alexandra Balfour were both tall and spare. They moved stiffly, obviously in pain, taking great care not to lean against the backs of their chairs. Each hung by their tail bone on the front four inches of their chairs to avoid touching their legs or backs to the wood. Carter was sure this was the only part of their anatomies not completely fried.

Upon their arrival they rented a car and went in search of a beach. Finding one, they proceeded to bake lily white skin in the strong rays of the sun. After four hours of sun worship they returned to the pension to find themselves burned everywhere except in those areas covered by cloth and heavy hair. Even the soles of their feet were blistered and the unrelenting pain kept them awake most of the night. Their shirts were all unbuttoned as far as their sense of decency would allow, trying to lessen the fire. They were a dour group, who regretted having ever left England for what promised to be a sojourn in hell.

Carter attempted conversation with them, but they were too preoccupied with their discomfort. After a few minutes he wished them luck and excused himself.

In the hallway he met Mrs. Daskaloyanni coming from the kitchen with a pot of hot water for tea. He greeted her, rolled his eyes in the direction of the living room and went outside. He followed the street to the square, where the normal daytime hustle and bustle was considerably less frantic than the nighttime crowd. He continued across the square and entered a main street heading into the center of town.

A shop with several icons in the window caught his eye and he stopped to admire them. From inside the shop came a heavily accented man's voice, "Greetings! Come in! You want to look around?"

Peering around the door frame, Carter could see a short, portly man approaching from the back of the shop. He wore heavy, dark-rimmed glasses and his thick, dark hair, slicked straight back, glistened with oil. As he walked across the dusty wooden floor he dug the fingers of his right hand into his oily hair, scratching his scalp vigorously. With the other he pushed his glasses back up from the tip of his nose. When he walked into the light nearer Carter he pulled his hand from his hair, cleaned the nails of his right hand with the nails of his left, wiped his right hand on his trousers, adjusted his crotch and then offered to shake hands. Carter responded reluctantly. The man's grasp was soft and fleshy, offering no return pressure. Carter pulled his hand away as quickly as he could without offering offense, struggling to keep from wiping his palm on his pants leg.

"Come in. My name is Manoli. This my shop. You American? What you like to see? We have many, many traysures here. Old Greek traysures. Icons. Rugs. Blankets. What you like? You look."

"OK, thanks," responded Carter. He walked around, peering at dusty shelves filled with what looked like the common trinkets tourists bought and carried back to Kansas City, Lyon, Baden-Baden, Eastbourne, or wherever else they called home.

"Manoli, you have some icons in the windows, but they look new. Is it possible to buy old icons?"

"Sure, sometimes. When the church needs money the priest sell icons. Very dangerous for foreigner to buy. Many icons in churches Byzantine traysures. Forbidden to take them out of Kriti."

"Oh, I see," said Carter, pleased with his performance as a tourist. "What are these strings of beads in the window? I saw a man playing with some."

"Kómpoloi," answered Manoli. "Worry beads. Most English speaking people call them worry beads. I have one very nice one here. Made from amber. You buy. A real traysure."

Carter looked at the worry beads held out to him. They were a rich yellow/orange color with bits of dark debris suspended in some of them. In the very end piece he recognized the form of a small fly. Attached to the beads by a piece of soiled string was a tag with the price of 1200 drachmae scribbled in ink. Although taken by the amber beads he resisted the impulse to buy. "They're beautiful, but I don't think I'd better spend that much money right now."

"How long you be here? When you leave?"

"I don't know. I'm planning on being here a long time." He then gave a version of how he had come to be in Crete.

"Po, po, po," exclaimed the shop keeper. "You are planning to be Kritikós...man from Crete. That's very different. I like for us to be friends." He rushed to the door and looked up and down the street. On the other side was a young boy wearing a white apron and carrying a tray. Manoli hailed him and the boy hurried across the street toward the front of the shop.

"What you want? You like Turkish coffee? Turkish coffee. Very good. I order you a varígliko. Plenty of sugar. You like it, I'm sure."

Manoli rattled off an order to the boy, who hurried away. "Come. We sit at the table on the sidewalk."

He ushered Carter outside then followed a moment later with two cane bottom chairs, which he set on opposite sides of a small table. Five minutes later the boy returned, this time his tray laden with two of the small cups of coffee, two pastries and two glasses of water. Manoli dug into his pocket and tossed some coins on the boy's tray. Deftly palming them, the young waiter hurried off down the street, looking for others to serve.

"Drink. Eat. We talk." Manoli dug in, finishing before Carter had hardly begun. He then picked up his glass of water, took a large draught in his mouth, swished it around noisily, and swallowed. He drained the glass and, with a contented sigh and a belch, settled himself back in his chair.

"I noticed your sign in the window with all the languages spoken in your shop. Do you speak all of them?"

"Sure. All of them."

"I'm impressed. Do you speak them well?"

"Well enough, I think. Oh, you know, I have some trouble with Spanish. Do you know Spanish?"

"Sure, I took it in school," answered Carter.

"You teach me Spanish," said Manoli with excitement, "and I teach you Greek."

"Wonderful," exclaimed Carter. "Go get two pieces of paper and two pens and we'll begin."

Manoli heaved his bulk from the chair, pushed his glasses up on his nose once more, and entered the shop. In a moment he was back. He gave Carter lessons in all the little phrases one needs when they are new to a country. In turn Carter taught Manoli numbers into the thousands. Additionally, he taught him to say, "This is a very important piece"; "This costs..."; "Where do you come from in Spain?"; "How long are you staying in Crete?"; "Are you married?"; "Where is your husband?"; and "Which hotel are you staying in?"

When a group of tourists paused on the sidewalk and entered the shop Manoli excused himself and followed them inside. Carter prepared to wait until they left, but just as the first group exited another walked in. Seeing that Manoli would be occupied for some time, Carter stood up and waved at Manoli through the door mouthing that he would come back later. Manoli nodded his understanding and Carter left.

At the corner he turned right and headed toward the port. Just past Fountain Square and the national bank he came upon two tall wrought iron gates hanging ajar in a narrow opening leading to the interior of a ruined building. Stopping, he looked up at the gates and was astonished to see wrought iron swastikas prominently included in the ironwork of each gate. He could not imagine why that hated symbol of Nazism could still be found here in Crete, particularly since he knew the German occupation was not known for its benevolence. He resolved to broach the subject with Mr. Daskaloyanni when he returned to the pension that evening.

Then the reality of why he was in this fascinating old city intruded upon his thoughts. His mission was of prime importance. He was aware of that, for it had been drummed into him from the very first day of his training. How long until he would be able to make contact with Bonisseur? Where was Abu Bekr at this very moment? Could he possibly already be on the island and preparing his own plans? He pushed the thoughts from his mind. There was yet time to work out all the details. Right now he was more interested in this birthplace of the Minoan civilization.

Knossos! It suddenly dawned upon him that Knossos, the seat of one of the great, but least known, civilizations of the ancient world, awaited his visit. He quickly reversed his steps, found a bus going west out of the city and climbed aboard.

That afternoon he wandered the grounds for several hours, sometimes looking at the ruins, sometimes watching the tourists as they passed. There were no guides and everyone toured by themselves. There were few signs, but Carter felt they were really not needed.

By midafternoon he was no longer able to ignore his hunger pangs. He had not even begun to fully explore the wonders of the reconstructed ruins, but he knew he would have many opportunities to return. He walked to the parking lot and, as there was not a bus present, crossed over to the small restaurant he had noticed that morning. He would be able to see the bus when it arrived and could simply run back across the sparsely traveled road and jump aboard.

As he ate he listened halfheartedly to the conversation of four Greek men seated at a table near him. They were carrying on a heated debate about the present government in Athens, its faults and shortcomings. He smiled to himself. He had heard this same topic many times before and always marveled at how vehement these discussions became.

What really caught his attention, however, was when one of the men mentioned a tomb having been found recently at a road construction site on the south coast. When the officials from the museum in Iraklion finally arrived nothing remained. One of the peasants who was suspected of having been present that day, and almost certainly one of the ones to steal part of the treasure, was fingered by the bulldozer driver. He was from a village on the south coast and was identified to police. Although they had gone to his village looking for him he was not found at his aunt's house. No one had been able to find a trace of him. According to gossip, the tomb was comparable to the royal tombs of the Egyptian pharaohs. Carter smiled at the obvious exaggeration, but the description of the alleged treasures piqued his interest.

Just then the bus pulled into the parking lot across the street. He hated to miss out on the rest of the conversation, but did not know when the next bus would arrive. Laying some coins on the table for a tip, he ran across the street.

When he arrived at the pension Mr. Daskaloyanni called amiably to him from the porch. "Kalispéra, Car-tear. Good evening! Where did you go today?"

"Into town. I walked around, made a friend in one of the shops on the main street off the square, visited the port and then took the bus to Knossos. I spent almost four hours there. Before leaving for Knossos I made a deal with the owner of the shop, who wants to learn Spanish. I told him I would teach him Spanish if he would teach me Greek."

"That sounds like a good idea." It was important that he appear to be a novice and anything he could do, including taking a few lessons from either Mr. Daskaloyanni or Nikos would help preserve his cover. When Carter spoke of making friends in Iraklion, Daskaloyanni's eyes lit up. "You must find Greek girl. Very nice, Greek girl." A lascivious chuckle and a knowing dig in the ribs from the old man's elbow accompanied his statement.

Carter said he would try to find one and bade him a good evening. He wanted to return to his room, take a shower and lie down for awhile. He was tired from being on his feet in the sun all day. Maybe he was not yet over his jet lag. He put his head back, enjoying the feel of the tepid water as it coursed over his body. He thought about going back into town later, spending a few minutes with Manoli and then finding a little sidewalk cafe where he could eat dinner and people watch. When he turned off the water he heard the deep whistle of a boat in the harbor. Another boat load of tourists for our economy, he thought to himself, and smiled at the thought.

Naked, with beads of moisture on his back and shoulders, he lay down. Just a few minutes to rest the eyes and he would be as good as new. He let his thoughts drift to the overheard conversation about the plundered tomb and promptly fell asleep.

The trumpeting of a rooster interrupted his dreams. He could hear movement below, so he knew it was probably time for breakfast. His stomach ached with hunger as he threw on his clothes and went downstairs.

Several young people were already seated at the table. All looked to be in their early twenties or late teens and talked animatedly as they enjoyed bread and coffee. They greeted him in German as he sat down and he replied in English. Five of the group of eight spoke English and they included him in their conversation. They had arrived the night before from Athens. All were students from the university in Tubingen in northern Germany and were hiking through Greece and the islands that summer. Carter watched the girls with particular relish. Their tanned legs and bare feet below white shorts completed the picture. None of the girls wore bras and pert nipples pushed against barely resistant tee shirts. He was captivated by their total lack of self-consciousness.

The boys were pleasant enough, but were content to converse in German. None in the group seemed to have any personal attachment to anyone else, other than the fact they were friends.

Two of the girls, Hanne Lore from Wiesbaden and Traudel from Munich, centered their attention on Carter, asking him numerous questions about where he lived and what brought him to Crete. They expressed envy because he chose to live here, saying they wished they could live in a place where there was so much sunshine and sea. He told them of the things he had seen in the short time he had been on the island, advising them to visit Knossos.

They already had plans to travel to Phaistos that day and invited him to come along with them. He thanked them for the invitation but declined, feeling obliged to see if he could turn up anything on the Frenchman. They said they would be back that night and asked if he would like to have dinner with them. They mentioned a restaurant in one of the back streets where the fish was wonderful. Carter said he would love to join them and they agreed to meet back at the pension at six that evening. When they rose Carter wished them a pleasant day, saying he looked forward to seeing them that evening. Before passing out the door, Traudel turned in his direction and smiled and waved. They intrigued him and he was glad for the opportunity to spend more time with the one called Traudel. He was sorry he could not join them, but was already looking forward to the evening.

As he turned once more to his breakfast he heard the sound of leather slippers scuffing on the tile floor and looked up to see Mr. Daskaloyanni enter the room. He put down his cup of tea and sat down across from Carter, a scowl on his face.

"Germans. You see the Germans this morning? We have to take them in, too," he spat.

Puzzled, Carter asked him, "Do you mean those students that just left?"

"Malista. Students, tourists, young, old. If they are Germans they are all the same. But what can we do. The government makes us take them in. If we don't, we lose our license. We cannot refuse them."

Carter nodded as if he understood his attitude and asked him what it had been like during the war.

"They killed my father and older brother. Put them in front of a wall and shoot them!" As he talked pain was visible in his eyes.

"Oh, I'm sorry. I see why you wouldn't like them. May I ask why they were shot?"

"Black market. Very little food. The Germans took it all to feed their soldiers. Many Greek people starved, many children die. After the war we hear stories of parents who ate their dead children to stay alive to fight the Germans. Greek woman very ferocious sometimes. They make good soldiers. Guerrillas. Good in Resistance. You see now why we don't like Germans?"

"Yesterday when I was in town I saw some tall iron gates with the Nazi symbol, the swastika, on them. What was that building?"

"In the street going down to the harbor? That was the headquarters of the high command. They say many terrible things happen in that building. No one will go inside now. No one will touch the gates. It has been like that since the Germans left. Now the building falls down and no one cares. People still afraid of that building."

The old man was interrupted by the entry of the two English couples. Their sunburn looked no less painful, although they appeared to move more easily. Daskaloyanni greeted them as he rose from the table and left the room. As he passed he patted Carter on the shoulder.

Carter, too, rose after greeting them and went to his room to change clothes. He had not been fully aware of the vehemence of the Cretan's hatred of the Germans. It must have been a terrible time indeed. He could not imagine what it must have been like to live through such a time.

The morning and early afternoon passed slowly. Carter found himself looking at people around him, particularly the men, wondering how he was going to find Bonisseur. At one point he almost asked Manoli if perhaps he knew the Frenchman, but refrained from doing so. He wandered the streets most of the day, feeling as if his search was in limbo. Finding one Frenchman in a city of Greeks should not be so difficult.

Late that afternoon he returned to the pension, hoping that Traudel and her group would have returned from Phaistos. He chatted clumsily with Mrs. Daskaloyanni for several minutes. She told him the tours usually did not return until after six. He thanked her for the information and went upstairs.

Chapter 9

Zakari watched the old man's broad back until he passed out of sight between the boulders. He was bathed in cold sweat, his stomach churning and knotting painfully. He had been so careful. How could Barba Yorgi know or even suspect him? Where was Detorakis? Why had he disappeared? His mind was filled with unanswered questions, questions that for him contained life and death implications.

He moved about his property, mulling over the turn of events. He milked his nanny and staked her out in the open where forage was plentiful. These were things he did by rote. The performance of these daily tasks did not interfere with his thought processes. His eyes continued to stray in the direction of the path. He assumed Barba Yorgi had continued on his way, but he wanted to give him time to get well away from the vicinity of the house. It was a struggle not to rush to the spot where he had hidden the statue. He was fearful of even looking in that direction lest he provide a clue to anyone who might be watching.

The sun grew hotter as it rose into the sky. Zakari stripped off his soiled shirt, threw it carelessly across a boulder, and dropped the bucket into the well. He heard it splash in the darkness below, waited a moment, allowing it to fill before pulling it back to the top. Setting the brimming bucket on the boulder next to his shirt, he plunged both hands into the water then vigorously rubbed his stubbled face. The cold water seemed to help focus his thoughts. He bent over from the waist and poured the remainder of the bucket over his head, gasping involuntarily as rivulets fell from his tousled hair onto the bare skin of his back when he straightened. He moved from the shade near the well into the sunlight, seeking its warmth. Droplets glistened like gems on the coarse hair of his chest and shoulders. He slapped his upper arms with his open palms trying to generate heat and aid circulation. An involuntary shiver passed through him.

Walking purposefully toward the house, he emerged a moment later with a rough bar of homemade soap. He stripped off his clothes and let them lay where they fell. Naked, he reached for the bucket, filled it once more and then, without hesitation, poured its contents over his head and body. Once more he filled the bucket and left it on the well while he soaped and scoured his entire body. Only then did he empty the third bucketful over his head. The contrast between the skin of his face, neck, hands and the rest of his body was startling. The former were nut brown. Skin normally covered by clothing was almost pasty white. His hands and face were also wrinkled and weathered, belying his age. The rest of his body looked years younger.

Still naked, he strode to the house and entered the open door. Picking up the container of goat's milk, he poured its entire contents into a blackened and battered saucepan, lit the one gas burner with a wooden match and put the pan over the flame. From a tin container on a shelf he took four spoonfuls of sugar, measured them into the pan and stirred the mixture vigorously. Turning toward the portion of the room containing his bed, he pushed back the curtain covering the front of a rough armoire, took a white cotton shirt folded haphazardly from one of the uneven shelves, and put it on. Its tail was long, falling to mid-thigh, leaving his hairy, slightly bowed legs and wide, flat feet bare. With a comb from which several teeth were missing, he raked at his wet hair, pulling it straight back from his forehead and temples.

By the time he finished the milk had begun to boil. He opened the top on a large tin box with an advertisement for tea on it and extracted the remains of a loaf of bread. From the table he picked up a knife, cut off the dry portion and threw it out the door. His chickens, who were busily scratching for insects in the dirt in another part of the yard, quickly converged on the morsels, each vying to claim the largest piece. Once they had been devoured, the rooster, bolder than the rest, moved through the doorway into the kitchen, head cocked inquisitively, looking at the half loaf Zakari still held in his hand. Making an amused sound resembling a short, harsh bark, he tore off another small piece and threw it outside. The rooster followed its trajectory with his keen eyes and ran after it.

He tore a hunk from the loaf and plunged it into the steaming pot now sitting on the table. Lifting the soaked bread to his mouth he bit off the soggy portion, burning his mouth in the process.

"Panagia!" he exclaimed in pain. "Zestos!" Hot.

His hunger overcame the pain, however, and soon the entire half kilo was gone. Picking up a battered metal cup, he poured the remainder of the milk from the saucepan into it, and drained its contents, tapped his stomach appreciatively, belched loudly and walked from the house toward the boulder near the well. Amongst his discarded clothes he found a flat orange box, took a cigarette, lit it and inhaled deeply to take as much of the harsh but satisfying smoke into his lungs as possible.

Everything seemed normal once more. Nothing was out of place. Lifting his eyes toward the sky he noted a number of vultures had congregated and were circling on the currents of morning air a few kilometers away. They seemed to have found food this morning for they circled lower and lower. To the south Zakari could see two more black dots in the sky winging their way closer. From kilometers away they had spied the gathering to the north and were headed toward the promise of breakfast. Eat heartily, Zakari thought to himself. Probably a rabbit or a dog who has died. God provides for his creatures, even the most disgusting.

Forgetting the vultures, he now scanned the surrounding high ground. Nothing amiss there, either. Satisfied, he began walking his property in a random manner. The statue was his goal, however, and he approached its hiding place circuitously. It took him thirty minutes to arrive near the cache. Everything looked normal here, as well. The dead branches he had placed over the small opening were still there. He examined the dust on the ground looking for tell-tale signs of an intruder. He saw none. He was as satisfied as he could be that the statue was still there without actually seeing it. Now to find Detorakis, he muttered to himself. He turned his back on the hiding place and returned to the house. He ignored the two vultures flapping soundlessly in the sky overhead, flying in the same direction as the others he noticed earlier.

When Barba Yorgi had stepped between the boulders onto the path he continued to walk for several hundred meters. Periodically he glanced back over his shoulders to see if Zakari followed. The house and Zakari were lost from sight. Taking no chances, the old man stepped to the side of the path just before it took a sharp turn, waiting to see if anyone would appear behind him. Satisfied that he was alone, he emerged from his hiding place and crossed to the other side of the path with surprising speed. Once more hidden from sight, he wended his way uphill through a jumble of boulders and stunted trees. Each step took him both higher and closer to the point which overlooked Zakari's land. Within a short time he was 75 meters above the path in a position affording him an unobstructed view of the monoliths marking the path and Zakari's house and olive grove.

He sat quietly among the boulders in the dappled shade of a gnarled tree. Unwinding his dark headband from his forehead, he spread it out on his knees and then tied it like a scarf over his head to cover his white hair and beard. Unless someone knew exactly where he was he would be invisible to searching eyes from below. The combination of shadows and his dark clothing broke up any outline of his body as effectively as hunter's camouflage.

Raising his head carefully, he spied Zakari below, sitting on a short stool beside his goat, milking her. His head was down, his back facing the hillside on which the old man sat. With his left hand he held her right rear leg tightly to make sure she remained in one place, while with the other hand he pulled her teats. The rich milk spurted into the container he had placed under her, making a tinny sound that carried up the hill on the still summer air.

Satisfied that he could not be seen, Barba Yorgi relaxed in the shade. The combination of the warmth of the morning air and his recent exertion caused his eyes to droop, but not close. As watchful as an old lion he did not move as Zakari went about his morning chores. He saw him go to the well, draw a full bucket and pour it over his head. He watched him strip and bathe beside the well, then walk naked into his house. He waited patiently for his reappearance and saw him walk out again, now clothed in only a long shirt, take a cigarette and light it. He watched especially closely as Zakari began to wander aimlessly about. There seemed to be no rhyme or reason to his movements now. Barba Yorgi sensed a change in the pattern of activity, however, and leaned slightly forward, his attention riveted on the figure below.

Zakari had appeared nervous when the old man had arrived that morning. Barba Yorgi had noticed the darting eyes, the shaking hands and the film of sweat on his face. What was he nervous about? What did he need to hide? He did not know, but he wanted to find out. It was for this reason he had doubled back and was now hidden on the hillside. He remembered Zakari's reaction when asked if he had heard the news of yesterday's discovery. The eyes. The eyes told the story. Zakari knew more than he let on. And then his reaction when he was told of Detorakis. He saw him furtively try to wet his lips with a tongue suddenly dry. Never mind that Zakari professed to know nothing of the discovery. Barba Yorgi knew he was lying. He knew he had been there. Poor simple Detorakis told him just this morning. Poor Detorakis. The little fool.

Late the night before Barba Yorgi passed through Plakias where, in the kafeneion, he encountered some of the old men of the village, some of whom he had known since he was a young man. They drank coffee together, then switched to raki. They talked of old times when, as virtual children, they had fought the hated Turks. The conversation naturally turned to the German occupation and they relived their experiences in the Resistance. Then someone brought up the discovery on the new road just that day. There was speculation about who had been involved and even greater speculation about what was taken from the tomb. Everyone had an idea of what must have been found. Everyone dreamed of what they could do with the drachmas the sale of such contraband could bring when sold to the right buyer. It was common knowledge that every village in Crete was located either on or near a site from which artifacts turned up every year. Many homes contained a piece of pottery or statuary. Colored seals of stone, beads with pictures and funny markings on them, probably Minoan writing, were still found in quantity. They learned early on not to divulge the location of their site or even to let anyone outside of the community know when they found something.

Years ago they sometimes took pieces from the earth to the authorities thinking they might be rewarded for their honesty. They quickly learned, however, that the authorities would most often confiscate their find and then begin to show up in their villages at strange hours under one pretext or another. Taking their finds to the museum for authentication was no better. The curator would express an interest in the pieces, wanting to know exactly where they had been found. He never believed the truth in their stories of a pot's having been dug up while plowing. Soon the police were again at the door, prying, meddling.

As early as that very evening the police had come to Plakias looking for young Detorakis. It seemed as if he was recognized as one who was at the construction site. The driver of the bulldozer remembered having met him before and told this to the people from the museum and the commissioner of police, who rode out with them to see this unexpected treasure. Detorakis returned home right after nightfall, ate dinner with his aunt, and then went out. He was already gone when the police arrived to question him.

Barba Yorgi listened to this story and to speculation of what was probably taken from the tomb. After midnight he left the kafeneion to begin the walk of several kilometers to his home in the mountains. His friend Vangelis offered to lend him his gaidouros, his sturdy little ass, to ride home. Barba Yorgi demurred, thanking him, telling him he did not know when he would be back this way. Having said his goodbyes, he went out into the night.

Shortly after leaving Plakias, the old man left the dusty, rutted road and took a path, which soon began to grow steeper. He walked steadily, guided by the faint glow of the path under the canopy of stars. The moon had not yet risen over the rocky crags towering above him, but he had known and traveled these paths since childhood.

He had been walking for almost three quarters of an hour when he thought he detected a glow among the rocks above and ahead of him. Stopping, he raised his head, not sure he had actually seen anything at all. For his age, his eyes and ears were still keen. Cocking his head, he held his breath, listening for any sound that might confirm his suspicion that someone or something was up among the boulders. Glancing to his left, where the edge of the path dropped off precipitously to the coastal plain far below, he could see a few lights still burning in Plakias. The moon had finally crested the tops of the mountains, making him unsure whether or not he had actually seen a light or just the reflection of the moon among the rocks. He stood for several minutes, unmoving, when he heard the muffled sound of metal striking something. This was quickly followed by a faint shadow flickering across the face of one of the boulders above.

Now sure he was not alone on the mountain, he gripped the staff in both hands, creeping along the path. He advanced with a stealthy tread, keeping to the path which continued to climb the mountainside. When he had climbed another 200 meters he left it and began to double back towards the spot where he had seen the glow. He was careful not to let his bloused pants catch on the stiff brush growing in the sparse soil, or to dislodge a pebble that might give him away. The closer he drew to the rocks above, the more visible the glow became. He could soon hear grunts and labored breathing, as well.

Circling above and behind the spot he saw the top of someone's head and the rise and fall of a short shovel. Barba Yorgi leaned against a boulder and eased himself into a position giving him a clear view of what was happening. To his surprise he recognized young Detorakis on his knees. He was intent upon making a hole in the dry, rocky soil using a shovel with a broken handle. The old man's eyes opened wide when, craning his neck further, he could plainly see a heavy cloth sack lying on the ground, some of the contents of which had spilled out. An involuntary gasp of surprise escaped his lips.

"Po, po, po, po!" he exclaimed under his breath. "Just look at the nuts this little squirrel is trying to bury!"

In the low light cast by a small, shielded lantern on the ground could be seen two small pieces of pottery covered with designs. In one of the bowls were what appeared to be seals or colored beads. Among the beads were two flat pieces of ivory or bone cut to anthropomorphic shapes. Other shapes could be seen in the cloth of the bag and he wondered what else little Mitzos had found. He surmised this must be a part of the treasure from the tomb. What a shame it would be to put all of this treasure back into the ground when it had just seen the light of day for the first time in thousands of years.

Mitzos was not making much progress. Sweat streamed down his neck and dripped from the tip of his nose. Periodically he stopped digging to swipe at his face with his sleeve, leaving it streaked with dirt, which quickly turned to mud. When at last he felt he could go no deeper he threw the broken shovel to the side, where it bounced off a rock, ringing clearly in the still night. He rubbed his hands vigorously on the rough material of his pants, then, still on his knees, reached for the sack. Barba Yorgi watched as he carefully extricated the remaining contents one by one and set them on the pile of dirt beside the hole.

There were three more pieces of pottery, one of which was rather small and long with a narrow neck, looking as if it had held either perfume or scented oils. One of the others was a larger vase, painted with what appeared to be leaping fish. The final piece in the sack was a statue standing twenty five to thirty centimeters in height with the green patina acquired by old bronze. It was of a boy or man, wearing a peaked cap and a girdle. The bronze figure was carrying something around its shoulders, what exactly Barba Yorgi could not make out. Mitzos fondled each piece as he removed it from the sack, squinting closely at the details in the light of the lantern. His mind raced with the possibilities provided by this unexpected fortune. He need only sell these things to the right buyer and he would have many drachmas. He might even have enough to buy passage to Germany where he could learn a trade. Then he could come back to Crete and be a rich man. So engrossed was Mitzos in the objects that he did not hear the old man move around the boulder behind which he was watching and into the light directly behind him.

"Kalispera, paidi mou," said Barba Yorgi softly.

The unexpected sound of a voice behind him caused Mitzos to cry out in alarm. Dropping the bronze statue in the dirt, he picked up the broken shovel, leapt to his feet and whirled clumsily to face the intruder. The old man towered over him and he cowered back, the shovel raised, ready to strike. The whites of his eyes showed clearly and his breath was labored.

"Siga, siga. Mi fovasis," the old man said reassuringly. Easy, easy. Don't be afraid. Nevertheless, he gripped his staff tightly, ready to defend himself should the young man swing the shovel. "It's just me. Pseramanolis. You know me." Barba Yorgi identified himself to Mitzos.

"Ba...Ba...Barba Yorgi?! What are you doing here? How long have you been standing here?" In spite of recognizing the intruder, he continued to hold the shovel at the ready.

"Long enough, little Mitzos. What have you found? A few baubles perhaps?" he continued to speak softly in his rumbling voice, hoping to reassure the young man. Mitzos' grip on the shovel eased perceptibly and he slowly lowered it. His eyes left those of Barba Yorgi and fell on his recently acquired treasures lying in the dirt. There was no use denying what he was doing. The evidence was all too apparent. Heaving a deep sigh he tossed the shovel aside, his shoulders sagging and his head hanging dejectedly.

"Nai, a few things. I just wanted to keep them safe here. You know how people are."

"Very interesting things, little Mitzos. Would you mind telling me where you found them?"

Mitzos gestured vaguely with his hand as he responded, "Oh, not far from the village. There was a cave, you see, that I found the other day. I'd noticed bats in the evening and thought to take their guano. Sell it in Rethymnon. I found these things in the cave. Nothing important, I'm sure."

"Is that why the police came looking for you tonight?" he queried, watching closely for a reaction. "Do the police come all the way to Plakias to talk to you just because you want to sell bat shit?"

Mitzos' reaction was immediate. Alarmed, he jerked his head up to find himself staring into the guileless eyes of the old man.

"Police!!? The police came to Plakias? Looking for me? They said they were looking for me? Did they go to my aunt's house? Why would they come asking for me?" His breathing once more quickened and fear shone in his bulging eyes. Barba Yorgi was satisfied.

"How should I know? I'm just an old man who was passing through. There was talk in the kafeneion of a discovery down where they're building the new road. Something about the bulldozer falling into a hole. A tomb, I think they said. The driver of the machine told the police there were several people watching him while he worked each day. When he went to call the authorities about what happened everything in the tomb disappeared. The 'watchers', too. He seemed to think he recognized you. Uh, were you one of the 'watchers', little Mitzos? I believe they said in the village the police were ready to pay for information."

Mitzos suddenly became frantic. "I wasn't the only one! The others were there, too! Everyone took all they could carry. Even Forakis, who fell into the hole. I wasn't the only one. Why would the police just come looking for me? Everyone took something!"

"Forakis? Which Forakis? You mean Zakari who lives on the mountain?" interrupted Barba Yorgi.

"Nai, nai, Zakari. He fell into the hole. We thought he hurt himself. We all rushed in after him. Then he stood up and ran away. He was bent over like this." Mitzos showed how Zakari had run with his arms wrapped around his stomach.

"That's strange," mused the old man aloud. "Why would Forakis run away? Unless... Of course! Why wouldn't he run away?"

In the meantime, Mitzos continued to babble on, confirming not his innocence, but his complicity. He wanted to make sure Barba Yorgi understood he was only one of several who plundered the tomb.

"Tell me, little Mitzos, who else was there?" he cajoled, his mind ready to file the names away for future reference.

"Who else was there? Uh, Annemoyannis...and, uh, Mavrodakis. His sister Popi was there with him. Nai, Mavrodakis! And, um, Tsipas and his wife. You know, Panagioti. Ah, also a man from Khora Sfakion named Petrides." As Mitzos ticked off the names of those who had been there a look of speculation passed across the old man's features.

"So! There must have been much to take in the tomb," he thought to himself. "But, Forakis. Why would he have run away without taking something? I must pay a little visit to my friend Zakari very soon."

Mitzos had run out of names and now stood looking up into the face of the old man. The enormity of what he revealed was beginning to dawn upon him and a feeling of desperation began to replace fear. Barba Yorgi said the police were willing to pay for information and he told the old man things for which the police would be happy to pay handsomely. If he told them everything he knew then he, Mitzos, would not have a chance to sell these things. Even if he didn't go to prison he would remain a prisoner of his village. He must stop the old man from telling anyone anything. If people like Forakis found out that he had been the source of the information they would certainly kill him, even if they were all in prison together. He did not want to die. These pots and statues represented a new life for him, away from his village. He could see his dreams of Germany, or even of Athens, slowly beginning to crumble. Perhaps if he offered half of what he had to Barba Yorgi then he would go away and leave him and the rest alone.

But no! He could take half of the treasure, but would still be able to turn them in to the police for even more money. Just look at him. He seemed to be already counting his drachmas. Moving stealthily, Mitzos reached for the broken shovel, which was lying in the dirt at his feet.

Barba Yorgi was, indeed, weighing the options open to him. His mind was sorting through the opportunities this situation presented when the soft metallic sound of the shovel's metal blade scraping against the dirt and small rocks as it was being picked up alerted him to the danger. Almost too late he saw the broken shovel in the hands of Mitzos, beginning its arc towards his head. Reacting instinctively and with the speed of a striking asp, he raised his staff just in time. The blade of the shovel struck the end of the upraised staff, its impact ringing in the still night air and stinging the old man's hands. The expression on Mitzos' face was that of a crazed man. His teeth were bared and spittle flecked the corners of his mouth.

Recovering his equilibrium, Barba Yorgi struck back. The large knob of wood on the end of his staff caught Mitzos under the chin, knocking his head back sharply and shattering his jaw. The shovel, cocked for another swing, flew from his hands. His eyes rolled back in his head and he began to slump forward. Before he could fall, however, Barba Yorgi struck again, this time from the side. With the other end of the staff he caught Mitzos on the neck, neatly snapping it. He was dead before he hit the ground. His knees struck the earth first, then his body folded back on his legs. His head lolled grotesquely at an unnatural angle.

"Trellós! Trellá!" rasped Barba Yorgi to the inanimate Mitzos. You are crazy! This is madness! He reached out with the end of this staff and prodded him in the side. "Get up! Come on. Enough of this. Get up!"

When there was no movement on the part of the young man, he dropped to his knees beside him. He turned Mitzos' face toward him, slapping first one cheek then the other. He looked for a fluttering of the eyes, but there was no response. As soon as he removed his hand the head fell back into its original awkward position. Barba Yorgi leaned down and placed his ear close to the boy's slack mouth. Nothing. The realization finally dawned that he was dead.

Death was no stranger to Barba Yorgi. He had met him face to face many times before. This time he greeted him almost casually, grunting acknowledgement of his presence before pushing himself to his feet. Standing over the body, the old man shook his head and uttered one word: "Vlákas!" Stupid.

Kneeling once more, he gathered the artifacts lying in the dirt and replaced them one by one in the sack. He picked up the shovel and, looking around him, threw it up the hill from where he was standing. He followed its flight through the moonlight, watching it disappear into the midst of more boulders and brush. With his boot he raked the dirt and stones dug up by Mitzos back into the hole, tamped and smoothed it carefully. He then walked out of the circle of boulders, found four more stones of varying size, and placed them haphazardly on the evidence of the freshly filled hole. With the morning sun the moisture in the slightly darker dirt would evaporate, blending in perfectly with the surrounding area. There would be no evidence of there having been any activity among the rocks.

He then moved downhill from the body and dropped to his knees. With no hesitation he grasped one hand and pulled Mitzos to a sitting position facing him. He reached under the boy's armpits, lifted the body, pulling toward his broad, powerful shoulders. He quickly transferred one hand and then the other to the belt holding up the boy's pants and lifted, draping the boy across his shoulders. Reaching for his staff which lay by his leg, he planted the end on the ground and levered himself to his feet. Mitzos' head hung down the old man's back, his legs down the front.

Barba Yorgi angled away up the face of the mountain. When he felt he had gone far enough he stopped and dumped the body unceremoniously in the midst of more boulders and brush. Breathing hard, he bent over to catch his breath, holding onto the staff with both hands and resting his face in the crook of his arm. When he recovered his composure, he surveyed the area around him. There was no possibility of anyone's finding the body here so far above the path. There was not even a need to cover it up. Barba Yorgi looked once more at Mitzos and again shook his head. "Sleep well, Mitzaki." Having delivered this benediction, he turned around and made his way back down the mountain to retrieve the sack.

Now hidden among the rocks above Zakari's house, Barba Yorgi caught a movement in the bright sunny sky. A pair of vultures sailing effortlessly on the currents of air. Zakari still wandered about below and did not see them. As he watched, the old man saw them turn in the sky and begin to flap their wings. There was purpose to their movement now as they flew off toward the southeast. From his vantage point he could not see the other vultures converging on a spot high on the mountainside. Had he been able to see the others, he would have known Mitzos' final resting place was no longer secret.

Below him Zakari approached the face of the mountain. As he neared the rocks and gnarled trees bordering his land, he scanned the terrain among the boulders. He stopped, craning his neck to get a better view, even raised himself up on his bare toes, and then lowered himself to the ground once more. He stood in that position for several moments, then nodded almost imperceptibly, turned around and walked straight back to the house.

"Ah, Zakaraki, my child, you're not as clever as you think." In spite of himself, an exultant smile creased the weathered features of Barba Yorgi's face. "Your secret is now mine!" Satisfied at last, he leaned back against a boulder and prepared to wait for the moment when he could slip away unnoticed.

Zakari entered his house, but reappeared within minutes, fully dressed. He walked straight to the tethered goat, untied her and led her unresisting to her pen. From a large clay jar with a heavy lid he took a handful of grain and placed it in a shallow stone trough in the pen. The goat concentrated on the treat, not noticing when her master walked out and closed the rough wooden gate behind him. Moments later he came out of the house again, this time closing the door behind him. Without hesitation he walked away from the house and to the path, passing between the two monoliths. The only sound now was that of the rooster chasing one of the hens, who ran squawking before his assault.

Barba Yorgi remained motionless for another half hour before deciding he was really alone. Cautiously he raised himself. His legs had grown stiff and he stamped his feet and rubbed his backsides vigorously. Standing to his full height, he could see the entrance to the path, which was deserted. Still taking no chances, he crept cautiously back through the boulders parallel to the path for a considerable distance, just to make sure he would not be surprised by Zakari. Convinced he was now safe from prying eyes, he scrabbled straight down the hill to the path, looked around once more, and began to walk in the direction of Zakari's house.

He arrived shortly, emerging from the path to the cleared area beyond. Not wanting to take any chances, he stopped under an olive tree and set the sack of artifacts among its roots. "Zakari!" he called in a loud voice. "Zakari!!" When there was still no answer he circled the house once and walked to the goat pen. She looked at him quizzically as she chewed her cud.

"Kanenas etho, eh, katsika? Mono mas. Kala." No one here, huh, goat? Only us.

The goat gave a short bleat then went back to chewing her cud. Barba Yorgi chuckled to himself. Sure he was alone, he walked back to the olive tree, picked up the sack and strode directly to the spot where he last saw Zakari. Bare footprints in the dusty soil led straight into the undergrowth. He was sure that whatever it was Zakari had hidden must be in this general area. Probably no higher than his head. With his staff he pushed aside bushes and poked among the rocks without success. Finally, he began to pull at the bushes covering some rocks at head height. He was surprised to find they came away in his hand. Moving quickly he uncovered a small opening.

He sensed he was close to making a discovery and climbed up onto a rock to peer into the hole. He could see nothing. He poked his staff into the opening and felt it hit something. Laying the stick aside, he reached inside, feeling on all sides. With a grunt of satisfaction, he felt cloth and his hand closed around it. Taking care not to drop it, he withdrew the object from the hole, placing it gently on the rock forming part of the entrance to the small cave. For such a small bundle it was very heavy. Whatever was inside was wrapped in a dirty piece of heavy cloth and tied with a slender rope.

"The squirrels of Kriti are very active this year," he exclaimed under his breath. "Here's another parcel of nuts hidden away. They must be looking forward to a very bad winter." So saying, he untied the knot in the rope and began to unwrap the cloth.

When the cloth fell open his eyes widened in amazement. "Panagia! This can't be real!!" Lying before him was the statue of a youth. It had obviously been crafted by a master artisan, for the detail was both realistic and anatomically correct. He supposed it represented an athlete, for the body was in an unnatural attitude, with knees slightly bent and arms reaching over its head. He had never seen or heard of anything like this. The subject of the statue was not where his immediate interest lay, however. The real interest was the fact that this statue gave off a rich metallic glow. It was not green, as was so often the case when bronze was disinterred. This was a golden color from which the sun glinted. Picking it up in both hands he turned it over, studying it from every angle. On the back were strange markings, as if someone had taken a knife and scored the surface. Also, the weight, in relation to the size, was extraordinary. It must be gold. There was no question about it. This statue was gold! Judging from its weight and size, the old man was sure it was solid.

Looking about him for a stone, he picked up several before finding one that approximated the weight of the statue. He held the statue in one hand, the stone in the other, weighing them, looking at each in turn. When he had found one that satisfied him, he dropped it at his feet, looked at the statue lovingly, caressed it with his palm, rubbed it against his cheek, felt its smooth coolness. He then placed it once more in the middle of the cloth, wrapped it up as he had found it and reached into the opening in the rocks to return it to its hiding place. Moving quickly now, he re-covered the opening with the branches and stepped back to observe. It looked the same to him as when he had first seen it.

He retrieved the stone from between his feet and backed up, checking all the while to make sure there were no tell-tale signs of his visit. There appeared to be none. He moved out from among the rocks into the open area of Zakari's field. There among the bare footprints Zakari had left earlier were the marks of his own boots. Barba Yorgi picked up a branch lying nearby and neatly swept the ground, thinking to obliterate any traces of his having been there. He then dropped the stone down into the open neck of his shirt. Its weight pulled on his shirt and the gritty roughness of its surface scratched the skin of his stomach. He went back to where he had left the artifacts, wrapped the neck of the sack twice around his hand and left.

His staff in his right hand, he moved toward the path, his mind awhirl with all that had happened to him since last night. He needed to hide the sack and its contents in a safe place. He also needed to distance himself from Zakari's house and land. It would not be good for him to be found here now. The value of his discovery and what he knew was incalculable. No wonder Zakari acted so strangely this morning! He had every reason to be nervous, thought Barba Yorgi.

"I must go to Candia as quickly as possible," said the old man to himself, using the old name for Iraklion. "Someone there will know what to do with these things. Someone like Deaf Yanni. Nai, Deaf Yanni! Of course! I must go to see him today."

Chapter 10

Carter was in his room thumbing through brochures picked up the day before at Knossos when he heard the door open at the top of the stairs. The narrow hallway resounded to the scuffing of sandaled feet and the sound of female voices conversing in German. He glanced at his watch, saw it was 6:30 and rose from the bed. When he opened the door Traudel stood in the hallway with her hand raised ready to knock.

"Oh, good evening, Carter," she said. "I was coming to see you. We have just returned from Phaestos. As soon as we have taken a shower we are going to eat. Do you still want to come with us?" Her face was flushed from a day in the sun.

"Hi! Good to see you... Madame D said the buses usually returned after six. I've been out all day myself. Got back about an hour ago and have been waiting for you to return. Go ahead and take your shower. Just give me a call when you're ready. I'm starved. I'll either be here in my room or on the terrace."

Hanne Lore's tanned face, framed by tousled blonde hair, appeared over Traudel's shoulder. "Hallo!" Her smile shone brightly against her tan and her blue eyes sparkled.

"Hey, Hanne Lore," Carter greeted her.

"Do you come have dinner with us tonight? We found a little restaurant in an alley when we come back from the bus. It looks wunderbar, uh, wonderful"

"Traudel and I were just talking about dinner. Sure. I wouldn't miss it."

"OK. We call you when we are ready." With that pronouncement she bobbed her head, gave a little wave and disappeared from the doorway.

Carter turned his eyes back to Traudel, who still stood in his doorway. "The shower is going to be full for a few minutes yet. You want a cigarette?"

She nodded and he stepped aside to let her enter. As soon as she was in the room he closed the door, picked up a pack of cigarettes from the writing table, shook out two and lit both. As she took hers their fingers brushed momentarily and a spark passed between them. He sat down on one end of the bed and invited her to join him. She slipped off her sandals, sat at the other end of the bed and crossed her long legs under her. They smoked in silence for a moment, listening to the comings and goings in the hall as the others took their showers and visited with each other in their rooms.

"Last year when I came with another group from the university we stayed in the youth hostel in town. This is a much nicer place. The hostel was too crowded. Many of the people were dirty and there was too much noise. Hannie came with me last year, too. She didn't have much fun. She was sick from something she ate. I begged her to come back with me this year."

"She seems to be having fun this year," remarked Carter. "Who're the boys?"

"They are just some boys who wanted to come, too. Two of them were in my classes. The others I never met until after the trip was all planned. They are friends of the others. One of them, Klaus, has fallen in love with Hannie, but she doesn't want anything to do with him. He tries to get close to her and she just ignores him. We stayed in Spetsai for three days before coming to Crete and he followed her around like a little puppy dog. We laugh a lot about it. We try everything to get away from him, but it was hard. He is very persistent. We even made fun of him to his face and he just turned red, but he comes back for more. Maybe he is masochist."

Carter laughed at the image Traudel painted of Klaus. He could understand Klaus' being attracted to Hanne Lore, for she was a lovely girl. Finishing their cigarettes, he asked about Phaestos. She described an unbelievably beautiful location. The ruins, high up on a hill looked out over the Plain of Messara, virtually surrounded by mountains, one of which contains the cave touted as the birthplace of Zeus. When she paused, she stretched out one of her legs and tapped him on the thigh with her toe. "Tell me about your day."

"Ah, well, there's not much to tell. I've been trying to find someone. A man I knew long ago. He's supposed to be here on the island but I'm not having very good luck. I was wrong not to agree to go to Phaestos with you and the others. I thought about y...., uh, the fun you must be having today. It sounds as if your day went well."

Reaching out her foot again, she put it on his bare leg
and left it there. He placed his hand over it and began to stroke it
as he would a small animal. He loved the sweet warmth
emanating from her skin. They both fell silent as he caressed her
foot, then moved his hand past her ankle and massaged her calf.
Traudel reached down to place her hand over his and scooted
toward him, her eyes locked on his. A soft knock at the door
stopped her in mid-motion.

"Traudelein?"

Carter reluctantly swung his legs over the side of the bed and
reached for the door knob. Hanne Lore stood outside wearing a
terry cloth robe, her hair pinned up on top of her head. Tendrils
of hair over her forehead and at the nape of her neck were still
damp from her shower and she dabbed at the moisture on her
face with the end of her towel.

"Come on in," said Carter. "We were just talking about
what we did today."

Hanne Lore entered the room and smiled at Traudel,
who still sat in the middle of the bed. "You can take your shower
now. The boys have already finish. Klaus ask me if he can wash
my back."

Both girls giggled and Traudel said something in
German Carter did not understand. Hanne Lore turned and told
him it was time for Traudel to take her shower. "I am so hungry I
think I will die. Let her take her shower and then we go to eat."
To Traudel she said, "Go now, before someone else go in. I will
keep Carter company until you have finish." With that
pronouncement she flopped down on the bed.

"OK. It will just take me a minute, then Hannie and I
will get dressed in a hurry. I'm starving, too."

As she left she put her hand fleetingly on his arm, then
was gone. Hanne Lore took Traudel's place on the bed and fished
awkwardly in the pocket of her robe. As she twisted to facilitate
her search, the robe fell open at the top, revealing firm bare
breasts. His attention was momentarily drawn to the smoothness
and color of her bronzed skin and he fought a sudden urge to
reach out and trace the underside of her breast from her rib cage
to the dark, pouting nipple. If aware of his gaze she gave no
evidence of the fact. Unconcerned, she finally drew a blue pack

of cigarettes from her pocket. Only then did she rearrange her robe unhurriedly. Offering the pack to Carter, she asked, "Do you know Gitanes? They are French cigarettes. Do you want one?"

He declined, but picked up the matches from the bed and struck one. She leaned forward to accept the light, inhaled deeply, blew a stream of smoke toward the ceiling and leaned back again against the head of the bed. In making herself more comfortable she put one leg underneath her and raised the other knee, resting her elbow on it. It was immediately apparent she was totally naked under her robe. He followed the remainder of the conversation with difficulty, hoping she would not notice his difficulty concentrating on the conversation...

True to her word, Traudel was back in five minutes. She shooed Hanne Lore out of the room, promising Carter they would soon be ready to leave. Ten minutes later they were all on their way down the quickly darkening street. Every time Carter glanced at Hanne Lore, however, a vivid image remained of golden bare skin set off by narrow strips of smooth white skin, normally covered by what must have been a tiny bikini. One thing about Hannie: there was no doubt about her being a true blonde. That much was evident.

Within minutes they strolled to the center of town. In a narrow street above the open air market was a small restaurant with tables set up on the very edges of the street itself. The waiter arranged three tables end to end and set chairs for all of them. Carter sat at one end with Traudel on his left. Next to her was a tall, dark haired boy Carter vaguely remembered was named Rainer. Hannie was seated between two of the boys on the other side of the table directly across from the ubiquitous Klaus. His adoring eyes seemed to never leave her face.

Dinner conversation consisted mainly of Traudel and Carter's experiences since coming to Greece. He found out from her the boys all worked during the year in addition to attending classes. The girls' parents could afford to pay for the luxury of their travel throughout Europe. Actually, they did not seem to require an inordinate amount of money or comfort. Much of their travel was by thumbing, or what they termed 'auto stop'. When they took trains or boats it was always the cheapest fare available. They arrived on Crete aboard the Keftiu, the inter-island ferry from Piraeus. Since the trip was overnight, they paid only for the privilege of coming aboard and spent all their time on deck. If they slept, they stretched out on a bench on deck or below, using their rucksacks as pillows. They were young, healthy and adventurous.

The remains of their feast littered the table as Carter and Traudel sat smoking and enjoying each other's company. So immersed were they in each other that the rest of the group ceased to exist. He studied the fine bone structure of her face, her generous and sensitive mouth and thick, lustrous hair. She sat deep in thought for a moment, watching the smoke from her cigarette curl up and dissipate on the gentle night breeze. He turned to look at the others at the table, particularly the interaction between Hannie and the boys on either side of her. Excluded from their conversation, Klaus looked miserable. Every time he tried to address Hannie she either ignored him or laughed in his face.

The feeling of being watched caused Carter to look around again. He found Traudel staring at him, a bemused look on her face. She leaned towards him, put her elbows on the table and cradled her chin in her hands. "Too bad Hannie came into your room when she did," she said softly. "I was enjoying talking with you. It felt so good when you were rubbing my foot and leg. I didn't want you to stop."

"Me either. Maybe next time we should lock the door. Better yet, next time maybe we should lock the door of the shower - with Hanne Lore inside."

Traudel dissolved into a fit of giggles that caused the others at the table to stop their conversations and look at her questioningly. Rainer, who remained aloof since their first meeting at breakfast at the pension now leaned forward and addressed Carter in heavily accented English. "Why do you Americans think you can just take any woman you want?" he asked with ill-disguised disdain.

Obviously eavesdropping on their conversations during dinner, Carter was nonplussed by the revelation he spoke English. He also seemed upset by something and Carter deduced it was probably because his interest in Traudel was something more than a simple traveling companion. He looked straight into the tall boy's eyes and said the first thing that came to mind.

"Bravo, Rainer. That is your name isn't it? Rainer? Where did you learn to speak English so well? Why, I thought you were only monolingual. Heard anything of interest tonight?"

Stung by Carter's words, Rainer turned crimson. Traudel quickly put her hand on Carter's arm, remarking at how full and uncomfortable she felt. Carter turned to her and asked if she would like to take a walk before heading back to the pension. He totally dismissed Rainer, whose features darkened in anger as they rose from the table.

Carter took the bill lying near him, added their two meals in his head and laid some money beside his plate. As he pushed his chair back and rose from the table he backed into an old man who stood unnoticed slightly to his right and behind him. He grasped the man's arm to steady him, noting the stout staff he held in his right hand.

"Excuse me, uh, uh, siggnomi," he muttered apologetically. The old man's face was suffused with anger and at first Carter thought it was because of bumping into him. Then he noticed it was at the other occupants of the table that he glared. The other thing Carter noticed immediately was the strength of the arm under his steadying hand. It felt like the limb of an oak tree. There were none of the slack muscles one would expect to find in a man of such advanced years.

Mustache bristling, the old man pulled away from Carter, spit an expletive toward those at the table then continued on his way down the street. Carter stared after him, unsure what prompted such a reaction. He watched his retreating back as he made his way down the street, noticing the dark, bloused pants tucked into the tops of heavy-soled, scuffed high topped boots.

"Didn't you see him?" asked Traudel. "He stood there for over a minute just watching everyone at the table. I thought maybe he was hungry and was looking at the food left on the table. He seemed very angry just now. I don't think it was because you bumped into him."

"Jesus, no, I didn't even know he was there. He was solid as a rock! I don't know why he needs that walking stick he was carrying."

Rainer, forgotten in the confusion of the moment, said something in German to Traudel. She whirled and levelled a withering stare at him, which caused him to lower his eyes to his littered plate. She took Carter's arm and steered him away from the table, but not before stopping briefly to whisper something in Hannie's ear. Hannie shook her head, looked up at Carter with a smile, and said, "Viel spa! Have a good time!" Carter thanked her, nodded at the others at the table, and he and Traudel made their way down the street towards the open air market. Glancing back before turning the corner, he noticed Rainer conversing animatedly with the others. He still appeared visibly upset.

"What in the world's the matter with Rainer? I can't believe he sat there and listened to everything we said tonight. He was really angry. What did he say when you got up?"

She pressed her breast against his arm, clutching him tightly with her hand. Looking down at the cobbled pavement as they walked, she told him Rainer was a little like Klaus. The only difference was that she and Rainer dated awhile the year before.

"He was so terribly jealous and possessive. He followed me everywhere and always made a scene when I would speak with another boy. Finally I told him I would be his friend, but that was all. He was not very gracious. When I found out he would be joining our group this summer I went to him and told him I would do what I wanted, when I wanted. If that meant I would be with another boy, then he could say nothing. He is still... what is it you say in English?"

"Carrying a torch?"

"Exactly! Carrying a torch. He drives me mad! At the table he told me not to go with you. He said something very uncomplimentary. You saw how I looked at him. Never mind. He is the one who is stupid and immature. I am where I want to be - with you."

She ran her nails down the inside of his arm from his elbow to his hand before lacing her fingers in his. Pressing even closer to him, she lifted her face to his and kissed him quickly on the cheek. Carter turned to her and returned her kiss full on the mouth. She responded by taking her hand from his and putting it around his waist. He put his arm around her shoulders and they continued through the market. They might as well have been alone. Neither of them noticed the people who walked past them, so totally engrossed were they in each other.

Seated in the gloom of a poorly-illuminated storefront, his staff propped against the wall beside his chair, the old man Carter encountered at the restaurant watched them from under bushy white brows. He was seated beside another man, a few years younger than he. The younger man spoke rapidly and earnestly in a soft voice. The old man listened intently to what was being said to him, but did not reply. Before him sat a narghile, a water pipe, through which flowed the smoke from the packet of tobacco sitting atop its clay bowl. As his companion talked, the old man drew deeply on the mouthpiece, setting the water in the body of the pipe abubble. He recognized Carter and Traudel from the encounter in the restaurant, but his expression did not change. He was more interested in what his companion was saying. He followed them with his eyes for a moment, but did not miss a word of the conversation at hand.

They continued through the open air market, which was closing down for the night. At the entrance to a small alley, Carter guided her off the more heavily traveled street into the relative seclusion of the narrower artery. Although deeply engrossed in each other, they nevertheless sidestepped a porter struggling along with a large sack on his hunched back. As they rounded a corner, Carter noticed an open doorway giving access to stone stairs leading to an upper level of a darkened building. He pulled her into the gloom under the stairs, where she melted into his arms and molded her warm body to his. As their lips met in a hungry, urgent kiss his hands caressed her body, finally cupping her firm buttocks and pulling her even tighter against him.

Carter became aware of moaning and pleading that he at first thought was coming from Traudel. There was something almost animalistic about it, however, and he opened his eyes to verify its source. In the dim light cast by a weak bulb outside their niche, he could see they were not alone. Someone stood in the alcove with them, an undulating silhouette, between them and the opening. The figure moved closer and Carter could now see his face. His jaw was slack and his eyes gleamed from shadows cast by heavy brows. Both his hands were thrust into the crotch of his pants. Over and over he repeated a two word litany, "Kaí egó, Kaí egó." Me, too.

Carter pulled the unsuspecting Traudel behind him and, with a savage shove, sent the interloper smashing into the stone wall. With both hands busily fondling himself the man was caught totally by surprise and fell backwards, hitting the wall head first with a sound like a dropped melon. Eyes glazed and with knees of rubber, he slid down the wall, his mouth working but making no sound.

"What is it?" asked Traudel, coming out of her daze. It all happened so quickly she was only aware of Carter's violent motion as he pulled her behind him.

"Just a fucking pervert," he spat. "Come on. We need to get out of here." They stepped over the still prone body of the man who was struggling to turn over and leapt the three steps down into the street. Rather than retrace their route, they turned left and hurried into the labyrinth of the old city. Behind them a gabble of sound came from the darkened doorway, spurring them to greater speed. Carter pulled her by the hand, both of them fearful of being caught in the warren of small alleys. Several twisting turns, made not through knowledge of where they were, but through pure luck, led them into the wide boulevard around the square.

The bright lights of the square's restaurants, hundreds of strollers, normal humanity, brought them to a halt. Far away Carter thought he could still hear the man's screams.

Still holding tightly onto Traudel's hand, he pulled her into the street where they found anonymity among the throng. Calmer now, he explained to Traudel the circumstances prompting his actions and dwelt on the possible results. What if the man were killed by his fall? What were the possibilities of their being attacked in the winding maze? He could have perhaps handled two or three of the porters, but there would be little chance of success against more.

They moved to find a table in front of one of the restaurants, summoned a waiter and ordered drinks for both of them. Traudel was incensed. She could not imagine anyone being so low as to expose himself. Naively she asked, "What do you suppose he wanted?"

Carter knew what he was after. He wanted to be included in their tryst. His adrenaline was still flowing and his muscles quivered. It was only after he downed his drink and ordered another that he began to return to normal. Their after dinner stroll was most memorable up until the incident in the alley.

They finished their drinks and turned to walk in the direction of the pension. They were both calmer now and walked once more with their arms around each other. Traudel kissed him gently and chuckled, "Too much excitement, too much excitement." Carter laughed with her now, as he began to see the humor in the situation. Their little friend would certainly think twice about repeating a stunt such as this, he thought.

When they arrived at the pension the rest of the group was already there and most still stood in the yard. Hannie ran up to them and asked what brought them back so early. When Traudel told her the story Hannie found a great deal of humor in it. Two of the other boys sidled up to them and heard most of the recounting.

Leaning down to Hanne Lore, Carter whispered conspiratorially, "And how was your evening? I see you still have your shadow with you."

"Ach! You mean poor Klaus. If that happen to him I'm afraid he make peepee in his lederhosen. Were you frightened, Traudelein?"

"No," she responded. "It all happened so quickly. Carter pulled me along the street so fast I thought my arm was going to come off! I only knew everything that happened after we came to the square."

"Well, you come to bed now. We have a long trip tomorrow and must get up early," admonished Hannie with a gleam in her eye.

"What do you mean a long trip?" asked Carter. "I know I didn't ask you how long you would be here, but I thought sure it would be longer than two days. Where are you going tomorrow?"

Traudel took his hand in both of hers and faced him. She told him they were leaving by bus early the next day for Chania, where they would spend one night. From there they would return to Piraeus by boat the day after. From Athens they planned to take a train to Skopje, Yugoslavia.

Carter neglected to consider the length of time they would have together. He assumed it would be at least a week. What was the good of a whirlwind tour? There is never enough time to really enjoy one place. They talked for a few more minutes then walked up the stairs together, followed closely by Hannie. At her door Traudel threw her arms around Carter's neck and kissed him lingeringly. He could feel the renewal of excitement and was reluctant to release her. Hannie, too, kissed him warmly, wishing him luck. Then both girls entered their room. Traudel looked back at him over her shoulder with a mixture of sadness and longing on her face.

Carter stood for a moment in front of the closed door, but finally went to his own room. He brushed his teeth, took off his sweaty shirt, washed quickly in the basin and turned off the light. Not feeling sleepy, he walked naked to the window and sat in the deep opening looking out at the stars and lights of the harbor. He felt frustrated not to have more time with her. He recalled their conversations before and during dinner, remembered the feel of her skin, her lips, and the lushness of her body. He thought of the promise. "What promise?" he asked himself.

He lit a cigarette and brooded in the darkness. He almost finished it when he heard the gentle click of his doorknob being turned. Looking toward the far end of the room he saw a female figure silhouetted in the dim light of the door.

Without a word she entered his room, closed the door quietly and locked it.

Chapter 11

By noon Zakari was on the path to Plakias. To the south he could see the sunlight shimmering off the sea in the distance. Far below him the village of Plakias baked in the sunlight, its olive trees dark against the dusty brown earth. From his vantage point on the mountain it looked deserted. The only sign of life was a plume of dust on the dirt road leading away from the village, caused no doubt by one of the contrivances some of the more affluent peasants owned, called a mikaní, which literally meant machine. It consisted of a large two-wheeled cultivator with ribbed tractor tires and was attached to a trailer-like cart. The driver sat in the cart and steered by holding onto the long handles of the cultivator. It was not fast, but it was better than walking.

Among the rocks of the mountainside to his left, over 200 meters above the path itself, Zakari could hear the squabbling of vultures. Earlier that morning he remarked their convergence. From far away others arrived. Now he was close enough to hear them. A few were still airborne. As they squabbled over their share of the carrion the light breeze carried the sound to his ears. A sweetish odor hung in the air, causing him to wrinkle his nose.

Adding to the general clamor were the large ravens. Not as big as the vultures, these thieves hopped around on the rocks, darting in when they could to claim a morsel dropped by the larger birds. Some of the vultures sat and preened on the tops of boulders, their wings spread in the noon day sun. The first to arrive following the discovery, they ate quickly, gorging themselves. They would have difficulty launching their heavy bodies into the air now, such was the burden carried in their distended crops. Zakari shuddered at the sight of their naked heads, long necks and cruel beaks. "Xristós kaí Panagiá!" he muttered to himself and quickly made the sign of the cross. No doubt they would make short work of whatever they found. Those not engaged in eating spied him walking below them and followed his progress with sharp eyes. Seeing them turn his way he felt as if he were being sized up for a future meal. A rock picked up from the path and thrown in their direction fell far short, clattering among the boulders. Those perched above turned to face the breeze, prepared for flight, but quickly realized they were in no danger as this human continued to descend the mountain.

Within thirty minutes he was passing the orchards and fields surrounding the village. As he passed a low stone wall separating a garden plot from the path, he was hailed by a peasant lying in the shade. Seated near him were a woman and a child, his wife and daughter, who brought him his noon meal each day. The midday break always lasted at least two hours, time to eat lunch and take a nap.

"Periménite!" Wait a minute, the man called. Zakari saw him touch his finger tips to his mouth. "Ela na sou pó. Ela na psoúme." Come over here and let's talk. Come have a drink.

Zakari wondered why this man would want to talk to him. He considered the summons and the invitation for a moment. Finally, nodding in assent, he climbed over the wall and walked toward the little group in the shade. Thirsty from his hot walk, a drink would taste good.

With no further word of greeting, other than to invite him to join them, the man asked Zakari if he came down the mountain. When he responded affirmatively he was asked if he met anyone up on the path, a young man a little shorter than Zakari, named Demetrios.

"What's his family name?"

"Detorakis. Everyone calls him Mitzos. He lives with his aunt, the widow Marika here in Plakias. Krasi thelate i nero?" the man asked, wiping the lip of a glass on his sleeve. On the ground before him rested a wicker covered bottle of red wine and a clay jug of water, the opening covered with a piece of gauze-like cheesecloth to keep insects and dirt from falling inside.

Zakari chose the water. "No, I saw no one on the mountain. Why do you ask? What's happened to this Detorakis?"

"Xero ego," he responded with a wave of his hand. Who knows? "Last night he went out and hasn't been seen since. The police are looking for him, too. Something about antikas; some things taken from a tomb out where they're building the new road. Did you hear about the tomb? Many, many things of great value."

Zakari's mumbled response was ignored as the peasant continued. "I thought maybe you'd seen him on the mountain. Everyone's been looking for him. His aunt's worried. Eh! Den Peirazei. Never mind. He'll be back." With a smirk he continued, "Probably went to visit a girl in one of the other villages."

Zakari thanked him for the water, wished him and his family a good day, and turned to walk away. So, little Mitzos is still missing. At least the police have yet to talk to him. That means I may still have a chance of finding him before anyone else does.

Relieved, he continued into the village, where he found a number of older men, including the village priest, sitting in the kafeneion. Recognized by several of them, he returned their greetings and took a seat. All conversation ceased as soon as he entered, then picked up again. As he sipped at a tepid bottle of Fix beer he listened to the conversations around him. The subjects were mostly mundane: crops, weather, prices and Papandreou's government. No one talked of Detorakis or the treasure. He was sure they would discuss every aspect of the events of the past days among themselves. Anything out of the ordinary was always welcome, for it added spice to lives that were otherwise monotone.

It was obvious there was nothing else to be learned here. To avoid appearing nosy, Zakari decided not to mention Mitzos. It would not be good to appear too interested in this domestic affair. He was not from Plakias and considered an outsider. If Mitzos returned to the village he would hear of it soon enough. It was important he find the boy before anyone else saw him, however. He nodded to the men seated next to him and walked once more into the sunlight.

While Zakari passed the vultures on his way down the mountainside, yet another scavenger was descending, searching for prey. Feeling it was safe to leave his hiding place, Barba Yorgi began to wend his way down to Zakari's property. By the time Zakari arrived in Plakias, the old man was just pulling the last of the branches away from the statue's hiding place. As Zakari left the kafeneion, frustrated with his inability to find Mitzos, Barba Yorgi replaced the statue, swept the ground and was on his way down the mountain by way of a path that was little more than an animal trail. When it reached the road running north from Spili he turned left onto it, hoping someone would come along with whom he could ride. He walked almost halfway to Armenoi before he finally heard the distinctive sound of an approaching mikani. Barba Yorgi hailed the driver, who stopped and picked him up. He sat in the little trailer, arms wrapped around his knees, head bent forward. Fatigued from hours without sleep and, in spite of the jostling, he dozed fitfully.

Within 45 minutes they reached the main east-west highway running along the north coast. Barba Yorgi indicated he would like to stop and the man pulled over and let him off. His muscles, already sore from the vigorous exercise over the past 24 hours were stiff and it took him several minutes to work out the kinks. He now needed only to wait for one of the inevitable buses, which ran every two hours during the day. He entered a kafenieon, ordered an ouzo and asked about the bus schedule. One passed not fifteen minutes earlier, which meant almost two more hours to wait. He finished his drink, asked where he might find a telephone and went to place a call to Deaf Yanni in Iraklion.

Yanni's son answered the phone, said his father was not there, but that he would give him a message. Barba Yorgi instructed him to tell his father to meet him at the normal place in the open air market at 8:00 that evening. The boy said he would give him the message and hung up. With nothing more to do than wait, he returned to the kafeneion. He asked the owner where he might find a set of scales and was directed to the back of the kafeneion, where local fishermen weighed their catches. He slipped the rock from his shirt and placed it in the chipped enamel scoop, chose a 10 kilogram weight, placed it on the hanging spindle, then nudged the indicator to the right until the arm was balanced in the middle. With surprise he saw the arrow point to 10-1/2 kilos.

"Opa!" he exclaimed under his breath. He knew the rock seemed to become weightier as he walked, but ten and a half kilos of gold! His mind could hardly register how many thousands of drachmas the statue represented. He removed the stone, turned it over in his hands absentmindedly, and then let it fall to the ground.

As the five o'clock bus pulled into view Barba Yorgi went to the side of the road and raised his arm to get the driver's attention. He settled himself into a seat near the back and was soon asleep. He did not awake again until the bus stopped outside the city gates to let someone off. They soon reached the terminus, where he got off and began to walk through the evening crowds to his rendezvous. His progress stopped when his attention was drawn to a street-side table at which were seated several young men and two young women. Stopping near the table as if to look at something else, he listened to the conversation, immediately recognizing it as German. At the head of the table was a young man in earnest conversation with one of the girls. He could not hear their words very well, but thought they were speaking either French or English. But the others were definitely Germans. Almost unable to contain himself, he gripped his staff and glared in their direction. The girl talking to the boy at the end of the table glanced up at him momentarily and then returned to her conversation. The boy with whom she was talking rose from his seat bumping into the old man in the process. So intent was he on the others at the table Barba Yorgi hardly noticed the collision. The young man said something Barba Yorgi did not understand and then apologized in Greek. Hearing even one word of his native language brought him back to his senses. He glanced at the boy, muttered an insult aimed at those still at the table, and proceeded down the street.

Within moments he found himself in front of a small butcher shop where he was to meet Deaf Yanni. Glancing at the clock through the open door he saw it was still a few minutes before eight. He greeted the owner of the shop, a man known to him for many years, and sat down on a chair within the shadows in front of the shop to await Yanni's arrival.

Shortly after eight he saw him coming up the street. Yanni recognized him from afar and acknowledged his presence with a slight nod. Barba Yorgi reached over and pulled another straight back chair close to where he was sitting and indicated Yanni should take a seat.

"Kalosto, Giorgos," Yanni greeted him softly. "Did you have a good trip, my friend? Kafes?"

The owner of the shop, watching for Yanni, as well, walked to the door where he stood wiping his hands on his bloody apron. He reached down and touched Yanni on the shoulder to get his attention. When Yanni turned toward him the butcher mouthed the words for coffee. Yanni nodded, said 'narghile', and turned back to Barba Yorgi.

The butcher knew it would do no good to speak in normal tones or even to shout. Yanni lived with almost total deafness since the war, the result of an injury from an Italian grenade thrown into a cave where he and three other members of the Resistance were hiding. The grenade exploded, killing his companions and covering him with gore. When the Italians saw the carnage they thought all four were certainly dead. No one could have lived through such a blast in that confined area. Stunned and deafened by the blast, Yanni lay unmoving until he thought the enemy soldiers were gone. Moving slowly and carefully, he crawled to the opening and peered out. With the approach of night, the two Italians sat close to a small fire. They shared a bottle of Cretan brandy stolen from one of the villages.

Yanni could see their lips moving, but he could hear nothing. He could also see they were quickly becoming intoxicated from the strong liqueur. From his boot he pulled his razor-sharp knife and waited. Soon one of the men fell over sideways, asleep. The other finished the bottle, got up and walked to the mouth of the cave, leaving his rifle lying beside his sleeping comrade. As he walked unsteadily in the direction of the cave he fumbled with the buttons of his pants, finally pulling his penis out to urinate into the cave. Quick as an adder Yanni rose from the ground in a fluid motion and sank the knife to the hilt below the soldier's Adam's apple. The man's mouth opened in surprise, but he uttered no sound. The knife stroke severed his larynx and spinal cord with one deadly blow. Yanni eased his body to the ground and withdrew the knife, watching the remains of life bubble out of the wound, as if from a bloody mouth.

Leaving him on the ground, Yanni crept across the few meters to the dead man's sleeping comrade, who snored softly in front of the fire with his mouth wide open and his head tilted back. He stood over him a moment, watching him sleep, and then knelt with his knee on the man's forehead and almost severed his head with his knife. He barely twitched.

Scanning the area from side to side to see if there were any others about, he knelt once more beside the dead man, cut off both his ears and put them in his pocket. Returning to the body at the mouth of the cave he repeated the action. Standing once more he noticed the dead man's flaccid penis still lying outside his open fly. With a crooked smile he reached for the exposed member, pulled it as far out of his pants as it would come and sliced it off at the base. He stood with it in his hand for a moment, undecided what to do with it. Coming to a decision, he stuffed it into the open mouth of the other soldier. Without another glance at the two dead men, he gathered up all the weapons left laying about and melted into the scrub.

He ultimately strung the two pairs of ears on a length of hemp cord and wore them around his neck as a trophy. In the hot Cretan sun they shriveled and dried until they looked like mushrooms. He wore them proudly, adding to his collection twice more before the end of the war. He never fully regained his hearing following the incident and was thereafter known as Deaf Yanni.

Many hearing impaired tend to speak overly loud. Yanni always spoke very softly. When he did speak he opened his mouth wide and spoke with a great deal of animation. Over the years he also became adept at reading lips. For this reason, when his friends spoke with him, they normally mimed a conversation.

Moments after ordering the coffee a young boy arrived with a tray bearing the small cups. The butcher followed him out of the shop carrying the narghile, a water pipe with a long hose made of red leather. He placed it in front of Barba Yorgi, applied a hot coal to the packet of tobacco, actually hashish, sitting atop the clay bowl, and the narghile was ready to smoke. Both men picked up their cups, raised them to one another, slurped noisily at the contents and set them down again. Barba Yorgi picked up the ivory and brass mouthpiece and drew deeply on it. In the street he caught sight of the young couple from the restaurant passing arm in arm. Before they walked out of sight, however, they were forgotten.

He turned to Yanni and began a convoluted discussion of why he called to meet with him. He told of a friend of his who found an item he wanted to dispose of. Not having any contacts, Barba Yorgi asked him to intercede for him and perhaps find a buyer. Yanni's eyes widened when he was finally told the item was gold. They widened even more when told it weighed over ten kilos.

During their conversation they were interrupted only once when a commotion began in an alley off the market place. One of the porters, a man everyone called 'Tzitzikas', Grasshopper, claimed someone attacked him for no reason at all. He howled in dismay and pain as blood streamed from his head and ran down his back. As he reeled through the market, he was forced to hold up his pants with one hand while with the other he held his bloody head. Hoots of laughter and derision followed his progress up the street, continuing until he disappeared from sight.

Hearing the commotion, the butcher came to the doorway to see what was happening. Deeply involved in discussion, Yanni did not notice anything until the butcher touched him on the shoulder and pointed out Tzitzikas to him. He nodded his head and laughed soundlessly at the spectacle. Barba Yorgi merely drew on his pipe, soothed by the sound of the bubbles in the water and the smoke in his lungs.

Again, the grapevine proved itself efficient and far-reaching. Shortly after its discovery, Yanni learned of the find on the south coast. He also heard that everything in the tomb was taken before the museum officials and police arrived at the site. He knew it was only a matter of time until someone approached him with some of the stolen items, but this news from Barba Yorgi was mind-boggling. The value of the gold itself was immense. In relation to the item's value on the clandestine antiques market, however, the value of the gold alone was paltry.

"Tell me, Giorgos," said Yanni, "who is this friend of yours who has this highly mysterious 'item'?"

"Ah, not yet, koubare," answered Barba Yorgi with a soft chuckle. "I will tell you one thing, however. I know the names of everyone who 'found' the antikas. Everyone. I'm their guardian angel. I protect them and their secret. Right now I'm only asking you if there would be a market for such an item as I describe. Give me a satisfactory answer and very soon I'll bring the item and put it in your hands. Right now I'm just an agent, working for a syndicate of interested shareholders, you might say."

"Without knowing what the item is, my old friend, I can't say just what it would be worth. It would be necessary to know where it came from and how old it is. Is it Greek, Roman or Minoan? These are all things I need to know first. Then, perhaps, just perhaps, we might be able to do some business for your 'clients'."

Barba Yorgi realized he dared not give more information at this time. In reality he felt his statements exceeded the caution to which he normally subscribed. Hopefully Yanni would not suspect. Siga, he thought to himself. Slowly. There is always danger in trying to rush things.

Yanni watched the old man closely. I think maybe he said more than he wanted tonight, he thought. I'd like to be inside the head of this Pseramonoli. Know what he knows. But then again, how much does he know and how much is the boasting of the hashish? At least he came to me first.

Barba Yorgi reached for his staff and pushed himself out of his seat. Looking down at Yanni he extended his ham-like hand. "Good to have seen you again, old friend. I must go, but I'll be back soon."

"Kalo taxidi," said Deaf Yanni, wishing him a safe journey.

The old man nodded and turned to make his way down the street. Yanni turned his head to see the butcher standing at the door watching him. Without a word he inclined his head in the direction of Barba Yorgi's disappearing back. The butcher looked across the street and jerked his head almost imperceptibly in Barba Yorgi's direction. A shadowy figure detached itself from the darkness of a recess in the wall facing them and glided away down the street.

CHAPTER 12

Carter did not begin to awake until almost 10 o'clock the next morning. Opening his eyes, he looked around the room. An involuntary smile crept across his features as he remembered the night before. He could still smell her scent on his pillow, on the sheets and on his skin. Looking at his watch he realized it was too late for breakfast, but did not care. He stretched, threw back the sheet and sat up. She would be gone by now, already far away on the bus with her friends heading towards Chania.

Getting to his feet he walked to the sink and brushed his teeth, then slipped on a pair of shorts, picked up his towel and went to take a shower. As he opened the door a slip of paper stuck into a crack of the door frame caught his attention. He reached for it, noticing the feminine handwriting. "Danke und viel Glück. Bis nächster Zeit!" It was signed simply "Hertzlich Grüßen." He understood the first word meant "Thank you," but only vaguely understood the rest of it. Never mind. He would ask Madame D to translate for him when he saw her. Laying the note on his writing table, he walked out the door.

He thought about his discussion the previous day with Mr. D concerning his desire to find some job – any job – in Iraklion. He mentioned to Carter the possibility that the English Institute in Iraklion would perhaps have a position he could handle. At the time of that conversation Carter smiled inwardly. It amused him that the old man's suggestion was the very place he knew that Matejowski in Athens mentioned as possible solution for employment..

Once back in his room, he looked through the clothes hanging from the rack next to the window, trying to find something that would be presentable to wear for an interview. He ruled out wearing a tie, for he rarely saw one worn other than by some of the bureaucrats in town. His pants were a little wrinkled from having been packed in his valise, but he felt that wearing them would cause most of their wrinkles to quickly disappear.

He stuck his head in the front door of the house to say hello, but Nikos was the only one there. He told Carter how to find the English Institute and that the director was named

Malcom Cruikshank. Carter jotted down the information, thanked the boy and left for town.

His first stop was Manoli's shop. The portly shopkeeper's effusive greeting rang out from the back of the shop when he saw Carter looking in his door. "Ah, kaliméra, Carter! Good morning! Come in, come in! How are you today?" He advanced toward the front, arms spread wide, the delight at seeing his new American friend evident on his face.

Carter shook the pudgy hand offered him. "Kaliméra to you, too, Manoli. I'm fine, thank you. Can I offer you a cup of coffee and a pastry? Today's my treat. You bought the other day, so call one of the waiters."

"Of course, of course," he replied, advancing to the door and scanning the street for one of the young boys with his tray. Spying one, he called him over and gave him the order.

"What do you do since the last time I see you?"

Carter gave him a brief account of almost all his activities during the past day or so, casually mentioning Traudel and Hannie. Manoli nodded his approval and leaned forward in anticipation of hearing the details. Carter was purposefully vague in his response and told him that she was already on her way to Chania with her friends and would leave by boat tonight for Athens.

"Ah, too bad for you, Carter. Never mind. There are many tourists in summer. You will see. How do you say, 'there are many fishes in the water'?"

"Many fish in the ocean," corrected Carter, smiling good-naturedly.

The waiter returned with two cups of Turkish coffee and two pastries, for which Carter paid. He and Manoli sat down in front of the store at the round table which was already in place. They slurped their coffee in unison and smacked their lips appropriately over the pastries dripping with honey. Afterward, as they smoked Papastratos from the flat orange box Manoli laid on the table between them, they gave each other brief lessons in Spanish and Greek. Carter continued the charade by writing down words and phrases as Manoli gave them to him, practicing each new addition before going to the next one. Manoli, on the other hand, wanted very few phrases which would lead to the increase of commerce. Most of his questions dealt with finding female companionship.

When Carter looked at his watch and saw it was almost 11:30, he excused himself, thanked Manoli for the Greek lesson, telling him he would see him later that day. Manoli pushed his glasses back up on his nose, rose to shake Carter's hand and wished him a good day.

Carter quickly found his way to the English Institute, which was located in an old three story building near a residential area just south of the business area. A wrought iron fence set into blocks of stone enclosed the front courtyard of the school. On the stone gate post hung a tarnished engraved brass plaque announcing:

ΤΟΝ ΙΝΣΤΙΤΟΥΤΟΝ ΑΓΓΛΙΚΟΝ ΙΡΑΚΛΙΟΥ'.

In smaller letters underneath was 'Heraklion English Institute'. He pushed open the gate and entered. Three teenage girls standing in front of the tall double doors addressed him in English as he approached, obviously proud of their ability. When he asked if Mr. Cruikshank was in the girls directed him to the lady at the reception desk. Thanking them, he went inside.

In a cramped corner of the entrance hall at a desk covered with papers, sat an officious-looking middle aged woman struggling to type a letter on a very old black typewriter. Carter stood waiting for a moment before she acknowledged his presence. She looked him up and down quickly, apparently trying to decide if he spoke English or some other language. Finally deciding he probably was an English speaker, she raised one eyebrow, pulled her glasses down on her nose, turned down the corners of her mouth and asked, "Yes? May I help you?"

"Yes, please. My name is Carter Martin. I would like to see Mr. Cruikshank, if I may."

"Do you have an appointment?" she asked, removing her glasses entirely.

"Why, no, I don't. I wasn't aware I would need one. I just have a question I would like to ask him and was hoping he could give me a moment of his time."

"The director is really a very busy man this morning, but I will see if he is available. You say your name is Mr. Carter?"

"Uh, no. Mr. Martin. Carter Martin."

"You are English or American?" she asked as she picked up the receiver of a battered black telephone.

"American. I'm American."

She dialed the phone and from somewhere above another phone began to buzz. Steps thudded on the wooden floor over his head, the distant buzzing stopped and she began to speak in Greek.

While she listened to whoever was on the other end of the line, or waited for an answer, she played with the beads around her neck. Pouring water into a glass from a carafe sitting on her desk, she took a swig, swished it around in her mouth, and then swallowed noisily.

"Málista. En táxei." She replaced the phone on its cradle and looked up at Carter again. "Please take a seat. The director will see you presently."

Carter thanked her and sat down on a straight backed arm chair, the leather covering its seat and arms cracked and black. The receptionist perched her glasses back on her nose and returned to her typing, totally ignoring him. He did not mind. It gave him a chance to evaluate his surroundings. In a prominent place on the wall was a large picture of King Constantine. On another wall was a photograph of Queen Elizabeth II, Queen of England. There were other photographs, some of them quite old, that Carter did not recognize at all, although one reminded him of pictures seen here and there of Eleftheros Venezelos, the renowned Cretan patriot. Periodically a child, or a group of young people, would clatter down the uncarpeted wooden stairs from the second story. They chattered gaily among themselves and several of them greeted him shyly in English. No one spoke to the receptionist.

A heavy tread in the upstairs hallway caused Carter to look up. At the head of the stairs stood a pleasant faced, sandy haired man of medium build, who looked to be about 30 years old. He looked down at Carter and began to descend the staircase. The receptionist leapt to her feet and with much animation and show of obeisance moved around her desk to wait at the foot of the stairs. Carter expected her to curtsy. She waved her hand in the general direction of Carter and said, "This is Mr. Martin."

He totally ignored her and walked toward Carter with his hand extended. "Mr. Martin! How do you do? My name is Cruikshank, Malcom Cruikshank. I'm the director of the English Institute. How may I help you? My secretary said you'd like to ask me a question."

He was friendly and offered a firm, warm grip. Carter liked his clipped accent, just the way he thought the head of an English institute should speak. He smiled, as he continued, "You're American, are you not?"

"Why, yes, I am, Mr. Cruikshank. I do have something I hoped to discuss with you and really do appreciate your taking time to meet with me. I apologize for arriving unannounced, but I wasn't sure what custom called for in this instance."

"Don't apologize, Mr. Martin. No bother at all. I was in the middle of the most damnably boring meeting of the planning committee. These things come up every three months and I absolutely detest them. When I learned of your arrival I jumped at the opportunity. Shooed them all out of the meeting room, saying an emergency required his immediate attention. Actually, the emergency was that I was about to go to sleep. Their droning sounding like flies batting against the inside of a window on a sunny day. It was a damn dreary prospect, I must say.

"Follow me. We'll go up to my office so we can talk in private. Would you like something to drink? A gazoza, say?"

"Please. A gazoza sounds fine," Carter replied, relishing the thought of the sparkling carbonated lemon drink.

"A gazoza it is, then." Turning to the receptionist who still waited at the foot of the stairs, he said, "Athena, have two bottles of gazoza and two glasses of ice sent up to my office. Right this way, Mr. Martin."

As Carter mounted the stairs he noticed Athena wasted no time, for she was already on the phone ordering the drinks. Cruikshank led him along a hallway into an office, which was not much larger than Carter's small room at the pension. He was surprised at the spartan surrounding. As if sensing Carter's reaction, Cruikshank turned and said, "It's tiny, isn't it? The first time I saw it I thought they led me into a closet by mistake. Here, let me move those books and you can take that seat there. Actually, I've grown quite accustomed to it. There's plenty of light and I can see out into the garden of the school. It's reasonably cool in the summer time, but damn cold in the winter. I sit here with my little brazier, which they supply me, all bundled up with my scarf around my neck..."

A knock at the door interrupted him and brought him to his feet. He opened the door to reveal Athena standing outside with a small tray containing two open bottles of gazoza and two glasses filled with ice.

"Ah, thank you, Athena." He took one of the bottles and a glass and handed them to Carter, then took the others and set them on his scarred desk top. Without another word he shut the door and returned to his chair, which protested as he sat back. Leaning to the side, he reached under his desk and produced a half-empty bottle of Gordon's gin.

"A tot of gin with these gazozas makes a very nice drink resembling gin and tonic. Quite refreshing. Care for some?" Before Carter could answer he leaned across the desk and splashed a generous portion of the gin into Carter's glass. "Now pour some of that gazoza on top of it, stir it with your finger and bottoms up! Oh, wait. Try a little of this, too." From his desk he produced a lemon, which he sliced with a knife and gave a wedge to Carter. "A little twist makes it look authentic, at least. Well, cheers!" He saluted Carter with his glass and drained it. Carter did the same, finding the taste to be as described. "Well, that takes the edge off! Here, one more, and then we'll get down to business."

Carter held his glass across the desk, accepting another healthy measure of gin, to which he added a splash of gazoza. Cruikshank raised his glass in salute again, took a large swallow and set his glass on the desk. "Now then, Mr. Martin. What business brings you to the Instituton Anglicon Irakliou?"

As Carter began to speak he could feel the pleasant warmth of the gin in his stomach. He told the director how and why he came to Crete and why he was in his office. "I'd like to be able to do something I can enjoy, which will enable me to learn at the same time. My Greek is just rudimentary at the present time, but then, I've been on the island less than a week. In college I was an English major and have a good command of the language. I saw some of your more advanced students this morning and even spoke with them. I think I could teach them with no problem at all."

"Capital idea, Mr. Martin!" said the director, slapping his desk with the palm of his hand. "Capital idea! In the planning meeting this morning we were discussing the hiring of an additional tutor, preferably one who is a native English speaker. Being an American I suppose one could say you are somewhat of a native speaker. Ha-ha-ha!! Have you ever been to England, Mr. Martin? No? Well, never mind. I'm sure we could fit you in very well here. This is most propitious. The gods must have been looking out for us. I'll call my secretary, who'll have you fill out the necessary paper work. You don't mind my calling you Carter, do you? Fine, then. Carter it is. Please call me Malcom, if you like. Actually, my friends call me Bunny. Just don't do it in front of the staff. These Greeks can be so damnably stuffy at times. No sense of humor whatsoever. They're almost as rigid as the Brits, you know. Heh-heh-heh! Well, anyway, I hope you'll be happy here. I want you to know I'm delighted! I could just see myself having to put up with some effete young man from Eton and Oxford, or else some crusty old professor from some public school in the Cotswolds.

"But here, where are my manners? What do you think? Would you like to come work with us? We can't pay what you Americans are used to getting, but then, we aren't in America, are we? The cost of living is so much lower here than either the United States or the UK. We can start you out at 1000 drachmas a week. At the current rate of exchange that would be a little more than, oh, let me see...that would be, right...right, $130.00 per month. Where are you living now? Oh, that's right. You told me. In that pension near the port. You know, Carter, in the suburbs you can find a very nice place for about 1000 drachmas per month. It's not all that plush, but it would do very nicely indeed. That would give you plenty to spend on food and leave you a bit to have some fun with. I feel sure that after a few months we can talk the board into increasing your salary somewhat. Well, what do you think?"

During the entire monologue Carter was only able to nod in agreement or occasionally shake his head. His image of the reserved English was shattered. He was overwhelmed not only by Cruikshank's verbosity, but by the way the question of his working at the institute was resolved. Should anyone have been listening they would have never guessed this interview was anything other than a young American being hired for a teaching job. What was it Manoli said this morning when he told him he was going to talk to the director of the English Institute? Something about the status of a teacher, a 'Dáskalos'. Carter thought of his days in school in Athens and the respect his teachers enjoyed. He would be known as Kyrie Daskalos. Perfect! It could not have worked out better.

"Malcom,..."

"Bunny. Please, just call me Bunny," Cruikshank interrupted.

"Yes, sorry. Bunny, it sounds very good to me. When do I start?"

"Capital, Carter, capital! I'll call my secretary right now so we can get the paperwork started. That'll only take a few days. Then I'd like for you to start work on Monday the first week in September. Let me look at my calendar. Here it is. September second. Mark that date and circle it in red."

He picked up his telephone and dialed a number, which was answered shortly. "Vasilia, come into my office, please," then hung up. Almost immediately after replacing the receiver a knock sounded at the door. The door opened and an attractive, titian haired young woman entered.

"Vasilia, this is Mr. Carter Martin. I want to hire him as a tutor. Take him into your office and have him fill out the appropriate forms. I'm going to present his application to the board and tell them I absolutely have to have him here." Standing up, he came around his desk and shook Carter's hand warmly. "Carter, I'm immensely pleased you came in today. This is a stroke of luck for the both of us. We'll do everything necessary at this end to make sure you can meet your first class by the first week in September. I'll be calling you from time to time, for I'm sure there'll be many questions you'll have. Also,

I'd like for you to sit in on several of our more advanced classes as an observer. Will you be able to do that?"

"Of course. I'll look forward to it. Thank you very much for your time and interest. I'm sure I can do a good job. The additional time before I begin will give me a chance to improve my Greek, as well."

"Fine, Carter. Now, please go with Vasilia. She'll take care of everything. If you have any questions, please ring me up."

Carter said he would and followed Vasilia down the hall to the cubbyhole she called her office. When he left an hour later he was walking on air. As he descended the stairs he noticed the receptionist push herself away from her desk and stand beside it, her attitude remarkably changed.

"It was nice to have met you, Mr. Martin. We look forward to having you here at the Institute."

"My, news travels fast," he thought to himself. He thanked her for her good wishes and walked out the door.

He stuck his head inside Manoli's shop and shouted, "I got it!" An older couple browsing through Manoli's 'traysures' whirled in surprise at his cry. The lady put her hand to her throat and her mouth gaped open.

"The job? Bravo, Carter!" responded Manoli with apparent delight. The lady and gentleman both whirled now to face the shopkeeper. "Now we will call you Daskalocarter. You live with Daskaloyanni. It is a pension full of dáskali! We must celebrate your good fortune?"

"You take care of your customers, Manoli. I have to run, but I'll be back later." He waved and turned to walk back to the pension.

That evening he returned to town to find Manoli sitting out front with a man he introduced as his brother, Alexandros. They talked for a moment, but Alexandros spoke no English and soon left. Manoli entered the store to straighten some shelves and Carter followed him inside to talk while he worked. They were there for only a few minutes when Manoli turned his head toward the door, smiled and exclaimed, "Ah, bon soir, Monsieur le Comte. Comment allez-vous?"

Before he could turn to see to whom Manoli spoke Carter heard a well-modulated, refined voice reply, "Très bien, merci, monsieur Manoli. Et vous?"

Manoli rushed from behind the counter and scurried toward the newcomer. The patter of polite greetings completed, he took the man by the arm and led him toward Carter. "Je veux vous présenter à mon ami, Carter," he said. "Il est américain. Carter, I want to introduce you to an old and very special friend, monsieur le Comte Yves de Givry."

"Allo, did Manoli say your name is Carter? 'Ow do you do, Carter? Pleased to meet you. I am Yves de Givry. Please call me Yves." His English was good, if heavily accented, his handshake brief but firm.

"Hello. Nice to meet you," Carter replied.

Manoli continued. "The count lives in Paris and comes to Kriti every year in summer time. I know him for many years. He writes for a newspaper in Paris. Travel column. He says many nice things about Crete and the Greek people. Pas vrai, monsieur? He tell all of Paris to come to Greece and Kriti in summer." Turning to the count, Manoli asked. "What do you do tonight?"

"Tonight, mon cher Manoli, I am going to the Club Fez. There will be many French people there tonight."

"The Club Fez? Very good club. How is my friend, Bonisseur?"

"Jean Paul is fine. You should close this shop down earlier and come have a drink wiz us."

Carter paid no more attention to the conversation. The name Jean Paul Bonisseur caused his eyes to involuntarily open wide in astonishment. Bonisseur! This was too good to be true. But then how many Frenchmen named Jean Paul Bonisseur could one expect to find in Iraklion? This must be the one he sought.

Carter suddenly noticed the pause in the conversation and that both men were looking at him.

"Oh, I'm sorry. I didn't realize you were talking to me," he said lamely.

"I was just saying to Monsieur Yves that he should take you to the Club Fez tonight. Do you have anything else to do?"

A look of delight appeared on the older man's face. "Why, yes. Zat would be wonder-fool. The owner of the club is a Frenchman from North Africa. He is maybe a little older than you are, but a very interesting person. Yes! You must come to the club tonight with me."

"You must go," urged Manoli. "He can introduce you to everyone. There are many beautiful girls there. French girls."

Carter nodded his agreement. The Count, obviously pleased with the decision, beamed. "Excellent! Are you ready to go now? Manoli, would you like to join us also?" When Manoli demurred they bade him good night and left the shop.

De Givry talked constantly as they walked, asking what brought Carter to Crete and if his travels ever took him to Paris. Carter was quickly finding the older gentleman to be quite charming. He was very well spoken and evinced an interest in everything Carter mentioned since coming to the island. He was particularly interested in the fact Carter would be going to work at the English Institute. He said the director of the French School would probably be at the club and that he would introduce Carter to him.

Carter's thoughts were not totally on their conversation. Part of his mind raced, thinking of the coincidence of his meeting the Count and to learn that this man probably knew the very person he sought. As Bunny remarked only that afternoon, the gods were looking after him. Everything was falling into place. Now Carter would have an introduction to Bonisseur and he could now begin his efforts at recruitment.

The Club Fez, a short walk past Fountain Square and across the street from a public park, was located behind a high wall covered with vines. Inside the wall was a courtyard with an overhead arbor from which hung jasmine, the sweet perfume of its blossoms pervading the area. Small round tables, accommodating two comfortably, were set up along the whitewashed stucco walls. Through the open doorway of the club itself, and the large, paned windows flanking the entrance, they could see a good crowd gathered. The sound of a piano playing could be heard above the hubbub and a man's voice sang 'Un Petit Bock" to a tune Carter recognized as the American song, 'One Meatball'.

Their arrival was met by a chorus of greetings from various groups at the tables. Everyone seemed to know De Givry. He took Carter from table to table, speaking to everyone and introducing him. Some of those to whom he was introduced spoke to him in English, most only in French. By the time they came to the director of the French School, Maurice Canif, he could only remember the names of a few of the people he met.

A puckish man, approximately 35 years of age, of medium height and stocky build, Canif was seated between two well-bronzed, attractive ladies. When Yves introduced Carter to Canif the Frenchman jumped to his feet, shook hands vigorously, and said, "I speak English." He pointed to one foot, then the other. "One foot, two foots."

Those at nearby tables exploded in laughter as he sat down to a round of applause. Carter simply smiled and congratulated the smug pedagogue. Someone produced two chairs from another table and he and the Count sat down.

Carter followed the rapid fire conversation, full of nuance and repartee, but acted as if he understood not a word. Nevertheless, it was a distinct pleasure for him to be there, even if only as a spectator, for it reminded him of his student days in Belgium and his French and Belgian classmates. He followed the different conversations raptly, at the same time maintaining his pretense of being just another monolingual American. Occasionally someone made an attempt to engage him in conversation, always in French. He would make a game attempt at replying but kept his vocabulary purposefully at a minimal and painfully inadequate level.

The women obviously adored Yves, finding him witty, urbane and charming. He chatted with the ladies as if he were one of them. Carter knew he was the subject of the conversation, but he maintained his role. He occasionally caught one or another giving him a look of appraisal. These women were mostly deeply bronzed, lithe and attractive and he would have loved to join in. There were many things he would have loved to discuss with these vivacious creatures.

A patter of applause came from several of the tables and Carter realized the pianist was no longer playing. Turning in the direction of the piano, he saw a tall, dark-haired man who looked vaguely familiar greeting individuals from several groups as he made his way across the floor. Carter watched him move slowly toward them, accepting accolades and gestures of familiarity from his clientele. A moment later Canif raised his hands over his head in a raucous greeting. A huge grin split the man's face. He stopped behind Yves, caught the eye of the barman and motioned for a round of drinks for everyone at the table. A young couple came up at that moment to introduce themselves and told him how much they enjoyed his playing. He thanked them for their kindness and invited them to join the group. One of the women moved closer to Canif and patted the bench beside her. The pianist accepted and seated himself across from Carter.

Yves hurried to make introductions. "Carter, I would like to present to you Jean Paul Bonisseur, ze owner of Le Club Fez. He is ze one I was telling you about earlier at Manoli's shop. I sink the two of you should become acquainted. Bose of you are expatriates."

So this was Bonisseur! Carter's heart leapt to his throat. He could not believe this turn of events. He looked nothing like the picture Ware showed him. Of course, the photo obviously was taken some years before and was of poor quality. Carter could not shake the feeling of recognition, however. Jean Paul half rose and leaned across the table to shake his hand.

"Allo, I am Bonisseur. Where did you find this old man?" As he spoke he jerked his thumb in Yves' direction. "You must be careful. He's always on the lookout for handsome young men. It's the only reason he comes to Crete every year."

The Count leaned back, clasped his hands together below his chin and smiled wryly. "I'm so sorry, Carter. I forgot to tell you he's also very crude. Pied-noir, you know. Zat means a Frenchman from Algeria." Someone who spoke English translated for those who did not and the whole table burst into raucous laughter.

Jean Paul leaned toward one of the girls who sat next to Canif and quickly glanced at Carter as she spoke. Not realizing Carter understood every word that was being said he laughed, shook his head and said, "She says you do not look like one of Monsieur le Comte's types. I tell her I don't think you are either. You are not, are you?"

"I love women, if that's what you mean," Carter replied with a smile.

Still laughing, Jean Paul told Carter, "The ladies at the table say they are glad. Speaking of le Comte, you know, Carter, one day Yves tell me that I am the most intelligent pied-noir in Paris. To me that means I am the most intelligent man in all of Paris, because I believe pied-noirs are much more intelligent than any French man. I thanked him for the compliment." The translation provoked another round of hilarity.

The barman arrived at the table with a bottle of Cretan red and extra glasses for the newcomers. He also brought a basket of pretzels, which were attacked by everyone. Jean Paul and Carter continued to talk, each telling the other briefly their reasons for coming to Crete. Jean Paul talked to Carter as if he was a lifelong acquaintance. During their talk Carter was able to confirm some of the information given him by the Agency on why he was forced to leave Algeria following its independence in 1962. Because, he said, of some difficulty concerning his returning to France at that time, he slipped across the Tunisian border and eventually found himself in Sfax. According to his account, he took odd jobs in Tunisia for almost six months before borrowing money from a friend and coming to Crete. Once on Crete he began to look for business opportunities. A Greek acquaintance told him of wanting to open a bar, but money was the major concern. Jean Paul saw a good thing and he jumped. He advanced the money and he and the Greek became partners in a small but potentially lucrative business.

This was almost two years ago. Since that time he rented a house in one of the suburbs and was comfortably situated. He invited Carter to come up at any time. "As a matter of fact, why don't you come tonight? I am giving a little party for a small group of friends. Would you like to join us? You can ride with me. Yves, would you like to come, too?"

Yves thanked him, but said an important engagement was planned for the next day and he needed to return to his hotel. He encouraged Carter to go, assuring him it would give him a chance to practice and improve his French. Carter accepted the invitation readily. It would be good to make new friends, particularly among the French-speaking community. This would also give him time to get to know the pied-noir even better.

Yves left around eleven and by midnight many of the others drifted out into the night, prompting Jean Paul to announce his imminent departure. He would take as many as possible in his car, the rest would ride with Canif.

"Carter, come on with me," said Jean Paul. "We'll take a few bottles of wine to make sure we have enough." Carter rose and followed him behind the bar, where he was handed three bottles of red wine. The Frenchman took three more, told his partner to close up in one hour, and they left.

On the far side of the park under some trees Jean Paul stopped beside a canary yellow convertible. It was then that Carter realized why he experienced the feeling of déjà-vu when they first met. Bonisseur was the driver of the yellow car on the airport road the night he arrived.

Squealing with pleasure, the girls climbed over the sides of the car into the back seat. Jean Paul handed his bottles to one of them and opened the door on the passenger side. "Here, Carter. You sit in front." One of the two remaining girls got in ahead of Carter, moving to the middle of the seat. Carter handed the bottles to her and turned to the girl he remembered as Christine still standing beside him. Several times during the evening when he thought she would not notice he cast frankly admiring glances in her direction.

"Zat's all right. You get in first and I will sit on you," she said.

He climbed in and she followed to sit on his lap. She immediately turned her body to the side, asking if she were too heavy. As soon as he assured her she was not she turned to continue a conversation with one of the girls in the back seat.

The engine started with a roar, as if the muffler were broken. "What kind of car is this?" asked Carter

"Mercury. An American car. I bought it from a Jew on an Israeli ship that stopped in the harbor. They were on their way to Haifa from New York. He bought two of them, one to keep and the other to take back and sell in Israel. He said it has something called 'glass packs'. That is what makes so much noise. I hope the neighbors are not asleep!"

He slammed it into gear, let out a whoop and roared away from the curb. They were not able to go fast through the narrow streets, but in the early morning quiet Carter was sure there were those who would be shaken from their beds by the engine's growl. They took the road out of town, the same one Carter took when he went by bus to Knossos. Before reaching the palace, however, Jean Paul turned left into a narrow lane and they soon found themselves confronted by the bars of a wide iron gate. Jean Paul slowed to a crawl, nudged the gates open with the front bumper, and drove into a large paved courtyard ringed by tall pine trees. He pulled around to the far end of the house and shut off the motor. Everyone spilled from the car laughing and talking.

Even in the dark Carter could see the house was of typical Greek design, and huge. Switches were flicked on, flooding the courtyard with light. In an immense room at one end of the house, someone turned on a stereo. Two couples began dancing on the flagstones under the pines, while others merely sat, drank and talked. While waiting for the others to arrive, Carter took the opportunity to explore the rest of the house. Off what he dubbed the 'ball room' were two doors leading to separate bedrooms. Both of the double beds were rumpled and were strewn with clothes and suitcases. On the far side of the entrance hall was yet another bedroom, a very large one, with two doors leading into yet another bedroom and a large kitchen. From the far side of the kitchen a double door led to a bathroom and a separate shower room, which was twice as large as the kitchen. Upstairs were six more bedrooms, all showing signs of occupancy. From one of them toward the end of the house containing the ball room a door lead onto a large rooftop terrace surrounded by an iron railing. Carter could not wait to see the house and grounds in daylight. From the terrace he could see a large yard adjoining the paved courtyard. At the far end of the side yard was a high hedge with a passageway cut into it. He could only guess where it led.

As he descended the stairs to the ground floor someone handed him a glass of wine. The long trestle table from the ball room was set outside on the paving stones of the courtyard and several people were seated around it. From high in the trees and on the ends of the house spotlights were positioned illuminating the entire area. Carter walked toward the grassy side yard and noticed a rectangular opening in the ground with steps leading down into total darkness. Another similar opening with descending steps could be seen twenty five feet further on. The walls on either side of the stairs, as well as the ceiling over the stairs, were constructed of thick concrete. He tried to peer in, but was unable to see beyond the sixth step.

A soft noise behind him caused him to turn. Christine walked barefoot across the grass toward him. As she approached she spoke to him in French and he replied without thinking. When he realized his inadvertent slip he covered himself by asking in a stumbling manner if she knew where the steps led. Her reply surprised him. Occupying Germans used the house during the Second World War. In fact, this very house was the residence of the Gestapo commander for over a year. The stairs led to two underground rooms where 'special' interrogations were carried out. This meant that few survived them. The Greeks were afraid of the house and its ghosts. None would even consider living there. A very successful exporter, whose family owned the house for over a century, could neither sell nor rent it. As a result, it remained empty from 1944 until the crazy Frenchman came to town 20 years later. Jean Paul agreed to 700 drachmas a month. That amount would only pay the taxes, but their only other choice would be to let it remain empty.

Carter was fascinated by all he learned from Christine, but conversation was tedious. Because of his feigned ineptitude, Christine switched to her limited English. In her estimation, although basic, it was still better than Carter's French.

Still curious about the house and surrounding gardens, Carter asked what was beyond the hedge. She replied it was a large area that looks like the remains of a formal garden. In it were grapevines, fig, kumquat, orange, lemon, grapefruit, apple and pear trees. A wide variety of flowers also grew there among the weeds and briars. Like the house, it remained untended since the war years, although the fruit trees continued to bear copiously. At the other end of the garden was another underground bunker over which, the neighbors told Jean Paul, an anti-aircraft gun once stood. At the bottom of a steep set of steps was a large room, constructed of reinforced concrete, closed off from the outside by a heavy steel door. Christine told him the door was so well-balanced that one person could open and close it with one finger. She said he would have to go and explore it in the daylight, to which Carter agreed.

They wandered around the property, talking for over an hour, even taking a stroll along the narrow, winding cobbled street, which ran past the house. All the surrounding houses were dark, their inhabitants having retired hours before. When they returned to the house, some of the partiers from the club were already gone. Others were in bed. Christine yawned, stretched like a bronzed, blonde cat and excused herself for the night. Carter found a half-full bottle of wine, poured another glass and wandered back outside. Jean Paul and Canif were seated at the table talking quietly. They looked up as Carter approached the table and Jean Paul invited him to sit with them.

They talked for a while longer before Canif said, "Bon, au lit! Bonne nuit tout le monde." With that pronouncement he waved goodbye and left for town.

Jean Paul and Carter were the only ones left awake. The stereo was silent and quiet reigned. The half-moon was no longer visible and the sky above the pine trees boasted a twinkling canopy of stars. Bonisseur got up and flipped the switch inside the door and all the outside lights went off. Coming back to his chair, he poured himself another glass of wine, topping off Carter's glass in the process, and propped his feet up on the table. "I never did ask you," he began, "where do you stay. Have you found a house yet?"

"I'm staying in a pension near the port. The Daskaloyanni family."

"Really?! They are wonderful people. When I first come to Iraklion I stay with them. Do you think you will stay there long?"

"No, I don't think so," Carter replied. "I've been hired by the English Institute as a tutor. Maybe you know the director, Malcom Cruikshank. He said I could find a house in the suburbs. That's what I'd really like to do. The Daskaloyanni's are nice people, but I'd like to have more than just one room in someone else's home."

"I agree with you. It is much better. Tell me, Carter, what brings you to Crete? I mean, what really brings you to this place? It is most unlikely to find an American who just leaves everything and come to a small corner of the world like Crete."

Carter told him briefly of having graduated from the university a few months before and of his wanting to simply get away for a while before he truly needed to earn a living. Jean Paul listened without comment, lighting a fresh cigarette from the burning butt of the one smoked down to his nicotine-stained finger tips. When Carter paused at the end of his recitation the Frenchman's expression contained a hint of skepticism. At the end of the long moment of silence he uncrossed his ankles from atop the table, dropped his chair purposefully to the flagstones, leaned across the table top on his elbows and forearms and dropped his voice to a conspiratorial whisper. "Eh, oh, mon pote! Mais qu'est-ce que tu me racontes?"

The slangy argot almost made Carter forget himself. He struggled to bite back the grin that tried to force its way to his lips and swallowed hard to keep from responding in kind. This was the kind of language, give and take between good friends, he used growing up in Belgium. At the last moment he concealed his delight and brought himself under control.

"Moputt? What does that mean?"

Bonisseur ignored the question. This time he said in English, "I just have a feeling you are not totally truthful with me. I told you I have a hard time believing you are just some, how you say it, footloose American who has come to Europe, much less to the island of Crete, to teach English to native children. There is something more to this story than you are telling me."

Carter looked Jean Paul in the eye for a moment and then down at his own hands clasped in front of him on the table. His racing mind sought a plausible answer, one which would be acceptable. He felt it was too early to tell the whole truth to this man he just met, but the opportunity was too good to waste. He was amazed when he heard himself begin to speak. "Well, my friend, you're right. I am here for more than just the fun of it. You really are quite astute.

A small smile tugged at the corners of Jean Paul's mouth. "Astucieux? Moi? Well, maybe. So, tell me."

"The truth of the matter is that I work as a freelance writer for a number of magazines."

Bonisseur's mouth dropped open and then snapped shut again. A knowing look appeared on his face as he leaned even closer.

"I'm in search of material for a story I've been commissioned to do for one of them on the Middle Eastern situation. I trust this will go no further than from me to you, but there has been speculation recently that the Palestinians, you know, the Fedayeen, at least some of them, are moving to work out of areas off the coast of Israel."

"Cyprus? Do you mean Cyprus?"

"Other than Cyprus. If you've been following their activities you know they've already launched some raids against Israel, probably from Cyprus."

"Ah, ouais, that's true! I read something not long ago in Le Monde about that. Putain! But tell me, what are you writing about?"

"I'm not exactly sure I should be telling you this."

"But, of course you can tell me. Trust me! I may know much more about them than you think. Perhaps I can even help you."

'Oh, mon pote!' thought Carter, 'that's exactly what I'm counting on.' Seeming to weigh his words, he said, "The fact of the matter is, I'm not so sure I'm not on a wild goose chase. I have no firm evidence or information the group I'm looking for is here or someplace else in the eastern Mediterranean. It's just a chance I'm taking. I don't even know the name of the group I'm looking for. The only thing I have is a name...the name of a man. I'm afraid it's just a nom de guerre and it won't be much help in the long run."

"A name? What name? Is it someone working with these sals Fedayeen?"

"His name is Bekr. Abu Bekr. Have you ever heard of him?

"Abu Bekr. Non, the name is not familiar. As you say, it's probably a nom de guerre. Do you have any idea of his real name?"

At first Carter thought of denying any knowledge of Abu Bekr's true name. He was still not certain he was not acting too hastily. In the end, however, what did he have to lose? In reality this man across from him was the only person who could help him. With that realization in mind he decided to give it a try. He acted as if he was wracking his memory for an answer. "Uh-h-h, maybe I have heard it before. What was it? Boudie? Bougie? Boulaid? Boulaid, yeah, I think that's what it is. Sure, that's it. Boulaid."

Jean Paul's eyes suddenly widened and again his mouth dropped open. In unison the two men spoke the name, the one name. "Belkacem ben Boulaid"

Instantly Bonisseur pushed himself back away from the table and rose to his feet. He was breathing hard and evidently in a highly agitated state. "Belkacem ben Boulaid! I know him! I know exactly who you are talking about!" He was almost shouting now as he paced quickly beside the table.

"You know him? That's fantastic! But wait a minute. How would you possibly know this man? I heard he'd been living in Syria and Lebanon for the past few years."

"But, no, mon vieux, don't you see? If this is the same man I knew he is not from the Levant. He is originally from Algeria. Besides, he is a most dangerous man and one I would very much like to see again."

Jean Paul talked non-stop for the next hour, telling Carter how he came to know ben Boulaid and of their relationship. He told of ben Boulaid's role with the F.L.N. in Algeria and of his own role with the 10th Parachute Battalion. During the entire monologue Carter sat entranced as everything he learned from the Agency was confirmed. When Bonisseur finally finished he stood with his arms wrapped tightly across his chest.

"I have two questions to ask you." When the Frenchman nodded Carter continued. "First of all, do you think you would know him if you saw him again?"

"Know him!? I would know this bastard anywhere. Unless his appearance has been totally changed by surgery I could not mistake him."

Carter nodded and then posed his second question. "Do you think you would be interested in helping me find him? Wait, before you answer. Let me tell you one thing. I do not want to talk to him or to interview him. All I want is for you to tell me if you recognize him and point him out to me. There will be no need for you to make yourself known to him in any way. Do you understand?"

"Yes, I do understand. But do you understand also that I would very much like to kill this man with my bare hands. I missed that opportunity once before when he escaped from custody after killing four of my men. He was wanted by all of the OAS. Wait, are you sure this is the same man you are searching for?"

"All I know is that he was born in Algeria and fought with the F.L.N. until independence in 1962. After that he disappeared and has only recently turned up in the ranks of the Fedayeen. If you could help me find him I would be forever grateful."

Jean Paul's thoughts seemed far away when he responded. "Agreed."

Carter was beside himself with joy. He never imagined that things could possibly fall into place so quickly or with so little trouble. It was almost too good to be true. Not eight hours before he did not even know where to begin looking for this man and now they were allies. His head spun with the import of his success. He accomplished all he dared tonight and sought now to divert his new friend's attention to something else, to something that would allow him to consider every aspect of what he was to undertake.

The first thing that came to his mind was archaeology. In an attempt to change the subject he mentioned his interest in the many archaeological sites on the island. Immediately the tall pied-noir's eyes lit up.

"That's interesting to me also. Since coming here I dig a little bit here and there. Once or twice I found some things of interest, but nothing big. I think there is many, many things here.

Very valuable treasures that the government is not letting the archaeologist dig for." As Jean Paul talked he pointed out things of which Carter was totally unaware, such as the priorities of the Archaeological Commission.

"What I'd really like to do is find a place to dig where I wouldn't have to worry about someone coming along and turning me in to the authorities," said Carter. "With all the undiscovered sites there has to be a world of treasure out there. I think it would be fun to go live in one of the villages with the peasants."

Jean Paul shook his head in agreement. "You know, the peasants find things all the time. I heard they've tried taking these things to the authorities, but they end up getting in trouble over having found them in the first place. The authorities always thank the peasants for doing their patriotic duty by coming to them, and then want to know where they are hiding the rest! They always want the peasants to show where they found the objects."

"If it's true they find things and no longer feel comfortable taking them to the authorities, what good is it to them if they sit on a shelf in their houses? Don't you think it would be far better if they could sell them? Why not take them to one of the larger cities in Europe and find someone who would buy them?"

"I've thought of that and it's interesting you would, as well. I've sometimes thought of going to Zürich or Basel and finding a contact, someone who buys antiquities such as these..."

"The first step would be to have access to these things, wouldn't it? I mean, how are you going to set up contacts if you don't have anything to show them? Something to offer to them. You've been in Crete long enough to have maybe run across someone who would be willing to sell their finds, haven't you? Hell, what am I saying? I'm sure people just don't walk up to a foreigner on the street and offer things of archaeological value for them to buy."

Jean Paul did not answer for a long moment. He sat gazing at the stars through the trees. He thought of what Carter said. There was a lot of truth in his statements. He liked this American. As Yves pointed out, they were both expatriates.

From the short time Jean Paul met and talked to him, Carter seemed to have a good head on his shoulders. He also seemed trustworthy, which he realized was only a snap judgment, but he said he was interested in putting down roots in Greece. They were also compatible, with many of the same interests. Carter seemed naive, as were most Americans. He also seemed to have some money and would be earning more when he went to work at the English Institute. To make his plan work he was going to need a partner to supply some seed money; a partner who would share in the profits, the benefits and, yes, even the risks. The idea of such an alliance came to him for some time now. He decided he would have to take a chance on Carter. He wouldn't tell him all he knew for the time being. He would also give him a chance to back out before he knew too much. In his mind he weighed the consequences of such a move and finally came to a decision. It would be much smarter to trust this Carter Martin than to try taking one of the Greeks into his confidence.

His main concern with sharing his ideas with the natives was that he did not totally trust them as business partners. He learned that lesson when he opened the club. There was a large element of greed where they were concerned. They seemed to feel there was nothing wrong with taking advantage of a foreigner. Dealing with them as their agent would be much better. That way he would be working in their interests, but he would have all the knowledge about where to sell their antiquities. He felt good about Carter. He would have to take a chance.

"Several months ago there was a man, a peasant from a village in the mountains in central Crete who came into the club. It was a busy night, but I noticed he sat at a table in the corner all by himself for a very long time. I became curious and approached him, as all good club owners will do, just to find out if I could get him something. He invited me to sit down. I bought him a drink and after some time he began to talk about some things that were being found by someone near his village. To make a long story short, he showed me two small ivory statues in a cigarette box and asked me if I would be interested in buying them. I told him I didn't have much money, but that perhaps I could find someone who would pay for them. I met a man, a

Belgian, some time ago. We discussed much the same topic as you and I tonight. In the end he gave me the name of a man in Switzerland who is the supplier for many private collectors in Europe. He also sells to museums sometimes. He gave me a letter of introduction to this man."

"Have you gone yet?" asked Carter with growing excitement.

"No, not yet. Money is a consideration. I must fly to Zürich and there isn't any money for such a trip. I put all my money into the Club Fez."

Carter leaned back in his chair and looked speculatively at Jean Paul. "Before we talk about finding money for a ticket, tell me more about the man who came to see you. Did he have a lot of things to offer, or just the two statues?"

"He said there were many more things in his village and in other villages all over Crete. He tells me there is a man here in Iraklion who has been able to sell some things for certain peasants from other villages. This man told the man who was in the club to come see me. They have secretly sold to foreigners one or two times, but he feels that outside of this country he can make more money. He cannot take his antiquitès out of the country and felt it would be much better to have someone, say a foreigner living in Crete, to act as a courier. He would say how much he would want for the things and whatever the courier could sell them for over what the middle man is asking, well, then, he can keep the extra money as his commission. He thinks this is a better idea than offering a pourcentage. You know, a percentage."

Carter's sense of adventure overcame any shred of caution that might have existed. For the moment he even forgot how important it was that he cultivate Jean Paul's friendship. He was convinced this scheme would work. He did not even consider the inherent dangers of such an undertaking. All he could see was the chance to do something that to him was fraught with intrigue. It was akin to being a spy.

"Well, tell me, how much money would it take to fly to Zürich and back? I have some money I can spare right now, that is, if you're considering including me in your plan."

Bonisseur knew there was a reason he liked this American. He felt his decision to confide in Carter was the right one. For the present he would have to keep him from becoming too involved. Above all, he would have to impress upon him the necessity of complete secrecy. He must discuss this with no one else, certainly not the Greeks. Once their operation was established he could consider taking Carter with him, perhaps even let him make one of the trips himself. It would be a good way to allay any suspicions the authorities might have. He must also keep Carter where he could teach him and guide him in making the right decisions. He was sure he would even be a good source for new ideas. He sensed this right away.

"Carter, let's talk about you. You said you wanted to find a house outside of town. Why don't you think about coming here to live? I have so much room and you can have any of the rooms you want for your own. In the winter I live here by myself anyway and it would be nice to have some company. You would like my friends who stay here. There is always someone new. In the summertime there are always tourists from the boat, girls of course, who will cook for us. Also, there are many interesting people, people who can teach you much."

"Do you mean just come here and live? Jesus, that sounds great, but from the looks of things the house is full right now."

"Never mind that. Most will be leaving in two or three days. Come then. Just move your things from the pension. I'll pick you up in my car and help you move. D'accord?"

"It sounds fantastic. That means I'm going to have to learn French in a hurry, doesn't it?"

"Sure, but what better way to learn than with people who speak it all the time! It's settled then. You'll move here by the end of the week." Jean Paul stood up, stretching. "It's getting late. Come on and I'll give you a ride back to town. But come to the club tomorrow night."

During the ride back to the pension Carter mulled over this day's turn of events. Not only was he employed, but now he would be well-lodged. Most importantly he now knew the very person the Agency sent him to find. Most unbelievable of all

Bonisseur was willing to work with him. He could hardly wait to call Horiatis and tell him the news.

Jean Paul tried once more to bring the discussion back to Abu Bekr, wanting to know when they would try to find him and where. Carter told him he was not sure, that he was waiting for information that would indicate Bekr and his group were on the island. Jean Paul accepted that explanation and reiterated his interest in helping him in his quest. Carter reminded him once more that he must not speak of this to anyone.

The yellow convertible growled to a halt in front of the gate of the pension. Carter got out and turned to thank him for the ride and the interesting evening. "By the way, the man at the club with the two statues: did he tell you who his contact is here in Iraklion? You know, the one who has access to artifacts from the other villages? The one who sent him to you?"

"He finally did after I insisted on meeting him. He has a small business in the center of town. One day soon I'll take you to meet him. It's a little difficult talking to him, however. He's deaf. Bon soir, mon ami. A demain."

CHAPTER 13

Barba Yorgi's path took him in the direction of the port. He shrugged off the slight sense of unease, the sense of being watched, he felt as he passed through the streets. He attributed it to his being in the midst of the city. Although not as comfortable here as among his mountains, he was nevertheless unconcerned for his safety. The fact that he might be followed never occurred to him. He was satisfied with his meeting with Deaf Yanni. Through him there existed the opportunity to make some money through the efforts of others. All he needed to do was utilize the knowledge gained from his talk with Mitzos. He would contact each of those who were at the tomb. Everyone there took something and each tried to formulate a plan of what he would do with it. He was almost certain, however, they were totally ignorant of how to dispose of their sudden potential wealth. This fit Barba Yorgi's plans perfectly, for he knew exactly how to turn the items into a profit. It did not concern him that they might not want to go along with his plans. When they discovered how much he knew they would only be too happy to cooperate.

Nearer the port the crowds thinned appreciably. There were fewer lights here too. Passing along one of the streets fronting on a small park he heard the sounds of gaiety issuing from an opening in a high whitewashed wall. On the wall was a sign announcing 'Club Fez'. Underneath were small letters that he could read, "ΚΛΑΜΠ ΦΕΖ''. As he passed the entrance he glanced in and saw the candlelit tables and dancing couples. From a record player on the bar came the sweet refrains of Theodorakis' To Kaimós. Giving it little notice he continued down the street. Thirty meters further on, he turned right and passed through a gate. Immediately afterwards he entered a narrow passageway and began to mount a flight of stairs lit only by a small fly-spotted bulb.

Behind him the person following him stopped outside the gate and peered around cautiously. He caught a glimpse of the old man's back as he ascended the stairs. Noting the address, he crossed the street and stood inconspicuously among several palm trees, his outline blending into the shadows cast by the trunks and their overhead fronds.

Mounting to the second floor, Barba Yorgi squinted as he peered at the nameplates on several doors. Apparently satisfied, he rapped three times on the door in front of him. After a pause of five seconds, he rapped again four times. From behind the door came the sound of a deadbolt's being pulled back and a key turning in the lock. As the door swung inward Barba Yorgi entered without a word and the door closed behind him. Lights from another room at the end of the entrance hall reflected through a door, but provided little illumination. He followed the silhouetted sloped shoulders and the shuffling sound of the slippers of the person who admitted him down the hallway toward the light. When they reached the lighted room, his host turned, his hands clasped behind him, looked at Barba Yorgi closely, studying his visitor for a moment through hooded eyes. Suddenly his lips drew back in a vulpine smile, revealing yellowed and crooked teeth streaked and mottled with brown. "Pseramanoli." It was a statement of fact. "Kalóstos, Yorgos. Tí kánis?"

Barba Yorgi responded to the greeting with a nod and reached out a ham-like hand to clasp his host firmly by the shoulder. "Andreas! I'm fine. It's good to see you again. I see you still remember the knock. I was hoping you would."

"Of course I remember it. The war hasn't been over as long as that. Come! Sit down. A little raki to wash the dust from your throat? Sit! Sit and tell me what brings you to town and what brings you to my house so late at night after such a long time. Stay the night here. My house is yours."

The two men talked until well after midnight. In the beginning they talked in generalities, catching up on news of each other, the bottle of raki sitting between them. As the hours progressed, Barba Yorgi's fatigue, the alcohol and the hashish began to take their toll. Shortly before 3 AM he told Andreas why he was there. Omitting the part concerning Mitzos' death, he told him about the treasure and the statue of gold hidden close to Zakari's house. During the latter part of the conversation Andreas merely listened, probing gently now and again for additional information.

When they parted to different rooms of the flat, Barba Yorgi fell into a dreamless slumber as soon as his head touched the pillow. Andreas, on the other hand, was wide awake. Having drunk much less than his old friend, thoughts of what he learned swirled in his head. He knew Zakari from his time as a runner for the Resistance, a young man who took many chances for them. The more Andreas mulled over tonight's information, the more he was convinced he should make a point of renewing old acquaintances. The light of dawn was beginning to paint the eastern sky rose when he at last dropped off to sleep. When he awoke five hours later Barba Yorgi was gone.

ϒ ϒ ϒ

Zakari did not arrive home until almost dark the evening before. The path from Plakias was steep, but he took no notice of the long walk. He was too preoccupied with thoughts of Mitzos and where he might be. Having finished their meal the vultures departed on the warm air currents rising from the coastal plain. What was left would provide nourishment for the ants, mice and dung beetles that lived among the rocks. The bones would bleach white in the dry air and incessant sunshine. When he entered his house he took a loaf of bread from the sack he carried, tore off a hunk with his teeth and chewed distractedly as he brought out the remainder of a kilo of cheese, some olives and dried chickpeas. He drew a glass of wine from the small wooden barrel lying on its side in a niche in the kitchen wall and took a seat on the bench in front of his house. He wanted to check on the statue, but it was already too dark. He felt sure it would wait until morning.

Having finished his dinner, he stripped off his vest and sweat stained shirt, drew a full bucket of water from the well and poured it over his head. Sleepy interrogatory clucks sounded from his chickens roosting in the olive trees as he passed beneath them. Returning to the house he pried off his boots with his toes, took off his pants and stretched full length on the bed. Worries concerning what could have happened to Little Mitzos writhed in his consciousness like a knot of worms, making it difficult for him to sleep. He rose once to smoke a cigarette then tried again to put these niggling thoughts aside. Closing his eyes he again attempted to sleep.

When he opened them again the sun was climbing over the slopes and the clarion call of the rooster, peremptorily announcing the start of a new day, sounded just outside his door. Astonished to discover it was light outside, he quickly sat up and rubbed his face vigorously with his callused palms, digging his knuckles deeply into his eye sockets. He pulled on his pants and, still barefoot, went outside to let the goat out of her pen. He staked her in a spot where she could easily reach the brown stalks of grass and prickly thistles she so adored. She bleated her delight as he turned in the direction of the hiding place.

He walked only a few paces before stopping to inspect the ground closely. Something was out of place. Someone other than him walked this ground recently. He could plainly see the marks of heavy soles in the dust, as well as round indentations in the dust that appeared to be the diameter of a five-drachma piece. The round marks paralleled the footprints for several meters and then disappeared. Soon, too, the footprints disappeared and he saw evidence that the ground still showed the marks of having been swept. There were even a few leaves lying about where there should have been none. Looking in the direction the footprints took his heart leaped into his throat, for he realized they led directly to the hole where he cached the statue the day before. They lead unerringly in that direction. Whoever they belonged to knew exactly where to look! The evidence was too plain. Barba Yorgi's staff would have made the circular impressions in the dust. There was no doubt of the interloper's identity.

Zakari's mouth was dry; his heart pounded in his chest and an involuntary groan escaped his lips as he hurried to the hiding place. He anticipated the worst possible scenario. But, how?! How could he have known? With trembling hands he tore the screening brush away from the hole and plunged his hand and arm deep inside. At first he felt nothing as he frantically swept his hand from side to side, top to bottom. His breathing sounded as harsh rasps in his ears. When his hand brushed against the rough cloth enveloping the statue he grasped it and pulled the bundle from the darkness. He felt its weight and he dropped to his knees as relief rushed over him. Sitting down upon a rock he tore the cord from around the package and peeled aside the layers of cloth. With a silent prayer of thanks to the gods he gazed raptly upon the sun glinting off the precious metal. It was safe. Safe!

He could not believe his good fortune. What was Barba Yorgi's reason for not taking it? This puzzled him. He certainly found it. There was clear evidence of his presence in front of the hiding place, for here, too, the dust was smooth. He must have thought no one would be aware of his discovery and planned to return at a later date to spirit it away. No other answer could explain this turn of events to his satisfaction. One thing was certain: neither he nor his treasure were safe for the moment. Now two people, Mitzos and Barba Yorgi, represented real danger to him. His first thought must be to hide it in a place where no one else could ever find it. For now, he must remove it from this spot and then await the cover of darkness. He must leave nothing to chance this time. There were watchful eyes everywhere. He wrapped the statue once more in the cloth and stood to push it into the waistband of his pants. Its bulk and the pressure of his stomach against it would hold it there until he could return to his house where he would hide it until nightfall.

He entered his house and looked for a place to put it temporarily. He decided the best location would be inside the chimney of the cook stove built into the wall. He reached as high as he could in the sooty blackness and placed it carefully on top of a stone projecting from the side of the chimney. He then took another piece of cloth similar to the one in which he wrapped the statue and took it outside. Searching among the rocks he soon found one that approximated the size of the statue. From behind his house he took a short length of lead pipe and placed it with the rock to give additional weight, then wrapped the two together. With another piece of cord he tied it to resemble the original package and once more left the house. He walked directly to the hole, inserted the bogus bundle, carefully replaced the brush across the opening and swept the ground in the immediate area with a branch. To his eyes all looked the same as before Barba Yorgi walked there. Finally satisfied that he could do no more, he took a circuitous route away from the hiding place taking care not to leave any more evidence of his having been there and returned to his house. He would not leave the area again until he found a safe place where only he could ever find the precious statue.

CHAPTER 14

Horiatis seemed pleased, if non-committal, when Carter first called him to report his meeting with Bonisseur. Carter said nothing about the conversation in the courtyard concerning Abu Bekr or Jean Paul's willingness to help him. When he called barely two days later to advise him of his plans to move into the villa in Aghios Vasilis, he could clearly hear Horiatis' surprised exhalation of breath through the static of the telephone line. Carter smiled inwardly, pleased at the unexpected speed with which he accomplished the first part of his mission. Then, in an offhanded manner, he broke the news that Bonisseur admitted knowing Abu Bekr and was more than ready to point him out should they find him.

"Agreed!? Just like that? What did you have to offer him?"

"Nothing."

Through the silence at the other end of the line Carter imagined he could hear wheels turning. His contact was obviously searching for the correct response and when it came Carter was taken aback for a moment.

"You little bastard! Whoever said you knew anything about recruitment? Whadda you mean you got our frog friend for nothing?" A raucous laugh gave him away and suddenly he was anxious to hear all the details.

"Actually, I don't know where the idea about being a freelance writer came from. It just popped out. Nevertheless, he took it hook, line and sinker. He was ready to leave immediately, but I told him ben Boulaid would have to wait for word that he was on the island from the publisher that commissioned the article. Did I do good?"

Once more Horiatis became serious. "Yes, yes you did better than good. How you did it is commendable. Now, let me ask you something. Where are you calling from?"

"From the telephone exchange. The last time was from a private residence."

"I think it would be best if you limited your calls to times of extreme importance or urgency. There's no need for you to waste money making long distance calls. I suggest we set up a drop." Matejowski in Athens advised him of a specific location they would use for such activities. "Do you still have the address?"

"Sure. Any information can be routed there." He remembered the drop in the neighborhood of Kazantzakis' tomb. "Is that all right with you?"

"Of course," said Horiatis. I'll look forward to hearing from you on a regular basis. Also, you might want to check your mail daily."

"Oh, incidentally," Carter interrupted, "I really would appreciate it if you would let me know as soon as you hear our friend is coming to town. I would hate to miss him."

"Don't worry. You'll be the first to know. Thanks for the scoop. I'll pass it on."

Carter was sure Athens and Ware would also be suitably impressed.

He was just about to hang up the phone when a thought occurred to him. "Oh, wait! Are you still on the line? Listen, there is one more thing I've been meaning to ask you. What should I do until I hear from you about our friend?"

"Nothing. Nothing at all. You just sit there and do what you do to look like you're what you say you are. Got it? When the time comes for you to do otherwise we'll be in touch."

♈   ♈   ♈

Monday, the second of September was Carter's first day at the Iraklion English Institute. None other than Bunny introduced him to his first class at 10 AM that morning, a group of nine 14 - 16 year olds. The previous week he observed classes on three separate occasions and soon came to realize all the students were there because they wanted to learn English.

"You shouldn't be surprised, "explained Cruikshank. "You must remember that Greek is really a very small language. The country's not large and Greek speakers are relatively few. I've always felt Greeks were an intelligent people. They realize their ability to expand their social and economic horizons is directly proportional to their aptitude in learning another tongue.

You'll find the longer you live here that, for the most part, it's difficult to carry on a private conversation in public that will not be overheard or understood. English is of prime importance to them, with German and French next. It's for this reason the students here are so willing to learn. They hunger for it. Even your most unlikely tradesman will have a command of one or more languages that will promote his success. You'll be astonished at the number of peasants in the most remote villages who are able to converse somewhat in German or Italian."

This was not the same attitude he remembered from schools in the US. Most American students took a foreign language only because they needed it both to graduate and be accepted at a university. The desire of these young people was evident. Even though their scholarship might have been unequal, their resolve to learn was not. Carter was delighted and launched himself into pedagogy with zeal.

Three days earlier, at the end of August, he moved into the house in Aghios Vasilis with Jean Paul. The obliging Frenchman, good as his word, came to the pension and helped Carter load his clothes and luggage into the yellow convertible and drove him to his new home. Carter chose an upstairs bedroom, the one from which he could step onto the rooftop terrace. It was like having two rooms, for he could rise in the morning and step out into the open air. He reveled in this luxury, often descending to the first floor to make himself a cup of coffee, which he would take back upstairs. He loved to sit on the terrace, reared back in an old wicker armchair, his feet on the railing, cupping his heavy mug with both hands as he sipped from it. The view was extraordinary, for he could look west and see the mountains dominated by snow-capped Ida. To the north, across the rooftops of Iraklion, lay the incomparable blue of the sea. From his vantage point, as well, he could observe unnoticed the neighbors feeding their chickens and goats, watering their plants, or simply wandering about their gardens.

Jean Paul was a night person. He rarely rose before 10:30 any morning after spending late hours at the club. Carter loved the early mornings and looked forward to the time alone, spending it either exploring the neighborhood or the grounds of the house itself. Should he want company there was generally another early riser among the varied guests who was only too glad to share coffee, cigarettes and conversation (or at least company) on the terrace.

The constantly changing stream of tourists or friends usually occupied several of the bedrooms. Carter found he could learn much from talking to them, finding out where they came from, what brought them to Crete and of their experiences during their travels. He was fascinated by their independence. Americans of his acquaintance never exhibited much interest in just picking up and leaving to explore the world. It was rare to find a young American among the group. When one did appear, he or she was usually accompanied by a European companion. They invariably expressed their surprise at finding a fellow countryman who left the States with no prospects, only high hopes. All were envious of his decisions and of the fact that he would be there long after they returned to wherever they called home.

When not occupied otherwise, Carter occasionally went to the beach near the airport, Florida Beach. He enjoyed spending time under the shade of the restaurant pavilion with Yves and his friend, Pierre from London. Carter thought it was unusual the Englishman should have a French name, but never thought to ask if it might really be Peter. With Yves and Pierre, when they were not talking about the "wonderful Greek boys", the conversations delved into philosophy, religion, politics, poetry, literature and the arts. Both were very learned and could converse interestingly and at length on a wide variety of subjects. As he learned from them he also found them to be highly amusing. They were not averse to interrupting the flow of talk to point out this or that choice specimen strolling the beach and, periodically, one or the other would excuse himself to pursue a particularly handsome young man.

When Carter asked Jean Paul about the Count, he found the Frenchman only too eager to recount what he knew of him.

"Let me tell you a story about Yves. During the war, when the Germans occupied Paris, this man was in heaven. You have seen documentaries of what happened to the collaborateurs. When the Allies arrived the people of Paris searched out those who profited from the Germans. They shot many who helped les boches and, for the women, they shaved their heads and paraded them before their friends and neighbors. Yves speaks fondly of this time of occupation. He loved the blond German soldiers and they loved him in return. He hosted many cocktail parties for them in his apartment on the Boulevard St. Germain. Many liaisons."

"Why wasn't he treated like the others?"

"Money and position. People overlooked what people of his class did and really didn't dare do anything to them. Maybe he thought that by, uh, what is the word...enculant? I heard this word from some Irish men in the club the other night. Ah! I remember now: by fucking these Aryan supermen he was somehow doing his part for the Resistance."

Carter laughed. He visualized the suave, worldly Count standing on the Champs Elysées dressed in the latest French fashion - with the strap of his knit shoulder bag clasped firmly in his hand, as the first time Carter saw him – searching out willing members of the occupation forces.

"He really is quite harmless," continued Jean Paul. "Actually, he's not a bad person to know. If he likes you he'll do anything he can for you. When I first met him in Paris I was living with a friend of mine, an ex-paratrooper. One day the phone rang and it was Yves, inviting us to a cocktail party at his house. I told him to wait one moment while I asked my friend, who was shaving in the bathroom. When I told him who was calling and why, he screamed back at me, 'Not unless he invited some real women! I'm tired of going to parties with a bunch of old faggots.' I forgot to cover the mouthpiece of the phone and Yves heard every word. When I got back on the phone Yves told me to tell him not to worry. Among the invited were the French film producer, Roger Vadim, and his young American wife. I don't remember her name, but her father is a very famous American actor."

"You mean Henry Fonda?"

"Yes, that's him. Well, they didn't show up, but there were many, many very rich women there, young and old. They treated us like guests of honor. The men were only interested in each other. I must tell you, I never miss one of his parties."

"What about your friend?"

"My friend? Oh, he was never invited back."

One night later that week Carter went to the club to meet Jean Paul. They were talking to some of his friends from Paris when Carter noticed Jean Paul's attention riveted in the direction of the entry. Carter glanced back over his shoulder and noticed a man who appeared to be Greek standing in the doorway. He was dressed in a dark blue suit, white shirt, tie and vest and his hands were in the pockets of his baggy blue suit coat as he stood scanning the room. From the corner of his mouth hung a cigarette from which a long gray ash dangled precariously.

Jean Paul excused himself and went to greet the new arrival, shook his hand and walked with him to a table in the back of the club. After taking their seats they talked for a few moments and then Carter noticed their heads close together across the table. The man was talking quietly and Jean Paul listened intently. When the waiter approached them they stopped talking and both sat back in their seats. They ordered and, as the waiter walked away, they resumed their conversation. Carter returned his attention to those at his own table and forgot about the other two men. Sometime later he felt a hand on his shoulder and turned to see Jean Paul standing behind him. Leaning down he spoke into Carter's ear, "Come outside with me a moment. There is someone here I want you to meet."

Carter got up immediately and followed him outside, curious as to whom this man might be and why Jean Paul wanted him to make his acquaintance.

"I want to present you to Andreas Aspropatos, an old friend. Andreas, this is Carter Martin, my American friend I was telling you about."

"Bon soir, monsieur Carter," said Andreas. "Jean Paul tells me you have come to Kriti to seek your fortune. He also tells me you are dáskalos at the English Institute. An honorable profession. I'm happy to meet you. I'm sure we will see very much of each other through the coming months. We were just talking about taking a little trip to the mountains to see someone I haven't seen in many years. I hope you'll join us on this petit voyage.

"A trip to the mountains? Sounds great! Sure, I'd love to go. I've wanted to spend time in the villages ever since I came to

Crete. I told Jean Paul that my goal is to be able to go into the villages and talk with the peasants. Get to know them."

As he talked, Carter studied Andreas. He looked to be about 60, with gray hair and cheeks stubbled with gray whiskers. The ubiquitous cigarette, with its long ash, hung from the corner of his mouth. On the lapel of his rumpled suit was a trail of ashes. His eyelids were like wrinkled visors and dark bags of loose skin sagged under his eyes.

"Well, I must be going," he said with finality. "It's very nice to meet you, Carter. Welcome to Kriti. Jean Paul, I'll talk to you later. Thank you for the drink." He waved his hand as he turned and walked out into the night.

Carter turned to Jean Paul to say something, but Jean Paul held up his hand for silence. He stood looking through the archway where Andreas disappeared. From down the street he heard an exchange of greetings and then there was nothing. Carter waited, wondering what was going on, looking expectantly at his friend. After a moment he turned to Carter, a gleam in his eyes and a look of ill-concealed excitement on his face.

"It's starting!" he said. "We'll talk more later at the house. All I'll say for now is that I must make arrangements to leave within a day or two for Switzerland. Can you still lend me some money?"

"Of course, but what...?"

"Not here! We'll talk tonight. Come! Let's have a drink?"

They stayed at the club for another hour before Jean Paul rose to leave. Carter was beside himself with curiosity, but did not bring the subject up again. On the ride home Jean Paul began to tell him what was happening. Andreas came into the club tonight to tell of his meeting with someone in town the night before.

"Do you remember the first night we met, as I was taking you back to the pension, I told you about a man in town?"

"I think so. Do you mean the deaf man? You never said any more about him and I forgot to ask you about him again."

"Yes, that's him. Tomorrow we're going to town to meet him. Tomorrow you are going to make the acquaintance of Deaf Yanni."

They talked far into the night of Andreas and his reason for coming to the club. Jean Paul met him when he first came to Iraklion and their friendship grew during the ensuing two years. While talking to him one day, Jean Paul expressed an interest in the archaeology of Crete. Andreas proved to be quite knowledgeable and told of the many things turned up virtually every year by the peasants. It was through Andreas that Jean Paul learned of Deaf Yanni.

"The most important thing is that Andreas can be trusted. He also trusts me and he knows I can do things a Greek cannot because I am a foreigner. I told him all about you and that you were now living at the villa. When he asked me if I could trust you I told him I could. That was good enough for him.

"Deaf Yanni has some small statues he would like for me to take to Zürich to sell. That is why I need to make arrangements to leave within a day or two. Can you give me the money that soon?"

"Sure, I just need to go to the bank. Since I started work I opened an account in the bank downtown near the Greek Orthodox Church. Do you want it in dollars or drachmas?"

"Drachmas will be fine. This is all exciting, but nothing compared to what Andreas also told me tonight. He didn't give me many details, but a tomb has been discovered on the south coast. Things were taken from it. He didn't tell me exactly what, because he doesn't know himself, but there is one thing that would make the archaeological world turn flips. He knows where it is and also knows the person who has it. It's someone who was in the Resistance with him. Merde! He wants to take me to see this man!"

Carter leaned forward and peered at his friend. "Can I go, too?"

"I told him I wanted to take you with us. At first he didn't like the idea, but when I told him he could trust you and that you and I were working together he finally agreed to your coming along."

"Jesus, this is exciting! When are we going?"

"Du calme. I know how you feel. Andreas just found out about whatever it is last night. He wants to contact the man who has the artifacts first. We can't just show up on his man's doorstep! A very important thing is that we must not tell anyone else, no matter what. Don't even write your mother about it. We just can't take any chances. Do you understand? There is a certain amount of danger involved, for there are people who would do anything to get their hands on these artifacts."

"Danger? What kind of danger?" asked Carter, not the least bothered by the prospects.

"Well, the police are already involved. They're looking for the ones who plundered the tomb. Of course, the museum people are furious. Then there is the man who told Andreas about it. It seems he is trying to get everything for himself. He's a man Andreas knows since they were young boys in his village. He says he's an old friend."

As if talking to himself, he looked down at his hands and muttered under his breath, "I wonder, however."

Looking quickly back at Carter, he continued. "They were in the war together, too. It's perhaps Andreas' friend who poses the greatest danger. We'll know more as time goes on. Please remember, you must say nothing to anyone. Nothing! We must take care even when we talk to one another to make sure we cannot be overheard."

The rest of that night and the next, whenever they talked about the artifacts, it was with a conspiratorial air. Even when they were at the villa they walked into the garden and sat on the ground under the fruit trees near the remains of the anti-aircraft site before discussing the subject.

Jean Paul drove to the airport to price a round trip ticket from Iraklion to Zürich. With the necessary information Carter went immediately to the bank and made a withdrawal. The price amounted to $170.00, but, to be on the safe side, to make sure all incidentals such as taxis, hotel and food were covered, he withdrew an additional $200.00. Jean Paul would only be gone for a maximum of three days and they felt this amount would cover any eventuality. Carter felt no misgivings as he handed the money to Jean Paul. Indeed, to his way of thinking, this was an excellent investment, one that could realize a substantial benefit for them both after the agreed upon sum was paid to the deaf man.

The afternoon of the third day Jean Paul took Carter with him to see Deaf Yanni, with no real appreciation of what they were undertaking. It all seemed to be a lark to Carter. 'Danger' and 'consequences', when associated with Minoan artifacts, were only words with no significance. Like many young people, he was imbued with a sense of his own invulnerability and immortality. These were just games he and his French friend were playing, much like the games of cops and robbers, or cowboys and Indians he and his friends played as children.

As they approached Deaf Yanni's workshop Jean Paul was watchful. He looked around, taking note of any idlers standing in the narrow street.

He told Carter before leaving the house he would only be an observer. "You don't need to say anything. Not a word. I'll introduce you as an associate, but I want you to just listen and look. I'll tell him you don't understand Greek, so that will put him more at ease."

When they entered the workshop they were greeted by a young man about 20 years old. He introduced himself as Deaf Yanni's son and immediately ushered them into a darkened brick enclosure in the rear. It looked like a storeroom, full of dusty shelves lined with various sized clay pots. Upon entering the room, the boy flipped a switch, which turned on a naked bulb filthy with the accumulation of terra cotta dust. The diffused light did little to pierce the gloom. Over the door a dark piece of cloth like a wool blanket, as encrusted with dirt and dust as the light bulb, was hung in lieu of a door and provided the only separation between the two rooms.

They did not have long to wait. An older man of medium build, whose face lit up when he saw Jean Paul, soon joined them. He went to the Frenchman and greeted him in a soft voice, clasping Jean Paul's right hand in both of his. Following closely on the heels of the first man, who Carter took to be Deaf Yanni, was another man, taller, with powerful sloping shoulders and massive forearms. He did not speak, but stood to one side of the door. Even in the dim light Carter noticed his hands were beefy, red and chapped.

Jean Paul spoke slowly, enunciating clearly, exaggerating the movement of his lips as he talked. Carter followed the conversation but pretended not to understand as it was explained who he was. Yanni turned to Carter and said to him wide-eyed, "Americanós? Brávo! Thávma! Miláte 'ellinicá?" Do you speak Greek?

Carter responded before he could think, "Nai, miláo lígo. Móno lígo." Yes, I speak a little. Only a little.

Yanni turned a huge smile on Carter while addressing his remarks to Jean Paul. Carter just smiled and nodded. Apparently satisfied, Yanni nodded and returned his attention to Jean Paul.

For the next fifteen minutes the conversation between the two was almost in pantomime. Carter followed it while allowing his eyes to drift to the man standing beside the door. He never moved and his eyes never left the two men engrossed in conversation. His expression was not unpleasant, but reflected the intensity with which he attempted to follow the flow of information.

Carter suddenly realized this man was here to provide some sort of protection to Deaf Yanni. It was with this new realization that some of the seriousness came home to the young American. These people were not playing games! Carter now looked at the situation from an entirely new perspective.

A pause in the conversation brought his attention back to the two men seated before him. Yanni looked back over his shoulder and snapped his fingers in the direction of the man standing at the door. Heaving himself away from the wall with a shrug of his shoulders, the man advanced toward the two who were seated in the rickety chairs. As he covered the short space from the door to the chairs, he reached into a side pocket of his baggy pants and pulled out a flat cigarette box. Yanni took it from him then held it between himself and Jean Paul. When he lifted the lid Carter leaned forward to see what was inside, but the only thing in evidence was a layer of cotton. When the cotton was removed, Jean Paul's involuntary gasp of delight punctuated the stillness. Carter was not half as impressed. Inside the box, lying on another layer of cotton, were four small figures, which to Carter resembled nothing more than likenesses of Casper the Ghost.

Jean Paul took one from the box and laid it flat in the palm of his hand. It was then that Carter saw its true form. The material was white like bone or ivory, cut to a thickness of mere millimeters. The form was, indeed, much like Casper the Ghost. The head was rounded and two indentations for the eyes and one for the mouth were the sole features of the face. The rest of the body was represented by the vaguest outline. He wanted to know more. He wanted particulars, such as: why would anyone become excited over such primitive and seeming insignificant pieces!? He remembered Jean Paul's admonitions, however, and said nothing. He was sure he would know soon enough.

The meeting was shortly terminated. Jean Paul put the statue back in the box with its companions, laid the cotton back on top and shut the lid. Yanni leaned forward, said a few words and patted the Frenchman on the shoulder, stood up and left. In the meantime Jean Paul secreted the small box in the inside pocket of a light jacket he wore. Once on the street he turned to Carter, indicating by a look that no questions were to be asked and took a path different from the one by which they arrived. It was only when they reached the car and were roaring through town towards Aghi Vasili that Jean Paul answered some of the questions bubbling inside Carter.

"The statues are ivory. There have been very few examples such as this brought to light, so they are considered very rare. Their form is only anthropomorphique and, no, we have no idea why they were made in this fashion or what purpose they served."

"Where were they found and how?" asked Carter, holding the open box in his hand while turning one of the statues over and over, studying it in detail.

"There is a place on the south coast called Kokino Pirgo. A peasant who lives near there found them and brought them to Yanni, hoping he could dispose of them. Through past experience he knew he could not sell them himself."

"What do you think they're worth?"

"Merde, I don't know! Deaf Yanni says he would like to have a thousand to fifteen hundred drachmas for the four of them. Whatever we can get over that amount we can keep for ourselves. He wanted more, but I explained to him we have expenses: plane tickets, food, et cetera. We finally settled on that range. It is much more than they could have hoped to get for them in Crete. Also, we don't know how much we'll be able to sell them for in Switzerland. This much I do know, after this trip we'll have a much better idea of the market for things such as this. Right now we're just guessing at their value."

Later that evening the two friends sat in the garden. The warmth of the day was tempered by a soft sea breeze as dusk fell. They talked of Jean Paul's leaving tomorrow evening for Athens on the inter-island ferry, the Keftiu. He would travel overnight to Piraeus and then take a Swissair flight from Athens to Zürich.

"Have you thought of how you're going to get the statues past customs? You know there's a chance they'll search your bags."

"I know. These are so small that I think I'll just wrap them in cotton and carry them in mon cul. You know, just put them in between the cheeks of my bottom. They should stay there all right. I just have to be careful not to sit down and break them before I can take them out. As soon as I'm on the boat I'll remove them, but I'll have to put them back before I pass through customs in the Athens airport. Once I'm on the plane there will be no more danger. I can go to the toilet and take them out before we take off. Swiss customs will not bother me, so I have nothing to worry about there."

"Well, no one on Crete has any reason to suspect you or why you're leaving the country. All you have to worry about are routine customs inspections. It would be a shame to get all the way to Athens and then have an inspector find them inadvertently."

Jean Paul agreed with him and laughed. "If anyone notices I walk funny, I'll just tell them I have a bad case of hémorroïdes!"

The next day seemed to pass at a snail's pace, but pass it did and the two friends descended to the port an hour before the Keftiu was to sail. Upon their arrival Jean Paul took his small suitcase with him to the men's room and went into a stall, where he pulled his pants down around his ankles and inserted the carefully wrapped statues. Standing normally, he found the pressure of his buttocks held the parcel in place. He pulled his pants back up and walked out to rejoin Carter. Carter could not help laughing as he saw his friend approaching. He walked with a self-conscious gate, only noticeable if one knew what he was carrying and where.

"Does everything fit all right?"

"I don't want to talk about it," replied Jean Paul with a barely suppressed grin. "Let's go aboard and find my cabin. You can come have a drink with me before we sail."

His was a second class cabin, which for the moment was unoccupied. He put his shoulder bag onto a shelf in a small closet, and then relocked the door when they left. They wended their way through the passageways until they found the second class lounge. At the bar they ordered Fix beers and stood drinking as they watched other passengers crowd into the room. Too soon the whistle sounded for those to go ashore who were not making the voyage. Carter walked out onto the deck, closely followed by Jean Paul.

"Well, good luck. I'll see you in three or four days. If you run into any problems, just leave a call with the Daskaloyanni's. You have their number, don't you? I'll check with them from time to time. If I don't hear from you I'll figure everything's OK?"

They said their final goodbyes and Carter turned to leave. Almost as soon as his feet were once more on the quay, the crews began to remove the gangplank and the heavy ropes mooring the ship to the dock. Carter found Jean Paul among the people crowding the railings and waved to him as the ship's screws began to turn and the vessel eased away from shore. Jean Paul was soon lost to sight as the ship passed between the lights marking the harbor's entrance and out into the open sea. Carter stood among the thinning crowds for another fifteen minutes, watching the lights of the ship grow smaller as it headed north. Not until then did he make his way back to the car.

Chapter 15

"Tí thà kánome?" asked a worried looking Panayoti Tsipas. He, like his companions, was at his wits end. He felt threatened and powerless, with no place to turn for relief. He was a simple peasant, who scratched and grubbed in the rocky Cretan soil for a living, as his father and grandfather before him. One day, out of the blue, the gods smiled upon him and granted his fondest dream.

Every Cretan was familiar with the Minoans. Each of them believed Minoan blood coursed through their veins, the blood of the great King Minos himself. Descended from the founders of that grand civilization, they were the inheritors of their legacy. When the civilization died, or was overrun by invaders from the mainland, the legacy, the treasures of the Minoans, were lost. These treasures remained hidden for millennia and only recently, in the past sixty-five years did they again begin to see the light of day. The inheritors, he, Panayoti Tsipas included, were present when the gift was laid bare by the probing blade of the bulldozer. But disaster followed on the heels of this discovery. Disaster, yes, in the form of 'The Bull' himself, the old man of the mountains: Barba Yorgi.

In Panayoti's case things changed dramatically just a few days earlier as he made his way home from the kafeneion. It was already dark as he walked along, musing to himself about the events of the day, the hard work in his field, his pregnant wife, his hope that his olive trees and grape vines would provide for them through the coming winter. He thought of market prices for his produce, the prices of food and fertilizer and gas for his mikaní. He walked along, minding his own business, when suddenly he was no longer alone. Standing in the middle of the path was the old man, his full white beard that seemed to glow in the starlight. He blocked the path and accosted Panayoti, seeming at first to simply want to pass the time of day. Panayoti thought this must be a chance encounter. They talked of crops and weather for a time, but then the subject changed and his blood ran cold. This old man knew of the treasure!

At first he tried to feign ignorance. Why, yes, there was some talk of something found along the south coast, but he knew nothing more than that it was unsubstantiated rumor. To his consternation, Barba Yorgi recounted the exact events of that day, even named the names of each person present. Finally realizing that denial of the facts would avail him nothing, Panayoti admitted all. He then asked why Barba Yorgi wanted to talk to him about it.

A low, rumbling laugh issued from deep inside was the first response. Then the old man advised him of his reason for accosting him that evening. It was very simple: he wanted a share of the treasure! For exactly half the antíkas Tsipas could be assured of his continued silence.

Panayoti was aghast. How could he possibly give up even a portion of the things he took from the tomb? He quickly weighed the alternatives. What if he were to say no? He looked at the stout staff in the huge hand of the man facing him and realized there was only one answer he could give. Even if he were not attacked, what would happen to him if Barba Yorgi went to the police with this story? The police would certainly be found sitting on his doorstep the next morning. He knew it was true. The police treated the treasures of the Minoans as if they were their own.

At last he agreed to what Barba Yorgi asked, or rather, demanded of him. There was no other choice. With a feeling of utter defeat and helplessness, he acquiesced. Satisfied, the old man told him he would be contacted soon to set up a meeting. There Tsipas would share half of the treasure with him.

Before continuing on his way, he turned to Barba Yorgi and asked how he knew the names of those at the site of the discovery. Who told him that he took part of the treasure before the police and the director of the museum returned? By the pale light of the stars and the new moon, he saw the gleam of triumph in his adversary's eyes.

"I'm the Bull of Crete," he responded dramatically. "I'm the mountains and the trees. I have ears everywhere and my eyes see everything. There's nothing that happens on my island that's a secret from me. Don't try to deceive Barba Yorgi. Always look back over your shoulder, no matter where you are. Keep a close watch. You may not see me, but you'll know I'm there...watching."

As Barba Yorgi made this dramatic pronouncement Panayoti felt the hairs rise on his arms and the back of his neck. He was familiar with stories of this man and was petrified of him and what he could do. Silently he nodded his head in agreement and, without another word, stepped off the path to continue on his way. Just as he was passing the old man, however, Barba Yorgi reached out his huge hand and grasped the smaller man's shoulder in his steely grasp. "You'll hear from me, Tsipas."

Panayoti wanted to run away as fast as possible, but it was all he could do to put one foot in front of the other. He stumbled home despondently, all the while trying to sort out this new development in his mind. He found sleep impossible that night and arose before the sun.

Later that morning he happened to meet Stavros Petrides, also present the day they plundered the tomb. He did not know what to say to him, but finally decided he must share the events of the night before with someone. He was almost relieved to discover Stavros experienced the same sort of discussion with Barba Yorgi when he appeared only a day or so before in his fields during the midday siesta. They discussed this between them, trying to come to some solution of what they should and could do. Together they went to the house of Vasili Annemoyannis, for he was also a co-conspirator. They found that he, too, received a visitor. They contacted each person present that day, with the exception of Zakari and Mitzos, discovering that each of them told similar stories of being approached by the old man. They were all frightened, but felt some consolation in numbers. They finally decided the three of them would go to Plakias to see Mitzos and then all four would climb the mountain to talk with Zakari.

The next day they met early and set out for Plakias, where they discovered Mitzos could not be found. This was disturbing news to them. Could he have left Crete? Did Barba Yorgi figure into his disappearance?

From Plakias they immediately set out for Zakari's house. As they made their way up the mountain they spoke little, each immersed in his own thoughts. High above Plakias they climbed, the sun burning down on them. Because of the narrowness of the path they made their way single file. It was by chance that Panayoti, the last in line, noticed a singular occurrence.

He stopped for a moment to remove his cloth headband, using it to wipe the perspiration from his face and neck. As he did so he happened to glance up among the rocks. A raven caught his eye as it swept out of the sky and lit on a boulder some way above them. It hopped from the boulder and disappeared from view. This was not unusual. What made this incident so remarkable was the fact that the raven suddenly reappeared to perch once more on the boulder. In his beak was something Panayoti at first thought was a twig or a vine. But then, as the bird spread its wings to launch himself into the air, the sun glinted off something metallic. The raven turned into the wind rising from the coast below and sailed out over the head of the watching man. Once more he saw a glint of sunlight. Panayoti focused his attention on the object the bird carried in his beak and realized it was a chain with something attached to it. As the raven passed overhead he was sure he recognized a chain and crucifix.

Without thinking he shouted. The startled raven opened his beak to voice his surprise and the chain dropped from his grasp. Panayoti watched it fall, marking the place among the rocks below him where it landed. The other men stopped in mid-stride, as startled as the bird by Tsipas' sudden cry. They turned just as their companion left the path and descended into the boulders below them. They called after him, but he continued to weave among the rocks and brush, intent upon reaching a spot below. For several moments they lost sight of him and each time they called out they received no response. Mystified by his behavior, they thought he must have lost his mind. Both decided they should try to follow him, but as they left the path they heard a shout from among the rocks below.

At the sound of his cry they stopped again, uncertain what to do. Stavros was the first to see Panayoti's head reappear among the boulders. He was climbing back towards them. As he came nearer they barraged him with questions. Without saying a word he held out his tightly clenched fist. They regarded it questioningly, but he said nothing. Finally, Vasili extended his hand tentatively to Panayoti, who slowly opened his fist and let the chain and crucifix cascade into the upturned palm.

"A crucifix!" exclaimed Stavros incredulously. "Where did you find it? Down among the rocks?"

"Màlista, among the rocks. Didn't you see the raven? He flew from the rocks above us and I saw it in his beak. When I shouted at him he dropped it and flew away. I saw where it fell and ran down to look for it." In spite of looks of skepticism he continued to explain. "I saw him fly down and pick up something shiny, the way ravens do, but it wasn't until he was overhead that I recognized what it was. I stopped to wipe my face and saw him land among the boulder above us. He hopped down and when he flew back up to the top of the rock I saw the sunlight glint off of it. He took off with it in his beak and, as he flew over me, I saw it was a crucifix hanging from a chain. It was at that moment I shouted and he dropped it."

Vasili, who still held the objects in his hands, turned the cross over. A sound of forcefully expelled air made the other two turn towards him. "Look! Look at this," he cried, holding the crucifix out to them. Panayoti took it from him and squinted at the back. He could see words engraved into the metal and tried to focus in the bright sunlight.
When he adjusted the distance so he could read the words leapt up at him. Engraved into the metal were a name and a date. . ΔΙΜΙΤΡΙΟΣ ΔΕΤΟΡΑΚΙΣ,, 22.3.52. "Dimitrios Detorakis. Mitzos!" said Panayoti, stunned.

"Mitzos? What about Mitzos?"

Panayoti handed the chain to Stavros. "This is Mitzos' crucifix. See? There's his name engraved on the back and the date must be when it was given to him."

"Where did the raven pick it up? I know you said up among the rocks, but where?" asked Vasili.

"Come on," urged Stavros. "Let's go up and see what we can find. In Plakias they say they haven't seen Mitzos since the day the tomb was discovered. What would he have been doing among the boulders here on the mountain? Do you suppose something could have happened to him?"

Without another word they left the path and began to climb the steep slope. Panayoti tried to remember exactly where the raven landed and headed in that general direction. The other two followed as closely as possible, struggling among the thorny underbrush, loose soil and rocks. The sun glared down unmercifully, causing them to sweat profusely. At first they were unsuccessful, for it was difficult to keep the particular boulder in view as they climbed. When they reached the general area they spread out and began to look everywhere. They looked for several minutes before Vasili called to the others.

"A shoe! Look, I found a shoe!"

"Is it one of Mitzos'?"

"I don't know," answered Vasili. "Maybe. Keep looking. You go a little higher and we'll continue looking here."

A sharp whistle brought the other two climbing towards Panayoti. "A shirt! This is Mitzos' shirt. I remember it from the day at the tomb. And look! Here's a bone! And more bones! There are the pants! Look how they're all torn."

The three men stood in silence as they looked at the evidence. There could be no doubt that before them were the remains of little Mitzos. They recognized his shirt and they held his crucifix with his name on it in their hands. The bones were scattered around as if from a desecrated ossuary.

Panayoti walked around the confines of the small space, kicking at the dirt with the toe of his boot. The other two talked in hushed tones as if in a church or graveyard. Panayoti walked close to a low bush and absentmindedly picked one of the tough leaves from a gnarled branch. When he pulled at the leaf the branch lifted for an instant and something he thought was a rock rolled into the open and came to rest against his foot. Panayoti looked down and then jumped back with a screech of terror.

Lying on the ground, staring up at him with empty sockets, was a skull, its shattered jawbone loosely attached by whatever ligaments still held it to the rest of the skull. The mouth gaped as if in a silent scream. The sun glinted from a gold tooth that was part of the ghastly open mouth.

At that moment a dull roar, felt more than heard, arose from the earth and Panayoti, looking down at the skull, felt as if he were going to vomit. The ground seemed to sway and twist beneath his feet and he was forced to reach out to brace himself against one of the boulders nearby. He lost all sense of equilibrium. From nearby came a muttered oath from one of his companions and a cry of fright from the other. When he swiveled his head to look at them the feeling of nausea increased and he saw Stavros struggle to remain upright. A pall of dust rose from the mountainside and then Panayoti was down among the boulders and the bones, flat on his stomach.

How long he lay there he did not know, but when he opened his eyes he was face to face with the skull. In panic he pushed himself up from the ground and flattened his back against one of the boulders. He fought to bring his labored breathing under control and looked around him. He realized he no longer felt the overwhelming sense of nausea. Sunlight filtered through clouds of dust and the silence was now pervasive.

Not total silence, however. There was music floating on the still air, the distinctive sound of a Cretan líra. Resembling a mandolin, it could be heard playing a lament, but he could not pinpoint its source. In renewed panic he leapt to his feet and saw his friends rising, as well. Stavros looked at Panayoti, his face ashen. "Earthquake! They say that when the bull roars the earth trembles. I heard him roar."

Vasili, equally pale, turned to him and said, "For a moment I thought I heard music. It was the strangest thing. Wait! Listen! There is music! It's not possible! How can I hear music here on the mountain?!"

"You hear it, too?" queried Panayoti. "I thought I was just imagining it. Is this spot haunted? How could there be music up here when there's no one else around?"

All three cocked their heads, again feeling the thrill of terror rush over them. In spite of the sun's heat, they succumbed to chills brought on by this new fear. They looked wide-eyed about them for the source. Stavros was the first to react. He ran screaming toward the path lying below them. After several steps he fell, tripping over some obstacle. He fell hard, hitting a boulder a glancing blow with his head, stunning him. The other two, seeing him fall, rushed down to him as quickly as possible, concerned for the safety of their friend. As they reached him he groaned and gingerly touched a bump already visible above his temple. A thin trickle of blood ran out from his thick hair and down his stubbled cheek.

"Stavros, are you all right?" asked Vasili, as he slid to a halt on the loose soil beside his still-prone friend.

Stavros did not reply immediately, but continued to gingerly probe the side of his head with his fingers. Panayoti joined the other two, a shovel in his hand.

"Where did you find the shovel?"

"Right up there where you fell. You must have tripped over it."

"What's a shovel doing here on the mountain? Do you think Mitzos brought it up with him?" questioned Vasili.

"Stavros groaned again and sat up. "I still hear music," he said.

The other two raised their heads and agreed that they did too, although it was closer now. This incident seemed to have brought them to their senses and they were thinking more clearly. "Come on," said Vasili. "Let's find out where it's coming from."

They helped Stavros to his feet and began looking for the source of the music. As they walked it became louder and more distinct, so they knew they were headed in the right direction. They also knew they were very close to the source, because it was so clear. Then it stopped. There was a moment of silence and then a voice announced the name of the tune and another voice began to give the weather. All three looked at one another and, as one, began to laugh.

"A radio!" said Stavros, the relief obvious in his voice. "First a shovel and now a radio.
Where is it? Do either of you see it?"

Vasili looked behind a boulder and there it was, lying on the ground, a transistor radio in a brown leather case. It was lying on a mound of soft dirt. The radio itself was partially imbedded in the dirt, sitting up on one end.

"Well, that explains the shovel," said Stavros. "Evidently Mitzos came up here to bury his part of the treasure and someone must have followed him, killed him and took his things. As for the radio, I don't know if it belonged to Mitzos or to the person who was here with him. The great mystery is why the radio suddenly began to play."

Panayoti looked at the evidence pensively and then said, "Oh, I don't know that it's that much of a mystery. From the way it's laying on that pile of dirt it must have been sitting up on one of the nearby boulders. The earthquake probably jarred it loose and it fell, hitting that stone next to where it was laying. That caused it to start playing. I'll admit, for a moment I thought I was dead and could hear the angels playing their harps." The others agreed, laughing with embarrassment. "Who was here with Mitzos and did they kill him and take whatever he was trying to bury?"

"I don't know," said Vasili. "Maybe Zakari would have some idea."

"Zakari!" said the other two simultaneously. "Has anyone seen Zakari since the treasure was found? Maybe the same person who killed Mitzos killed Zakari, as well." A sense of foreboding descended upon all three men and they looked at each other with concern in their eyes.

"Well, there's nothing we can do for poor Mitzos, but we must find Zakari. We still need to talk to him," said Panayoti. "Stavros, take his shirt and go get his skull. Wrap it in the shirt. I have the chain and cross. Leave the shovel here. It's of no use to any of us. Let's hope Zakari will know what must be done."

Stavros climbed back up the hill, rubbing his head as he went. The wound no longer bled, but the knot remained. He found the shirt where they dropped it and walked to the spot where the bones of their friend lay scattered. When he reached the skull he bent over, gingerly picked it up with his fingertips and laid it gently on the shirt spread on the ground. On the uneven ground the skull rolled to the side and a large beetle crawled from one of the eye sockets. Stavros crossed himself and quickly finished wrapping it in the shirt, then picked it up and returned to where his friends awaited him.

"Páme," said Vasili. "That does it. Let's go. There are so many questions. Hopefully Zakari will have the answers to some of them at least. I have the radio. Stavros, be careful with the skull. Are you all right, or do you want me to carry it for you?"

"No, no, I'm fine. Let's just get off this accursed mountain. I feel as if there are ghosts up here and the sooner we're away from here the happier I'll be."

Zakari was outside pruning his grapevines when he heard approaching voices. He was surprised to see the three of them, for he expected no visitors and certainly not these three. They were not close friends. He knew Panayoti well enough, but only saw Stavros and Vasili before the discovery of the tomb. Nevertheless, he greeted them warmly, as they did him. Panayoti shouted out his name with delight as soon as he saw him. "Kalósto, Zakari! Tí kánis?"

Zakari grinned at him. "Did you lose your way or did that little earthquake chase you up here to the top of the mountain where nothing can fall down on you? What brings you to my house? Come have a seat. Welcome! Can I offer you some coffee? Stavros, what do you have in your bundle?"

"Efkarístos, fílemou." With pleasure, my friend, said Panayoti, ignoring for the moment the second question. "It's been a hot trip from Plakias. Some coffee would be welcome, but first a little water from your well."

As Zakari went into his house he looked back over his shoulder, "Of course, please, drink all the water you want. Plakias, huh? What were you doing in Plakias? Did you hear any news of Mitzos?"

The three men looked at one another. "No," said Panayoti. Then, in a low voice, he addressed the others. "Wait until he brings the coffee and can sit down and talk."

The other two nodded and continued in the direction of the well. They refreshed themselves at the well and Stavros washed the dried blood from the side of his head. Then they returned to the shaded front of the house, where they sat on the bench. Zakari came out bearing a tin tray with four cups of Turkish coffee on it, as well as a plate of paximadi, some olives and a hunk of the delicious white cheese known as Kefálo tirí.

"Here, drink this. I made all four métrios. It was quicker like that." Looking more closely at the bundle sitting on Stavros' knees, Zakari remarked, "Stavros, is that a kilo of bread from Plakias you're taking home for dinner tonight?"

Zakari laughed, but he noticed the others did not join him. Rather than answering they looked at one another.

"Here, here, what's the matter? You all look as if you just lost your best friend." Zakari again noticed the look that passed among the three. Something was on their minds, that much was evident. They were not on his doorstep because they happened to be passing by. Their presence did not represent a neighborly call, by any means.

"I feel there's something that's happened I know nothing about. What is it and what can I do to help you?"

When Vasili and Stavros looked at Panayoti he realized it would be up to him as the chosen spokesman to explain why they were here today. He looked down at his feet for a moment, then up into the sky, beseeching the gods for assistance. Zakari watched him and waited for him to begin.

"Zakari, fílemou, I'm not sure where to begin. There've been some things happening you probably know nothing about. I'm not at all sure how you or any of us are affected by these events, but they're bothersome. We're here today to tell you of them and to ask if you have any answers.

"When we were all together where they're building the road the treasure from the tomb was put into our hands and we all felt excitement over our shares of it. We thought no one knew who we were and that we would never be found out. It seems as if we're perhaps not quite as fortunate as we thought." Taking a deep breath he continued. "Do you know Pseramanoli?"

"Pseramanoli? Which Pseramanoli?"

"Yorgos, Yorgos Pseramanolis."

"Of course, Yorgos! Barba Yorgi. It's strange you should bring up his name. The day after the tomb was discovered he came to my house. He just suddenly appeared the next morning. He sat right there where you're sitting now and told me about the discovery of the treasure. He didn't name any names, but he led me to believe he knew, or at least suspected, I was there. He said some things that made me wonder how much he knew. Why're you asking?"

Zakari carefully omitted his rushing with the gold statue back to his house and hiding it. These men did not know of its existence and Zakari was sure his secret would be safer the fewer people who were aware of it. Right now only two people knew of it, he thought wryly to himself: Barba Yorgi and me.

Panayoti leaned forward earnestly and looked directly at Zakari. "So, the old man came to see you, as well. What you don't know is that he's made separate visits to each of us. Did he threaten you? With us he said he wanted a share of the things we found - exactly half. He threatened us and said that if we didn't cooperate he would tell the police what he knows. We've all talked to one another and you know about his visits to us, but we didn't know about you and Mitzos. This morning Vasili, Stavros and I came to Plakias to find Mitzos and talk with him. We were told in the village he's not been seen since the day of the discovery."

More to himself than to the others, Zakari muttered, "So, he's still not returned." He looked at the three men and spoke softly. "I have hoped he would come back within a few days. I've heard nothing from him or any more about him. I have no idea where he is. You know the bulldozer driver recognized him, don't you? The police even came looking for him. Went to his aunt's house. At first I was afraid of what he would say if they found him. You know how he is and how the police can be when they question someone. But by the time they arrived in Plakias he was gone and hasn't been seen since. Now I'm beginning to worry maybe something happened to him."

"You need not worry about Mitzos' telling anyone anymore. He's beyond that now," said Panayoti, reaching into his pocket and taking out the chain and crucifix. He held them out to Zakari, who took them with a puzzled look on his face.

"Turn it over and look at the back," said Vasili.

As he did so, he saw the name and date engraved into the silver. His stomach knotted and his eyes searched the faces of the men for answers. "This belongs to Mitzos! Where did you find it?"

Panayoti motioned to Stavros to open the bundle. He laid it on the ground and untied it. When he uncovered the contents he saw Zakari's mouth drop open.

"Panagía!" Madonna! Zakari crossed himself as he stared wide-eyed at the skull with the gold tooth and shattered jaw. "Is that...?"

"Naí," answered Panayoti. "Mitzos. As we were on our way to see you today we were on the path from Plakias and, by the oddest of chances, we found him, or what was left of him."

"But where did you find him and how?"

With Stavros and Vasili eagerly filling in any blanks, Panayoti told of events leading to the discovery of Mitzos' remains, the earthquake and then the bizarre music seeming to come from nowhere. Zakari sat spellbound until the mention was made of the music.

"Music!? On the mountain, right after the earthquake?"

Stavros took up the narrative and told of their terror, but that they eventually found the shovel and the radio. "We think the radio must have been sitting up on a boulder. The earthquake probably caused it to fall and hit a rock. That's what caused it to start playing. We found it laying in a pile of dirt showing signs of recent digging. We think Mitzos must have come to the mountain to bury his part of the treasure and been surprised there by someone who killed him. We looked in the dirt, dug into the turned earth but found no antiques. Nothing. Whoever killed Mitzos must have taken his body higher and left it for the vultures and carrion eaters, then come back and taken away what he was trying to bury."

"Let me see the radio," demanded Zakari. When Vasili showed it to him Zakari jumped to his feet. "Pseramanoli! That's the radio Barba Yorgi always carries in his vest. I've seen it before many times. He must have put it up on a boulder after he attacked Mitzos then forgot to pick it up when he left. He didn't have it with him the day he visited me. I thought it was strange that he should be without it, but I didn't think too much about it at the time."

The other three looked at one another and nodded in agreement. "Naí, Barba Yorgi. He must have forced Mitzos to tell him who was with him at the tomb. That's the only way he could have known our names. Then Barba Yorgi must have killed him. Maybe Mitzos tried to run away and Barba Yorgi caught and killed him with his staff. Look at the skull. The jaw is totally broken. He must have hit him with the staff he always carries.

They looked at Zakari, who took his seat once more and sat with his head in his hands. When he raised his head he looked at them through eyes that were raw and red. "Poor little Mitzos. I think I know the spot on the mountain you're talking about. The day after we found the tomb I went to Plakias to see Mitzos.

Barba Yorgi told me the bulldozer driver remembered seeing him. I remember vultures sitting on the rocks and flying about overhead. I thought...I thought there was some animal dead among the rocks. A sheep, or a goat. I never thought it could have been a man up there. Little Mitzos.

"When I returned home I found signs of Barba Yorgi having come back to my house. From the traces of his having been in the yard I was sure he was looking for something. He was gone by the time I returned. Poor Mitzos. Yes, you must be right. He must've made him tell who was at the tomb. That's the only way he could have come to see me, and then you, so soon afterwards. When he was here little Mitzos was certainly already dead. Barba Yorgi probably came directly here. I remember how surprised I was by his visit. Filthy, murdering old man! Pseramanoli! He must be made to pay. This time he's gone too far. I swear on my mother's grave I'll see him dead and in Hell!"

Panayoti put his hand on Zakari's arm. "We agree with you, Zakari, but how are we going to do this? How are we going to avenge Mitzos' death without implicating ourselves and perhaps losing everything we've found?"

Through clenched teeth Zakari replied, "For the moment I don't know. He must be made to pay for what he's done, however. He's lived too long. I don't know right now, but I'll find a way that'll rid us of the threat of that old vulture. I'll find a way.

"Thank you for coming. You brought sad news, but believe me, we'll find a way. Go on home, all of you. Watch yourselves. I'd suggest you take the treasures you took from the tomb and hide them where no one can find them. I'll send a message to you as soon as I know what we're going to do. If anyone hears from Barba Yorgi you must let me know immediately. Don't wait before contacting me.

"Wait, before you go, leave the chain and cross, the radio and Mitzos' skull with me. I'll keep them safe. Also, when you return home don't go by Plakias. There's another path a little way from here. An animal trail. It goes directly down the mountain to the coast. Take it. No one's to know you came to see me this morning. Swear to me that this will be our secret. Also, tell no one, not even your families, about Mitzos. I don't want there to be any chance of Pseramanoli's finding out we know he's dead."

The three men swore an oath of silence. They thanked Zakari profusely, promising to let him know as soon as anything happened. Zakari watched them until they were out of sight, then turned and went into the house. He wrapped the chain and radio up in the shirt with the skull and carefully hid them on the same ledge high up inside the chimney, beside the gold statue.

By god, he would make that old man pay for what he'd done. He, Zakari Forakis, swore he would avenge this death. He would find a way.

Chapter 16

As soon as the boat pulled away from the quay and began to traverse the harbor Jean Paul returned to his cabin. He was pleasantly surprised to discover he would be travelling alone. There was no guarantee of sharing quarters with someone who was pleasant or compatible, unless you paid for first class passage and brought your traveling companion along with you.

He locked the door behind him, dropped his pants and removed the package. It appeared none the worse for wear, but just to make sure he carefully removed the contents. The four small statues lay nested on their bed of cotton. He saw no reason why he should be suspected of anything other than taking a trip, but one could never be too careful.

He looked about the small room for a place to hide these precious artifacts. It would not do to simply put them in his valise, particularly if there were any thieves aboard. Standing up he pushed gently on the stained acoustical tiles of the low ceiling to find they were simply lying on aluminum channels. He chose a spot close to the overhead lamp and slipped the small packet between the lamp socket and a rib of aluminum. He then let the tile fall back into place and stood back to admire his handiwork. There was no telltale sign to give away the fact something might be hidden there.

A glance at his watch told him it was just a little after nine. It was too early to even think of going to bed. He was alone on a boat full of tourists heading for several destinations around Europe. There was also no chance anyone could stumble across the statues by hazard, so there was no reason he should cloister himself in his cabin all night. Getting up from the bed he patted his pocket to make sure the money was still there, took a light jacket from the valise and walked out the door.

Before going into the second class lounge he walked along the deck, which still teemed with people. From the stern of the ship he could make out the mass of Crete rising darkly into the fast-fading light of the evening sky. The lights of Iraklion could still be seen low on the horizon, but they, too, were slipping into the dark of the sea. The ship's phosphorescent wake marked their passage through the calm waters, while overhead the first stars twinkled in the night sky.

The night was not a loss as Jean Paul judged it. In the bar he encountered an English girl who held a simple boarding ticket and planned to sleep on the deck with the other wanderers of summer. Several ouzos later, she accompanied him to his cabin, where she spent the night, abandoning herself to the dark good looks and seductive magnetism of the tall Frenchman. Jean Paul was delighted to have the company and even more happy not to have to spend the night with someone not of his own choosing.

With the morning sun the girl arose, said her goodbyes and slipped out the door. Jean Paul dozed in bed for a while longer, luxuriating in the afterglow of his night of sex. Then his thoughts turned to the trip ahead and he quickly forgot the girl. He arose, shaved at the rust-stained sink, put on the same clothes he wore to come aboard, hefted the shoulder bag and went to the lounge for his normal breakfast of coffee and cigarettes. Through the windows of the lounge could be seen the dark blue of the mainland and he knew they would be arriving in Piraeus within the hour. He took his time, however, and docking was already in process before he finally left his table.

With his bag safely between his feet he leaned against the rail to watch the comings and goings on the polluted waters of Piraeus. Other cruise ships were at dock, pennants flying. Rusted freighters and those sporting fresh coats of paint were berthed side by side. Each was attended by an army of workers and cranes lading cargo or emptying holds full of goods from around the Mediterranean. The sight reminded him of his last visit to the port of Marseilles not so many years before, when he returned to Algeria from France.

The night before his departure, unable to sleep, he and Carter talked well into the wee hours of the morning. They sat on the terrace outside Carter's room with glasses of cognac, the bottle resting between them. Jean Paul told Carter of his birth in Oran 31 years earlier, where his family prospered for five generations. His father was a well-known and respected physician and yes, Jean Paul planned to follow in his footsteps. He finished college in Oran and then enrolled in the university in

Montpelier, where he studied medicine until 1959. After two and a half years of study the 'unpleasantness' taking place across Algeria became a full-scale civil war.

The Algerians, that is to say the Arabs, fought for their independence. The colons, the pied-noirs, as they were popularly called, fought just as ferociously to retain their hold on the profitable colony. Sometime after the French lost Indochina, following the debacle at Dienbien-phu in 1954, the Arabs began to push for independence. Rhetoric turned to acts of violence and sabotage, by 1959 it reached such a pitch that Jean Paul withdrew from medical school, rushed to Marseilles and took a boat home to Oran.

Upon his arrival he greeted his family, found some of his friends who were still in town, got drunk and enlisted in the French army. He was shipped back to France for basic training and jump school. Because of his time in medical school, he was made a medic in a parachute regiment to which he was assigned, sent back to Algeria, and stationed near Oran.

Jean Paul's return to Algeria coincided with the growth of discontent within the ranks of the French military, including the Foreign Legion, historically based at the Legion's headquarters in Sidi bel Abbes. General Raoul Salan, veteran of World War II and the war in Indochina, was much disturbed by the turn of events in France. Under the leadership of De Gaulle, France set into motion the mechanism which would ultimately grant independence to Algeria and return it to the control of the indigenous population. Those closest to Colonial Algeria, the colonists themselves and the Foreign Legion were bitterly opposed to such an action. Most of the pied noirs in the army and the Legion deserted, to follow men named Salan, Zeller, Jouhaud and Challe. The result was civil war, with Frenchman fighting Frenchman. The pied noirs battled both the Algerians and their compatriots from Metropolitan France who were sent to quell the uprising.

In the midst of this turmoil was Jean Paul. He allied himself with the first group of deserters and, during the course of the next two years, was heavily involved in the fray. He became a member of the OAS (the Secret Army Organization), the paramilitary force headquartered in Bab-el-Oued.

In the OAS he was accorded the rank of sous officier. His duties included leading forays into the interior to root out suspected terrorists. One such sortie took him and two ex-Legionnaires into a small village in the Atlas Mountains. There they took into custody a man suspected of planting a bomb. The prisoner, surly and combative, was led away between his two burly captors with Jean Paul walking ahead of them. The Arab quickly realized his struggles and epithets were to no avail and, in a moment of extreme frustration, turned to one of the men holding his arm and spit full in his face. The insults were difficult enough for the ex-Legionnaire to stomach, but the gobbet of warm spittle proved to be the last straw.

At that moment the small group was crossing one of the old Roman bridges spanning a rushing stream far below. Jean Paul heard the sounds of expectoration and the resultant splat. He turned just in time to see the unfortunate wretch sail over the parapet, arms and legs flailing, his trajectory describing a magnificent arc. The man's screams echoing down the deep, rocky ravine were cut short by his sudden and violent arrival on the jagged boulders awash in the torrent below. Jean Paul's interrogatory, "Putain, s'qui s'passe!?" was met with a typical Gallic shrug. "Ben, il sautait!" He jumped!

Jean Paul and his group were also instrumental in the assassination of two of De Gaulle's secret agents, referred to by the pied noirs as 'Barbouzes'. A particularly lethal bomb planted in their car exploded when they turned the key to start it after coming out of a restaurant. The resultant explosion shattered windows in the vicinity and killed the hated agents instantly, to the delight of the pied noir population.

In 1962, when it became evident that all hope of saving his homeland was lost, Jean Paul made his way out of the country - on the run. Because of his activities during the struggle, a price was placed on his head both in Algeria and in France. He eventually landed upon the shores of Crete, which reminded him somewhat of his native North Africa. With borrowed money and a partnership with a rail-thin, oily fellow named Stephano, he opened the Club Fez near the port in Iraklion. In spite of the fact that Jean Paul was not a good businessman, the club enjoyed a moderate success and drew its share of the under 30 tourist trade.

His mind drifted to Belkacem ben Boulaid, who now called himself Abu Bekr. The mere thought of him caused Jean Paul to grind his teeth in frustration. How strange that this Carter Martin, an American, should suddenly turn up in his life and perhaps bring ben Boulaid back into it, as well. What a strange turn of events. Who would have ever dreamed he would ever even hear the name of this bloody individual again?

His recalled the night in Oran when he participated in a sweep through the souks of the city looking for a terrorist group believed to be hiding there. They found them purely by accident, when one of his men literally fell into their hiding place. There were eight of them, most already known to the OAS. The leader was the most sought after of them all, a man known only by reputation. No one knew his name or what he looked like. Vicious interrogations finally provided the torturers with his name. At the limits of resistance, one of the wretches babbled that ben Boulaid was one of those in the holding cell. He was even able to point him out from photographs which of those in the holding cell was their sought-after leader.

Jean Paul was present at most of the interrogations, watching from a chair in a corner of the room. As soon as ben Boulaid's identity was learned it was Jean Paul who gave the nod that ended the session. A final kick to the head from a heavy boot caused massive brain damage and the prisoner died on the floor. He told the other four to get rid of the body and to fetch ben Boulaid from the holding cell. While they busied themselves with carrying out his orders, Jean Paul left to retrieve a fresh pack of cigarettes from the floor above the interrogation room. What happened in the interim still remained a mystery to him.

All four guards were armed. A trail of blood down the hallway attested to the fact that two of them apparently took the body by the legs and drug it away. The other two went to the holding cell to identify the leader and bring him to the interrogation room. Somehow, when they entered the cell, those crowded inside set upon them. One of the guns was torn from the grasp of the soldier and turned on its owner. In the resulting melee one of the pied-noirs was killed instantly by a short burst.

The room was so small and crowded that the remaining guard could not maneuver sufficiently to protect himself as the prisoners attacked him. He succeeded in shooting two of them before he went down. The five remaining prisoners, now armed with two mitrailleuses, spilled into the narrow hallway, eager to make good their escape. The two guards moving the body heard the first shot, but thought it was their friends shooting. When the shooting continued they ran toward the uproar, their arms at the ready. A bloody shootout in the hallway ensued and both of the remaining guards were killed, as well as two more of the prisoners. A third, badly wounded, was left unconscious where he fell. The two remaining prisoners, now well armed, took to their heels. In their frantic rush to escape they discovered a back stairway leading to the floor above. An unguarded exit provided an escape route and they once more regained anonymity among the general populace.

On the floor above, Jean Paul heard the firing and shouts and descended the nearest staircase at a run. By the time he arrived it was over. All that remained were his four dead comrades, the four dead terrorists and their wounded companion. The wounded man almost lost an arm from a fusillade and was also wounded in the neck. He remained unconscious until he died some thirty minutes later. From comparing the dead to the photographs of each of them, they discovered that one of those who got away was Belkacem ben Boulaid. Two weeks later he was again seen and identified in the key region of Kabylia, but successfully evaded capture.

Bonisseur heaved a sigh as his thoughts returned to the present. He remained at the railing on deck until after the other passengers began to stream ashore. It was only a little after 7 in the morning and his flight would not leave until around noon. The crush of departing passengers abated considerably before he finally bent to pick up his small bag and make his way down the gangplank. There he boarded a bus headed for Syntagma Square. This would take him into the center of Athens, from where he would hail a taxi to the airport.

He spent an hour in Syntagma, reading that day's issue of Le Monde and drinking coffee. At 9:30 he folded his paper and put it under his arm, picked up his valise and headed towards

Amalias to find a taxi to the airport. Arriving shortly after 10, he immediately went to the public toilets where he carefully replaced the flat box of statues in its hiding place. He would be forced to stand now until he could board his flight. Rather than putting off the inevitable any longer, he headed for customs. As he approached he took deep breaths to calm himself. He knew the agents were trained to look for any signs of nervousness. Inner turmoil churned his insides and he felt a trickle of sweat begin to course down his spine. A queue of several passengers waited to pass through customs and Jean Paul took a place at the end of the line. The package of statuettes between his buttocks felt enormous. His every movement made him aware of its presence. He licked his lips surreptitiously trying to wet them. A drink of water would be wonderful, but he dared not even move out of the slowly inching line to go to the water fountain for fear he would call attention to himself.

When he finally faced the customs agent he slid his passport under the glass and forced himself to look at him. The agent nonchalantly flipped the pages open to his picture and then raised expressionless eyes to compare the photograph to the face in front of him. The moment seemed interminable to Jean Paul. He wanted to drop his eyes, to look away, but dared not do so.

"Rien à déclarer?"

"No, just a carton of cigarettes I'm taking with me."

For a moment the agent looked as if he were considering having Jean Paul open his shoulder bag, which would have been fine, for there were only two changes of clothes and some clean underwear and socks, in addition to the packs of Greek cigarettes. He experienced a rush of relief when the agent finally reached for his rubber stamp, slammed it down on the page, closed the passport and pushed it back through the window. "Bon voyage."

Without saying a word Jean Paul picked up the passport and headed toward the Swissair gate. There was nothing left to do now but wait until his flight boarded. He could not sit and dared not go into the men's room to remove the statues. That would have to wait until his flight was ready for boarding. He would take no chances. Time seemed to crawl as he watched the comings and goings of the other passengers in the lounge. He was hopeful his demeanor matched that of any of the international travelers.

When the call came for boarding he remained leaning against a concrete column, smoking a last cigarette. He did not move toward the gate until most passengers for his flight were already aboard. By waiting he did not have to jockey for position with the others crowding to be the first to find seats. He showed the agent his ticket and boarding pass and went directly onto the airplane. Once he found his seat he placed his newspaper and jacket on it, then made his way to the toilets. He quickly removed the package and opened it to see that all was in order. They were each as he last saw them, no worse for wear. He breathed a sigh of relief and slipped the box containing them into his jacket pocket. Moving to the washbasin he turned on the cold water, washed his hands and splashed refreshing water on his face. As he dried his face and hands he looked into the mirror, gave his reflection a thumbs-up sign and returned to his seat.

He was mentally and emotionally drained from the ordeal of passing through customs, but now he was as good as out of Greece. Safely ensconced in the Swissair jet, he could be considered to be on Swiss soil. He buckled himself in, put his head back on the seat, closed his eyes and murmured a heartfelt, "Merci, mon dieu!" Moments later, even before the engines began their whine he drifted off to sleep.

He awoke as the plane started its bumpy descent through the clouds into Zürich. The sleep alleviated his fatigue somewhat, but his eyes still felt gritty. Upon awakening he immediately patted the pocket of his jacket where the statues were cached, just to make sure they were still there. When they finally broke through the heavy overcast and he could see the countryside below, he thrilled at the pelting rain that obscured the surrounding mountains. This was his first view of rain since the last showers in early May. For him the rain signified the essence of continental Europe. He could hardly wait to disembark.

After passing through customs and leaving the terminal he found a bus destined for the Hauptbanhof, the central railway station. He knew he could find cheap but comfortable lodgings in this section of the city. At the information kiosk he was given the names of several nice small hotels on the other side of the Limmat, the river that flowed through the center of the city. He made his way across the Bahnhofplatz and took the closest bridge, the Bahnhofbrücke, across the river to the Limmatquai, where he soon found the Limmathof, a small hotel facing the river. It was located just west of the university and within easy walking distance of the Old Town. It was there he felt his chances of finding a buyer for the statues would be the greatest.

He checked into the hotel and took his bag to his room. Once more he unwrapped and examined the statues closely. Much to his relief, they remained in fine condition. He bundled them once more in their blanket of cotton and slipped them back into the inside pocket of his jacket.

By evening the rain stopped and the weather was cool and overcast, with the clouds perched on the tops of the surrounding mountains. He put on the London Fog raincoat Carter insisted he take and left the hotel. He ate a spare meal and then walked in the direction of the Old Town. Here he was sure would be someone who would be interested in the artifacts. As he walked through the narrow streets of the old city he marked in his mind three small shops which showed promise. Only a short walk from his hotel, they would be easy to find the next day.

With nothing else to do he found a movie and enjoyed an American film subtitled in German. By the time it was over it was almost midnight and Jean Paul strolled back toward the hotel. He stopped for a quick cup of coffee and a pastry before turning in for the night.

The next morning he looked from his window as soon as he arose and was pleased to see the sun peeking from behind puffy clouds in a blue sky. He quickly shaved and dressed, then descended to the street. A nearby Konditorei offered fresh baked breads, sweet rolls and coffee. He took his breakfast at one of the small round tables while perusing the Geneva newspaper. Thirty minutes later he began his quest for a buyer.

The owners of the first two antique stores he approached looked at the statues with appreciative eyes, but felt they would not be able to find a suitable buyer for them. Jean Paul thanked them and headed for the third, a small storefront in a narrow cobbled street resembling an alley. Its owner was somewhat more knowledgeable, but was disinclined to make a purchase of this nature. They fascinated him, however, and he asked Jean Paul all about Crete and the types of things one could find. Jean Paul spent almost an hour with him, regaling him with stories of things seen and experienced. Like most Swiss, the shopkeeper was bilingual and their conversation was conducted in French. In his native tongue Jean Paul was eloquent, weaving a conversational tapestry, which came alive with the telling.

The old gentleman's eyes gleamed with interest. "I've always thought I'd like to be in the position you're in now, monsieur. I have read that the Minoan civilization is just beginning to be uncovered and rediscovered after all these centuries. How fortunate for you, being in the vanguard of those making those discoveries. I just wish I knew more about such things as you have here. I have no doubt they're authentic. I simply couldn't find a buyer for them. Besides, I have no idea what to give you for something like this. In one sense their value is immeasurable, yet, as you know, they are only worth what someone will pay for them."

Jean Paul nodded his head in agreement. "Yes, I know. So, how am I to find someone here in Zürich, or in Switzerland, who's knowledgeable enough to realize their value?"

The old man pondered for a moment then disappeared into the back of his store. He soon reappeared with a slip of paper in his hand and gave it to Jean Paul. "I'm not sure whether or not this will bring you any success. It's worth a try, however. This man's name is Katz, Moritz Katz. He doesn't have a shop but I know he has a great deal of interest in Mideastern and Mediterranean artifacts. I've heard he sometimes buys not only for himself, but also for collectors and museums in Europe. He's said to be particularly interested in Egyptian items, as well as some others. Who knows? Perhaps he's the person to contact."

"Where's this address?" asked Jean Paul, studying the writing on the piece of paper.

"It's in the Unterstrass district near the university. To save yourself a trip for nothing, call him first. I wrote down his telephone number. Give him an idea of what you have and tell him you would like to meet with him. You may tell him I suggested you call. My name is Peter Bullinger."

Jean Paul stood up to leave and thanked Herr Bullinger for his time and the information.

"Ach, it's nothing," he replied. "It is I who thanks you for stopping by and for taking the time to tell me of all you are discovering. I can only wish you the greatest of success. If I were younger I would like to join you. But...perhaps in the next life," he added wistfully.

With the slip of paper in his pocket Jean Paul retraced his steps up the narrow cobbled street and soon found a public phone. Next to it was a kiosk selling newspapers and magazines, where he purchased a jeton to pay for his call. Returning to the telephone he inserted the token and began to dial. From the other end of the line could be heard tinny, insistent ringing. After almost a minute the receiver was picked up and he heard a woman's voice.

"Ja?"

In halting German Jean Paul asked if this were the residence of Herr Katz.

"Ja."

He asked if he could speak with him and the voice answered, "Moment mal, bitte."

The phone was laid carefully on a hard surface and then the sound of retreating footsteps could be heard. After a minute of silence he heard a door slam, footsteps walking towards the receiver, and then a voice announcing, "Katz hier."

"Herr Katz, my name is Jean Paul Bonisseur. May we speak French?"

Switching immediately to heavily accented French, Herr Katz replied, "Of course."

"Thank you very much. I've just come from talking to Peter Bullinger, who has a shop in the old city. I arrived from Crete with some things Herr Bullinger thought might interest you."

"Herr Bullinger. Hm-m-m. The antikenhändler from Altstadt Antikitäten. Why did he think I might be interested in what you have to offer?"

"He mentioned that you're interested in Mideastern artifacts, archaeological artifacts. Do you prefer only items which come from the Mideast itself, or do you also take an interest in those which might come from, say, Turkey or Greece?"

"Hm-m-m, Turkey or Greece? Which country specifically? Yes, you must be more specific."
"Greece. To be more specific still, Crete."
"Kreta! That depends, you know. Do you have any idea of the age of the items? By age I mean are they Greek, Turkish, Venetian, Roman...?" His voice trailed off, leaving the question hanging.

"Oh, no, Herr Katz. I know very little about those periods. No, what I have is definitely Minoan."

"Minoan!?" The surprise in his voice was evident. "Hm-m-m, yes, Minoan. That could be interesting. How do you know they are Minoan?"

"Herr Katz, I've lived in Crete for the past two years. During that time I've learned a great deal about its archaeology. I know exactly where these pieces were found, at what depth and, most importantly, what was found with them. There's no doubt of their authenticity."

"Ja, I see what you mean. There is the possibility they could be Minoan. Where are you now, Monsieur Bonisseur?"

"Near the university. Would you be able to see me today?"

"I think that could be arranged. I am going to be busy for the next two hours; however, if you could arrange to meet me at five o'clock at my home I will be free to see you then."

"Thank you, Herr Katz. Five would be fine. How will I find your house?"

Katz explained how to come to his house from the area of the university and Jean Paul scribbled the directions on the reverse side of Peter Bullinger's instructions, thanked Katz again for taking time to meet with him and hung up. This proposed meeting was a positive sign. If Katz were interested enough to purchase the pieces, Jean Paul's mission could be counted as complete and successful. Otherwise, he would have to look elsewhere, which would mean having to go to either Bern, Basel, Lausanne or Geneva. He walked with a new spring in his step as he again crossed the Limmat and headed for his hotel.

By 4:30 he was once more in the Unterstrass district and found the home of Moritz Katz. He passed the next thirty minutes nervously drinking coffee and chain smoking in a small restaurant. Punctually at five, however, he was standing before Katz's door with his finger on the doorbell.

The door was answered by an old woman wearing a shapeless sweater and felt slippers. When he identified himself and told her of his appointment with Katz, she moved back from the door and motioned for him to enter. The hallway in which he found himself was long and narrow with wide double sliding doors, now closed, on either side. Although the ceilings were high there was almost a claustrophobic feeling. There was only one light, a lustra hanging from a chain in the entryway, which did little to pierce the gloom. To the right a narrow stairway mounted to the deeper gloom of the second story. Glancing up the stairs, Jean Paul found he was unable to see beyond the first landing.

He followed the old woman down the hall to a low doorway set into the wall on the left. She opened the door, entered and he followed her inside to find himself in a library. Hundreds of volumes covered the floor to ceiling shelves. A ladder on rollers top and bottom was located on a far wall, which would have been the only way even the tallest occupant could have reached the books on the highest shelves. One corner of the room held an immense desk covered with books and papers in total disarray. In front of it was a heavy, high-backed chair covered in dark brocade.

Behind the desk sat a small man, resembling a withered child. His head appeared much too large for his frail looking body and the spindly neck supporting it. On his prominent nose was perched a pair of gold wire glasses, the ear pieces of which were hooked over ears that stood out from his head and were covered with wiry black bristles. A translucent eyeshade on his forehead gave a greenish cast to the face below it. In front of him on the desk was an open book, on which the man rested his hands, hands that looked as if they belonged to someone five times larger. Jean Paul could not take his eyes from them. From thin bony wrists sprouted long narrow hands with huge knuckles and spread fingers. On their backs and between the knuckles of his fingers grew coarse, black hair, which covered the large liver spots and ropy veins like a mat. Jean Paul's only thought at that moment was that here before him was the fabled Gnome of Zürich.

Neither said a word and the apparition before him did not raise his head to acknowledge Jean Paul's presence. The noise of the door's closing softly caused him to turn his head to look over his shoulder where he realized the old woman no longer was in the room. When he turned back to face Katz he saw the old man was now studying him with dark eyes shadowed by heavy black eyebrows.

"Herr Bonisseur? Ich bin Katz."

Jean Paul advanced toward the desk and held out his hand. "Bon jour, Monsieur Katz. I'm pleased to meet you."

Katz took Jean Paul's hand, but did not return the pressure. Jean Paul was surprised to notice that the old man was now standing behind the desk, for there was no apparent change in his height.

"Please, Monsieur Bonisseur, have a seat," he said, indicating the large chair in front of the desk. When Jean Paul sat down Katz continued with no further niceties. "Hm-m-m, so, Monsieur Bonisseur, you have something you think would be of interest to me." It was not a question, but a statement of fact.

Nonplused at the beginning, Jean Paul quickly recovered his equilibrium and reached inside his jacket to withdraw the small box. He set it gently on the fine wood of the desk and opened the top. As he was doing this he found the silence in the library oppressive, but could think of nothing appropriate to say. The only sound was that of Katz's breath being expelled with a slight whistling through his great nose as he watched the unveiling with interest. With the statues finally uncovered, Jean Paul spread them neatly on top of their cotton wrappings and pushed them diffidently across the desk.

"Les voilà."

Katz sat forward with his elbows on the desk and his fingers interlaced. He lifted his head as if attempting to focus his eyes. For a long moment he seemed content to examine the ivories as they lay there in front of him, but he soon reached out a long forefinger to touch each of the three. From a drawer he extracted a large magnifying glass and studied them before picking up one and turning it over to look at the back. Each piece received detailed scrutiny.

"Hm-m-m, well, monsieur, please be so kind as to tell me about these pieces. You mentioned on the telephone you know where they came from and all the details. You were present when they were discovered?"

"Of course," Jean Paul lied without hesitation. "It would be difficult to authenticate their provenance were I not there. I regret only that I have no photographs taken in situ. You must realize this affair is not totally within the law. Time and secrecy are of the utmost importance. Otherwise, neither I, nor certainly anyone else with whom you do business, would have anything to show you."

For the first time Katz showed a glimmer of emotion as the corners of his mouth lifted in what might be interpreted as a hint of a smile. "Ja, you are quite correct. This is a difficult product to deliver to those who await its arrival so anxiously. Tell me about them."

During the next hour Katz listened as Jean Paul spun his narrative of the world of clandestine archaeology on Crete. Occasionally Katz offered a comment or posed a question, but most of the time he merely sat, elbows on desk, attentive to what was being said. The only interruption was the arrival of the old woman with a tray containing a teapot and two fine china cups and saucers. She withdrew again without saying a word and the one-sided discussion continued. When he finished he sat back in his chair and reached for his cup. For a long moment there was no sound in the room.

"Well, monsieur," began Katz, "I must tell you I am interested in what you have to say, as well as in these little tidbits you have brought me. I assume you have access to more artifacts, nicht wahr? Some of what I find through people such as you I keep, but there are some gentlemen who come to me from time to time to try to add to their collections. As you are probably aware, there is not a great deal coming out of Crete at this time. Some pieces have begun to arrive on the continent from Santorini, and a Minoan piece from Egypt was identified and found its way into my hands two years ago, but there is a dearth of quality. Fortunately, up until this time, because there is so little known of the Minoans when compared to the Greeks or Romans, there is little counterfeiting. Hm-m-m, you have convinced me these pieces are authentic and, quite frankly, I would be willing to consider others you might have. I ask only that if you come to me in the future you bring with you at least an example of the pottery found with, or in the general vicinity of your find. A fragment will do. It will help date the artifact itself. Also, pictures of the site would be extremely useful.

"Now then Monsieur Bonisseur, what are you asking for these three?" Having posed the question he sat back in his chair and waited for Jean Paul's reply, while absentmindedly caressing the wood with his fingertips.

Jean Paul anticipated the question, but he still hesitated dramatically before giving his answer. Leaning forward in his chair, he looked across at the dealer and said, "I can only assume your interest in these pieces means you already have a buyer in mind, or...is it to your own collection you would like to add them? There are no pieces similar to these in the Iraklion Archaeological Museum, nor have I heard mention of them anywhere else. Perhaps in the Ashmolean, but I'm not sure. I would like twenty-five hundred dollars for them."

"Hm-m-m, twenty-five hundred dollars. For all three?"

"No. Each."

"I see. Well, monsieur, that's a very steep price. I could never resell them for that much, you understand. Business is business and I must realize a profit should I decide to sell them to someone else. I think I could see my way clear to give you that amount for all three, but not for each."

Not having any idea of the market value of such artifacts, Jean Paul put forward the figure just to test Katz's reaction. Now he was being offered over eight hundred and thirty dollars apiece for them, much more than Deaf Yanni wanted for himself and the person to whom they belonged. Of course, everyone who handles these things wants to be paid for his part in it, he thought to himself. Twenty-five hundred makes a nice profit for me. Nevertheless, nothing ventured, nothing gained.

"You said yourself, Herr Katz, how unique these pieces are. I'm sorry, but I don't see how I could take any less than thirty-five hundred for all three of them together."

The thrust and parry of negotiations continued unabated for the next few minutes. During the entire time the old man kept the statues in front of him, reaching out from time to time to touch them. When Jean Paul finally countered with a proposal of three thousand dollars for all three Katz hesitated a moment and then said, "Agreed, Monsieur Bonisseur. You will accept dollars?"

Jean Paul's heart leaped into his throat. Only with the greatest self-control did he contain himself. This was far more than he dreamed he would see for his efforts, and he would have settled for less. He realized Katz was probably already figuring his own profits, for there was surely someone just waiting to take statues such as these off his hands. There was no doubt in Jean Paul's mind that Katz would make a handsome profit. It was a lesson learned and one that would be useful in the future.

Katz left his chair and went to a sidewall of the library where he pulled open the steel door of his wall safe. He counted out thirty $100 bills and returned to his desk, where he again counted the money for Jean Paul's benefit. Jean Paul noticed immediately there was not a single wrinkle or stain on the bills. They were as pristine as the day they were printed. He reached for them with his left hand while removing his passport wallet from his inside pocket with the other. He hated to even fold them. In his mind he quickly converted this sum into French francs, old francs, to be sure, and his mind screamed, "Quinze cent mille bals! Une brique et demie!" A million and a half anciens francs did sound like a great deal of money.

Outwardly calm, Jean Paul rose from his chair and extended his hand to Katz, who still stood beside the desk. It was when he rose to his full height that he saw just how small the old Schweizer really was. "Thank you again for meeting with me and especially for your knowledge and appreciation of Minoan artifacts. There aren't many people with a true understanding of how valuable these things are and will become."

Katz walked with him to the front door and opened it. "Na, ja, Herr Bonisseur, I must thank Peter Bullinger for sending you to me. Think of me the next time you come to Zürich with something to sell. I trust you will come to me first?"

"But, of course, Herr Katz!" responded Jean Paul with true pleasure. "You may count on it. Well, until next time."

"Bis nächste mal, monsieur," answered Katz with a nod of his head. "Auf wiedersehen!"

Jean Paul turned and walked down the steps into the street. When he glanced back at the house the front door was already closed. He walked calmly to the corner and turned up the next street. Out of sight of Katz's house he leapt into the air with a whoop of glee. A heavyset matron, coming home from market pulling a small two-wheeled cart with a string bag of groceries on it, saw him leap and stopped in astonishment. When he continued down the block she watched his retreating back for a moment more, shook her head in bewilderment, and went on her way.

That evening he chose to dine rather than just eat. At the Mère Catherine, Im Nägelhof am Rüdenplatz in the heart of the Old Town, he feasted à la française on côtelette de mouton and a delicious, if somewhat expensive, Pinot Noir. The cost was not important. He was rich, and he was going to become much wealthier! Tomorrow he would return to the realities of Greece. Tonight he was an international antiques merchant dining in style, the style to which he could quickly become accustomed.

He awoke the next morning with somewhat of a hangover, but a long shower and a good breakfast at the local Konditorei quickly set him straight. After checking out of the hotel he hailed a taxi to take him to the airport. No more buses for him! No, sir! He was already planning his next trip to Zürich and could not wait to get back to Crete to put together his next clandestine package.

Chapter 17

As Carter opened the door to the car and got in to drive away, he wondered what he was going to do during the next three days. He glanced out to sea where the lights of the Keftiu twinkled in the rapidly growing dusk, wishing he were also aboard making this voyage that promised to be so momentous. Should everything work out as they hoped, he would have loved to make this trip as well as the next. To him it was still a game they were playing. He did not fully grasp the seriousness of the venture upon which they were now embarked. For him, finding and identifying Abu Bekr and his group was serious business. Archaeology, even clandestine, was a game he and Jean Paul played, and its appeal grew with each passing day.

Carter pulled out of the parking space, noticing the looks from pedestrians on the quay. He knew the convertible aroused interest and covetousness in many that saw it, particularly when he pressed the accelerator and the grumbling throatiness of the glass packs roared and was thrown back at him from the stone walls of ancient warehouses. Taxi drivers cast poisonous glances in his direction as he passed. When he and Jean Paul picked up tourists the taxi drivers felt they were interfering with their livelihood. Carter was sure they were only jealous of the yellow convertible. Of course, the fact he and Jean Paul were often seen with female tourists in the car: lovely, tanned, mostly blonde, carefree young women the Cretan men looked upon with ill-concealed envy.

He threaded his way carefully among those taking their evening vólta alongside the harbor, before turning into the main street leading towards the center of town. After only one block he realized he would be better advised to take another route, for ahead was a mass of strolling humanity. At the post office he turned right and soon found himself on the street that ran alongside the park. Ahead and to the left was the Club Fez, where Carter considered stopping for a drink before heading home. A man walking along looked familiar. When he looked up and saw Carter he stopped, turned and walked in his direction.

"Carter! Kalispéra! Comment vas-tu?" he said with a wide smile.

As soon as he saw the cigarette dangling from the corner of his mouth and the baggy navy blue suit, Carter knew immediately who it was.

"Andreas! Kalispéra to you, too! How are you tonight?" Carter answered, pleased Andreas remembered him. "Where are you going this time of night? Are you just out for a walk?"

"No, no, no, no, I was headed home. When I saw the car I thought it was Jean Paul at first. Where is that crazy Frenchman?"

"I've just come from the port where I saw him off on the Keftiu. He left for a few days."

"The Keftiu? Ah, O.K., I remember now. He was leaving tonight for Zürich. I saw him yesterday and he told me of this trip." Leaning towards Carter, he said in a conspiratorial voice, "Did he take the commissions for Yanni?"

"Yes, we met with him day before yesterday and picked them up then. Did you see them?"

"No, but Yanni told me about them. By the way, did Jean Paul mention to you about a trip I've asked him to take with me to the mountains?"

"He mentioned you'd talked to him about someone you know who found something of value. He said you wanted him to go with you. I'd really like to go as well."

"Of course! If he finds a buyer in Zürich on this trip he will have a great many things to take to him in the future. Jean Paul said he would like for you to make the next trip with him, as well. He told me you gave him money for this trip. Kalo paidí! Good boy!"

He leaned toward Carter and glanced to each side before speaking, "You must remember not to mention this with anyone. This could be very dangerous. You do understand that, don't you?"

"You don't have to worry about me. Besides, who could I possibly talk to about it? No, my mouth is shut," he replied, making a zipping motion across his lips with his fingers.

"Good, good!" said Andreas with a nod of his head. "Now, there is one other thing: I met a man today who tells me of something important that is to take place near Chania next week. There's going to be a private sale of antiquités, in a village just south of there. The peasants who live in the area have been finding things for many years and from time to time someone organizes a market for them. Some people, usually dealers or their agents come in from Europe and the United States. They meet to look over what is being offered. This happens almost every year and provides the peasants with money for their families. I want for you and Jean Paul to go with me this year."

"An auction? Does Jean Paul know about this?"

"No, he will not even have heard rumors, because there are not many people who know about it. There are only some very special people who are told. This way the peasants can dispose of the pieces they find without risk. It is a secret from all except a few. Certainly the police and the people from the museum know nothing about it."

"A private sale? Can just anyone buy? Do you think we could possibly pick up something, too?"

"Well, my friend, that's the reason I thought the two of you might like to go see what they are offering this year. If you have the money you can buy something. Tell Jean Paul as soon as he returns. Also, have him come see me the day the gets back and we will make arrangements for the trip to Plakias. We don't have much time and must move quickly. Will you tell him for me?"

"With pleasure! Say, I was just going to the club for a drink. Would you like to join me?"

"Thank you, Carter, but not tonight. I have something I must do. Another time. I really must go now."

"OK, well, I'm sorry. Maybe we can get together before Jean Paul returns. Good talking to you."

Carter watched as Andreas turned and continued down the street. He could hardly wait until Jean Paul returned. He looked at the entrance of the Club Fez and decided he really did not care for a drink after all. It was still too early for the tourists to start coming in and he wanted to avoid talking to Jean Paul's partner, Stephano. He returned to the car and drove in the direction of Aghi Vasili. He would decide after he got home what to do about dinner.

When he arrived at the house he nosed the car through the iron gates, opening them with a gentle nudge of the front bumper. Spotlights in the trees illuminated the courtyard and the lights were on downstairs, but he saw no one. He rolled to a stop and shut off the engine, listening in the sudden quiet. From inside the house he could hear the plaintive strains of a ballad coming from the radio tuned to one of the Greek stations. Sounds of water splashing on the concrete floor of the shower room could also be heard. He opened the car door and stepped out onto the flagstones, then headed for the door leading to the shower room. He and Jean Paul spent the past few days alone. All those staying with them either returned home or continued their voyages to other parts of the Mediterranean. He was curious to know who was taking a shower. It was obviously someone they knew, for he did not think a complete stranger would have moved in and made himself so completely at home without an invitation.

The splash of water echoing in the large room masked his footsteps as he entered and traversed the short passageway. When he reached the door leading into the shower room he stopped and craned his neck trying to see through the opening. His first impression was of blonde hair and honey-colored nakedness. Standing with her face lifted to the stream of tepid water, she arched her back, making her finely curved buttocks and calf muscles tense under the silky smoothness of her flawless skin. Her high breasts curved proudly away from the line of her chest, their tips laved in the flow of water that cascaded from them. Her stomach was flat and firm under her rib cage and descended uninterrupted to her blond pubis, trimmed to allow her to wear a tiny bikini. There was hardly any bikini or bra line, however, indicating she sunbathed nude far more often than otherwise. Her hands were held to each side of her face making it difficult for him to make out who she was. Between the doorway and the shower her towel hung on one of several wall hooks. She was totally unaware she was being observed and apparently gave no thought to someone's walking in on her.

Carter slipped through the open door and leaned against it, fascinated by this naked wet woman. When he plucked her towel from the peg on which she hung it she moved her hands from the sides of her face and he recognized Christine. She was the last person he expected to find here. She left for Tunisia before Carter moved in. She looked like a dream. A wet dream. His first inclination was to silently slip away into another part of the house to wait for her to finish. Instead, he remained at his vantage point, her towel draped over his shoulder and his hands on his hips. In a moment she rubbed her face and eyes with her hands, wiped the excess water from them, and then reached over her shoulder to pull her long blond hair forward, twist it and squeeze the water from it. At that moment she opened her eyes and caught a glimpse of Carter standing there. When Carter saw her eyes open he smirked and called out a cheery greeting, "Salut!"

Her surprised shriek echoed in the large room and instantly made him feel like the Peeping Tom he was. Her arms flew to cover her bare breasts and she crouched defensively.

"Carter!" she screamed at him. "Mais quel salaud! Qu'est-ce que tu fais là? Donne moi mon linge, espèce de con!"

Not waiting for him to respond, she dropped her arms from her breasts, stood upright, turned off the water and walked towards him, jerked the towel from his shoulder, wiped her face and eyes before wrapping it around herself. Carter stood transfixed. Once covered, she put her hand on her hip and fixed him with a stony stare. Suddenly she dissolved into giggles and swept her free arm around his neck. He thought she was going to hit him and flinched involuntarily, sending her into a gale of uncontrolled laughter. She pulled him to her, quickly gave him a wet kiss on the mouth, pulled away, patted him on the cheek and swept out of the room, leaving him standing there.

A trail of wet footprints led out of the shower room, across the rear access hall and through the double doors of the kitchen. Carter began to follow them into Jean Paul's bedroom. Her tracks exited the bedroom through the doorway leading to the entry hall and he could hear her walking on the wooden floor of the bedroom directly over his head. She slept there when she was here before and she naturally reclaimed ownership. Within a few minutes he heard her descending the staircase anew and waited to see what her reaction would be this time. He sat in the chair beside the round wooden table placed before the tall double window. She entered the room wearing a loose-fitting, multicolored djellabah she probably brought from Tunis and a towel wound around her head like a turban. Her cornflower blue eyes sparkled when she saw Carter sitting there and she greeted him with a mock-fierce glare, which soon turned into a mischievous grin.

"Alors, petit voyou, je suis contente de te voir. C'est bien d'être de nouveau là."

Carter only smiled in response to her gibe. With little thought he stood and addressed her in French, "Welcome, little blond lady. You were the last person I expected to see here tonight. I apologize for staring at you, but...well, you understand."

She laughed good-naturedly and gave him a meaningful look. "I could tell you were sorry. Menteur! Anyway, it's good to be here. Where's Jean Paul?"

"Switzerland. Business. He left tonight on the Keftiu. I've just come from taking him to the port. I expect him back in a few days."

"Switzerland? What kind of business?"

"I'm not sure. Something about having to see a man. Hey, I was thinking about going back into town for dinner. Want to come?"

Christine thought for a moment and then responded, "Thanks, but I don't think so tonight. I'm so tired I can hardly walk. I left Tunis early this morning and arrived not long before you. I took the evening flight from Athens. No, you go ahead, I'm not hungry. I think I'll dry my hair and then go to bed. Is that your room off the terrace?"

"Yeah, when I moved in I took that one. I wanted it because it's like having two rooms. I sit out there in the evenings. Every morning before I go to work I drink my coffee and watch the sunrise."

"Well, I'm right across the hall in my old room. When you come in please enter quietly. If you bring someone with you, don't make too much noise. And, please, don't bother waking me up tomorrow morning. I think I'm going to sleep all day. By the way, your French has really improved. Congratulations."

Carter smiled and replied, "Thanks. You know, I'm around Jean Paul so much and he insists we speak French as much as possible. Then, too, with the Daskaloyanni family I have to speak French with her. Besides, the Count has taken it upon himself to make me Francophone. I felt so inept when I first met you. I really wanted to talk with you that first night, but just couldn't do it. Anyway, I'm much more comfortable with the language now. Jean Paul is teaching me pied-noir slang and I'm teaching him to swear à l'américaine."

She laughed again and said, "I can just hear you now. Be careful, though. Something that's humorous in Algiers can be very, very pejorative to Parisian ears."

"Thanks, I'll keep that in mind. Well, I'm off. Hope you sleep well. I'm glad you're back. Jean Paul will be surprised. See you tomorrow. You can tell me about Tunisia then."

She walked with him to the door, squeezed his arm with both hands and stood on tiptoe to kiss him affectionately on the cheek. "A demain."

"Until tomorrow," he responded.

Driving into town he tried to decide where he would eat. There was such a large choice of restaurants and cafes that a decision was difficult. Rather than trying to plunge through the crowd of promenaders who clogged the streets, he parked the car on the west edge of the city square and walked across it. As he was making his way among the diners and drinkers seated all around the square, he heard his name being called. He turned to search the sea of faces, but saw none that looked familiar. Again someone called to him and he stopped. To his right next to the trunk of a tall palm tree he saw Yves rise from his chair and wave to him. Carter waved back and made his way to where Yves stood. At the table with him was a young man of about twenty he did not recognize.

The Count greeted him warmly and introduced him to his companion, Guy Chatain. He was small of stature like Yves and extremely pretty. Carter thought how strange to describe another man as being pretty, but Guy's appearance was much more than handsome. When he sat down Yves explained how he and Guy met just that afternoon and invited him to come along with him.

Yves told Carter they were at the beach that afternoon and came to the square for a drink before dinner. He invited him to join them and Carter readily accepted. It would be more fun than eating alone. He ordered ouzo with ice on the side and savored the licorice taste of the refreshing aperitif as he visited with the two men. As soon as he finished his drink all three rose and walked down the street toward Adoni's restaurant off Fountain Square.

It was almost 9:30 when they were shown to a table. Because of the late hour the restaurants were already full and they found themselves sitting at a small table in the narrow cobbled roadway that permitted only foot traffic in the evening. A cooling breeze wended its way from the sea to the square and into the space where they were located, adding to the pleasant atmosphere. A waiter came to them immediately and took their order, then weaved his way among the other tables to disappear into the interior of the restaurant. While waiting for their meals Carter and Yves discussed their activities since they last met. The Count raved about a sexy young baker he and Pierre met at the beach two days earlier. When the discussion took this turn Guy jumped in immediately, wanting to know all the details. Carter simply smiled and nodded, letting the two queens regale each other.

His attention wandered as he idly watched the other diners. From the corner of his eye he noted the arrival of two women, who were seated three tables away. One was rather elderly and obviously Greek. She wore a dark gray dress and a humorless expression. Her companion, who commanded his full attention, was her antithesis: tall, blond, willowy, and wearing a colorfully printed short-sleeved summer dress. The design of her clothing was of the latest fashion and she exuded class. From where he sat Carter could discern her tasteful gold jewelry and slender, well-manicured hands. Because of her companion Carter thought she might be Greek herself, but from the cut of her clothes and bearing he was not sure. He completely forgot those sitting with him, as well as his food, devouring her with his eyes instead. Whatever light makeup she wore was perfectly applied and gave her eyes the look of two large pools of blue in which the naked bulbs strung over the dining area sparkled like sunlight on the Mediterranean. The older woman said something to her as they sat down and she responded with a smile of pure radiance. Her teeth, straight and white, were framed by well-formed pink lips. He found himself wanting to reach out and touch them, to trace their outline with his fingertips.

A voice, gently and insistently calling his name, brought him back from his reverie. He turned his attention back to those at his table and found Yves looking at him with an amused expression. His eyes flicked from Carter, to the woman and back again. One eyebrow rose questioningly and Carter felt compelled to say something.

"Isn't she the most marvelous person you've ever seen?" he asked enthusiastically.

"Yes, she is quite beautiful, but she seems to be well-chaperoned."

Carter nodded his head in reluctant agreement and turned his eyes once more in her direction, watching her pick up a glass of water and sip from it with a grace that seemed to him pure poetry.

"I don't think I've ever seen you so taken with someone since I've known you. This is after watching you react and interact with the women at the Club Fez, so I think I know that of which I speak," he observed stiltedly. "Would you like to meet her?"

"Christ, yes! Do you know her? Just look how beautiful she is!" he rhapsodized, an observation meant more for himself than for the older man.

"Bon, alors, attends içi. Je reviendrai tout de suite." With those words he pushed his chair back from the table and rose.

"What in the world are you doing, Yves!? Sit back down! You can't just walk over to her like that. Wait! Where are you going?" His protests came too late, however, for the diminutive Frenchman made his way purposefully to the table where the two women sat. Carter was hesitant to look, but he could not keep his eyes from the scene unfolding in front of him. Yves walked around the table and stopped by the side of the younger woman. He could not hear what was being said, but both women looked up at him as he bowed slightly from the waist. He held out his hand and the younger woman placed her elegant hand in his. Yves brought it to his lips, kissed it gallantly and then waited as she slowly withdrew hers. When he began to speak the women gave him their rapt attention, the younger with a bemused expression on her face. As Yves spoke she nodded her head several times in apparent acquiescence to what he was saying. A sudden glance from her in Carter's direction almost caused him to drop his gaze, but the look was so fleeting he was unable to react. Yves continued to speak and she to smile and respond. He inclined his torso once more towards her, then took her willing hand and kissed it again. Straightening, he looked at the older woman, gave her a brief smile and a word, which she answered in like manner, then he returned to his table. From the corner of his eye he could see the younger woman following his progress back to where Carter and Guy were seated.

Yves took his seat once more, picked up his bread from beside his plate, tore off a small piece, dipped it in the juices from the grilled fish on his plate and placed it in his mouth. He savored the aroma and the flavor before he spoke. "Well, mon grand Carter, you'll be pleased to know that she'll come to the Club Fez tonight after dinner. I invited her to join us there. She's coming to be with you, however. Her name is Madame Carlton. Her prenom is Evgenia. The older woman is her aunt who lives here in Iraklion. She'll take her aunt home before coming to the club."

Unable to believe either his eyes or his ears, Carter's mouth hung open in amazement. His glance stole involuntarily to the other table, where he caught the eye of the younger woman, who gave him an almost imperceptible nod. He surprised himself by having the presence of mind to return the nod before he turned once more to the older man. When he finally found his voice he could only stammer, "But...what...how...you're joking, of course! Why...?

"No, no, not at all. She's married to an American and lives in Boston. They own hotels here and in Boston. She came to Crete to check on a hotel that belongs to her alone. It's located near the park. Her husband did not come with her, but chose to stay in the US. She's looking forward to meeting you and says she noticed you when they first sat down. Is there anything else you would like to know before your dinner gets cold?"

Carter could only look at Yves in amazement. During one of their conversations Jean Paul told Carter that Yves was like an old woman and that the women of Paris adored him. He was always invited to their luncheons and dinners, sometimes the only man present. He knew everyone who was anyone in the capitol and was also a wonderful gossip and conversationalist. But this! It was too much for him to comprehend. Several minutes passed before Carter could organize his thoughts well enough to even make a coherent comment.

"Yves, what I find so difficult to comprehend is how you could just walk up to her like that, introduce yourself and set up a...a...a rendezvous with someone she's never seen before in her life! Jean Paul said you were amazing, but I never dreamed.... Are you sure you don't know her?"

"I've never seen her before, but she is a woman, albeit a most beautiful one. I understand some things about women," he stated, continuing to eat.

Finally, resigning himself to the fact he would probably never understand what he witnessed, he addressed himself to his own plate, which was already beginning to cool. No matter. He hardly tasted it anyway.

After dinner, over coffee, they discussed art and literature. When they rose to leave after paying their bill, Yves turned toward Evgenia's table and bowed. Both women responded with smiles and inclined their heads toward him. Evgenia, her fork suspended halfway between her plate and her mouth, shifted her gaze to Carter, who smiled at her and gave a brief nod. She smiled gently at him as he turned to follow his two companions in the direction of Fountain Square.

"Evgenia," thought Carter. "Beautiful name to go with a beautiful lady."

Guy and Yves awaited him at the end of the cobbled alley, looking out onto the square, which was filled with an undulating and colorful sea of strollers and diners. At the various restaurants waiters moved to and fro, catering to patrons who filled each table. Guy decided to return to his hotel and was just saying his goodbyes when Carter walked up. He assured Yves he would meet him the next morning for breakfast and the older man watched his retreating back fondly as he turned and walked away.

"May I offer you an after dinner drink?" asked Carter.

"Why, yes, thank you very much. Shall we stroll on down to the club and have it there? There should be a good crowd there already and I told some colleagues who flew in from Paris today to meet me there tonight. If they've arrived it'll give me the opportunity to introduce you to them."

"Fine, let's go."

As they walked Yves told him of his friends. "I think you'll be very interested in this couple I just mentioned. He and his wife own an art gallery in the 7th Arrondissement in Paris. He's much older than she, and very charming. I know you'll like his wife, as well. They've been coming to Crete longer than I and have even purchased a villa in Aghios Vasilios, not far from where you and Jean Paul live. Their name is Crozet and they spend most of the summer here. They arrived late this year, because Hervé has been very busy. They plan to stay until October this year, however."

"Do they know Jean Paul?"

"Mai, oui, everyone knows Jean Paul. Well, here we are! Listen, it sounds as if there's quite a group here tonight."

From the interior of the Club Carter could hear the sound of someone singing in French. Every table was full and Stephano, the barman, was busy filling orders for drinks and snacks. When Carter and Yves walked through the door a raucous chorus greeted them. Seated on the arm of a long low sofa was Maurice Canif. He was in obvious good humor this evening, for when he saw Carter he jumped up and did his "one foot, two foots" routine.

A distinguished looking gray haired gentleman rose and came towards Yves with hand extended. He greeted him effusively and Yves turned to introduce him to Carter. "I would like you to meet my good friend, Carter Martin. Carter, this is Monsieur Crozet, and seated there on the sofa looking ravissante as ever is his wife, Marie-Claire."

Crozet beamed and greeted Carter warmly. "Ah, l'américain!" he exclaimed. "I've heard all about you. Welcome to Crete! I'm Hervé Crozet and this is my wife, Marie-Claire," he said with a wave of his hand in the direction of the sofa.

Madame Crozet leaned forward and held out her hand to Carter. For an instant he considered kissing it, but decided it was not expected of him. Besides, he would feel awkward.

"Bon jour, monsieur," she said brightly. "J'imagine que vous parlez français, non?"

"Je vien de commençer, madame, mais je me débrouille un peu. Et vous, est-ce que vous parlez anglais?" asked Carter

Her husband, who stood with his hand on Carter's arm, now squeezed it and exclaimed in a hearty baritone, as smooth as fine cognac, "Bravo, an American who speaks French. But this is marvelous! Where did you learn your French?"

"This is my teacher," said Carter, indicating Yves standing next to him. "He has been an exacting taskmaster. Besides, living with Jean Paul, he insists I speak only French with him and those who stay with us. He told me I'll never have a better opportunity to learn and I agree with him. It's just difficult in the beginning because you're afraid everyone is going to laugh at you. Actually, only Canif makes fun of me."

Canif, who was following the conversation, leapt to his feet. "One foot, two foots!"

Crozet rolled his eyes, muttered con under his breath, and invited Yves and Carter to join them. Others already seated moved over to make room. Carter knew several of those present and they greeted him as he took a place. A young waiter picked up empty glasses from the low table as he took orders for another round of drinks.

On the small dance floor couples were packed so tightly there was only room for them to hold their partners in their arms and sway. The music was eclectic, going from Piaf's Non, Rien de Rien and Mon Joujou, to Enrico Macias' J'ai Quitté Mon Pays, to popular music by Greek composers, such as Theodorakis and Hadzidakis. When To Kaimos or Strosai to Stroma Sou played everyone joined in and sang along with the familiar words of the melodic and haunting refrains.

Periodically newcomers joined them at their table while others left. Acquaintances stopped by to say hello, then found a table elsewhere. Carter felt very much at home in the ambiance of the bar, surrounded by friends who were interesting and congenial. He was accepted by them all, casual tourist and expatriate alike, which gave him a satisfying feeling of belonging.

It was almost midnight when Yves, sitting opposite Carter, waved to someone and got up from his seat. Turning to look over his shoulder, he saw Evgenia standing alone in the doorway. She smiled and advanced to meet Yves, who again kissed her hand and led her to where the others were seated. Carter stood up, delighted to see her. She smiled warmly as soon as she recognized him in the gloom of the candle-lit club. She held out her hand to him and he took it, remarking on the cool smoothness of her skin. The gentle pressure of her fingers pleased him. He could not remember ever being so taken with anyone. Yves stood looking at them, a bemused smile on his lips.

Taking her by the arm, Carter led her to the table and introduced her to everyone seated there. He could tell immediately Crozet was interested in her, for he leapt to his feet to greet her and kiss her hand. From her place on the sofa, Marie-Claire gave her an appraising look and smiled warmly when introduced. In a well-modulated and refined voice Evgenia apologized for not being able to speak French. This revelation did not bother Carter in the least. It meant he would have her virtually to himself. Manoli, the young, self-proclaimed Communist, who sat next to Carter, moved over as far as he could to allow room for Evgenia to join them.

Because of the language difficulty they immediately fell into a conversation between themselves that excluded the others. He half expected Canif to launch into his normal routine, but Maurice was too deeply involved with a slim German woman seated next to him. Evgenia talked of Boston and her reason for coming to Crete. She told Carter she was born and raised in Aghios Nikolaos and how she met her husband while in school in London a few years before. Her husband did not care for Greece, she said, and therefore rarely ever came back with her. Almost everyone in her immediate family was either dead or now lived in America. Her aunt was the only close relative still on the island. The hotel once belonged to her father and was left to Evgenia following his death.

They talked over drinks, learning about one another. Evgenia expressed her admiration of the fact that Carter simply pulled up stakes and moved to Crete. That he taught English to young Cretan scholars was a surprise to her. As they talked she maintained constant eye contact. She seemed to draw him to her, such was the intensity of her gaze. They spoke of Yves' having approached her and her aunt and both laughed when Carter mentioned his embarrassment.

"Never mind," she said softly, "I was glad he did it. Especially now."

A particularly pretty song began to play and in unison Carter and Evgenia said, "Let's dance." They got to their feet and made their way to the small dance floor, which, in spite of the late hour, was still crowded. He took her hand in his as they walked among the tables and when they finally were able to squeeze into an open space, he put his right hand on her waist and held out his left to her. Without hesitation she moved into his arms and nestled her cheek against his. The sweet smell of her perfume was enticing and made him want to nuzzle her ear and neck beneath her hair, which lay soft against his face. She fit her body close against his and the touch of her firm thighs against his and the pressure of her breasts against his chest warmed him. He was enchanted listening to her hum along with the music, but was most surprised when her hand, which was on his shoulder, crept to his neck. He was mesmerized by her gentle caress as she lightly ran her fingers through the hair at his nape. He responded by slightly increasing the pressure of his arm around her waist, pulling her even closer.

Across the room he could see Yves watching them, the same expression on his face he saw at dinner. Carter wore a pair of tight, white jeans and he noticed Yves' eyes were not watching their faces, but were fixed on a point somewhat lower. Evgenia's closeness aroused him, but Carter was unaware his excitement was evident to anyone else. Pulling back slightly to look her in the face, he glanced down between them and was appalled to see the very evident bulge along the front of his left thigh. There was no hiding it. Yves' stare was fixed upon it, although no one else seemed to have noticed. Carter shrugged inwardly, moved back close to Evgenia, and finished the dance, hoping the next one would be slow, as well. He realized, however, that as long as they danced closely there would be no chance his erection would disappear. She had to be aware of its presence, but did nothing to move away from its insistent nudging.

When the music of the first record stopped he and Evgenia maintained their positions in each other's arms. The next record was a slow, languorous ballad. He asked that they not return to the table yet and she put her soft lips against his ear to murmur her agreement. As the music continued they swayed in rhythm to its slow beat, barely moving their feet. Her hand tightened on the back of his neck. After a moment, as if by mutual agreement, they pulled back slightly from one another, and he found himself looking into her eyes. Her lids were half closed and a look of utter contentment dominated her face. She did not avert her face in the slightest when he kissed her fleetingly on the corner of the mouth. Her response was a soft moan and a sigh. She rolled her head back on her shoulders, which gave him an unobstructed view of the silken skin of her neck. A satisfied smile played across her lips.

He told her of admiring her mouth from afar while eating dinner; how he had wondered how her lips would feel and taste and of his desire to trace them with his fingers. Her response was to grasp him firmly by the back of the head and pull him to her once more. She turned her head slightly and he could feel her lips against his skin at the joint of his neck and shoulder. Her nails dug into the back of his head, as she grasped a handful of hair. He shifted slightly and her movement at the juncture of her thighs and lower belly caressed his erection. Neither seemed aware when the music stopped.

The floor was virtually empty when he finally took her hand and led her back to the table. Yves had just risen and was telling everyone good night. Several of the others had already left as the club was beginning to clear. Evgenia said that she, too, must go and Carter announced he would walk her back to her hotel.

Carter thanked Yves in French for his intervention.

"Ah, yes, I can see you are pleased. Are you satisfied with her? Does she live up to your imaginings of how she would be?"

"Certainly seems that way. I still don't know how you did it, but, believe me, I do appreciate it."

Yves smiled, then turned and went out the door. Carter and Evgenia left soon afterwards. As soon as they were outside, she moved into the circle of his arm, put her free hand on his biceps, and lay her head momentarily on his shoulder.

"My hotel is on the other side of the park and up that small street to the left. The shortest way is to cross the middle of the park here. This walkway comes out near the street we need to take."

Carter said nothing as he led her along the tree-lined walkway. It was almost two A.M. and the park was deserted. He did not want to spoil the moment by talking. Instead, he reveled in her warmth and the action of her long, supple fingers caressing his arm. When they arrived in front of the hotel she pulled away from him grudgingly and fluffed her hair with her fingers. They walked up the steps in front of the hotel and, before entering the lobby, Evgenia turned to him and asked, "Would you like to come up to my suite for a drink or a cup of coffee?"

"Love to."

When they entered the lobby Evgenia strode purposefully ahead of Carter. The only person present was the night clerk. He greeted Evgenia obsequiously and then cast a quick disapproving glance in Carter's direction. Carter stared directly at him, not caring what he thought. She gave the clerk instructions in Greek and he moved quickly away from the front desk and disappeared into a door in the paneling, which obviously led to an office. As soon as he was gone, they walked into the open elevator. She pushed the button for the sixth floor and they began to glide upward.

When the elevator door opened she preceded him into the corridor, stopping in front of a door at the end, inserted the key into the lock and pushed it open. From inside a soft light spilled into the corridor. She stood aside and Carter entered, walking down the short entrance hall. A large bed against one wall was scattered with discarded clothes and other accoutrements belying the fact this was a woman's room. Two double sliding glass doors led to separate balconies, on which he could see numerous plants growing. On one of the balconies were a white wrought iron, glass-topped table and two chairs. To his right, on one side of the bed, a door led to a small kitchen. On the other, a door led to a sitting room. Although unable to see clearly into the sitting room, he did notice another sliding glass door leading to yet another balcony. When he commented on the size of the two rooms and kitchen, Evgenia replied simply, "Owner's suite."

His perusal took but a moment. He still stood, hands clasped behind his back, facing away from the entry hall, when he heard the click of the shutting door. The sound of whispering footsteps behind him were a prelude to soft arms slipping between his arms and his body and encircling his waist. He tensed involuntarily as warm lips touched the back of his neck. Her body pressed against his, her lower belly against his open palms. Hands pulled his shirt from the waistband of his pants and her right hand, inserted under the shirt, raked long nails from the rigid flatness of his belly to the muscles of his chest, flicking tantalizingly and maddeningly over the sensitive flesh.

An intake of breath left a gap between his stomach and the top of his jeans. Her left hand, lightly resting on his bare navel, insinuated itself into the opening and her insistent fingers followed the trail of soft, curly hair down, down, down. He held his breath, his attention centered on her hand, unable and unwilling to move. First one fingertip, then another, reached the object of their quest, each caressing the exquisitely sensitive skin of the tip and then the heavy veins from tip to base, through which pulsed the blood that maintained his almost-painful erection.

Her right hand moved from his nipples to trace slowly and sensuously over his ribs, under his arm, to his back. She slid her palm and nails up the ridge of his spine, pushing up his shirt as she progressed. Her lips left the nape of his neck and kissed him gently between his shoulder blades. Tongue replaced lips, its firm, wet tip tasting, exploring. Her body undulated in a slow, sensuous, insistent dance against his open palms.

For the first time Carter experienced the heat, the wanton abandon of such refined concupiscence. His whole being was inflamed, aflame, nerve endings vibrating, fanning the fire, which threatened to consume them both. No longer able to hold his breath, he exhaled explosively, trapping her arm against his stomach. The increased pressure caused the metal snap to release and the heavy zipper to descend as if of its own accord. He turned to take her in his arms and her hands slipped to the muscles of his buttocks. She clutched him convulsively with her strong fingers, pulling him tightly against her rhythmically moving body. Her mouth, raised to his, opened and hungrily accepted his tongue deep inside, feinting, sparring, clashing with her own. She began to moan softly, unconsciously and her breathing became heavier and ever more rapid.

Without taking his mouth from hers, he bent his knees slightly and swept her into his arms. One shoe remained on the floor, the other dangled loosely from her toes. He turned and advanced with firm steps toward the bed scattered with clothes she tried on and discarded before going out that evening. He reached the bed and sat on the edge of it with her still in his arms. Even before breaking their kiss she began to pull at his shirt with frantic hands, trying to rid him of it. His hands were busy unfastening the long line of buttons on the back of her dress. He raised his arms and she yanked his shirt over his head and flung it to the floor. At the same time he pushed his topsiders off his bare feet with his toes. She freed herself from his arms and scrambled on her knees across the bed, lifting her dress as she moved. Once over her head, she discarded it in a crumpled heap in the direction of one of the glass double doors. Her eyes were dark pools reflecting intense desire. Her hands went to the hooks between the cups of her filmy, semitransparent bra.

Carter rolled back on the bed, pushed his jeans and underwear from his hips to his knees, before kicking them off. He never took his eyes from her as he watched her open her bra and shrug it from her shoulders. She ran both hands beneath her breasts, over her dark nipples to her chest, caressed the column of her neck and then through her hair on either side of her head. She ended with her arms stretched high in the air, her fingers extended and rigidly spread, her head thrown back and her mouth open in a silent scream. Her breasts stood firm and proudly bare before his gaze, the nipples erect and swollen. From where he lay on the bed, he reached out a hand and touched her flat stomach, then trailed his fingertips along the underside of the breast nearest him until he reached its tip. With one finger he traced its outline and caressed the pebbly skin of her turgid nipple. At his touch, she dropped her arms and clasped his hand tightly to her breast with both of hers.

He rolled slightly toward her and extended his tongue to flick it over the skin of her stomach around the cup of her navel. From there his tongue trailed down toward the ultra-feminine briefs she still wore. Releasing his hand, she inserted her thumbs into the waistband and, rising to her knees, pushed them down off her hips. His tongue continued its downward path, teasing, touching lightly, then moving away. She was transfixed before the delight of his questing tongue, every nerve ending tingling with the electricity of anticipation.

She was open to him, bedewed, inviting and welcoming his touch. When it came she collapsed on top of him, as if suddenly her finely toned muscles and sinews had turned to jelly and would no longer support the weight of her body. Grasping at the backs of his thighs with her hands, she engulfed him with her mouth, kissing him deeply as he kissed her. He slid his hands along her long smooth legs, pushed her lacy briefs over her knees and calves and off of one foot. There they dangled from one ankle, completely forgotten.

With a fluid motion that caught him unaware, she raised herself from his grasp and he saw her once more beside him on her knees. Before he could question what was happening, she lifted one bronzed leg over his body and, taking his penis in both hands, guided him to where just moments before his lips and tongue had driven her to distraction. Once impaled, she slid down onto him with a keening cry of ecstasy, her head thrown back, her eyes closed, her mouth wide in the intensity of the moment.

He reached up with both hands to caress her breasts before he pulled her down onto his chest. Their mouths locked upon each other as they fell into the rhythm that would bring them to the peak. Both cried out as they came almost simultaneously, her hands clutching at his back, his pressing down on her shoulders. After a breathless moment they began the long, sliding descent.

For the next hour they lay on the rumpled bed, their legs entwined, talking softly, touching, laughing contentedly, and reveling in the satisfaction they both felt and appreciated. Once more, near dawn they made love, sweetly, slowly, with great feeling and care. Then, as the sun crept out of the sea, Carter arose, picked up his scattered clothes and put them on. Once dressed, he leaned over and kissed the shoulder of the sleeping Evgenia before pulling the sheet gently over her, then slipped out the door, closing it quietly behind him.

Chapter 18

The city was just beginning to stir as Carter made his way back across the park and through the dusty streets. He took a seat on a cane-bottomed chair outside a small cafe where he wolfed down pastries fresh out of the oven with two Turkish coffees. When he finished he continued through the nearly empty streets to where he parked the car the previous evening. It was covered with a mixture of the early morning dew and dust, making him glad he put the top up before going off to have dinner with Yves.

On the drive to Aghi Vasili he thought of Evgenia. She told him as they talked after having made love the first time that she would be leaving for Athens on today's noon flight. She spent two weeks on Crete, a week longer than originally planned, so it was only through a splendid quirk of fate that they were allowed the time together the previous evening. He offered to take her to the airport, but her aunt planned to pick her up and would escort her herself. Carter was disappointed when she told him she could not say when she would return. These trips were becoming increasingly rare, now that the business of her hotel was running smoothly. When she did come again, she was certain her husband would not be coming with her. She promised she would write to him beforehand in care of the institute.

Carter felt himself sinking in spite of the rich pastries and coffee. Through bleary eyes he peered at the road ahead, wishing he were already in bed. The early morning breeze was cool and huge, fluffy clouds drifted across the sky. When he arrived at the house he drove right into the courtyard, not having closed the gate the night before. To avoid making too much noise, he cut the engine and coasted onto the paving stones.

The villa was quiet, meaning Christine was probably still asleep. In the shower room he found his toothbrush and a crumpled tube of toothpaste, turned on the shower and brushed his teeth while standing under the cold spray from the overhead nozzle. He thought about the coming winter and wondered how he would find the courage to shower. With no heat in the shower room and only cold water for bathing, it could prove to be quite an ordeal. At least the climate was temperate. After rinsing the soap from his body, he put his pants back on without drying off and walked out into the courtyard.

The sun was just rising and the birds were busy in the pine trees. Cicadas sang their endless song of summer and, from somewhere nearby, a rooster crowed. He stood drinking in the freshness of the morning before going back into the house to make his way carefully up the creaking wooden staircase to the second floor. At the landing he eased open the narrow double doors leading into Christine's room and stuck his head inside. Her face was turned away from the door and her tousled blond hair spilled across her pillow. Assuming she was still asleep he closed the door quietly and tiptoed across the hall to his own room.

His bed looked enormously inviting. Muscles ached and there were still faint red marks on his chest where Evgenia pulled her nails across his skin. His body retained the tingle and afterglow that made him wonder if it was from the intensity of their lovemaking or the cold of the shower. He smiled to himself, remembering, as he passed through the open door leading to the rooftop terrace and walked into the dappled sunlight.

To the west rose Mount Ida, its towering peak gleaming with traces of old snow in the early morning sunlight. In a neighbor's yard chickens scratched at the bare earth and muttered to themselves. In the narrow cobbled lane running alongside the house, an old man scuffing the stones with worn soles of battered brogans three sizes too large trudged arthritically to keep some obscure rendezvous.

The glory of the morning, the beauty of his life here on Crete, reminded him of the opening lines of a poem he was required to memorize as a freshman in college. The opening line, he recalled, aptly expressed his feelings: "I saw this morning morning's kingdom dawn, drawn falcon..."

He flicked the butt of his cigarette away over the railing and watched it fall to the courtyard. As it hit the stones below it threw out a small shower of sparks then lay still, mortally wounded, its soul escaping upward in a thin column of smoke.

"The bleak blue embers fall, gall themselves, and gash, gold vermilion."

What the hell was the name of that poem? Something about the wind. 'The Windhover". That was it. He loved it, but these two lines were the only remnants of verse he could bring to mind. No matter. He was too tired now to even try to think of anything other than the bed he knew awaited him. He stepped back into his room, kicked his pants off in the general direction of the chair in the corner and fell into bed. Within seconds he was sound asleep.

From the depths of sleep he was vaguely aware of his bed's shaking. It also seemed as if the mattress sloped from the head down to the foot. The feeling of being slightly out of balance interfered with and intruded upon his well-being. It bothered him, nagged and brought him closer and closer to wakefulness. He lay on his back with his arm thrown across his eyes. His mouth felt like leather, as he probed here and there with swollen tongue, looking for a bit of moisture to relieve the awful dryness. Another movement of the bed awakened him even more and he became aware of feeling uncomfortably warm under the single sheet. Without opening his eyes he tried to throw it off, but it was wrapped around one leg and wedged underneath his body. He struggled with it a moment before finally succeeding in kicking it away.

The breeze from the terrace stirring across his naked body was pleasant and he started to drift off once more. Again the bed moved and he raised his head with difficulty and opened one eye just a slit. Someone sat on the foot of his bed! Once more he raised his head, this time opening both eyes and squinting against the light. He was having great difficulty focusing on whoever was seated there.

"Salut!" came a cheery voice. "Are you planning to sleep all day? What time did you come home last night?"

This time he sat bolt upright, his eyes wide and staring. "Christine! Merde! What are you doing in here? What time is it?"

"Oh, I don't know," she replied coquettishly. "I thought I would come in and take pictures of this nude man I found."

"Nude man?" He stopped, looked down at himself, and reached for the sheet. Laughing, Christine held her coffee cup out over the floor while pulling the sheet just out of reach of his fingertips. He was forced to scramble after it, jerk it out of her hand and pull it back over himself. By this time Christine was laughing so hard the coffee sloshed out of her cup and onto the sheets and the floor.

"Are we even now?" she giggled. "This is what happens to those who sneak up on a lady in her shower. I certainly hope you've learned your lesson! Here," she said, getting up from the bed to retrieve a steaming cup of coffee from the windowsill. "I woke up a little while ago and made coffee. Thought you might like some."

Carter took the proffered cup and leaned back against the wall at the head of his bed. "Thanks. What time is it?"

"Almost 11:30. What time did you get home last night? I didn't hear a thing."

"Last night? You mean this morning. As a matter of fact, I got here about five thirty, took a shower, looked in on you, went out on the terrace and fell into bed around six. I've been sound asleep since then, although I feel like it's been only about five minutes. Hm-m. This coffee tastes good. Where'd you get it?"

"Tunis. Brought it back with me. I thought those cretins in customs were going to confiscate it from me."

"Cretans? Where did you have to go through customs on Crete? Customs is in Athens."

"Idiot!" laughed Christine. "Drink your coffee and wake up. I said cretins, not Cretans! Cre-tins, Cre-tins! Do you understand now?"

"Oh, cretins. Sorry. I was momentarily confused."

"Yes," she agreed with a shake of her head, "it's sometimes difficult to differentiate the two. So! You came in at 5:30 this morning. What kept you out so late?"

Carter told her of meeting Yves and Guy for dinner. She howled with laughter when he recounted how Yves accosted Evgenia and her aunt and his own discomfiture. He told her of going to the club, meeting the Crozets and of Evgenia's joining them.

"Crozet? The first summer I met Hervé he almost drove me crazy. Every time he came near me he found some excuse to put his hand on my bottom. Eventually, any time he was around I either tried to stand with my back against a wall or find protection by staying close to his wife. Then I discovered Marie-Claire was just as interested in my bottom as he was. I asked Jean Paul to say something to him, but he just laughed. Anyway, tell me about this Evgenia."

She sat silently while he told her of their evening at the club. When he finished she sat quietly for a moment, staring at the dregs of coffee he swirled absentmindedly around the bottom of his cup. "Well? Is that all? You were out until 5:30 this morning! What did you do between the time you left the club and the time you came home?"

"Nothing. Talked."

"Are you going to see her again?"

"Sais pas. Well, maybe I'll see her again sometime, but I don't know when. She's leaving for New York tonight and doesn't know when she'll be back. I've never known anyone like her. As I told you, she's married and, besides, I'm not sure what sort of relationship I would want with someone like her. She looks like an angel, though. I wish you could have seen the look on Yves' face when we were dancing. I thought his eyes were going to fall out of his head."

"Poor Yves, he does like boys," she agreed. "He's also a very good maquereau, isn't he?"

"Maquereau? Without a doubt. The smoothest pimp I have ever seen."

He glanced at his watch before leaping from the bed. "I'm sorry, but I just remembered I have a meeting at the English Institute at one this afternoon. I have a new job, by the way. I'll tell you about it later. Thanks for the coffee. I still want to hear about Tunisia. Are you going to be here tonight? If so, let's have dinner together and then come home early. What I really mean is, you can stay out if you like, but I want to come home and get some sleep."

"That sounds wonderful. What time will you be back?

He threw on his clothes as he talked. "Probably about six. Let's plan to leave about seven. That way we'll get into town before the worst of the crowds."

As he rushed down the stairs she called after him, "See you at six! I'll get a bottle of wine and we'll drink it before dinner. I'll tell you about Tunisia then. Also, you can tell me about your work." From the upper landing she walked back into his room and out onto the terrace, just in time to wave as he pulled out of the courtyard and drove away.

Vasilia was putting the finishing touches on a letter in her typewriter when he arrived at the Institute. Classes were generally scheduled to begin early in the morning so as to finish by noon and avoid the afternoon heat. In the evenings there were sometimes classes given for adults, which were well-attended. Carter's footsteps echoed on the wooden stairs and, by the time he entered Bunny's office he found him standing over his desk putting a twist of lemon in a well-iced glass of gin and gazoza.

"Top o' the mornin' to ye, boyo!" he boomed, his voice echoing down the bare corridor. "I thought I recognized the pitter patter of yer little footsteps. Right on time. Here, see if this will fit your hand," he said, offering the sweating glass to Carter.

"Hello, Bunny. Thanks. This should hit the spot." He took a swig of the refreshing drink and pulled a chair up to the front of the desk. "Well, how's your tí kánis this afternoon?" asked Carter with a mischievous grin on his face.

"My WHAT!? My tí kánis?!? What in the world do you mean?"

"You know how the Greeks see someone they know and greet them with kalispéra or tí kánis, good evening or how are you, or whatever? As you know, the answer is always, Kalá, efcharistó. Kaí eseis? Fine, thank you. And you? To which the person who started this whole thing responds, kalá, good, good, with much mutual bobbing of their heads. Then they go on their merry way, to repeat this same ritual ad nauseum. It's a formula and it happens to be an integral part of the evening vólta."

"Yes, yes, go on," Bunny urged.

"The other night Jean Paul and I were walking through the park at the height of the vólta when we noticed two young Americans ahead of us. One of them walked with his hands clasped behind his back in the standard attitude and the other slipped his arm through his companion's, just as the Greeks do. Everyone they greeted bobbed their heads, smiled and said Kalá. However, a few paces further on most of them would stop, look back at the two with a puzzled look on their faces, shake their heads and then continue on their way. The proverbial double-take. Intrigued, we moved up closer to them to be able to hear what they were saying. Each time they greeted someone it was always the same: "How's your tí kánis?"

Bunny's laughter echoed through the empty building. "My word! Now that's clever!" he exclaimed, tears of mirth running down his pink cheeks. 'How's your tí kánis?' Who would have ever thought...?"

"Once we even heard them ask two men walking along arm in arm, "How's your tí kánis hanging?"

Howling with laughter, the supposedly staid headmaster clapped his hands and whirled around in his swivel chair. "How rude!" he guffawed. "And how perfectly delightful! Leave it to you Yanks to come up with something like that. How's your tí kánis? Kalá. Kalá."

Carter glanced up and saw Vasilia pass by the doorway, a questioning look on her face. Bunny laid his head on his arm and, with the other, pounded the wooden desktop. She must certainly think we're crazy, mused Carter. He was sure she would not understand, for when he recently told Manoli of the incident the humor of it escaped him completely. Carter realized early on that something knee-slappingly funny in one language often fizzled and died in translation, and usually lacked any meaning at all.

Bunny sat back, swiped at his eyes with the back of his hand and took a drink from his glass. "Well, my friend, let's get down to business. I'm sure you have other things to do this afternoon and I want to get out of here too."

For the next half-hour they went over lesson plans together, working out a strategy designed to challenge their young pupils' entry into the world of the English language.

Finished at last, Bunny stood up and thanked Carter for meeting with him. "You know, you're doing a marvelous job," he complimented. "We've heard from several parents that their children are coming home with glowing accounts of Daskalocarter. You're to be commended. I hear from the staff that your Greek is improving each day, as well. That's good! If you like, we'll soon be able to give you more advanced classes. Those are really the ones that are much more interesting. Thanks, too, for assisting some of the other teachers with their English. They all have an adequate command of the language, but, as you know, there are some niceties that may take years to learn and understand, unless one is a native speaker. It's a welcome change to have the influence of American English to compliment the Queen's own. Well, see you on Monday. Thanks again for coming in."

When he was once more on the street he turned in the direction of the square and headed for the Daskaloyanni's pension. For over two weeks he was too occupied to visit them and in the past few days they were on his mind. He valued their friendship and did not want to lose contact. He spent almost an hour there before driving back to Aghi Vasili. He found Christine in the courtyard holding two envelopes in her hand. "Who're the letters for?"

"One is for you. From America."

He recognized his mother's handwriting and, as he started to tear it open, asked who the other was for.

"Jean Paul. The postmark is the 16th Arrondissement in Paris. I think I know who it's from. If it's who I think it is, you're going to be having some company soon. If it's who I think it is, she's going to love you," she smirked.

"Oh? Why?"

"You'll see."

Chapter 19

Intense afternoon sun hammered the south coast. Outside of town, on the baked soil of the fields, the heat was not so intolerable and a breeze occasionally stirred the green and silver leaves of the dusty olive trees. The low rooftops of Khora Sfakion shimmered in the heat. From the doorsteps of the town the azure expanse of the Mediterranean swept uninterrupted, except for the islands of Gavdhos and its smaller neighbor, Gavdhopoula, toward the horizon and the unseen shores of Libya.

In his perivóli, his garden plot, cloaked in dust, Stavros Petrides guided his all-purpose mechanical tiller down the rows. Before driving from home to the fields that morning he hitched a small trailer to the ubiquitous mikaní, mechanized agricultural implement, a two-wheeled tiller-tractor, and principal mode of transportation in rural areas. Into the trailer he carefully placed a bundle, along with his hand tools, lunch and a jug of water. Among the remnants of already harvested crops he turned under dry and desiccated stubble, attempting to loosen the compacted soil in preparation for late summer planting. He wanted to be ready when the fall and winter rains began. On another nearby plot inherited from his father grew a crop of tomatoes ripening quickly in the sun. This would be his second tomato harvest of the year. Normally either his wife or one of his sons worked with him, following closely behind with a mattock-like tool, breaking up any stubborn clods he might have missed, but today he was by himself. He felt more alone than any other time in his life. He tried hard to concentrate on the work at hand, but found it to be an almost impossible task. Periodically he threw furtive glances over his shoulder at the other fields bordering his own, wondering when and where he would appear.

Hidden inside the top of his boot was a knife. Its presence was far from reassuring, however, for he was aware of the reputation of his adversary, knew of his cunning and ruthlessness. He wondered if he would have the ability, or the time, to reach into the top of his boot to grab his weapon and strike.

That morning, when he secreted it there, he was full of confidence, ready to defend what was his. At first, the handle pressing against his shin and ankle was merely annoying. As time wore on, however, and the sweat began to roll down his body and dirt accumulated inside his boot, the handle formed a pressure sore. By the end of the morning the spot throbbed with annoying persistence. He wanted to remove it, but dared not. Who knew who could be watching him or for how long. Now, alone in his field without the reassuring presence of his family and friends, he was not so sure of himself. Anxiety grew, causing his stomach to churn like the rapidly spinning blades of the tiller.

At noon he stopped for the midday meal his wife prepared for him. Although not hungry, he forced himself to eat, but the bread and olives stuck in his throat, almost gagging him, and the wine tasted like vinegar. He finally wrapped the remains in a cloth and settled down under an olive tree, his back resting against its gnarled trunk. His eyes darted here and there trying to pick up movement. His ears pricked at each sound, each rustle in the grass. When after an hour no one appeared he began to wonder if he was being tested. Growing more and more nervous by the minute he finally stood and went back to work.

Stavros came to the end of a row he was tilling, where he was forced to stop by the stones piled there to form a wall between his field and the next. He thought he detected movement out of the corner of his eye and turned to face the olive tree under which he ate his lunch. Looking now he decided his imagination was playing tricks on him. He stood in the piercingly bright sunshine, shielded his eyes with his hand and looked again. Nothing seemed unusual. He started to turn back to his tiller when a dark shadow moved away from the trunk of a tree and stood in silhouette, unmoving, facing him. The still form looked huge and menacing. So dry was his throat from the fear that engulfed him that Stavros could barely swallow. His mouth dropped open, then closed again like a trap and a name formed silently on his parched lips: Pseramanoli.

Without taking his eyes from the figure under the trees, Stavros reached around the long handle and shut off the tiller's roaring motor. It slowed, coughed and stopped, its din replaced by crushing silence. Nervously he wiped the back of his hand across his dry mouth and began to walk across the tilled earth, trying not to limp. Barba Yorgi awaited him, his wrists crossed and resting on the top of his staff, his face impassive, his eyes watchful under bushy white eyebrows.

"Chéretai, kyrie Stavros," came his rumbling greeting. "Good to see you. Come, have a seat under this tree. It's time to talk."

The night before, while eating dinner with his wife and children in the communal room of their house, a knock came at the front door. His wife directed one of the older boys to see who was there. The boy rose from his place and left the room, but was gone for only a moment before he returned. Stavros looked up from his plate, his mouth crammed with food, his spoon poised, a questioning look on his face.

"Someone asking for Kyrie Petrides. A boy. Not from our village."

"What's his name?" Asked Stavros, chewing vigorously as he questioned his son.

"He didn't say, Papa."

"What does he want?"

"I don't know, Papa. He only asked if he could speak to you. He says he has a message for you from an old friend."

"Well, invite him to come inside. Who would be sending a message to....?"

He stopped in mid-sentence and the children at the table looked up at him. His wife came back into the room and asked the boy still standing by his father's chair who was at the door. Before he could answer, Stavros pushed himself back from the table and stood up, causing his chair to fall over and clatter on the bare cement floor.

"Sit down, boy," he ordered his son. "I'll go see about this."

His wife watched him as he left the room, then shrugged her shoulders and sat down in her chair. She took the youngest from her nine-year-old daughter and plopped him onto her own lap. She dug a piece out of the soft interior of a hunk of bread lying on the rough tabletop, dipped it into the juices on her plate, and held it before the face of the child. Like a small bird he opened his mouth wide and accepted the morsel, smacking his lips and nearly toothless gums. When his mother turned her attention to her own plate he reached out with chubby fingers, picked up a spoon lying within his reach and banged it clumsily on the edge of the table. An awkward backswing caused him to smack himself in the forehead. The blow surprised him and he dropped the spoon to the floor. A whimper escaped his lips and he held out his hand in the direction of the spoon. Immediately his big sister reached down to pick it up and handed it back to him.

Stavros walked slowly back into the room, a folded and smudged piece of lined paper in his hand. On the outside was written his family name, Petrides. When he reached the door there was no one there. He went out onto the top step, looked about but saw no one in the fast-fading light. As he stepped back into the house he happened to glance down and saw the folded sheet of paper lying on the floor where someone slid it through the gap under the heavy wooden door. He stooped to pick it up, a feeling of dread coming over him. He stood there a moment, wanting to unfold it, but he could only stare at it dully as he walked back to rejoin his family at the table.

His wife, Popi, saw the strange look on his face and questioned him about the paper he carried.

"Oh, this. It's nothing. Nothing," he replied haltingly.

"What does it say and who sent it to you? Where's the boy that brought it?" she insisted.

"Típote, I said! It's nothing!"

Popi saw the expression on his face and knew she would gain nothing by further insistence. Turning to the children she addressed them as a group. "You've all finished eating, I see. Fine! Pick up your plates and put them in a stack on the counter. Marika, take your brother, wash his face and then put him to bed. All of you, in bed now. It's getting late. Your father and I are going to have some coffee and then we'll go to bed as well."

Without a word of protest, the children left the table and did as their mother asked. Marika took charge of her baby brother, lifting him from his mother's lap, kissing him playfully on the neck and stomach as she carried him out of the room. His giggles and squeals could be heard as she shut the door of the room where they all slept. Before she went to bed Popi would gently retrieve him from his sister's bed and take him into the room where she and Stavros slept.

Stavros sat down and laid the folded paper on the table in front of him. He put his elbows on either side of it, laced his fingers together and rested his chin on the backs of his fingers as he stared into space.

Popi rose from the table and busied herself with the preparation of coffee. She turned her back to where Stavros was seated in order to watch the dark, bubbling brew, carefully poured it into small cups and picked up one in each hand before returning to the table. She set the cups down and went to fetch a bottle of raki from the shelf, along with a small glass, which she placed in front of her husband. He poured until the glass was filled to the brim, then picked it up, silently saluted his wife and downed it in a gulp.

"So," began Popi, "what does it say?"

"How should I know?" he replied testily. "I haven't opened it yet."

"But why are you waiting and why are you so upset? I thought it was a message from an old friend."

"An old friend!" answered Stavros, rolling his eyes and throwing both hands into the air. "If it's what I think it is, the person is old, but he's not a friend. Ah, well, the news won't get any better by letting it sit here." Saying this he unfolded the paper with reluctant hands.

The short message, written in big clumsy letters, contained but brief instructions. Tomorrow, midday, in your family garden plot on the Skaloti road. Tell no one. Come alone, bring everything. Pseramanolis. When he finished reading Stavros continued to stare at the paper, his eyes no longer focused on the words written there. There was no one to turn to for help, no alternative but to do as he was directed. With a sigh he refolded the paper and shoved it across the crumb-strewn tabletop to his wife.

Popi picked it up, unfolded it, scanned the words written on it, and then looked questioningly at her husband, who sat fingering his komboloi, his worry beads. "Is this the Barba Yorgi you told me about?"

"Yes, this is the one."

"What are you going to do?"

"What am I going to do? I'll tell you what I'm going to do. I'm going to do exactly as he says. I have no choice. I don't even have time to contact Zakari like he told us to do. For all I know, that old man is sitting outside my house right now, making sure I don't try to contact anyone. He knows I can't go to the police and he's not afraid of anyone else. Did you notice? He even signed his name."

Stavros rose from the table with another huge sigh and looked down at Popi. "Well, we have no choice. Help me gather the things together and we'll make a bundle. I'll take them with me on the mikaní tomorrow. As soon as he leaves I'll find Zakari. Maybe he'll know what to do."

They slipped out the back of the house to a small shed and carefully disinterred the pieces from the ground. When they were wrapped individually and placed in a stout wooden box for safekeeping, they put the box in their room and retired for the night. Stavros was emotionally drained, as well as physically tired from his day in the fields. He thought he would fall asleep quickly, but his eyes would not stay shut. He lay staring in the direction of the dark ceiling until the early hours of the morning. When the first rays of dawn peeked through his window he was surprised to find he slept at all.

Stavros met Barba Yorgi as directed. He did not greet the man, afraid his trembling voice would reveal his fear. But as he approached the tree he was unable to take his eyes from the forceful presence standing before him.

"You have everything with you?"

Stavros merely nodded his head.

"Good," he said with a smile. "If they're in that box on the wagon you can bring them over here under this tree. Don't worry, my friend. I appreciate your finding these things and keeping them safe. I don't intend to take everything from you. Oh, no! Not at all. I just think you should share with those who are less fortunate than you. What are a few trinkets between friends, huh?"

Barba Yorgi's attitude was like a slap in the face to Stavros, and growing anger threatened to overcome his fear. Who did this old man think he was? He was nothing more than a common thief, taking something that did not belong to him. Stavros' right hand began to creep toward his boot. If he could just pull out the knife quickly enough perhaps he would be able to use it in an unguarded moment. The old man's eyes caught the stealthy movement, however, and as he continued to talk, he removed the end of his staff from the ground and now stood holding it parallel to the ground in front of him. Stavros stopped as soon as he saw his adversary's new stance.

"Now, now, Stavrolaki," he said, using the diminutive of Stavros' name as one would with a child. "Why don't you just go ahead and bring the box over and we'll see what you have in there. I noticed you limping earlier and just now saw you moving your hand toward your boot. Did you hurt yourself?" he asked innocently. "I'm sure you were just going to rub your leg. Isn't that right? If your leg is hurting you so badly, why, I suppose I can help you carry the box. So, come. Let's end all this unpleasantness, my friend."

Stavros saw his only choice was to comply. The old man was too suspicious and too crafty by far. He pushed himself to his feet and then limped toward the box, his head hanging in resignation and defeat. With slow movements he dragged it to him and lifted it. It weighed heavily on his arms as he made his way back to the tree under the watchful eyes of Barba Yorgi. After setting it down as gently as possible, he gestured to the old man with his hand.

"No, no, my son. Please. You may do the honors. I'll just stand here and watch so as not to get in your way."

Stavros removed all the items and placed them haphazardly in the soft dirt. The old man's eyes widened in appreciation as he moved closer. There was a total of thirteen pieces, ranging from vials and vases to a small bronze statue and two votive offerings. Barba Yorgi wasted no time in making his choice. Without hesitation he picked out the two ivory votive offerings, the bronze statue and a slender vial, which at one time probably was stoppered to hold unguents or other oils.

"I want to thank you for being so reasonable, Stavrolaki. See, I left the larger number of antíkas for you."

There was very little consolation in these words. Without speaking or further acknowledging Barba Yorgi's presence, Stavros knelt to replace the remaining pieces in the box, lifted it and carried it back to the trailer, then turned his back and walked to where his tiller stood idle in the field. After starting the motor he engaged the gears and walked behind it as the machine once more pounded and macerated the earth. He was numb, filled with anguish and performed the last two acts without raising his eyes. As he did so now he stopped and looked quickly left and right. Barba Yorgi was gone. It was as if he vanished like a genie returning to his bottle. Stavros advanced into the shade, continuing to look for evidence of the old man but could find none.

He finally hitched the tongue of the trailer to the tiller, sat on the wooden seat and drove away. As he moved along the rough dirt road he glanced back once more trying to see Pseramanolis, but there was nothing to indicate he was ever there. Nothing other than the fact that Stavros' treasure was only a little more than half of what he possessed when he left home that morning.

Chapter 20

Carter and Christine walked along the narrow streets of Aghi Vasili, taking full advantage of the sweetness of the late afternoon. She told him of her sojourn in Tunisia, elaborating on the styles of architecture and the living conditions encountered there. Along with Morocco, Tunisia enjoyed a relatively high standard of living. This was perhaps due to the difference in circumstances under which the two countries shed their respective yokes of French colonialism and was in direct contrast to the turmoil that continued in Algeria.

Algeria was an embittered country, its economy in ruins under the leadership of the former shepherd, Achmed ben Bella. Tunisia, on the other hand, enjoyed the benevolent guidance of Habib Bourguiba. Life in Tunisia was good, and a particular joy to the thousands of Frenchmen who either visited or still lived there. Christine regaled him with accounts of the food and sights, making Carter wish he could drop everything and take the next flight out.

She also told him of her childhood in Cambodia, where she lived most of the first twelve years of her life. Her father, a minor functionary in the colonial government, chose to live there as long as possible. Born in Pnom Penh in late 1940, the only time she left until she turned twelve was during the early war years, just prior to the Japanese sweep across the western Pacific. From 1940, right after her birth, until late 1944, when her family was finally able to return to Pnom Penh, they took sanctuary in the Seychelles, also a French colony.

Carter was fascinated by her recollections of growing up in French Indochina, of being fluent in Chinese, because of her Chinese amah that raised her practically as her own, and of speaking two dialects to perfection because of her Cambodian playmates. He could imagine how she stood out from her friends with her blonde hair and blue eyes. She recounted how the Cambodians loved her hair and how even adults would approach her to touch the silky golden tresses.

"But, enough about North Africa and the Orient! Tell me about the English Institute. I'm so glad you were able to find a job there. How are you getting along?"

"Fine. I love it. The director, Malcom Cruikshank, who you may have seen at the club, is a wonderful person to work with. He's a little like Canif in temperament, good sense of humor, loves to drink, has a nice little bachelor apartment in town. He seems to be much more outgoing than most Englishmen I've known. Now granted, I haven't known all that many, but still, I told him about something that happened the other night in the square and I thought he was going to choke from laughter."

"What are your students like? Are you enjoying them?"

"They're the best part. Bunny told me they're anxious to learn another language and English in particular."

"What ages do you teach?"

"Mostly early teens. Most of the ones I've taught until just recently were second or third year students. Bunny seems to think my Greek has progressed to a point where I can handle beginners, so last week he put me in charge of a class of five kids with no background in English at all. That was a hoot."

"How do you start with beginners?"

"With the alphabet. If they were Athenians I don't think I'd have any problems. There they speak a kind of 'High Demotik'. Here in Crete, however, you have the Cretan dialect. Not that it's not understandable. It's just that so many of their X's and K's, those following a vowel, come out sounding pretty much alike. That's where I encountered a problem teaching them the alphabet."

"What do you mean 'sound alike'?"

"Well, I don't know if you've noticed, but when they say 'no', óxi, they pronounce it 'oshee', with a very definite 'sh' sound. Actually, the correct sound is a little like an H, but really nothing like in English. On the other hand, with the K, as in kalokéri, summertime or beautiful weather, they say 'kalochairy'. See what I mean?

"Let me give you another example. Manoli, the fat shopkeeper in town, the one who sometimes comes to the club. You know the one I mean. He's always scratching his head and pushing his glasses back up on his nose? Well, he has a real problem with the English H. When he tries to say 'he' it always comes out 'she'."

"She!?"

"Yeah. The other day he told me about something Yves did and he kept referring to him as 'she'. 'She is going to the club. She is a fine man.' At first I corrected him, but a minute later he would forget and go right back to calling him 'she'. I finally gave up. If Yves ever hears him talking like that he's going to think he's making fun of his...what shall we call it...predilection?"

"I've heard them say 'oshee' before, but I didn't think about it. I haven't spent enough time in Athens to notice the difference. At least it's easier than the TH sound in English," she said with a laugh.

"I know. Or the French R for Americans. Jean Paul has a terrible time with the TH sounds. I've tried and tried to get him to think about it, but he gets involved in his conversations and all his TH's sound like Z or S."

"So, how did you get the correct pronunciation across to your students?"

"Most of the English alphabet was a breeze for them, because it's so much like the Greek. When we got to H, however, I really ran into a problem. I searched for a word to illustrate it, one they would all know. Well, the only word I could come up with was Hitler."

"Hitler?" she said with surprise.

"Transliteration. What I did was spell it out, using their X as an English H. 'Xi, Iota, Tau, Lambda, Epsilon, Rho'. I told them, 'It's pronounced HEETLER. Now, you try it'. They looked up at me with their bright eyes and their intense expressions and out came, 'SHEETLER'. It was all I could do to keep a straight face, Christine, but I made them pronounce it once more, and again it came out 'SHEETLER'. So, then I thought, if they pronounce it slower and with more care it'll come out right. Sure enough, when done slowly and with precision, I heard a close approximation of 'HEETLER'. I praised them and told them how wonderful they were and, that now, I wanted them to say it at the normal speed. Sure enough, there it was: 'SHEETLER'.

Between fits of giggles Christine asked, "They were saying Shitler? Shit, as in merde?"

"Exactly. I finally gave up and told them we'd work on it later and went on to something else. That day after class I happened to be walking out with my students and met one of the fathers coming to pick up his little girl. Of course, he asked me how she was doing and I told him the story about the alphabet and Shitler. He didn't get it at first, but then I told him about the English word 'shit' and he thought it was the most marvelous story he ever heard.

"'O Shitler. Naí, katalavéno. Skatá énai! You know the Greek word for shit is skatá. He understood, all right. The first thing he did was to tell all his friends about it. You also know how much they still hate the Germans, and particularly Hitler. The next day I ran into two more parents in the street and they both wanted to talk about O Shitler. The story was all over town in two days! They think Daskalocarter is the finest teacher they've ever met. Bunny told me he even received a call from one of the parents telling him the story."

Christine was still laughing when they walked through the gates into the courtyard. The sun was quite low now and hung just above the peaks to the west. A cooling sea breeze whispered through the pine boughs overhead, stirring the branches.

A voice from above stopped them dead in their tracks. "Oh! Les gamins! S'qui s'passe?"

Both Carter and Christine looked up and saw the figure of Jean Paul silhouetted against the fading sky. He was completely naked and leaned on the iron railing surrounding the terrace. "Come on up," he urged them, "I have something I want to show you."

"Non, ça va," said Christine. We don't need to come up. We can see it from here. But just barely."

"Don't be silly. Come on upstairs. Quickly. I'll be waiting for both of you. Then he disappeared into Carter's room.

"When do you suppose he got home?" asked Carter. "Come on. Let's go see what he has that's so important."

"Knowing him as I do, there's no telling what he has waiting for us up there." At Carter's continued urging she followed him into the house and mounted the stairs behind him.

The door to Carter's room was closed and no sound came from the other side. Carter pushed it open and strode inside, then immediately gave a shout of laughter. Christine followed close behind, intrigued to see what could be going on.

Lying on the bed was the still-naked Jean Paul, his legs stretched out and crossed at the ankles, his hands clasped firmly behind his head. On his crotch was a pile of green bills, obviously dollars, and between each toe were more dollars folded lengthwise. A long, thin cigar was clamped firmly between his teeth and an open bottle of Martell sat on the wooden crate Carter used as bedside table and bookcase. He was trying to look serious, but was having difficulty containing his mirth.

"What the hell...?" began Carter, but was unable to finish his sentence.

"Wait! Don't say anything yet. You haven't seen the best." So saying, he flipped over onto his stomach to disclose several more $100 bills sticking from between his buttocks like tail feathers. "Have you ever seen a green tailed rooster? Cocorico!" he crowed in his best imitation of a Gallic cock. He scooped up the handful of bills and tossed them gleefully into the air. Ben Franklin stared from the center of each.

"Hundred dollar bills. Where in the world did you find these? You must've robbed a bank!"

"You might say that. It's called the Katz Bank of Zürich, and the gnome who owns it was most impressed and most generous. I'm feeling so good right now I think we should go into town and celebrate. Say, a fine dinner at the Peripteron? Anything either of you wants tonight is yours. By the way, welcome, Christine. When did you get back?"

"Two days ago. The same day you left. Carter told me you went to Zürich, but never did say exactly why. Something about your having to meet someone in Switzerland. From the looks of it he must be a rich uncle."

"No, just a casual acquaintance. I provided him with some information he wanted. That's the reason I flew up. Fortunately, he was willing to pay for it."

Carter could hardly wait to be alone with Jean Paul to hear of the trip. He was delighted at the success of the venture and particularly thrilled to discover he would be repaid the loan.

"Christine, Carter and I have to run into town right now to see someone, but we should be back here by 8:00. That'll give you time to do whatever you need to do before dinner. Do you mind?"

She looked a little puzzled, but nodded in agreement.

"Come on, Carter. We need to go see Yanni before it gets any later. Here, help me pick up this filthy lucre. I don't want to take a chance of any of it going down between the floorboards. If it's in my pocket I know it'll be in a safe place."

"Safety is a relative term where you're concerned," said Carter with a laugh. "I've seen money burn holes in your pockets before. Maybe we ought to find a tailor in town who'll line them with asbestos."

"Before you make any more cutting remarks like that, take this cigar I brought you and stick it in your face. That way you may be able to keep your filthy opinions to yourself. Christine, I'm glad you're here. Sorry to run off like this, but we won't be long."

Before Christine could reply Jean Paul and Carter hurried down the stairs. As she picked up the forgotten bottle of Martell from the bedside box and walked across the upstairs landing into her room, she heard the roar of the car's motor and the squeal of tires on the stones of the courtyard.

"Drôle de mec," she observed to herself as she shook her head. Strange guy. She put the bottle to her lips and took a drink, then went down to take a shower.

On the way into town Jean Paul covered the highlights of his trip, hardly pausing to breathe and giving Carter little chance to ask questions.

"If at all possible, you must come wis me next time," said Jean Paul, falling back into English. "You wouldn't believe how exciting it was. I just happened to find zis man, Moritz Katz, in Zürich, who is probably going to take everysing we can bring to him. He tried to hide his interest, but he didn't do a very good job."

"En français, s'il te plaît. I need the practice. If I have any questions, I'll interrupt. Ever since you left I've been forced into either French or Greek. Let's give it a try. I might surprise you. Secondly, where in the hell are we going?"

Jean Paul laughed good-naturedly. "French? Bon, d'accord. To answer your question, we're going to see Deaf Yanni. I told him I'd come see him as soon as we returned. I don't want to disappoint him. He needs to think he's the most important person on Crete right now. After all, he is our main source of supply. It'll reinforce his trust to give him the full measure of his money right away. That way he'll be more inclined to continue doing business with us. I want him to know that we can do what he can't. Also, I'd seriously consider leaving again for Zürich tomorrow with another consignment, but I don't want Herr Katz to think I'm too anxious."

"Just what did he give you for those four statues?"

Jean Paul turned with an amused expression on his face. "Are you sure you want to know?"

"Damn right, I'm sure," he answered.

"Trois mille," he said, pausing between the words for emphasis.

"You're kidding!"

"No, I'm not kidding at all. Three thousand dollars, all in one hundred dollar bills so crisp and new they looked as if the ink might still be wet. Do you realize how much that leaves for us?"

"Deaf Yanni told you he wanted a thousand to fifteen hundred drachmas for all of them. Drachmas, of which there are thirty to a dollar. We're sitting here with ninety thousand drachmas."

"I'm going to give him the full fifteen hundred. That still leaves us with two thousand nine hundred and fifty dollars. Don't you think we should give him all he asks for? He'll be much more inclined to do business with us in the future."

"Yeah, you're right. Fifteen hundred sounds like so much, but that's only fifty dollars. Well, in that case, why don't you give him a little more, like, oh, I don't know, say two thousand?"

"No, can't do that either. We don't want him to get too greedy. All we want him to do is to continue to feed us everything that comes to him. That way we don't have to take everything. Just the best things. Our only problem is that we won't always know what the best things are. If we're not sure of something, we can always take pictures of it and show it to Katz. Then he can tell us if he'd be interested or not. It's as simple as that. In the meantime...oh, no, the vólta has started."

Sure enough, where Dimokratia entered Eleftherios Square, the streets were already packed with evening strollers. "It'll take us forever to get through here. Merde!" he exclaimed, slamming the steering wheel with his fist.

"Never mind, just park it here and we'll walk across. It'll be quicker. Are we going back to his workshop to meet him?"

"Not this time. He said that if we wanted to contact him in the evening just to go to the butcher shop in the outdoor market. Do you remember the man standing by the door at the meeting? That was the butcher. We just need to go to his shop and if Yanni isn't there the butcher will send someone to bring him."

"Do you know where it is?

"Sure, it's in the middle of the outdoor market up from Morosini fountain." Jean Paul parked the car along the curb and started to get out. "Come on. Let's go pay our debts."

They quickly crossed the square, but rather than going down Lalolairinou, which ran in front of Manoli's shop, Jean Paul turned into a narrow alley. To Carter's surprise, it was the same alley in which he and Traudel found themselves the night he scuffled with the porter who wanted to share their moment under the stairs. He allowed Jean Paul to lead the way and they soon entered the open-air market with its stalls and its air of bustle and commerce. They turned left and slowed immediately. Hanging from racks were chickens and unidentifiable cuts of meat, being fanned by a young boy to chase away flies. Jean Paul passed beneath them and approached the large man in the bloody apron. Carter recognized him immediately as the 'body guard'.

He greeted Jean Paul and, with a word, sent the young boy with the fan flying through the crowded market. Chairs were produced and coffee was ordered. In five minutes a waiter appeared with two small cups of Turkish coffee and two glasses of water. The butcher paid and went back into his shop. They barely finished their coffees before the first boy could be seen returning with Deaf Yanni in tow. When he saw them sitting in front of the shop a broad smile creased his face.

Without speaking a word, he made an interrogatory gesture with his hand and a jerk of his head. Jean Paul responded with an affirmative nod of his head. Still grinning from ear to ear, Yanni motioned for them to enter the butcher shop.

The butcher led the three men through another door in the back of the shop into a cramped office containing a battered desk and chair. Yanni sat on the edge of the desk and motioned for Jean Paul to join him there. He asked about the success of the trip and what he was able to get for the statues. Jean Paul reached into his shirt pocket and pulled out a wad of red and green drachma notes, from which he peeled twelve hundreds and six fifties. While Yanni counted he expressed his pleasure over and over. He indicated they should come back to see him in two or three days, for he would have some more things he wanted them to try to sell.

Within five minutes the meeting ended and they were ushered back outside. This time the butcher also smiled and patted Jean Paul on the shoulder as he passed out onto the crowded street. Yanni stood in the door beside the butcher, waving to them as they melted into the stream of shoppers.

"Well, that's that," said Jean Paul with satisfaction. "Let's go get our little blonde friend and see if we can't find a friendly bottle of wine."

During the short trip back to the villa Carter told him of seeing Andreas the day he left on the Keftiu and of his insistence that Jean Paul come see him as soon as he returned. "He wants us to go with him to see a friend of his near Plakias on the south coast. He wants us to go as soon as possible. There are some problems he wouldn't elaborate on, but I suppose we'll find out."

"That's fine. When we go back into town tonight I'll see if I can find him. We'll go by his office first and if he's not there he'll probably come to the club. Otherwise, I'll run up to his flat before we leave. Thanks for telling me about this. It seems everything is coming together for us."

When they pulled into the courtyard Carter remembered the mail. "Have you seen the letter that arrived for you from Paris? It came the day you left. I suppose Christine put it in your room."

Jean Paul stopped the car and turned off the motor before responding. "I saw it earlier. It's from a friend of mine in Paris. Her name is Karine. Karine de Châtillon. I met her here last summer. Last fall I flew to Luxembourg from Athens, slipped into France and took the train from Metz to Paris. Once inside the country there was no problem getting around. She lives there with her parents and brothers. They're pied-noirs. From Algiers. She arranged for me to stay with them while I was there. I invited her to come spend some time in Crete this summer and the letter said she would be arriving next week."

"What is she like?"

"Karine? Let's see. She's about Christine's height, although thinner. She has dark brown hair and brown eyes, is considered to be beautiful by many and she thinks she's an author. The last time I talked to her she told me she was beginning a book, a romance of some sort, although she never said what it was about. You'll like her and I know she'll like you. I wouldn't encourage anything more than friendship with her if I were you, however. Besides, she probably won't be here that long. Here comes Christine. Let her in on your side, will you?"

As they drove into town a piercing whistle caught their attention. Standing on the curb waving at them, female companion in tow, was Canif. Jean Paul pulled over to the side of the street and invited both to join them for dinner. Canif quickly accepted and Carter got out of the car to allow them to climb into the back seat. He introduced the woman to everyone in the car and they settled back to enjoy the ride.

Jean Paul drove directly to the Peripteron, a seaside restaurant known to tourists as the Glass House, located on a shoulder of hard land by the sea in the western part of the city. As soon as they shut off the motor they could hear the sounds of music coming from inside. Once through the doors the sight of a sea of diners at candlelit tables greeted them. On a raised stage was a band performing on traditional Cretan instruments, including bazouki and lyra players. On the dance floor could be seen a line of dancers engaged in Cretan folk dancing.

The host approached and led them to a table on the edge of the dance floor. From there they enjoyed an unobstructed view of the dancers, who held hands and formed a long line that swirled and snaked around the floor. The lead dancer clutched a woman's hand with his left and held a handkerchief over his head with his right. The music, recognizable folk airs Carter remembered hearing time and again blaring from radios and jukeboxes all across Iraklion, was loud and rhythmic. Everyone at the tables joined in, clapping their hands and swaying in time to the music. When the waiter came to take their order they were forced to shout to make themselves heard above the din.

Several people waved at them and Carter was pleased to see how many people he recognized. A warm hand clasped his shoulder and when he looked around he found the father of one of his students smiling warmly at him. He insisted Carter come to his table for a moment and then led him across the floor to a table for eight. Another chair was produced and a space was made for him to sit down. Someone handed him a full glass of wine and placed a small plate with a half-eaten chicken wing in front of him. He took a token bite from the wing and raised his glass in toast to everyone at the table. "Stín í giásas!" To your health. His host stood up, clinked his glass against Carter's and replied at the top of his voice, "Aspro páto!" Bottoms up. All the men at the table drained their glasses and thumped them onto the checkered table cloth.

Theodoro, the father of young Manoli, told everyone the story of Carter's alphabet lesson and of O Shitler. It was received with great appreciation and the punch line was repeated over and over. Others at nearby tables saw the obvious foreigner at Theodoro's table and asked what everyone was laughing about. The entire story was repeated and Carter was sure it would make the rounds of the entire restaurant by the end of the evening.

He thanked Theodoro for the wine and shook hands with everyone at the table once more before returning to his own table. Jean Paul asked what was going on and Carter repeated the story. Canif did not understand any of it until Christine explained it in painstaking detail. The one word he retained was 'shit', which he promptly added to his vocabulary.

"I speak English. One foot, two foots! Shit!"

The band began playing again, but this time they chose music currently popular in northern Europe. The line of dancers gave way to couples and, as the floor began to fill, Jean Paul grabbed Carter's arm to get his attention.

"Look! Do you see who's on the dance floor?"

Carter craned his neck, peering in the direction Jean Paul pointed. It was a moment before he was able to pick out Adoni, the proprietor of one of their favorite restaurants located in the alley off Fountain Square. It was at Adoni's restaurant where Yves accosted Evgenia and her aunt. Middle-aged, rotund Adoni gyrated in an athletic dance with a lithe young woman who looked young enough to be his daughter. Sweat glistened on his bald pate and ran in rivulets down his neck, darkened his armpits and glued his shirt to his back. In spite of his bulk he moved with a certain grace, but seemed out of place in this milieu. A more appropriate place would have been at the head of one of the lines of folk dancers.

Canif saw him too, and was quick to act. He picked up one of the salad plates and launched it in the direction of the dance floor, where it shattered almost under the feet of Adoni and his partner. Adoni whirled to see what was happening and gave a huge grin when he saw Canif, Jean Paul and Carter standing on their chairs, clapping their hands and screaming, Opa! The first plate was quickly followed by more and the floor under the dancers' feet was soon covered with broken crockery. Nevertheless, the music played on and Adoni continued to jitterbug and sweat, trying to maintain a serious mien but failing in his attempt. It was obvious he was enjoying being the center of attention.

The waiter rushed to their table to replace plates as they were broken. The musicians, appreciative of what was happening, redoubled their efforts. Other dancers moved away from the target pair to give them a wide berth, being careful not to step on the debris littering the floor.

In the middle of the table was a huge white platter, heaped high with fleshy bunches of red and white grapes, strawberries, succulent oranges, pears, figs, apples, bananas and great, juicy slices of cantaloupe and watermelon. Looking around for fresh ammunition, eyes agleam with feverish delight, Canif espied the platter. Without hesitation he upended its contents in the middle of the table then flung the empty vessel towards the dance floor.

Time and motion slowed perceptibly as the platter described a magnificent and stately parabola. All eyes in the room followed its trajectory, everyone's gaze concentrated upon it. Faces were alight in breathless anticipation. Up rose the platter, turning gently, wobbling slightly on its axis, majestic in flight. A vapor trail of droplets of water and fruity juices marked its passage; glinting and glistening scintilla, diamonds caught in the sun-like spotlights suspended in the dark firmament of the ceiling.

Upon reaching its apogee, it began its floating descent. The dance floor rose up, met, embraced and ultimately shattered, scattered and dispersed its atoms. Even with the decibel level of the band rising to a climactic crescendo, the sound of the platter's detonation stood apart from all others. For an instant there was the impression of silence. Then sound returned and as one all who observed this marvelous flight in open-mouthed awe raised their voices in a thunderously tumultuous, unanimous and resounding, "OPA!"

Chapter 21

Dinner was a riotous affair. They feasted upon calamaraki, red snapper, saláta horiátika and bottle after bottle of Retsina. When the bill arrived the total doubled the anticipated amount. Upon questioning the waiter's math they were reminded that broken dinnerware was always factored in. Jean Paul waved away Canif's attempt at paying his part and laid a handful of notes, including a generous tip, on the waiter's tray.

From the Peripteron they drove to the club, which contained only a handful of people that evening. Jean Paul saw everyone seated and served, then excused himself and left to find Andreas. Canif and his date left after only one drink. The Crozets, who came in as the others were leaving, took their seats. The Crozets, too, only stayed long enough to have one drink, and then left for home. Before going, however, they invited Christine, Jean Paul and Carter to their house for dinner later in the week. With friends arriving from Geneva they planned to roast a whole lamb.

When Jean Paul returned he did not even bother to sit down. He leaned over and spoke directly to Carter. "We have to go right now. Both of us need to go to bed. We're meeting Andreas here in town at 6:30 tomorrow morning, picking up a car and driving to Plakias. He says it'll be better to be as inconspicuous as possible, so we won't take my car."

Christine begged to be allowed to go as well, but Jean Paul was adamant in his refusal. "I'm sorry, Christine, but this is to be a very quick trip up into the mountains along the south coast. Also, a woman would be out of place where we're going, particularly a very striking blond, blue-eyed one. Don't worry. When we come back we'll take you someplace else, probably Ierapetra, since you want to go to the south coast so much."

She pretended to pout for a moment, then got up and followed the two men out the door.

ϒ ϒ ϒ

When Carter's alarm went off at 5:30 he came instantly awake. He threw back the sheet, sat up, slipped on a pair of shorts, shirt and running shoes and headed down the stairs. It took him slightly longer to roust Jean Paul from his bed, for the Frenchman, a noted night person, rarely arose before noon. Carter's task was made somewhat easier by the fact that they were in bed by shortly after midnight. When Jean Paul was finally sitting on the edge of the bed, head in hands, Carter headed into the kitchen to heat water for their coffee. He soon returned with two large mugs full of steaming, heavily sugared coffee, liberally laced with Martell. By a few minutes after 6 they were on their way to town. Carter drove while Jean Paul slumped, eyes closed, in the passenger seat.

He parked on the narrow street across from the club, waving to Andreas who waited for them. Jean Paul groaned, opened his eyes and reluctantly slid out of the car. Andreas approached them with a smile on his face and a twinkle in his eye. A layer of cigarette ashes already dusted the front of his shirt and the lapels of his jacket.

"Kalimérasas pediá. We must take a short walk to pick up the car. Not far from here."

It was only two blocks to the garage where Andreas made arrangements for the rental. When they arrived the owner directed them to a dark blue Opel that had seen better days. Carter commented on its state, but Andreas told him not to worry. The owner assured them it was in good condition and would get them safely there and back with no problems. With these assurances in mind, all three men climbed in. Jean Paul squeezed into the back and promptly lay across the seat.

Carter drove through town and out the city gate below the Pantokrator Bastion known as the Haniaporta. Before long they turned south in the direction of Aghia Varvara and Gortyn. In the early morning sunlight peasants headed for their fields. On either side of the road were small settlements, with crops planted on steep hillsides above them. The road into the mountains was paved, but was barely wide enough to accommodate two cars. High above could be seen small white chapels perched on peaks here and there. The countryside was beautiful and rugged, with every inch of arable soil utilized. All along the way Andreas gave a running commentary, which Carter thoroughly enjoyed. The patient and informative Andreas readily answered his many questions.

South of Aghia Varvara the road flattened out and followed a valley nestled between mountains on either side. As they passed Gortyn, Andreas remarked that in Roman times it was the capital of Crete and the North African province of Cyrenaica. The ruins of the Second Century AD Praetorium, the residence of the Roman Governor, were visible from the road. What impressed Carter the most was the apparent age of the olive trees growing among the ruins, their gnarled toes dug into baked earth, keeping a silent, centuries-long watch over the history buried beneath the crust of soil.

Turning west they passed the road leading to the Minoan Palace of Phaistos and the summer palace of Aghia Triada. Carter remembered it was here Traudel and Hanni visited with their friends the day he met them. His mind wandered back to dinner that evening and the incident in the alley. He thought fondly of Traudel and their wonderful night spent together and wondered if he would ever see her again.

From Timbakion the road became progressively worse. At times they could see the sea to their left and at other times olive groves and rocky terrain surrounded them. At Aghia Galini, situated right on the South coast, they headed inland again. The road became so rough that Jean Paul gave up trying to sleep in the back seat. As they pulled into Plakias he directed Carter to pull over in front of the kafeneion.

Andreas disappeared down the street. Five minutes later they heard the sound of an approaching motor and looked up to see a mikaní chugging up the street with Andreas waving to them from the trailer where he rode. The driver pulled over in front of the kafeneion and Andreas beckoned for them to join him.

"Carter, take the car and follow us. You can leave it on the edge of town. I'll show you where," directed Andreas.

"Where in the hell do you think he found that and where are we going?" wondered Carter to Jean Paul, who rode with him in the car.

"I assume we can't drive to wherever it is he's taking us. Andreas says it's up in the mountains above Plakias and that's the contraption that's going to take us there. We're just along for the ride, so we might as well enjoy it."

Carter agreed and plowed through the clouds of dust thrown up by the mikaní. The driver turned onto another dusty path and pulled to a stop. Andreas immediately motioned for Carter to park the car off the road under some trees. Jean Paul and Carter climbed in the back of the trailer with Andreas and made themselves as comfortable as possible on some heavy sacks thrown onto its wooden bed. Andreas regarded them with a wide smile. "Sit back and enjoy it. It should take us about forty minutes."

Everyone braced as Agamemnon engaged the gears and chugged off up the narrowing dirt track. Peasants in fields delineated by stones stacked to form low walls stopped work at the sound of the mikaní. Seeing Agamemnon with the strangers, they straightened from their labors and stared fixedly as they passed, wondering who they could be. The next time they saw Agamemnon they would question him. By evening everyone in town would know about the visitors from the outside world. It was difficult to keep secrets of this sort, and the grapevine would prove its efficiency.

As soon as the track began to rise Agamemnon geared down to handle the additional load. The heavily ribbed tractor-style drive wheels bit into the loose dust and bounced over unavoidable rocks as the narrow coastal plane fell away behind and below them. The sun glistened on the sea, which looked perfectly flat from their vantage point of ever-increasing altitude. Carter thought of the mythical Icarus and his ability to fly from the ruggedness of Crete out over the dazzling blue waters below. He envied the birds, floating on air currents high above. Ravens, swooped and dived, protesting raucously at the mikaní's noisy intrusion into their domain. Few words passed among the men. Each dealt with his own thoughts.

Andreas remembered hardship and suffering among the rocks and caves not so many years before. Jean Paul was reminded of his beloved Atlas Mountains in Algeria. Both remembered good times. And they remembered death. For Carter it was all new.

Agamemnon said something to Andreas, who nodded. He turned to his two companions and told them they would be arriving in about ten more minutes. Carter sensed an uneasy anticipation. Something in Andreas' eyes and manner belied his outward calm.

♈ ♈ ♈

Zakari was already hard at work building a new pen for three lambs he agreed to buy from a shepherd near Skaloti. He arose at dawn and gathered olive branches from here and there in order to construct a sturdy framework into which he wove other branches to form an enclosure.

Sound traveled far on the still morning air and he heard the roar of the mikaní's laboring motor while it was still some distance away. He was mystified, for he expected no one. He dropped what he was doing and walked towards the well. He stopped and slaked his thirst from the bucket, then turned to face the stones marking the entrance from the track.

When the mikaní pulled into view Zakari recognized Agamemnon immediately, but wondered who the other three were. One of them, the older man, was surely Cretan, but the other two were obviously foreigners. The driver pulled onto Zakari's property and drove to where he stood. Andreas clambered to his feet as soon as their forward motion stopped and peered down from his perch.

"Well, Zakaraki, this is the way you greet old friends?"

Zakari looked puzzled for an instant and then his expression changed to one of joyful recognition. His eyes opened wide and he raised his arms over his head. "Kyrie Andreas! Is it really you? I can't believe it!"

With remarkable agility Andreas vaulted to the ground and took Zakari in his arms, kissing his stubbled cheeks. Carter and Jean Paul descended and stood watching the reunion. Andreas, his arm still around the shoulders of the younger man, guided him in their direction.

"Zakari, I want to present two very good friends of mine to you. This is Jean Paul Bonisseur, from France, and Carter Martin, my American friend."

As Zakari shook hands with both of them, Andreas turned to Agamemnon to give him instructions. He nodded his head, started the motor of the mikaní, made a wide circle around the yard and exited down the path.

"Kyrie Andreas, where is Agamemnon going?"

"Don't worry. He has an errand to run and will be back in two hours. As for you, my friend, it's a delight to see you again after so many years. Come, sit down over here. We have so much to talk about and so much catching up to do."

"Of course, of course. Pardon my lack of manners. Come, all of you, and have a seat. Let me offer you kafés, or wine or raki. What will you have?" asked Zakari, as he ushered them toward the bench in front of his house. He chased the rooster from the bench and picked up a rag to wipe away chicken droppings. "Now, have a seat, please. I'll fetch some refreshments for all of you in just a moment."

In less than five minutes he returned with four cups of coffee and glasses of water on the tin tray. "Kyrie Andreas, I can't believe you're here. Tell me about yourself. You look prosperous. What brings you to my mountain top?"

Before answering Andreas took a noisy slurp from his cup then set it on the bench beside him. He took out a box of cigarettes and offered them around, lit them, took another sip of his coffee and then leaned toward Zakari.

"Serious things."

Zakari was instantly on guard. "Serious? What do you mean serious? You suddenly sound as if what you have to say is a matter of life and death. This is a joyous occasion for me, old friend. This is not the time to be serious."

"Ah, but there you are wrong. I'm only sorry to be here on such a mission. And, you speak of time. Yes, time is of the utmost importance. Unfortunately, we don't have much of it."

Zakari glanced at the two foreigners and then looked back at Andreas with a questioning look in his eyes.

"My two friends are part of why I'm here, Zakari. You know how I've always been about trust. Well, I trust them completely and, therefore, I'm asking you to trust them, as well. I also ask for your complete honesty. There are some hard decisions which must be made today."

Although still wondering where this was leading, he nevertheless nodded in agreement.

Andreas paused to drain his cup and set it down again before speaking. He still appeared hesitant, as if not sure how to express what was on his mind. "Zakari, I hear there've been some interesting things happening here on the south coast. I, like most everyone with ears, heard of the tomb that was found and the things taken from it."

Zakari looked down at his feet and mumbled, "I've heard some things like that, yes..."

"Stop right there," interrupted Andreas, holding up his hand. "I told you time was of the essence and all you're doing is wasting your time...and mine."

The younger man started to protest, but Andreas cut him off again. "Would you like to show me the statue you took from the tomb? I think I'm correct when I tell you it weighs about 12-1/2 kilograms and is probably solid gold," he stated matter-of-factly.

"Panagía! But...how...you...I can't...!" Zakari stuttered as he leapt to his feet.

"Kátze, paidímou. Sit down. Listen to what I have to say. There were at least six of you, probably a few more, and you all came away with several things of value. It seems you were the most fortunate in that you fell into the tomb right on top of the statue you brought home with you. None of the others who were with you know you took anything. That's fortunate for you. But, like it or not, your secret is no longer safe."

Nodding his head in resigned acknowledgment, Zakari clenched his fists until his knuckles were white. "Say no more, Andreas. I know. Barba Yorgi."

"That's right. Pseramanoli. Somehow he discovered what you found and, as soon as he saw it with his own eyes, he rushed to Iraklion. His first stop was to see Deaf Yanni. Later he came to me. He smoked a pipe of hashish in the market place with several drinks on top of that at my house. It was then, in a moment of carelessness on his part, he told me of what he saw

here. The next day I went to Yanni and he confirmed Yorgos'
visit. One thing I know for sure, Yorgos didn't tell him where it
was or who took it. He just told him he 'knew where to find' this
marvel."

"But why would he go to Deaf Yanni? Why would he
tell him of it?"

"Because he thought Yanni would buy it from him, or at
least help him sell it. I think he was planning to come steal it
from its hiding place and carry it to Yanni for the money. He
heard Yanni could sometimes find buyers for some of the things
that are found. But after too much hashish and too much raki he
forgot to be careful. He came to my house looking to spend the
night. We talked until quite late and he told me all about the
statue. Otherwise, I would never have known it was in your
possession. That's the reason we've come here today. I don't
want to see you lose something of great value. After talking to
Yanni, I discovered he doesn't want you to be cheated either."

The revelation was stunning. It left Zakari sitting with
his elbows on his knees, head hanging down in an attitude of
utter defeat. Without lifting his head he began to speak.

"Your coming here answers many questions for me, old
friend. It answers questions that you know nothing about as yet."
He raised his head and looked at Andreas through red-rimmed
and bloodshot eyes. "What you don't know is, Barba Yorgi has
the names of everyone who took something from the tomb. He's
already contacted two of them, Stavros Petrides from Khora
Sfakion, and Ari Mavrodakis from near Plakias. I don't imagine
you know either of them, but he threatened to give both their
names to the police and, because they're afraid of being betrayed
to the police and also afraid of Pseramanolis, they showed him
what they found. Each time he's taken half of what's theirs. The
first two came to me as soon as he took their treasure. The rest
are awaiting their turn and are mad with fear. Quite frankly,
Kyrie Andreas, they don't know which way to turn. Neither do
I."

"I see," said Andreas pensively.

Carter and Jean Paul listened intently to the conversation
between the two men. Jean Paul's command of Greek was less
than Carter's, but he was used to the vagaries of the local dialect

and able to understand most of what was being said. Zakari's strong Cretan accent and his use of patois made it difficult to understand every word. There were things Carter wanted to question, but did not say anything that would interrupt the two older men.

"There's one more thing you should know, Andreas. Wait here a moment." He got up from the bench and went into the house. In a moment he returned with what looked to be a bundle of clothes. The three men craned their necks to have a better look at what he carried in his arms. Zakari sat down again, put the bundle on his knees and began to unwrap it. The outer part appeared to be a shirt, torn and dirty with great brown stains on it. Before unwrapping it entirely, Zakari stopped for a moment and looked up at Andreas to be sure of his full attention. Then, with an almost theatrical flair, he threw the cloth wrapping open. Lying in the middle of the shirt was a skull with a crucifix on a chain hanging out of one of the eye sockets. Next to the skull lay a transistor radio in a brown, imitation leather case. Andreas leaned closer to get a better look.

"And would you mind telling me what this is all about? Just who is this and what about the crucifix and the radio?" demanded Andreas.

"This is, or was, Dimitrios Detorakis, of Plakias." Zakari told him of what happened the day the treasure was discovered and of the bulldozer driver's having recognized Mitzos. He explained how Mitzos disappeared and how Barba Yorgi suddenly appeared at his door with vague information concerning the treasure. He also told him of the cryptic warning to watch his back. He continued by telling him of Stavros' finding the remains of Mitzos on the mountain side, and then of coming to him with the skull, the crucifix and the radio.

"See the jaw? It's shattered. The radio must belong to Pseramanoli. He's never without it and the first day he came here after we found the treasure he didn't have it with him. I remember that distinctly. What else can we think but that Pseramanoli found little Mitzos burying his part of the treasure, killed him, probably with his staff, and took the treasure? He didn't even bother trying to hide the body. Who would have thought anyone would ever find it so far up the mountain among the rocks? During the struggle, he must have lost the radio and then in his haste to be away from there he forgot it. He must have thought it could be replaced and that there would be no danger of its linking him to the murder. He must have been confident that the radio, like Mitzos' body, would never be found. He left him there on the mountain, probably already dead, thinking also that the vultures and the other carrion eaters would do away with all evidence. Instead, it was one of the carrion eaters themselves, the raven, which gave it all away.

"Now what can we do? We can't go to the police. You understand that. If we do nothing, however, we'll all lose at least half of what we have and Pseramanoli, who's calling himself 'The Bull', will once again go free. I don't know, Andreas, I just don't know. We're on the horns of a dilemma and the dilemma is called Yorgos. Someone should have taken care of him years ago when he caused so much pain and sorrow. Who would have thought he would come back to haunt us?"

Andreas heaved a great sigh before speaking again. "It seems as if we have no choice, Zakari. We must act now before it's too late. First of all, have you put the statue where it can't be found? I certainly hope you moved it from the place where Pseramanoli found it the first time."

"Yes, of course. I think it would take a miracle for him to find it again, although the first time was a miracle to my mind."

"Let me think for a moment, Zakaraki. While I'm thinking, would you mind showing us the statue? I know you wondered why I brought these men with me today," said Andreas, indicating Jean Paul and Carter with a sweep of his hand. "Well, they can take it and sell it for you. They take things like yours out of the country and find buyers. They wouldn't want to take it with them now, but suppose they came back in the next few days and took some pictures of it. They can take the pictures with them to show their buyers. There would be no harm in doing that."

Zakari thought for a moment about Andreas' comment before responding. When he finally answered, Andreas nodded at the logic of his argument. "My old friend, I'll show you the statue and they can come back to take pictures of it if they wish.

Please remember that this is not some piece of pottery or bronze. I'm not an educated man, but I do know the value of gold and I also know that pottery and other things of this nature only have value if you can find someone to give you money for them. As for the statue, it's gold, solid gold from the feel of it. The value someone puts on it as a piece of Minoan, or Roman, or even modern work, is only what someone is willing to pay for its historical worth. When I look at it in my hand, I'm holding something that has a value aside from what a scholar or an archaeologist would put on it. The value I'm talking about is the gold itself. I may never realize the historical value of it, but the value of the gold is always there."

"What you're telling me then is that you would take the statue and melt it down for the gold?" asked Andreas with grudging admiration.

"That's exactly what I mean. If I were to let it out of my hands I would stand to lose even the value of the gold. I realize these friends of yours are certainly honest men, and they would have a better chance of taking it out of the country than I ever would, but there's still the chance they could be caught with it before leaving the country. What would I have then? What? I'll tell you what! Mithén! Zero."

"But Zakari, if there's the chance you would receive much more money for the statue than the mere value of the gold itself, wouldn't you be willing to take that chance?"

The younger man looked intently at Andreas. "No, I wouldn't. There's too much sure value, a fixed amount that I know I could have. No matter what."

"All right, I understand what you're saying and when I think about it I have to agree with you. What do you suggest doing?"

"Andreas, I'm not a greedy man, but I try to be careful. Life is hard for someone like me. Actually, all I want is the assurance I'll have what the gold itself is worth. Let me make a proposition. If your friends will pay me for the gold itself, I'll let them walk away with it today. But we must weigh the statue on a good scale, figure the gold on today's market, or at least the day they pay for it, and they must pay for it not in drachmas or dollars, but in gold coins or bullion. That way I'll know I've been treated fairly and they can take their chances with it."

The man might be an uneducated peasant, but Andreas admired his good sense and sound reasoning. "Wait a minute and let me explain your proposal to them."

Zakari readily agreed. If the two foreigners were to accept his offer he would be assured a fair return and he would no longer have to worry about Barba Yorgi. As for the other men, hopefully Andreas would be able to find a solution that would protect them all.

Andreas turned to Jean Paul and Carter and told them briefly what Zakari said about the tomb and the problems with Pseramanoli. He also told them of his proposal to sell them the statue for the value of its gold content, as well as his readiness to melt it down. Both of the younger men were horrified at the thought of this unseen work of art being turned into a blob of yellow metal and both were quick to agree, on the condition that they are allowed to see and hold the statue and take pictures of it.

"Do you think you could come up with some money, Carter?" asked Jean Paul. "I think that working together we could find enough to cover the cost of it, don't you?"

Carter quickly went over in his mind some of the resources he might be able to tap for a short-term loan. He told Jean Paul that off the top of his head he could see no difficulty in finding someone to bankroll them. The return would be mind boggling and they could even pay a handsome percentage in interest to whoever agreed to let them have the money for a short-term loan.

"Of course," said Jean Paul," we need to see it first, and above all, take some pictures. Andreas, ask him how long he would give us to come up with the money." Jean Paul could have asked the questions himself, but was unwilling to let Zakari realize he spoke Greek as well as he did.

Andreas translated the Frenchman's question and Zakari thought for only a moment before answering.

"Until November first."

"The first of November. It's the first week of September now. Do you think we could come up with the money by then, Carter?"

"Probably before then. We need to get on it right away. I'll start writing letters tonight."

"In that case," said Andreas, "it's agreed." He turned to Zakari and spoke of their willingness. "They ask only to see the statue and take pictures of it."

Zakari stood and extended his hand to the two foreigners. It was decided and all parties seemed satisfied with the terms.

Andreas clapped Zakari solidly on the back and said, "Now, my old friend, show us this little treasure that's causing you so much trouble!"

Zakari rose from the bench and turned to face the three men still sitting there. "Wait here. I'll call you. You'll certainly understand why I'm being careful."

"Of course," answered Andreas. "We'll wait here for you."

When Zakari left Andreas turned to the two younger men. "Well, did you understand what that was all about?"

Both indicated they were able to follow the conversation more or less, but were not entirely clear on several points. Andreas clarified and explained as quickly and in as much detail as he could. There was little Carter missed, but Jean Paul wanted to hear it in French to make sure no nuances escaped him. Zakari called from inside the house and they arose from their seats with great anticipation.

Lying on the rough boards of the table was something wrapped in heavy canvas-like material, cloth streaked with soot and grime. Zakari waited until they gathered around the table before moving to unwrap it. All three men waited breathlessly, watching his every move. As the last layer of cloth was removed they edged closer to have a better look at what lay before them. Each gasped involuntarily in surprise and wonder at the beauty and artistry displayed before them. A youth wearing a girdle-like loin adornment, an acrobat from the looks of him, stood on tiptoes, his arms raised above his head. His eyes looked intently ahead, as if anticipating the charge of one of the bulls over whose horns he would vault. Both men recalled seeing a similar form in a statue from the museum in Iraklion, but never in gold and never this size. Jean Paul was the first to reach for it, but stopped in the midst of the motion. He looked questioningly at Zakari, who nodded without speaking.

"Merde, it's unbelievably heavy!" he exclaimed in a low voice. He traced the details with his index finger, amazed at this wonderful work of art. "Look at the detail! I never realized the Minoan artisans were this advanced."

"I know," agreed Carter. "Of all the things we've seen in the archaeological museum nothing, with the exception of perhaps the Goddess of the Serpents or the acrobat, even comes close to the detail. Here, let me hold it."

Jean Paul passed it to him reluctantly, but continued to stand and watch as Carter examined it, a look of awe on his face. Even Andreas seemed to be moved. Zakari stood to one side looking like a proud father showing off his first-born son to admiring friends. He addressed the two foreigners slowly, enunciating clearly so they would understand. "When do you think you will come back to take the pictures? Tell me today and I'll be sure to be here for you."

"Methavrio," answered Jean Paul with no hesitation. Day after tomorrow. "Can you be here then? We'll be here in mid-morning, say about 10:30. En táxei? Is it agreed?"

"En táxei," said Zakari with a smile. Agreed.

Andreas inspected the statue before returning it to Zakari, who took it lovingly in his rough hands. They watched as he once again wrapped and tied the length of cord around it. He nodded towards the door and they went back outside while he returned it to its hiding place. When he rejoined them Carter and Jean Paul were among the olive trees beyond the well, where they discussed the statue. Andreas awaited him, seated on the bench. He sat down beside Andreas and lit a cigarette before speaking.

"Pseramanoli. What are we going to do about him?"

"Yes, Pseramanoli. I was just thinking about that little problem. We must work quickly, old friend, and I'm going to need your help. You must immediately contact those who have not yet been approached by him. This is what you're going to tell them."

By the time he finished speaking the sound of Agamemnon's mikaní could be heard coming up the trail.

Chapter 22

Zakari's first objective was to travel as quickly as possible. Andreas made it clear to him he must contact the remaining individuals who were at the tomb before Barba Yorgi could further his devious plans.

The sounds of the mikaní barely faded before he shut the door of his house and slipped through the trees and rocks on the small path that ran straight down the mountain. Speed was imperative. As shaken as he was by the extent of Andreas' knowledge of the statue and the tomb, he was even more horrified to know Barba Yorgi not only knew of the statue's existence, but that he saw and told Deaf Yanni about it. If Andreas' plan could only be put into action before it was too late. The mere thought of all that was at stake pushed him even faster down the steep and torturous track.

Within half an hour he reached the lower levels of the mountain and began to pass fields, some being worked while others were deserted. As he passed each one he looked carefully to see who was there and then moved on. It was not until he almost reached the Plakias-Skalotí road that he finally found what he was searching for. As soon as he saw it he changed direction and rushed toward the two men hoeing around their grapevines.

"Vangeli! Vangeli! Ela ná sou pó!" Come here, I need to talk to you.

The older of the two, Evangelos, known as Vangeli, raised his hand in greeting. "Kalósto, Zakari! How've you been? I haven't seen you si..."

"Vangeli, let me use your motorbike," Zakari interrupted breathlessly. "I need to borrow it for one, maybe two hours. It's very important. I'll fill it up with gas before I bring it back to you."

Vangeli turned to his son, and gestured questioningly. The younger man wondered why Zakari would be in such a rush, but nodded his head in agreement. Zakari saw the gesture and the nod and, with a shout of thanks, leapt astride the motorbike. He kicked the motor to life, opened the throttle wide and roared off in a cloud of dust.

"Po, po, po, po!" said Vangeli. "He acts as if he has the devil on his tail."

His son watched the cloud of dust begin to settle, worried Zakari would lose control riding so recklessly on the dirt roads. Finally, with a resigned shrug, he returned to work.

With the added advantage of speed working for him, Zakari soon saw the remaining men. He was encouraged to discover Barba Yorgi had yet to contact them. To each he gave the same message: when the old man comes to see you, you must tell him you cannot give him his part of the treasure that day. Tell him you have hidden them in the mountains and that it will take some time to recover them. Urge him to meet you at the old talcum mill south of Arménoi at 7 o'clock in the evening in two days. Tell him you're willing to do as he asks, but you must have some time to get everything together. Don't let him talk you into bringing the things to him that day. You must stay as calm as possible. Remember, there are those who will help you through this.

As soon as he's gone you must come to me and let me know. I'll handle the rest. Talk with no one. You must tell no one else of my visit with you today. If you tell anyone of our plan you risk it's reaching the ears of Barba Yorgi."

Each of them said they understood and would do as he asked, but each was still frightened of Pseramanoli and the danger he represented.

"Don't worry," Zakari tried to reassure them, "the Bull's going to be tamed and then we'll all be safe again."

Within two hours he saw everyone, filled the almost empty tank with gas and returned the dusty motorbike to its owner. With a word of thanks and a hasty wave, he made his way back up the mountain.

♈ ♈ ♈

On the ride back down the mountain with Agamemnon Carter tried once to question Andreas about his discussion with Zakari. Andreas inclined his head toward the stolid Agamemnon and motioned Carter to silence. Now that they were once more in the car, however, he was willing to discuss what had been accomplished.

"What I don't understand," Carter wondered aloud, "is why this Barba Yorgi is taking these things from the people that found them. Also, why is he threatening them with exposure to the police?"

"Me, either," interjected Jean Paul before Andreas could answer. "What I'd really like to know..."

"Sigá, sigá," Andreas admonished them laughingly. "Slow down a moment and maybe I can satisfy both of you with the same answer.

"It's difficult for you to see how this could happen because you don't know what came before. This Barba Yorgi, o Yorgos Pseramanolis, was a fine young man. He was born in Rethymnon a few years before the Turks were chased from our island and worked with his father as a fisherman. He's a big man, larger than most Greeks I've known. Because of the type of back breaking work required on the boats, pulling the nets and fighting the sea at times, he became a legend even as quite a young man. Some of his feats of strength were prodigious. At Easter, when the priest threw the cross into the water of the harbor, it was almost always Yorgos who surfaced with it in his hand. He swam like a fish and fought like a shark to have the honor of retrieving it.

"In 1932, already a man of stature and renown, he married a young woman from Episkopi and brought her back to Rethymnon, where his father gave him some land. It was on this land that he built a house for her. Life was good to them. In 1933 his wife, Athena, gave birth to two fine boys, twins, who were the apples of his eye, but they almost caused him to lose his wife. She experienced difficulties in giving birth and the doctors told her she could never have any more children.

"Yorgos became very protective of her and the boys and, it's said, he treated her like a queen. When the boys were still just tiny babies he took them, one in each arm, to the port on the

Gulf of Almiroú to show them his boats and talk to them of the sea. When they began to crawl he let them play among his nets as he mended them on the quay. By the time they were three or four years old he began to take them for short trips on his boat.

"Those that knew him at that time will tell you those two boys were like little monkeys and were all over the boat helping their father where they could. He even allowed them to take the tiller from time to time, or let them help him remove fish from the nets. None of the other men dared laugh at him and all eventually came to admire his methods of initiating his sons into the life of the sea.

"In the spring of 1939 his father died in an accident on his boat. He was caught in a storm while out fishing by himself and the boat capsized. They never found the old man, but the boat washed up on shore a day or two later. Yorgos inherited his father's property and what business there was. He soon hired two men to work for him, as he built the business and prospered. He took his mother into his house, where she worked side-by-side with Athena and helped watch over her two grandsons.

"When the Germans came in May, 1941, Yorgos was among those who fought those first days to try to repel them. The north coastal area was quickly subdued, but not without a considerable loss of life on the part of the invading paratroopers. Many were dead before they hit the ground. In late June Yorgos decided to give up the fight and tried to go back to work. Crete has known occupation through the centuries and he, like many of the others, knew it would only be a matter of time until the Germans, like the Venetians and the Turks before them, would be pushed back into the sea. Life under the Germans became very difficult and in November of 1941 he joined the Resistance. This is where we first met.

"Ah, my young friends, he was a remorseless, crafty and vicious fighter. As in peacetime, he made a name for himself and before long the Germans became aware of him and his activities. They tried unsuccessfully to entrap him for several months, but he was always a step ahead of them.

"Early on he moved his wife, mother and the children to Athena's father's house in Episkopi to get them out of Rethymnon. Food was scarce and times were hard, but he felt they would be safe there. Little did he know just how ruthless the Germans could be. In the summer of 1942 they made a sweep into Episkopi, picked up Athena and the boys and took them to Iraklion. They beat his mother and an old man who worked on the property almost to death and left them in the wrecked house. As soon as he heard about it, Yorgos became like a crazy man. He was truly a raging bull, ready to charge into Iraklion to take on the whole German army with his bare hands. Unfortunately, cooler heads prevailed."

"What do you mean by 'unfortunately'?" asked Carter and Jean Paul simultaneously. "Had he done that he would almost certainly have been killed immediately."

"Exactly!" responded Andreas. "If that happened we wouldn't be in the situation we're in today."

"So, what did happen, Andreas?" prompted Carter, eager for him to continue.

"Well, no one knows for sure, but there's a strong suspicion that somehow or other he contacted the German authorities that autumn. To make a long story short, he became a double agent for them, giving them information from time to time about the Resistance and what the various groups were doing. We suddenly found it more and more difficult to surprise the enemy. We lost men every time we struck them. They kept Athena and the boys in custody to ensure his continued cooperation. Even though the tide began to turn in favor of the Allies in North Africa, our war remained pretty much the same. Oh, it became somewhat easier for us as the Germans lost their hold in the Mediterranean, but in 1945 they still controlled parts of the western end of the island.

"In March of 1943 the Gestapo, which held his family hostage, felt they could get more and better information from Yorgos and insisted upon greater cooperation from him. He must have been in a terrible turmoil, for as a father and husband, his first priority was to ensure the safety of his little family. On the other hand, coming from a long line of patriots and freedom fighters, he was betraying his country by cooperating with the occupation authorities.

"He became a virtual recluse, even from us who lived in caves in the mountains. He would disappear for days, sometimes weeks at a time, and then suddenly turn up again with no explanation of his whereabouts. It was not long before we realized that our successes were noticeably more numerous when he was away. So, when he did return, he was excluded from all planning.

"In July of that same year he abducted one of the Gestapo officers from Iraklion and questioned him in depth about the location and situation of his wife and sons. We don't know all the details, but from the little we do know the questioning was brutal and the man finally admitted that one of his sons died in a camp on the southern mainland where they were interned. He also admitted that Athena and the remaining son perished from malnutrition and pneumonia shortly afterwards. Although dead for almost six months, the Gestapo withheld the information from him, counting on his continued cooperation as long as he could hold onto the hope they might someday be returned alive.

"Yorgos' reaction was immediate and his rage knew no bounds. He literally tore the man apart with his bare hands and left the severed head in a box at the gate of Gestapo headquarters as a warning to all the other Germans of what would happen to them as long as they stayed on Crete. We very rarely saw him after that, but there was a strong suspicion among our group he was working alone. He assuaged his grief and outrage in a bloody personal vendetta against those who caused him so much pain. Doubtless, his guilt over having betrayed his countrymen was a major reason for his disappearance, as well."

"But why was he not treated as a collaborator after the war? I thought those who collaborated in all the occupied countries were severely dealt with by their own countrymen after it was all over," said Carter.

"We didn't know then, and don't even know to this day, all the circumstances. Much of what I've told you is supposition based upon the few things we knew for sure. Besides, there were many, many extenuating circumstances in his story, just as there were with every individual family who was on the island during that terrible time. You must understand that when the occupation ended everyone wanted to get back to normal and try to pick up the shattered pieces of their lives. Everyone was in a great deal of pain and suffered so much during those years. Yorgos was not amongst us at the end of the war, either. We suppose he went up into the mountains, for he was not seen by anyone until the late 1940's. That's the nature of Crete. It lends itself to guerrilla warfare - or disappearance. If someone wants to hide himself here it's difficult to find them.

"He's never really come back into society, back to the friends he knew. The old man, the retainer, died within a month of the beating he received from the Germans when they took Athena and the children. His mother starved herself and died in early 1943.

"Tales of Yorgos' exploits began to surface and, as with all such tales, grew with the telling. The early 50's saw him as a great patriot and freedom fighter. People regarded him as a living legend and held him in tremendous respect and awe whenever he appeared. He was a folk hero to the people of the mountains. Those of us who knew or suspected the true story kept our own counsel and didn't bother to try to enlighten the others.

"It seems this all affected his mind in a way that's difficult for us to understand. Now this specter from the past is returning to haunt those that knew him. He's not the same Pseramanolis, but a bitter old man. Yes, a bitter and a dangerous old man."

Andreas let his voice trail off and seemed lost in deep thought. Neither Carter nor Jean Paul spoke for several minutes after he finished his account of this Barba Yorgi. The thoughts of both of them were fixed upon the old man: what he endured and what he became. They both wondered, too, about Andreas' discussion with Zakari and what they were planning to do to protect the rest of the treasures from the tomb, and both felt it best they did not know. The rest of the journey back to Iraklion was marked by long periods of silence or inconsequential talk of weather and the surrounding countryside.

Night was beginning to fall as they passed once more through the gate in the city wall and drove through the growing crowds in the streets. Jean Paul dodged the insouciant walkers and they were soon at the garage where their journey began that morning. Carter was the first to alight and, as he held the door open for Andreas, he was amazed at how old their friend suddenly seemed. He appeared to have the cares of the world bearing down on his shoulders, bending his back under the strain of his inner turmoil. Heaving a sigh he turned to them.

"Thank you for coming with me pediámou. I really must leave you now. I feel so tired."

Jean Paul came around the car and was shocked at the transformation in their friend. "Are you all right?"

He looked at both of the young men through red-rimmed eyes set deep in the shadows of their sockets and gave a slight nod. "Tired. Tired and more than a little sad. Don't forget you have a rendezvous with Zakari day after tomorrow. Have you thought how you'll get to Plakias and Zakari's house?"

Both looked quickly at each other and shrugged their shoulders. "I thought we'd take my car," responded Jean Paul.

"No, no! I don't think that would be a good idea. My suggestion is for you to find a motorbike. It will carry a passenger easily enough and that way you can go directly up the mountain without having to go into town. We've caused enough discussion today and I don't think it would be a good idea to use Agamemnon again. Yes, I think a motorbike will be the best idea and will be much quicker than a car. Do you think you can borrow one?"

Carter was the first to answer. "Sure, that won't be a problem. Jean Paul, don't you think we could borrow Stasso's? He rides it to work from time to time, but I've noticed that most often he leaves it at home and takes the bus. Maybe he wouldn't mind taking the bus for one more day. We can offer to give him his fare. He let me ride it one day when I needed to go into town for something. I know it'll carry two people easily, for he takes his younger brother on it with him sometimes when they make the trip up to their grandparent's village near Lasithi."

"Fine, then. It's settled," said Andreas. "Come see me as soon as you return. Tell no one where we went or what we saw today. I'm counting on you to keep all this between us. Agreed?"

"Sure, fine. We aren't going to say anything to anybody," Jean Paul assured him. "Take care of yourself, old friend. Are you sure you won't come have a drink with us, or dinner?"

"No, but thank you both. Good night." He turned and moved slowly up the street. Jean Paul and Carter watched his departure in silence, both wondering the cause of this sudden change in him. As young men will, however, they quickly turned their minds to other things. They walked in the opposite direction, speaking in low, excited voices about the statue, what Katz would think of it, and where they were going to find the money to pay Zakari.

Chapter 23

As soon as they returned home Carter walked along the narrow cobbled street that ran beside their villa to see if Stasso was home. When he knocked on the heavy door that opened onto the street it was answered almost immediately by a heavyset older woman he recognized as being Stasso's mother. Her face broke into a pleased smile.

"Kyrie Kartos! Kalispérasas. Eláte." She greeted him warmly and invited him to come inside. Carter thanked her, but shook his head.

"I just came to see Stasso. I'd like to speak to him for a moment if he's here."

"Certainly, I'll call him for you. Just one moment."

Stasso ambled into the light of the entryway. His short legs gave him a rolling gait of a sailor just landed from a ship after having been at sea for months and a huge grin lit his face. From his manner of speech and the way he carried himself Carter suspected he might be slightly retarded. Whenever he saw Carter he always seemed delighted and made a habit of showing up in their courtyard to pass the time of day. He enjoyed watching the people who stayed at the villa, although he never understood a word that was said.

Yves referred to him in gentle derision as "le Nain," the dwarf, but always welcomed him when he appeared. He was allowed to stay, for he never bothered anyone. He was simply a fixture, his ubiquitous grin beaming upon Carter and Jean Paul. He was also handy when it came to problems with either the plumbing or electricity, neither of which they understood. Now he greeted Carter as he would an old friend, took his hand in both of his and pumped vigorously.

"Carter, tí kánis? Come inside. We're just sitting down to dinner. Come join us."

"Thanks, no, Stasso. I'm sorry to disturb you at dinner, but I have a favor to ask and wanted to talk to you as soon as possible."

"Sure. If there is ever anything I can do to help you and Zon Pawl, all you have to do is ask. That is what friends are for."

"Stasso, day after tomorrow Jean Paul and I want to visit a place outside of Iraklion. There's no bus that goes there and I was wondering if we might be able to borrow your motorbike. We'll be careful with it, but we'll need it for most of the day. We'll also put gas in it when we come back. I know you need to go to work, but I'll pay your bus fare so you won't be too inconvenienced."

"Of course, my friend, of course!" he beamed. "Keep it all week if you like."

"Thanks, I appreciate your generosity. If you don't mind I'll come get it tomorrow night so we can leave early the next morning. Will you need it then?"

"No, I'm glad for you to use it." He paused for a moment to collect his thoughts then changed the subject abruptly. "Carter, I have a surprise to tell you! Can you guess what it is?"

"You're going to get married! Congratulations, Stasso." shouted Carter joyously. "Who is she?"

Stasso giggled in delighted laughter, blushed and held up his hand.

"No, that's not it. Next week I'm going into the army! I have to go into training for about eight weeks and then they will send me to a base on the mainland, probably in Thessaloniki. I'm going to be a truck mechanic." When he stopped talking he stood expectantly waiting for Carter's reaction.

"In the army? That is exciting!" Carter responded appropriately. "I'm sure you'll make a good soldier and a good mechanic. Maybe you'll get to go to Cyprus to fight the Turks." Seeing how excited Stasso was Carter congratulated him by shaking his hand and pounding him on the back, genuinely happy for him. Stasso threw his shoulders back in pride and then popped to rigid attention before snapping a salute. Carter assumed an exaggerated pose, returned the salute, and both exploded in laughter.

His mother appeared from the back of the house and stood looking expectantly at Carter. When he acknowledged her presence she came and put her hand on his arm and attempted to guide him into the house. "Come, Kyrie Carter. I have set a place for you at our table. Come sit with us. Eat."

Carter refused as politely as he could. He knew it was bad form to have someone visit your home and not offer them something to eat, even if the cupboards were virtually bare. It would have been proper for him to sit with them for a few minutes and share a piece of bread, or whatever she offered, but he wanted to return to the villa as quickly as possible. She looked very disappointed, but said she understood.

"Well, congratulations again, Stasso, and thank you for letting us use your motorbike. Go back and eat your supper before it gets cold. I'll see you tomorrow evening. Good night."

"Kaliníkta, Kartos. Good night. See you tomorrow."

When he got back to the house he told Jean Paul of his conversation and of Stasso's willingness to let them use his motorbike. He also told him of Stasso's imminent induction. Jean Paul laughed ruefully.

"I'll need to talk to him before he leaves to give him some pointers on how to conduct himself."

The news that they would be able to use the motorbike to go photograph the statue put Jean Paul in a garrulous mood, not that he was normally taciturn. He regaled Carter with stories of cross-country jaunts by motorbike while in school in France and how he learned to ride as a young man in Algeria. He bragged of his motorcycle leathers and how they saved his life when, as a young daredevil, he laid his bike down on a country road one day.

"I'll show you how to ride one of these machines," he boasted. "All I ask is that you hold on tight and lean with me. These roads will be just like a motocross. You'll see."

"Just keep one thing in mind: we need to get there and back in one piece. I don't want to think I'm going off with some wild man. There's a motorcycle daredevil in America who's just gaining popularity. Name's Evel something or other. I understand he's broken just about every bone in his body and I don't want to be a statistic like that," Carter warned.

Jean Paul laughed it off and waved his hand in a gesture of dismissal. "You have to begin to live sometime. To dare! But don't worry. We'll get there and back without going airborne cross-country. I'm not going to endanger you. You're right about one thing. We are taking a lot of chances right now and we don't want to add to our liabilities. We have too much to live for to do anything foolish. Come on, let's go down to the club and see who's there. I feel like playing the piano tonight. My fingers are itching for the feel of the ivories.

While Jean Paul played and sang, Carter talked with Canif and then struck up a conversation with a group of Swedes who arrived in Crete a few days before. He found it difficult keeping up with the conversation, for his mind was elsewhere. He could still feel the weight of the gold in his hand and, in his mind's eye, could see himself sitting in Katz's house, showing the statue to him.

Sometime after ten they left and went to one of the cafes surrounding the city square for a bite before going home for the night. While eating Jean Paul brought up the subject of pied-noir street slang. Carter was fascinated, as always, for many of the words were so different from those he recognized from either Brussels or Paris. In turn Carter gave a lesson in Anglo-Saxonisms to the delight of his friend. By the time they finished eating and were on their way home they sounded like French and American sailors, each trying to outdo the other with filth and insults.

"Have you ever noticed Manoli when he tries to swear in English?" asked Carter. "It's hilarious! He thinks swear words give him a better command of the language. Every time he says 'goddamn' it comes out 'hoddamn' with that glottal 'G" sound only the Greeks can do."

Even after they went to their respective rooms that night, Carter upstairs and Jean Paul downstairs, they continued to act like teenagers. They swore at one another in their newly learned vocabularies and then exploded in laughter.

The next morning Carter arose early, as was his habit, and left for school. He needed to make arrangements for the following day, to find someone who would be willing to stand in for him at his morning class. If they left early for Zakari's, he felt as if they would be back by early afternoon and he would be able to take his own classes that began at three. He wanted to tell Bunny, or someone, about their trip to the south coast and about the statue, but he restrained himself. Instead he sat down between morning classes and wrote a long letter to his mother, explaining to her the wonder of holding an object in his hand last touched by the hand of man over 4000 years before.

He tried to write her at least once every two weeks to add to the travelogue he was providing her. His mother wrote that she was living every adventure vicariously through his letters. After writing to her of the four ivory statues Jean Paul sold to Katz he received a letter, couched in motherly idiom, about the dangers of such activities. He appreciated her concern, but was sure he could handle whatever situation might arise.

The day passed quickly and he was soon at the villa once more. After picking up the motorbike from Stasso, Jean Paul took it out for a trial spin and filled the gas tank before returning to the house. They were both excited about the next day's trip and fell asleep with difficulty. Bunny loaned his 35-millimeter camera to Carter after extracting a promise from him that he would guard it with his life. He found what he considered to be suitable lens for making high-resolution photographs. The photos were the next best thing to having the statue in hand and he fully intended to show it from every angle. He even borrowed Bunny's macro lens, which would show aspects not normally noticeable. From the school he took a small straight edge he thought would give a further touch of professionalism to his photographs, in addition to giving the viewer an exact idea of the statue's dimensions. As a gesture of good will toward Zakari, and hopefully to ingratiate themselves to him, they took two bottles of reasonably good red wine from the club's stock.

Instead of going back into town for dinner they walked down to the small cafe located along the side of the road which passed through Aghios Vasilis, The owner was frying smelts in the manner one found in the villages. The three to five inch fish were edible head to tail, including the bones, and the two downed several platters of them. They greeted patrons they knew or who recognized and spoke to them, of the weather or the economy. Only rarely did they speak of politics. They learned early upon their arrival on the island not to become embroiled in political discussions, or to discuss personalities in the government. These always ended in shouting matches and it was best to steer clear of them. If one was to talk politics it was much better, and probably safer, to comment only on those politicians

from one's own country. De Gaulle was a prime candidate for
Jean Paul. Carter would occasionally discuss his views of
Johnson and the late John Kennedy. The Cretans seemed to hold
a special affection for Kennedy, the reasons for which were
never made clear. They lamented his untimely death from
assassin's bullets.

Carter remarked the presence of two strangers in the
cafe. They entered and took seats at a table along the wall,
speaking only to order. They preferred to observe the two
foreigners as they ate or talked with others. To watch these
foreigners who were welcomed into the bosom of the clientele of
this little cafe on the road to Knossos was a treat for the idly
curious. Invariably they leaned over to someone near them to ask
who these two young men were and invariably asked if Carter
was German. When they found out he was American and a
teacher at the institute they bobbed their heads to the side in
understanding/amazement. The strangest thing of all to the
latecomers was that these two were conversant in Greek - and in
the Cretan dialect!

The men of Aghi Vasili pronounced Jean Paul and
Carter's names with difficulty. They called Carter Kartos and
Jean Paul they called to Gállos, the Frenchman. Neither minded
the butchering of their names. They were just delighted to be
admitted into the 'inner circle.' They regarded the inhabitants of
Aghi Vasili with true affection and, in most cases, this affection
was returned full measure. Even the priest of the local church
greeted them warmly when their paths crossed and, on more than
one occasion, joined them at their table.

The priest provided their introduction to many of the
men who came to the cafe. Upon his arrival one evening he
noticed them sitting at a small table near the back. He threaded
his way toward them, speaking to this group and that as he
progressed to where Carter and Jean Paul were seated. He
introduced himself and they invited him to join them in a drink.
He accepted gladly, for he was as curious about them as the rest.
As he sat and talked with the two foreigners he sipped his wine.
Others approached under the pretext of greeting the priest. Proud
of being invited to join them he introduced them to others that

approached. It was in this way they came to know, and be known, by the inhabitants of the quarter.

ႃ ႃ ႃ

At the same time that Jean Paul and Carter were in the cafe eating fried smelt and drinking icy retsina, there was another drama going on in the mountains to the south. Vasili Annemoyannis, one of the co-conspirators, was alone. Only moments before he experienced a visit that all but stopped his heart. He wiped his work-roughened palms across his eyes, trying to remove the stinging sweat that dripped into them from his bushy eyebrows and labored to control his breathing. For a moment he feared his bowels were going to release of their own accord and his knees threatened to buckle.

When suddenly confronted by the old man his mind became totally blank. He stammered and stuttered, trying to pull his thoughts together. He promised himself beforehand that he would not show emotion when this moment came, but the palpable miasma of his uncontrollable fear enveloped him. Barba Yorgi's nostrils flared like a mastiff that could smell Vasili's terror.

He did not know how he succeeded in getting through the moment that seemed interminable to him. In the end he was finally able to convince him that he did not have the artifacts nearby, but that they were hidden some distance away. Barba Yorgi, so sure of himself and his power over these little men, allowed himself to be persuaded Vasili would bring his treasure to him. Vasili pleaded for understanding and finally his nemesis, the bull, relented, agreeing to meet him the following night. The place agreed upon for the meeting would be the abandoned talcum mill, which resembled a stone silo, near Arménoi. The old man set the meeting for nine o'clock. With a final warning that he be on time, Barba Yorgi vanished into the night.

Vasili could stand it no longer and sat on some nearby stones, bridging his knees with his arms and cradling his head. His mind raced, trying to think what it was that he must do next.

Zakari! He must find Zakari! Zakari impressed upon him only two days before that if he were approached by Barba Yorgi he must come to him immediately. He gave the same instructions to all the others, telling them exactly what they were to do. He also assured them not to worry, for there were friends now who were going to help them - to protect them, he said. Yes, protect them!

He pushed himself to his feet, feeling stronger now. He moved purposefully for he knew what he must do. He must find a way to see Zakari tonight. There was no time to delay. He hurried into the village of Sellía where he lived and went directly to his house. He did not enter, but instead walked quickly to the back, his legs stronger, and started his mikaní, mounting it as soon as the motor roared to life. His wife heard the noise and came to the door to see what was happening, but was only in time to see its bobbing headlight probing the darkness as her husband negotiated the bumpy road at top speed.

Vasili turned in the direction of Plakias, feeling the night wind cooling his face and entering his shirt through its open collar. He bared his teeth as he tried to urge his mechanical steed to greater speed, but to no avail. The throttle would open no further.

A quarter mile from the first houses on the edge of Plakias Vasili turned off the main dirt road onto the path, which gave access to the garden plots at the base of the mountain. Because of the darkness and the roughness of the path, he was forced to slow down, for he feared losing control and either being thrown from his perch, or damaging his mikaní. As the path began to rise, however, it became smoother and less rutted. There was not much traffic that passed this way, and most of what did was either by foot or donkey. In spite of the better going he was unable to increase his speed, for the grade became progressively steeper and he was soon forced to shift into a lower gear. The roar of the motor and rush of wind past his ears gave him a sensation of speed, which assuaged his need to plunge up the mountain as quickly as possible.

As he passed the place where they discovered the bones of Little Mitzos he crossed himself and glanced up at the stars. Fifteen minutes later he passed between the upright stones marking the beginning of Zakari's property and began to shout for him as he neared the house. He stopped his machine some

twenty feet from the front of the house and shined the light
directly on the front door. He was gratified to see a light appear
and knew Zakari was there. As soon as he saw the light he shut
off the motor. The intensity of the headlight's beam diminished
in direct proportion to the revolutions of the motor, soon
plunging the clearing into silence and darkness. The door opened
and a naked arm with the lantern clutched in its hand appeared,
followed by the apparition of Zakari's tousled head.

"Poiòs enai?" he demanded. Who is it?

"Annemoyanni. O Vasili," he replied. "Zakari, I need to
talk to you. It's happened!" he continued in a shouted whisper.

Zakari, now fully awake, suspected Vasili's reason for
showing up at his house in what must be the middle of the night.
Holding the lantern high he could see his friend's wide eyes and
worried expression. He smiled with what he hoped was an
expression of reassurance and motioned for him to come inside.
As soon as Vasili entered Zakari shut the door behind them.
Should anyone have tried to eavesdrop they would have great
difficulty understanding the whispered conversation being
quickly conducted inside.

Less than five minutes later they both reappeared and
Zakari shut and locked the door. He followed Vasili to the
mikaní and stood next to it with the lantern held high while
Vasili restarted the motor. When it once more roared to life
Zakari walked to the back and climbed aboard, sat down on
some heavy sacks and extinguished the lantern. Vasili put the
machine into gear and swung a tight arc through the olive trees,
heading once more toward the path. During the entire trip back
down the mountain they did not speak. Zakari thought of the
chain of events he was about to initiate. The adrenaline flowed
through his veins, making him feel as if he could run faster than
the clattering conveyance.

Once into Plakias Vasili headed for the kafeneion, where
he knew he would find one of the three telephones in the village.
He pulled up in front of the door, which was closed, but he could
see a dim light glowing in the interior. He leapt from his seat and
began to rap lightly, but insistently at the door. In a moment it
was answered by the proprietor, who closed an hour earlier, but
who lived with his family in the rear. Vasili told him of their

urgent need to use the telephone. When he saw Zakari walk up behind the man at his door, he stepped aside and let them enter. Vasili stayed with the proprietor while Zakari went into a small room at the end of the counter and picked up the receiver.

After repeated attempts at raising an operator he finally succeeded. Fumbling in his pocket he pulled out a creased and grimy scrap of paper, unfolded it and squinted at the number written upon it. He gave the number to the operator, put the paper back into his pocket and waited. From a seeming great distance he could hear a final metallic click before the phone at the other end began to ring.

Chapter 24

It was almost midnight and the shop was closed. The day was long and arduous but not unusually so. His profession was one that required physical strength. He sat in a battered cane-bottomed chair tilted back against the wall. Its joints creaked every time he shifted position even slightly, protesting the weight of the large man seated upon it. The heels of his boots were hooked into the lower rung of the chair, his head tilted back against the wall; his ham-like hands rested in repose upon his thighs. Beside him on a small enameled table sat an empty cup of coffee, the sugary grounds coagulated in the bottom.

Although the lights in the shop were extinguished, the plate glass window and the glass pane in the front door in the front of the shop admitted light from naked 30-watt bulbs strung above now empty stalls. Only a few hours ago the area was crowded with a myriad of produce and the bustle of evening shoppers. From one of the small bars down the street the strains of the bouzouki could be heard backing up the nasal tones of a singer pouring out his heart to unrequited love.

The ringing of the telephone on the cluttered desk in the little cubicle that passed for an office insinuated itself into the consciousness of the man seated on the chair. It rang insistently several times before he groaned, flexed his shoulders and pushed himself away from the wall. The chair landed with a thump, followed immediately by the heavy soles of his boots upon the floor. He stood, stretched, yawned and walked toward the door of the office. When he entered he stopped before the desk and, in an action born of habit, wiped his hands on his bloody apron before reaching for the receiver.

"Naí." Yes.

At the other end of the line a voice spoke tersely, without preamble. No niceties were required, none expected. Information was passed and received. Each would know what to do.

"En táxei." O.K., was his only reply before he replaced the receiver. From the look in his hooded eyes it was difficult to tell what was going through his mind. It was obvious, however, from the way he sloughed off the mantle of fatigue and moved purposefully, catlike, from the office that this call was not unexpected.

With a quickness belying his size, he untied the strings of his apron, lifted it over his head, hung it on a hook on the wall, took a cloth cap from another hook and put it on as he opened the door and went out into the night.

Chapter 25

For once Carter did not need to badger his friend and drag him from his bed. He appreciated the importance of this day and awoke shortly before Carter's alarm sounded. This morning Jean Paul was awakened by his own alarm: the randy rooster belonging to the Karas family who lived on the other side of the vine-covered stone wall bordering the courtyard. At the first hint of dawn he flapped up onto the roof of a shed, surveyed his domain, and announced the arrival of the new day in ringing tones. By the time Carter thudded down the wooden stairs Jean Paul stepped from the door of his room with two steaming cups of coffee in his hands.

"Qui est-ce, ce putain de mec? Je le vois de temps en temps l'après midi, mais jamais le matin!" Exclaimed Carter upon seeing the Frenchman's face. "Don't tell me you're ready! I thought I'd be forced to get a bucket of cold water to get you going this morning. It's about time, I might add. Thanks for the coffee. Hm-m-m, Martell! Now this is the way to get the day started."

"If mossieu will wait one moment I have more than just a simple cup of coffee to offer him this morning." He disappeared into the kitchen and returned a moment later with fresh bread, still warm from the oven and several hunks of chocolate. "Here, I ran down to the bakery before you got up and bought us a real breakfast. As a child I ate bread and chocolate as often as possible. During the war an American Army Sergeant with the Allied soldiers in Oran gave me something called a Hershey Bar and some bread one morning. I quickly developed a taste for this delicacy. Try it. It's fantastic."

Carter did not need to be asked twice. He wrapped a roll around a hunk of the chocolate and dunked it into his steaming cup of coffee liberally laced with the fine cognac. Jean Paul busied himself with the final preparations for their departure. Ten minutes later breakfast was only a sweet memory and they walked out of the house into the early morning light.

Jean Paul mounted the motorbike and kicked it to life. The morning was cool and the sun was still below the horizon. It would be a marvelous day to set out for the south coast. Carter swung his leg over the back and seated himself on the padded passenger seat, barely having the time to put the back foot pegs down and plant his feet on them before Jean Paul gunned the small motor and popped the clutch. Carter grabbed a double handful of Jean Paul's shirt to keep himself astride the bike. Soon enough, however, he settled into the rhythm of the ride, leaning with the bike as they rolled down the winding road into town.

They passed quickly through the nearly deserted streets and were soon past the city gate and out into the countryside. Jean Paul increased their speed, but Carter soon realized that this bike, particularly with two grown men astride, was woefully underpowered. With that realization he settled back for the ride and stopped trying to peer over Jean Paul's shoulder to look for danger in the road ahead.

Both of them laughed when they reached the steep sections of road leading into Aghia Varvara, with its sharp switchbacks. Jean Paul was forced to shift down into the lower gears and the heat from the exhaust near Carter's right leg built until he was soon riding with his heel on the end of the right foot peg. Once they were able to build up speed again, however, the heat was dissipated by the wind.

Within an hour of leaving Iraklion they arrived on the outskirts of Plakias and were soon passing the mostly vacant perivólis. Prior to harvest time there was little to do to maintain them, not at all like springtime when preparation of the fields and planting were so labor intensive. The few peasants already working their fields hardly looked up as the pair bounced by in low gear over the bumpy path.

At first the ascent was not difficult, but by the time they arrived at the steepest part their little motor labored in first gear. They moved at scarcely more than a fast walk. Both leaned forward, unconsciously trying to provide just that ounce more impetus that would get them to the top of the mountain. They were relieved when the grade became more gradual and they could shift up once more.

Both men shouted to announce their arrival as Jean Paul guided them through the olive trees to the front of Zakari's house. Everything was quiet. When the motor was shut off they both looked around. All they could see were several chickens and a scruffy rooster scratching in the bare soil. Through the metallic popping of the cooling motor they could hear a goat or sheep bleating somewhere off to the left. Jean Paul thumbed the button on the handlebars causing the bike's tinny horn to bleat in reply. As there was no answer from inside the house they both got off and walked up to the door. Carter knocked gently, but there was no answer. The next time he knocked with greater authority, but there was still no sound to be heard. Jean Paul reached down and tried the door, but it was firmly locked.

"This is strange. It was today we were supposed to be here, wasn't it?

"That's what I thought. Let's walk around a little to see if maybe he's out on the property somewhere."

They walked to what appeared to be the limits of the property. The goat was still in her pen, pacing nervously while looking at them and bleating plaintively.

"He can't be too far away this early in the morning," stated Jean Paul. "It looks like the path we took is the only one to his house and we didn't pass him on the way up. Maybe it would be best if we wait awhile. He's sure to return before long."

Carter agreed, and they wandered around aimlessly before finally sitting down among the trees. Zakari's absence puzzled them. He seemed anxious enough to work with them. He was sure to return before long. But the minutes passed and they became restless and somewhat discouraged. Carter rose and wandered some more, finally drawing a bucket of water from the well.

They turned to idle speculation about where Zakari kept the statue hidden, even going so far as trying the front door. Common sense told them they would be the prime suspects should Zakari find his treasure missing. There could be no doubt of their presence for the tracks of the motorbike could be clearly seen in the dust of the yard. Besides, he agreed to meet them here this morning.

After two hours they dejectedly remounted the motorbike and started back down the mountain. Upon their return to town they would find Andreas and tell him how his friend failed to show up at the appointed time. They could not imagine where he could be. The ride down was considerably quicker than the morning's ride up. Upon reaching the main road they turned in the direction from which they arrived earlier, but at a fork in the road Jean Paul braked to a stop. The sign showed arrows pointing in different directions. To the right they would return via Spíli and Timbakion. To the left would take them directly north via Arménoi.

Intent upon the road ahead of them they paid no heed to the small track, which branched off to the left and disappeared behind a hillside covered with a jumble of scree. Where the path dipped into a small vale the talus hid the ruins of an ancient talcum mill. It was here, in years gone by, peasant miners brought their loads of steatite, common soapstone, taken from veins in the rugged surrounding hills by pick, shovel and muscle wrenching labor, to be ground into talcum powder. When the veins of green, brown and black steatite from the immediate vicinity petered out some forty years earlier it was abandoned and fell into total disrepair. Traces of white talc were still evident on the interior stones of the circular grinding pit itself. If a roof ever protected the interior from the elements there was none now. Those stones that remained stood as high as fifteen feet in some places. The mortar between them was weathered and rotten. Only gravity kept the remaining stones together and in some semblance of their original form. Several of the large hewn blocks forming the circular wall were displaced, with those at the top seeming to teeter, delicately balanced, on the verge of falling in on itself.

The site was abandoned, but not deserted. Activity began before daylight. Among those present was Zakari, who spent the night with Annemoyannis at his home in Sellía. He gave no thought to the two foreigners who were to meet him this morning at his house. Instead he arose after sleeping only fitfully and engaged in chores around the property for several hours. It was he who greeted the others upon their arrival with grim countenance. Preparations were carried out with quiet resolve and everything was in readiness for the curtain to rise on the last act of this drama, a Greek tragedy, which could only have one outcome.

The sound of the motorbike's passing came faintly to those so busily engaged, but they paid it no heed. The passengers on the bike would have been surprised to know they were so close to the one they set out to see in such a lighthearted mood this very morning. They were totally unaware of all that was happening just a few yards from where they motored by.

Carter and Jean Paul stopped in Arménoi for coffee and then continued north to Rethymnon and east to Iraklion. By one o'clock they were back in the city and immediately began searching for Andreas. They wanted to talk to him, tell him of how his friend failed to keep their appointment. They looked first in his office, the small cubbyhole near the center of town, but they last saw him the day before. When they tried to find him at home no one answered the door. They talked with several people who they knew to be his friends and business associates, but all told the same story. Puzzled by their inability to find him and frustrated by their experiences of the day, they stopped at a service station to fill the tank of Stasso's motorbike then headed for their villa.

Chapter 26

By 8 o'clock the light began to fade. The softness of the Cretan dusk descended, laying a mantle of peace upon the land. Insects buzzed through the still air, but the sound of their passing was thin and whispery, having lost its robustness in direct relation to the declining temperature and changing season. The quiet of the vale was broken only by the occasional calls of a raucous magpie. Other than the birds and the puffy, pink tinged clouds drifting across the deepening blue vault of sky, there was no movement. It was as if this corner of the earth would pass into night as for millennia past, to sleep tranquilly under the stars, undisturbed by man.

From afar the persistent buzz of a small motor insinuated itself into the quiet and anything or anyone listening pricked up their ears. As it came closer the level of noise increased, and all other ambient noise ceased. Whatever, or whoever, heard it held their breath and waited for it to pass. The level of noise dropped, picked up again, idled and stopped, giving way to total silence. For long moments there was no other sound, until muffled footfalls could be heard coming toward the vale. They approached the rise overlooking the mill site and paused. Silhouetted against the sky's remaining light appeared the form of a man bent under a load he carried slung across his left shoulder. He held the neck of the sack closed with both hands as he stood there. His head turned to the left and then right, peering up the hillside and back down to the jumble of scree. His shoulders lifted in an inaudible sigh before he moved forward again, slowly, as if measuring his steps in the direction of the ruins of the round stone structure.

When he reached the ruins he stopped again to glance quickly behind him before passing through the open doorway to the interior. In a moment he reappeared in the doorway without the sack, looked around again, lifted his head as if to smell the wind, and then began to pick up dry branches that dotted the area surrounding the ruin. With an armload he reentered the stone mill, from which could be heard the occasional sharp crack of splintering wood and muted scraping noises. All sounds from the interior ceased, however, when a wispy plume of smoke appeared from the top of the circular structure. It rose in the still air, unwavering, straight as a die, until it encountered a slight breeze. The top of the column of smoke was knocked off and dissipated to the southwest.

Flames licked at the dry wood, giving off less smoke and more light as they gained strength. The glow of the flames illuminated the face of Vasili Annemoyanni. He sat with his back against the rough interior stones, his knees drawn up in front of him, his hands resting atop his thighs. He seemed mesmerized by the fire, alone with his thoughts, withdrawn. Beside him lay the sack, its slack top closed with a piece of stout twine. Within easy reach was a stack of dry branches, fuel for the small fire. Its wavering light comforted and reassured him. He did not relish the prospect of being here with no light. Soon it would be dark and he wondered nervously how long he would have to wait here alone.

Vasili would have been more nervous if he knew he was not alone. In a carefully chosen vantage point, giving him an unobstructed view of most of the small clearing where the ruins of the mill stood crouched Barba Yorgi. To ensure there would be no unpleasant surprises he arrived early for this rendezvous, hiding himself in the talus. To cover the whiteness of his hair and beard, which would have shown like a beacon, he removed the sweat-rimed black cloth from around his head and retied it like a mask. His dark clothing blended with the uneven terrain, making him virtually invisible. He sat quietly awaiting his quarry, assuring himself that every eventuality was covered. He would be sure of the situation, know what and who would confront him, before showing himself. He might be an old man, but he was no fool. He remembered well the lessons learned while with the Resistance. For this reason it was he, Barba Yorgi, who was alive today while so many others suffered for their incaution.

Darkness was almost complete when the old man leaned forward and, with the aid of his staff, pushed himself to his feet. His eyes were fixed upon the doorway of the tower from which emanated the flickering glow of Vasili's fire. Standing erect he looked around, peering warily into the darkness, checking yet one more time. Satisfied, he moved quietly through the scree, being careful not to announce his presence by inadvertent noise. Once in the open he advanced with more confidence, no longer worried about stumbling. His concentration was upon the rectangle of light emanating from the interior of the ruined mill.

Vasili heard nothing until there came the sound of a soft, rumbling voice saying his name, "Annemoyanni."

Startled he leapt to his feet and searched wide-eyed for the source. Across the flames he saw the hooded apparition standing in the doorway. Barba Yorgi still wore the dark cloth wrapped around his head and the only feature visible to the frightened Annemoyanni was his eyes glinting in the firelight.

"Pseramanoli?"

"Yes, it's me. Did you think I wouldn't come tonight, even after we made plans for this meeting?"

"N-n-no, I just..."

"I see," the old man cut him off, his voice dripping with cynicism and irony. "You just hoped I wouldn't meet you tonight"

"W-why, no! No, I didn't think that at all. You just surprised me. I didn't hear you coming."

With uncharacteristic effusiveness Barba Yorgi swept the concealing cloth from his head and stepped across the stone threshold into the warm glow of firelight.

"Never mind, Vasilaki, never mind. You've kept your part of the bargain and, of course, you can be sure I'll keep mine. I see you have a sack there beside you. The antíkas, I suppose? Let's see what you've brought to share with old Yorgos."

The old man stepped further into the confines of the barrel-shaped structure, avarice evident on his face. Through the hair of his mustache and beard could be seen the pink tip of his tongue quickly wetting his lips. An unconscious expression of gleeful anticipation suffused his features. Vasili gestured resignedly towards the sack lying on the ground before moving to his left, edging uneasily to the far side of the fire.

Barba Yorgi, his attention riveted upon the sack lying unopened on the ground, appeared to have forgotten him. So confident was he that he turned his back entirely and leaned his staff against the wall. The flicker and flare of the fire behind him threw a gigantic wavering shadow up the curved wall of the mill. From the other side of the fire, near the ruined opening, which served as a door, Vasili watched in silent fascination. The scene before him held him in its powerful grasp, transfixed, as a small animal before a weaving, venomous cobra.

Barba Yorgi could no longer contain himself and reached for the filthy piece of heavy twine binding the neck of the sack. His thick fingers fumbled with the knot, but he was unable to pick it loose with his blunt and broken nails. In frustration he pulled his knife from his sash, quickly slicing through the stubborn binding. When the cord parted the old man gave a grunt of satisfaction and replaced the knife. Taking the cloth in both hands he spread it wide and let it fall to the ground, revealing the contents to his questing eyes.

At first he thought he was looking at the bottom of a clay pot or pitcher and he moved closer to the firelight to illuminate it. He stepped back to better focus his eyes and gave a small grunt. He moved closer to confirm what he was seeing and then leapt to his feet with surprising alacrity, an oath escaping his lips.

Lying before him, surrounded by the puddle of the collapsed sack, was a pile of dirty clothes. The shirt and torn pants were spotted in several places with dark reddish stains resembling rust. There was a pair of heavy shoes, both with their tongues hanging out like dogs on a hot day. The sole of one was more than twice as thick as the other. On top of the pile was a skull, its jaw askew and obviously broken. From one of the empty eye sockets a tear seemed to glisten, reflecting the light of the flames, and then run down the cheek bone, leaving a glistening, iridescent trace of its path. Taking a closer look Barba Yorgi discovered the trail was a silver chain, at the end of which, half hidden in a fold of the clothes, was a crucifix. Beside the skull piled atop the jumble of ruined clothes was a transistor radio in a case of brown imitation leather.

He was so surprised by this revelation that a moment passed before recognition dawned upon him and he knew for a certainty that this was little Mitzos. Barba Yorgi felt the hair rise on the nape of his neck. His head felt as if it was being slowly tightened in a vise and his legs threatened to give way beneath him. A hoarse, rasping sound filled the enclosed space and, as he became aware of it, he searched for its source. He was surprised to discover that it was he and struggled to bring his breathing under control.

He did not know how long he stood there faced with the damning evidence before he heard a small sound behind him. Although his body remained rooted where he stood, his head snapped to the right on his thick neck. His only visible eye was wide and staring.

On the far side of the fire was the hunched form of Vasili. Flanking him were Ari Mavrodakis, Panagioti Tsipas and Stavros Petrides, all men who were at the tomb the day it was found, all men from whom he took, or threatened to take, a share of the treasure. From beyond the limits of his vision came another voice.

"Pseramanoli!"

His head snapped back in the other direction. To his left behind him he could see Zakari Forakis standing upright, legs braced apart. To Zakari's left was another form, twice as broad as Zakari and over a head taller. Falling embers caused the flames to leap momentarily higher. In the flare he recognized the fifth man, Apostolo Moussis - the butcher - Deaf Yanni's man.

The old man felt as if he were in a dream. His limbs would not respond properly to the commands his brain gave them. He struggled to face the men there behind him, to face the accusation in their eyes. His mind, too, remained sluggish and his vision blurred. It seemed to take him forever to turn around. When he finally succeeded he saw them arranged in a semicircle behind him. With the blank face of the stone wall behind him and the group of determined men on the far side of the fire between him and the door he was trapped!

In the quiet, broken only by the soft sounds of the fire, movement through a half-hidden opening attracted his attention. He focused his eyes past the heads of his accusers and saw two dark forms move into the light cast by the fire. As soon as he recognized their faces in the flickering light his mouth dropped open once more in amazement, for behind the men standing close to the fire were Andreas and Deaf Yanni. Upon entering the enclosure both men stopped and surveyed the scene. When their gaze finally fell on Barba Yorgi they saw hope flicker across his face and in his eyes. The old man's tongue darted quickly over his dry lips.

"Andreas..." he began, but when he saw the icy stare fixed on him he stopped, although his lips continued to work soundlessly for a moment more. With the realization that all reasoning and supplication would be useless he let his hand drop to his side and the great head drooped, pillowed by his beard.

Andreas watched for long seconds, and then, to his amazement, a change came over Barba Yorgi. Without lifting his head, his eyes opened wide and he peered fixedly at each man in the group. A cynical smile, devoid of warmth or humor, suffused his features as he slowly raised his head. As it came up he straightened and threw his shoulders back in a proud gesture of someone supremely sure of himself. It was the Barba Yorgi of old who now looked out at the group of men facing him, projecting a fearless aura of authority and power. As he began to speak his words came low and rumbling from deep within his chest.

"My friends, we seem to have a little misunderstanding here. Yes, a misunderstanding. That's all it is. Nothing that can't be straightened out with a little discussion and straight talk. I'm glad you're all here together, for now we can correct any problems that may exist. Each of you knows I'm a reasonable man and a good friend to all of you. Why, I wouldn't let any harm come to such good friends as you. No, not at all. I say we just move outside, build a fire and sit down to discuss what's on each of your minds. Yes, that sounds like a good idea. Let's just go outside where we have more room and can sit down comfortably around a nice fire. Here, I'll help you gather some wood. Come, friends. Yes, I'm glad we're all here together."

While he talked he edged cautiously toward the back wall where his staff leaned just out of reach. He hoped his conversation would distract from his movements and that the others would not notice what he was attempting. Closer and closer he inched, until finally, with a glance out of the corner of his eye, he saw all he need do was reach out and take it in his hands. Once he could heft the familiar weight and bulk of his staff he would no longer be unarmed, no longer helpless.

Although he was outnumbered, these men would not have a chance of stopping him once the staff was within his grasp. Just a little closer now. Keep talking. Keep their attention. Easy! Easy! Just a little more...! NOW!

Barba Yorgi stopped in mid-sentence, his expression changing from one of placation to a wolfish grin, and his left hand shot out for the staff.

From the far side of the fire came a brief shout. Barba Yorgi saw the beginning of a movement and the blur of something in the air as it passed over the fire. With no time to react, no time to protect himself, the fist-sized stone smashed into his temple and knocked him back against the rough blocks of the wall. He heard the sound of its impact, followed immediately by a starburst of light. He was dimly aware of the ground rushing up at him, but before pain could overtake him he pitched headfirst into a vortex of darkness and oblivion.

An indefinable sense of discomfort and pain nagged and pulled at him. The ebb and flow of consciousness made him aware at times of the soft murmur of voices, words he could not understand. Behind his closed eyelids he sensed, rather than saw, flickering light. But before he could reach for that source of illumination, and define it, he sank once more into the pit-like darkness. Increasing discomfort caused him to try to ease the cramping he felt in his shoulders and legs, but he was unable to move. As he swam closer and closer to the light he became aware of the sharp pain in his head, as well as the unpleasant feeling of his face resting on a cold, rough surface. He tried to lift his hand to his head, wanting to probe the tender, throbbing area with his fingers, to rub away the sharpness of it, but he was unable to move.

The closer he returned to consciousness, the greater the realization of his situation. With his eyes still closed he took a mental inventory. He knew he was lying on his side and that he could not move his arms. His hands were numb and there was a great pressure on his wrists. His legs and feet were numb, as well, and the muscles of his thighs felt as if they were being torn apart. An involuntary groan escaped his lips and immediately the babble of soft voices ceased. On the other side of the curtain of his closed eyelids he sensed the others' attention shift toward him. His pain served to sweep the cobwebs from his brain and focus his thoughts.

A voice close to his ear called his name, "Pseramanoli! Pseramanoli! Yorgos!"

Barba Yorgi moved his head and tried to open his eyes. As soon as he attempted to move his cheek from where it rested a cymbal clash of pain caused him to squeeze his eyes tightly shut. A sharp slap to the cheek caused him to jerk back his head and again the pain assaulted him. The slap was repeated and he felt a hand grasp a handful of the hair of his long beard and jerk his face roughly to the side.

In spite of himself he emitted a low moan and one of his eyes opened for an instant. The firelight, although not so bright, stung his one opened eye and caused his already blurred vision to blur even more. The slap was repeated and his name called again.

"Yorgos, wake up! Open your eyes!"

Another slap followed.

"Pseramanoli! Come on, now. You've slept enough. Open your eyes!"

Waves of anger rolled through the recumbent form like electricity. All at once his senses were acute and he gathered himself to strike out at his tormentor. One eye flew open, but the other remained glued shut by the coagulated flow of blood from the wound in his temple where the stone struck. A trail of blood ran from his temple, across his cheek and puddled in the socket of his closed eye. There it congealed and effectively sealed his right eye shut. He tried to sit up, but his efforts were in vain. He was tied in such a manner that he would never be able to sit up or move without help.

His legs were bent at the knee and lashed with strong rope around his body, pulling his thighs tight against his abdomen. His arms were stretched along his body, which was bent slightly at the waist. His wrists were tied tightly to the outsides of his ankles and his elbows firmly bound to his knees. From knees to toes and elbows to fingertips his circulation was cut off, leaving him with no feeling in his extremities. Only his head remained free, but because of the enforced fetal position of his body his face pressed against the stone of the low ledge upon which he lay. His great muscles strained against the bonds holding him. He tried to turn himself in order that he might at least look full-face at his captors. The tendons of his neck bulged as he grunted and strained in frustration. Great drops of sweat appeared on his brow and his face was crimson against the white of his beard. In the dancing firelight it looked as if the eye socket where the blood pooled and dried, effectively gluing the eye shut, was a bloody hole from which the eye was gouged. An uneasy murmur was heard from one of the men in the group, voicing concern that the old man would be able to free himself.

"Don't worry," one of the others replied. "To break free he would need the strength of Samson, and I don't think this old one is going to bring down the pillars of the temple tonight." The not totally inappropriate imagery evoked nervous laughter, but none wronged by Barba Yorgi appeared willing to approach him too closely.

As he lay panting from exertion, unable to breathe comfortably or fully because of his position, one of the men standing on the far side of the fire spoke. "Why don't we just kill him now and rid ourselves of this parasite forever? Why should we wait and discuss what should be done with him. Andreas and Yanni are gone. We can do with him as we like. Apostolo, that knife you carry is all we need. Use it! Use it now and let's be done with it."

A universal murmur of approval caused Barba Yorgi to catch his breath. He watched as the butcher stepped into his line of sight, his great, beefy red, chapped hands massaging one another. His face was without expression as he looked down at the tortured and bound body before him. Once again Barba Yorgi's good eye was wide as he tried to see what the man standing over him intended to do. There was no fear in them, however, only a mocking look to match the sneer on his lips.

"Moussis. Fat little Apostolos Moussis. Kalispéra, Apostolaki. What are you doing here with these little men tonight? They always called you the village idiot when you were young. Are you still playing the idiot for these horiatí? These peasants?"

Apostolos' implacable expression never changed and his fleshy lips barely moved when he replied. "Naí."

"Naí? Yes!? What do you mean, yes? Do you mean 'yes', you are still the village idiot, or 'yes', you put yourself on the same level with these worthless wretches with whom you consort?" asked Barba Yorgi with a condescending laugh. "You know me, Moussis. I am The Bull. This is my island. These are my mountains. What do you think you can do to me?"

While Apostolos considered his answer, a rustle was heard in the underbrush outside the enclosure, followed immediately by the beating of wings as roosting birds beat the night air in alarm. Two of the men were startled by the interruption and looked quickly in the direction of the door. The blackness of the night was all that could be seen beyond the fire lit interior. They both thought it strange that birds should suddenly burst into flight in the middle of the night. Being superstitious men, they crossed themselves quickly, but the drama before them was more compelling than their fears.

Apostolos remained in place, but continued regarding the man lying before him. When he finally spoke a suggestion of a smile flickered across his face.

"When I say 'naí' I mean 'yes'. Yes, I'm going to kill you. You've been judged, Kyrie Yorgos, and you must die."

From somewhere far away the clarion crow of a rooster pierced the darkness, followed shortly by the raucous lament of an ass, all strange sounds in the middle of the night. As strange as the sounds were, to Zakari, who stood behind the other men watching the drama unfold, the diversion of the out-of-context noises was welcome. He tore his attention away from the imposing bulk of the butcher towering over the prostrate form of Barba Yorgi, raised his head and flared his nostrils as if trying to smell what was happening out in the darkness. Within him there was unease, a presentiment of something monstrous, something infinitely evil lurking in the darkness. The evil within this place he could see with his own eyes. The evil without he could only sense. The haunting cry of a screech owl floated down from up beyond the talus, to be answered by the cry of another coming from a different direction. As if of their own accord his feet began to move toward the door and the blackness beyond. The feeling of imminent danger was overwhelming, as was the urge to run. No one noticed him slip out the door. He ducked his head to avoid the low stone lintel as he moved from the glow of the firelight and was swallowed by the night.

Inside the ruins anticipation was palpable. Barba Yorgi felt no fear. Instead, he was consumed with helpless rage. His bloodshot eye glowed with a feral gleam, fixed upon the face of the butcher. He watched as Apostolos' hand moved resolutely toward the sheathed knife hanging from the worn leather belt and unfastened the thong which kept it from falling out of its sheath, wrapped his huge fist around its handle and began to bare the cold, razor sharp steel. The others watched, as well, from the far side of the fire, their collective breaths on hold. Here and there, a tongue licked at bone dry lips.

Barba Yorgi silently pitted all his great strength against the ropes restraining him. Sweat coursed down his brow, ran into his eye and dripped from the end of his nose. Barely visible through the matted hair of his beard and mustache his mouth stretched in a mad grimace, his teeth tightly clenched. The ropes at his hairy wrists creaked from the strain and bit into his tortured and swollen flesh until blood seeped from the wounds and soaked into the rough fibers.

Apostolos took a step toward the old man, stopped, watched him, and then approached another step closer. He held the knife comfortably, yet firmly, in his right hand, its finely honed blade with needle sharp tip pointed in the direction of its prey.

The point of the blade was a scant handbreadth away from Barba Yorgi's neck, its veins and tendons standing out in sharp relief, when words arose which sounded as if they came from a tomb. "You will not escape! None of you! The Bull damns you all!!" Spoken through clenched teeth, with lips barely moving, set in a face contorted in rictus, the effect of the words echoing in the chamber was powerful. The small smile froze on the face of the butcher and the others quickly crossed themselves. Still, in spite of their fear, they craned their necks forward to witness what would follow. Having paused for a heartbeat, the tip of the knife resumed its inexorable journey toward the point on the old man's exposed neck where it would inevitably find the carotid artery.

From Barba Yorgi came a low sound, as if from far away. His expression did not change and, for an instant, everyone wondered about the source of the drone. Again the movement of the knife stopped and hung in midair. It was not a moan or a groan, but rather a low keening, as if someone pushed one of the keys in the lower register of a great organ and held it down while slowly increasing the volume. In the reverberations set up by the tone a harmonic was created, filling the enclosed area with a mystical chord, which, in turn, invaded and filled the very being of each of the men present. It was as mesmerizing as the call of Homer's sirens, thrilling each in turn.

The chord ended only when there was no longer any air to be squeezed from the lungs of the sacrificial bull. At the precise instant it ended there came a subtle lurching of the ground, a shifting. It was not an up or down motion, but a movement to the side. The attention of the men was so riveted upon the scene unfolding before them that they did not even notice.

Some distance away on the outside Zakari heard the sound coming from inside the mill. He noticed the movement following the abrupt cessation of the droning. To his dismay he heard another sound, which sent a thrill of horror through him. From the hillside above him came a groan and a crack, followed by a distinct thump and the sound of movement. He listened for an instant trying to define what he was hearing. It did not take him long to realize that the small tremor was sufficient to dislodge one of the boulders from above.

The boulder was part of the landscape, perched in that precise position since time immemorial. Through the millennia winter rains slowly eroded the matrix fixing it upon the hillside, until it became delicately balanced against the force of gravity that pulled at it. At that precise moment in time only a suggestion of movement was required to set it in motion. Once the inertia was broken it became an animate object and moved down the side of the mountain with increasing velocity.

To Zakari It sounded as if it were aimed at him. He stood rooted to the spot where he first heard it, unable to make his feet move. His mind screamed at him to run, but where? Which direction? In panic he took one step and fell flat on his face. A second later the huge projectile passed directly over him, missing his prone form by mere inches and headed directly for the doorway through which flowed the soft light of the fire. For a brief instant Zakari saw it silhouetted between him and the glowing doorway.

Inside the drama continued, each participant totally ignorant of the approaching danger. The sudden explosive impact as the boulder crashed through the opening taking stones from the side and top of the low door with it startled them all. Apostolos, who was at the moment of pushing the point of the knife slowly into the stretched skin of Barba Yorgi's neck, lurched and fell forward. The knife entered the old man's neck, but missed the carotid artery. The blade sliced deeply into the wrinkled skin and opened a gaping wound before the point snapped against the stone shelf. A gout of hot, red blood followed. Confused, Apostolos withdrew the knife immediately and straightened himself, all the time looking down at the gore that covered the blade and his fingers. Behind him he could hear the clamoring of the others scrambling madly to get out as quickly as possible.

No sound came from Barba Yorgi, who bled profusely from his neck wound. Apostolos glanced from the blade to the face of his victim and was puzzled by the look of abject terror he saw. His head was turned as far to the left as humanly possible and his eye, opened wide and staring, was fixed upon a spot above the butcher's head. His mouth stretched open wider and wider to match the expression of his eye. Apostolos threw his head back in a jerky motion, searching for whatever was above his head that drew Barba Yorgi's attention.

What Apostolos saw never registered on his consciousness. No sooner was his head fully back than a large, hand-tailored block from atop the roofless wall, dropped out of the darkness above and smashed with brutal impact into his forehead, shearing off the top of his head from just below the hairline of his forehead to the nape of his neck. Such was the velocity of the blow that the butcher's body was left standing for an instant. A rain of others, smashing, pulverizing, destroying followed the first block. There were no screams, for there was no time to react and no conscious thought of their imminent demise.

The only sound other than that of the collapsing mill was a brief demonic laugh, silenced by the cascade of stones.

When Zakari saw the projectile flash between him and the lighted doorway he became transfixed. It all happened so quickly. And then the stone bowled into the doorway. Like a tower of loosely stacked dominoes the structure fell in upon itself. As the walls collapsed a gout of sparks flew into the air, twinkled like the stars in the sky and then winked into oblivion. In spite of the fact that it all happened in the blink of an eye, it was indelibly stamped upon his incredulous mind.

In the ensuing silence he pushed himself once more to his feet and advanced haltingly toward the mill. He heard no sound from what remained of the interior. Against the slightly lighter sky he could make out the remains of the truncated edifice. All that was left now was a cairn of stones, burying the evidence of what transpired here this evening. He stood rooted to the earth, tears running down his stubbled cheeks. In the end he turned and stumbled away into the night.

Chapter 27

The dawning of the new day found Carter already up and about. He slept fitfully. Zakari's failure to meet with them as promised concerned him. Before going to bed Jean Paul vowed to locate Andreas the first thing in the morning in order to learn why the carefully planned meeting did not take place. True to his word, and much to Carter's surprise, Jean Paul arose with a sense of purpose and determination. By nine he dropped Carter at the institute and began to make the rounds of places where his old friend would most likely be found. Andreas was usually at his cubbyhole of an office by that time, but this morning he was neither there nor at home. By 11:30 Jean Paul gave up in frustration and wandered by Manoli's shop on his way back to the car. Manoli was alone in his shop and insisted he stop for a while. Ordering coffee from one of the wandering waiters, he and Jean Paul sat out front in the morning sun.

For several days the two men had not seen each other and Manoli was full of questions about who was staying at the villa in Aghi Vasili. He was forever hopeful of an invitation to be included and was not shy about making his wishes known. Jean Paul was not receptive, however, and gave vague replies to his overtures, remaining preoccupied with his primary goal of finding Andreas. A familiar slump shouldered form walked around the corner, causing Jean Paul to jump to his feet. He cut Manoli off in mid-sentence and quickly crossed to the other side of the street.

Andreas was deep in thought and did not even notice Jean Paul until he ran up beside him and, matching strides with him, put his hand on his arm. Andreas looked up, surprised at the sudden appearance of the Frenchman. "Ah, bon jour, mon ami. What are you doing out so early this morning?" he asked lethargically.

His eyes were red and sunken with dark circles under them. The skin seemed to hang on his face and his shoulders slumped even more than normal.

"Where in the world have you been? I've looked all over town for you this morning. Carter and I went to the mountain to see your friend Zakari yesterday, but he never showed up. I don't have to tell you how upset we both were. That's a long way to ride double on a motorbike for nothing. What's going on?"

"Zakari? Ah yes, about the statue. You were supposed to meet him to take pictures of the statue. Well, all I can say is that Zakari was involved in some very important business yesterday and was unavailable to meet with you. I can tell you that it was something he couldn't avoid. Look, I'm very sorry, but I don't have time to talk with you right now."

Andreas raised his eyes and suddenly realized Jean Paul did not follow what he was saying. "Please forgive me, my friend. I'm just not myself this morning. And don't hold this against Zakari. It was not his fault. I'm sorry. I must leave now."

He patted Jean Paul on the arm and without another word continued down the street. Jean Paul watched his back until he turned the corner. He did not know what to think. Something was definitely bothering Andreas. If his appearance was any indication, something grave must have happened. He returned to Manoli's shop, told him he must leave for he needed to take care of some things and walked up the street to retrieve his car.

♈ ♈ ♈

None of those inside the ruins of the mill could have survived. The falling blocks must have crushed everyone as the walls crumbled. Zakari finally returned to the scene to search through the rubble for survivors, but was hampered by the darkness. He sweated and strained, lifting and shifting blocks of stone, but his efforts were fruitless. In despair he left the scene and wandered aimlessly until shortly after midnight.

He was so exhausted by his effort and the strain of the night that he crawled under some bushes and immediately fell into a troubled sleep. No sooner did he fall asleep than he began to dream. In the dream a stone tower rose, dark and forbidding. As he stood outside the tower the sky became dark and a chill wind arose. Thinking a storm was approaching he looked around for shelter, but seeing none decided to enter the tower. He began to run towards it, but did not seem to be making any progress. The harder he ran the further away the tower seemed.

A high pitched shriek from the sky caused him to stop running and look up. High above was a bird, black against the darkening sky, flapping its wings, seeming to struggle to gain altitude. He watched, fascinated, wondering why the bird should be trying to fly higher and higher in the face of the coming storm. Suddenly it wrapped itself in its wings and began to plunge earthwards. Down, down, down it came. The closer it came the larger it grew, until it filled the entire sky. Lightning flashed and its glare was reflected in something hanging from the neck of the giant bird. It was a chain! Attached to the chain was a skull, its ghastly mouth hanging open. It was at that moment Zakari realized it was not the bird that shrieked, but the skull! The bird continued its downward dive and did not spread its wings again until it was directly above the tower. When it finally unfurled them a tremendous wind was created that howled and shook the earth. He tried to run, but his legs refused to do his bidding. It was as if his feet were mired in mud. He did succeed in turning to run away, but no matter how hard he strained to escape he made no headway. In desperation he looked back over his shoulder in time to see the tower begin to crumble under the onslaught of the wind. It fell inward from the top, followed by row after row of stones. From the interior came the sound of cries, followed by a great gout of sparks and flame. To his astonishment the sparks mounted to the sky, where they became birds and flew away before the wind.

His attention now refocused on the ruins of the tower. All that remained was a pile of rubble with wisps of smoke rising from it. For a long moment there was nothing else, no movement, no sound. Without warning one of the huge stone blocks lifted slightly. Then another shifted and slid to the side, followed shortly by another and another. Something was rising from the ruins, pushing up from beneath the stones. A new thrill of terror ran through him and once more he tried to run.

This time he could not even turn away. To his horrified eyes came the vision of a huge head rising from the debris. He could only see the back of the head and the powerful shoulders supporting it, but on either side grew black, glistening horns. They were thick, massive and hooked.

A bull! A bull!! But what would a bull be doing in the ruins of the tower? In spite of his fear he took first one step then another in the direction of the vision. The great head swung first one way and then the other, as if searching for something. Without knowing why Zakari called out. His cry arrested the motion of the great head for an instant and then, with no warning, it snapped 180 degrees to face directly towards him. Eyes that flashed fire dominated the face of the bull. When they saw Zakari standing there they widened in recognition and a cavern of a mouth opened, a bottomless pit from which issued the foul odor of putrescence and death. A demonic laugh, more terrible and physically shocking than anything he remembered rolled up from the pit, surrounding and suffocating him. It was the face, however, that made him feel as if his heart would burst from his chest. That face! It was the face of Barba Yorgi!

Zakari screamed and sat straight upright. He was bathed in sweat and trembled violently. With palsied hands he scrubbed at his eyes and stubbled cheeks. He produced a cigarette then struggled to light it. He told himself it was only a dream, the vision was so real. As he smoked he fought to bring himself under control. The acuteness of his nightmare slowly receded, yet he was unable to put it out of his mind.

Andreas! He must call Andreas. Both he and Yanni needed to know what happened. He struggled to his feet and stumbled through the underbrush in the direction of Plakias.

Finding a telephone was no easy task at that hour of the morning on the south coast of Crete, but he finally succeeded and placed a call to Andreas. If only Barba Yorgi perished no thought would be given to providing clues to finding his body. In this case, however, there were men involved who left behind families. To cover the real reason why all of them were together that night, the three survivors needed to devise a plausible scenario, which would explain it.

For long moments Andreas said nothing. He was aghast by the panic apparent in Zakari's voice. When he began to speak it was in the attempt to calm the fears of his old friend. His mind raced through a list of possibilities, sorting and discarding. Time was the important consideration and he needed time.

"Listen, Zakaraki, don't worry about it. Yanni and I will take care of everything. Go home. As soon as it's light we'll send some men to the mill. They'll look for anything that might raise questions. We'll work out an explanation. You'll be fine. Just try to act normal. Do the things you usually do and let us handle this. I'll contact you in a day or two."

His fears somewhat allayed, Zakari agreed and hung up, thankful for good friends like Andreas and Yanni.

ϒ   ϒ   ϒ

Andreas came to the club that night to seek out Jean Paul and Carter. Although he did not look much better, at least he seemed less preoccupied. They seated themselves away from everyone else, a bottle of Cretan red in the middle of the table.

"I know you were both upset when Zakari wasn't there to meet you as planned. Don't worry. I'll be in touch with him again in the next day or so. When we talk I'll set up another rendezvous with him for you."

"I hope so," responded Jean Paul. "I want to return to Zürich early next week. If I could take along the pictures of his statue at that time we could perhaps get the ball rolling. Carter contacted his uncle in America asking to borrow money. It would be a crime if the statue were melted down for the gold. I even talked to Yves about lending us some money, Carter. I forgot to tell you about that, but he says he can't risk it."

"Listen, don't worry about it. We'll find it somewhere. Maybe we can raise a large part of it ourselves through the things we sell to Katz. Anyway, thanks, Andreas, for setting up another meeting for us with Zakari. We were both very upset when we went up there yesterday."

Before long Andreas bade them good night and rose to leave. Jean Paul followed him outside. He was gone only a few minutes and when he returned Carter could tell something was on his mind.

"The strangest thing just happened. When I walked out with Andreas we stood and talked a moment and then he walked away. As he was walking down the street a man came out of the park and stopped him. I couldn't hear what they were saying, but they talked for a minute. Suddenly Andreas stumbled back as if slapped. I started to go over to see if I could help, but before I took my first step Andreas rushed off down the street to his house. The other man crossed the street and disappeared into the park. Strange. Really strange."

Carter agreed with Jean Paul's assessment, but was more concerned with how they were going to come up with the necessary funds. Jean Paul sat down and the two men shared the rest of the bottle and how they could make Zakari's statue theirs. Both finally agreed they should approach Deaf Yanni about his sources. He appeared highly satisfied with their earlier efforts and trusted Jean Paul. Neither gave Andreas another thought.

Andreas, on the other hand, was frantic. Adrenaline pumped wildly through his veins and, in activity belying his age and weight, he took the steps leading up to his flat two at a time. When he reached his door he struggled with the key, trying by force of will to make it fit into the lock. He breathed in strained gasps and his heart thudded painfully in his chest. When he finally succeeded, he slammed the door back against the wall and rushed down the hallway, not even bothering to remove the keys or close the door. With trembling hands he knocked the telephone to the floor and fell to his knees as he scrambled to pick it up. Still on the floor he pulled the telephone into his lap and dialed four digits. He silently urged the ringing to begin at the other end, all the time rocking back and forth. An involuntary gasp of gratitude escaped his lips as the tinny paradiddle began to sound in his ear. Without even realizing he was doing so, he counted the rings. By the eighth he was rocking like a pear-shaped metronome, all the time imploring someone, anyone, to pick up. The tenth ring was cut short and, after a short pause, a sleepy voice came on the line.

"Emprós?"

"Taki! Taki, is that you?"

"Málista. Who is this?"

"Taki, this is Aspropatos. Is Yanni there?"

"Naí, my father's here. He's asleep. Do you want me to wake him?"

"Yes, but wait one minute. I have a very important message for him. As soon as I tell you what I have to say I want you to wake him and give it to him. All right?"

Before the boy could answer Andreas continued. "Listen, tell him I just talked to one of the men we sent to the south. He'll know what I'm talking about. Taki, listen carefully. Tell your father they went to the mill to do as we asked. Taki, tell him...tell him: Pseramanoli was gone!"

Chapter 28

For Carter and Jean Paul the weekend was spent conspiring to raise the necessary money to buy the statue from Zakari. They tried to contact Deaf Yanni, but he was away and would not be back until early the next week. Both thought his sources could supply them with the kind of artifacts Katz would be most interested in buying until they could present him with the photographs of the golden statue. If they could obtain some artifacts early enough Jean Paul could make a quick trip to Zürich to sell them.

Also, Carter was reminded, Karine would be arriving the following week. Jean Paul received a telegram from her announcing her arrival in Athens from Paris the following Friday. If he could get to Zürich soon enough he could be back in Athens in time to meet her there and they could fly back to Iraklion together.

Saturday afternoon they were sitting on the terrace adjacent to Carter's room when the sound of a car's stopping at the gate could be heard. Out of curiosity Jean Paul got up and walked to the railing. Carter heard him greet someone below and walked over to see who might be coming to visit. Below a young man with a backpack and suitcase handed the taxi driver the fare and walked into the yard.

"Who's that?"

"Philippe Moreau. A writer I met the last time I went to Paris. He's finishing a book and needed to get away, somewhere he could be alone and not bothered by telephones and friends always wanting him to come have a drink with them. I told him about the villa and invited him to come to Crete. I didn't know whether he would accept or not, but evidently it sounded good to him. You're going to like him. He's pied-noir. Comes from Tizi Ouzou. His father was a pharmacist."

Turning back to the waiting figure below, Jean Paul waved his arm. "Philippe! Come around to the courtyard and take the stairs inside the second door. Come on up. We have a bottle of wine up here ready to toast your arrival."

Carter quickly discovered he and Philippe were the same age and seemed to have a number of interests in common. The three of them finished the bottle of wine and Jean Paul told him to take any of the bedrooms he wished. That night they went into town for dinner and then to the club. By the end of the evening Philippe and Carter were fast friends.

On Monday Jean Paul went to Yanni's office in the market. He half expected to see the butcher coming to meet him, but the front was deserted. Yanni could be heard in his office talking to someone. As soon as he heard the person with Yanni leave by a back door he pushed against the half-open doorway and entered. Yanni, like Andreas, seemed preoccupied. Jean Paul's focus was on his own goals, however. Without the diplomacy and ritual normally expected, he announced to Yanni he planned a trip back to Switzerland and hoped Yanni would find something to take with him. Yanni nodded thoughtfully and then asked Jean Paul to wait for him in the office. Five minutes later he returned with what looked to be a cigar box in his hand. When he lifted the lid two cloth-wrapped bundles could be seen inside.

The smaller package contained 14 carved and inscribed beads. Because of the belief that if a nursing mother wore one on a string around her neck she would be blessed with plentiful milk, the peasant women called them 'milk stones'.

The larger package contained an 8-inch bronze statue of a young boy. Jean Paul held it in his hand and looked at it carefully. When he asked where it was found Yanni replied vaguely of a village near Rethymnon. Jean Paul was satisfied with that answer, for he could easily fabricate a story for Katz. There was no doubt in his mind it was authentic. He was just not sure of the period from which it came. He would go to the museum that afternoon and see what he could find similar to it. At least he would have an approximate date.

He leaned close to Yanni's ear. "How much for everything?"

"Eighteen hundred drachmas."

For appearance sake Jean Paul bargained briefly. But when he saw that Yanni's mind seemed to be elsewhere, he shrugged his shoulders and told him he would do his best.

In actuality he was delighted. For a mere $60 there would be almost no risk. Besides, the bronze might not be as old as the small ivory statues he took the first time, but it was almost as rare and should bring a good price. He took the box to the villa immediately and then returned to the airport to buy a plane ticket to Athens. From the airport he drove to town to search the museum displays for a similar bronze.

Tuesday night Jean Paul left for Athens. He decided to forego the boat this trip, for there was so little chance he would be stopped. Before leaving for the airport he taped the statue to the inside of his forearm. Security at the Athens airport was notably lax and, as long as he put nothing incriminating into his suitcase, he felt he would pass with no problem. As for the beads, they were secreted in various pockets. Their size and bulk were negligible and the loose change in his pocket kept them from being noticeable. He bought a ticket, passed immediately through customs and was on his way to Zürich 45 minutes after his flight from Iraklion landed. Success buoyed his confidence. He was sure he would never have any trouble in the future. As the plane flew north from Greece, he made plans to transport bigger and better things the next time.

Although he did not show it outwardly, Katz was pleased to see him return and their negotiations were quickly concluded. The statue traded hands for thirty-eight crisp new $100 bills. For each of the steatite beads he received another $50. He considered mentioning the gold statue to Katz, but decided to wait until they took pictures of it.

The next two days were spent relaxing in Zürich. He stayed in the same hotel he occupied on his earlier visit and ate in a different restaurant for each meal. Having money was much more pleasant than the type of existence he lived since leaving Algeria on the run, often not knowing from where his next meal, place to sleep or pack of cigarettes would come. On Thursday afternoon he took the train to Kloten and caught the Swissair flight for Athens and his planned rendezvous with Karine.

On Friday, in anticipation of Jean Paul's return, Carter bought a freshly slaughtered lamb and a five-liter demijohn of local red wine, krassí mávro. Next to the steps leading down to the underground rooms he and Philippe dug a pit in which they built a roaring fire from olive branches. While the fire burned itself into a white-hot bed of coals, they bent a concrete reinforcement rod to form a rotisserie. They removed as much of the rust as they could before running the rod through the carcass and tying it securely. At the local market they bought mustard and a rope of garlic, which they separated and peeled and inserted into pockets pierced in the meat of the lamb with a sharp knife.

From the overgrown lot on the far side of the hedge an old herb garden, which, in spite of years of neglect was still vigorous, provided them with fresh basil, thyme and rosemary. From one of the neighbors they borrowed sage. The entire lamb was then slathered with mustard to keep it moist. By the time they finished preparing the carcass Carter salivated just thinking of the treat awaiting them. Sturdy, forked green sticks driven into the ground provided support for the rotisserie.

By two o'clock they began to alternate turning the lamb over the coals. The demijohn rested within easy reach and the one not turning the spit kept the glasses full. By three the juices sizzled and spat among the coals and the delicious aroma of roasting lamb wafted on a gentle afternoon breeze throughout the neighborhood.

Philippe, an avid mariner, regaled Carter with stories of sailing the western Mediterranean. On one voyage from Oran to the Balearic Islands via Marseilles in his 8-meter sailboat he met a Spanish girl and fell in lust. The first and only problem seemed to be language. Philippe spoke no Spanish and she spoke no French.

"So, how did you talk to her?"

"Latin."

"Latin!?"

"Ben, oui. Et heureusement elle en parlait aussi!" Fortunately, she spoke it as well.

"And so your love affair was carried on in Latin?"

"Totalement."

In turn Carter told of all he learned of the Minoans and the history of Crete. Without divulging his and Jean Paul's clandestine activities he discussed archaeology in great detail. Philippe asked intelligent questions based upon his limited knowledge gained through reading about Crete before leaving Paris.

"Speaking of books, you know Jean Paul is writing a book, don't you?"

"He told me that when I met him in Paris. Have you read his manuscript?"

"Why, no, I haven't."

"Have you ever seen him working on it?"

"Uh, no. But I think he's well along in it. I've heard him discuss it several times with others. He quotes liberally from it. Naturally I assumed it's close to being published."

Philippe laughed and leaned forward. "Listen, Carter. One of the greatest dangers for a writer is to discuss the subject of his current work too often and in too much detail. He risks reaching a point where, in his own mind, the book is complete. He can quote passages and even page numbers. To him the book is a reality. He will even edit it in his head, but there will rarely, if ever, be another word put on paper.

"When I began to write my book I discussed the premise and what I planned to accomplish with a good friend who's a member of La Table Ronde, an elite group of authors in France. He warned me of too much talk of what I was doing. The best advice anyone could have possibly given me came from him. He told me, 'whatever you do, don't talk about it in any detail until it's already committed to paper'. Jean Paul falls into the category of those who will never see a single page of their own work. Strangely enough, that's not a problem for him. In his own mind his book is a reality. With your experiences here you'll have the material for a book of your own someday. You might even want to keep some sort of diary. I do. Right now you may think you'll never forget this or that detail because it's all so fresh and clear to you. Soon, however, you'll find yourself struggling to recall the details of something you experienced and you won't be able to. Then you'll wish you bothered to keep a daily log to jog your memory."

"I'm sure you're right. The only notes I keep now have to do with language. When I hear people use a term, particularly slang I'm not familiar with, I try to clarify it and then write it down."

"In French?"

"Uh-huh. And Greek."

"Good. I've noticed some of the slang you've used since I arrived. Obviously Jean Paul has been an influence on you. You've used terms that are common only in Algeria among pied-noirs."

Carter smiled at this, pleased that Philippe noticed. He took over the job of turning the rotisserie while Philippe talked about Parisian slang currently in vogue. Carter listened avidly, carefully cataloguing each new word and expression for future use.

By six thirty the air was redolent with the rich aroma of roasting lamb and echoing cicadae shrilling in the pines. The lamb was almost done, presque cuit, as were Carter and Philippe. The level of the demijohn dropped noticeably and both were impaired. Carter left him to turn the rotisserie and walked with an unsteady gait toward the house to gather plates, glasses and utensils for the evening feast. Earlier they moved the long table and four cane-bottomed chairs from the ballroom onto the worn stones of the courtyard.

Popi, the eighteen year old Greek girl from the house on the other side of the lower wall, she of the copper-colored hair and lush young body, appeared earlier. She came into the yard drawn by the arrival of this handsome new foreigner. He was as taken with her as she with him, but this time there was no common tongue. For more than two hours she and Philippe relied upon Carter as intermediary to communicate. When Philippe invited her to stay for dinner she willingly accepted. Eager to help, she left with a few drachmas from Carter in her pocket and walked to the nearby market to buy two kilos of bread. Before leaving on her errand she called to Athena, her family's housekeeper, to gather the necessary ingredients for a salad from her father's garden. When she returned to the house she brought a bowl from the kitchen out to the table in the courtyard and busied herself preparing the saláta. All the while she hummed to herself and cast frankly appraising glances in the direction of Philippe.

Carter was inside when he heard Philippe shout in greeting. He recognized Jean Paul's voice followed by

exclamations of wonder from an unknown female. As he passed
Jean Paul's bed a blue box of Eklekta, the Greek cigarettes he
smoked, caught his eye. He stopped to take one from the box, lit
it and made his way out of the room. As he crossed into the entry
hall he heard the voice of Jean Paul talking to Philippe.

"Il est où, Carter?"

"Ben, je pense bien qu'il est dans la maison," surmised a
thick-tongued Philippe.

"Carter! T'es où? Viens dehors!"

When he turned the corner Jean Paul saw Carter leaning
against the doorway, shoulders slumped, both hands stuffed in
his pockets. From a cigarette dangling at the corner of his mouth,
acrid smoke from the strong tobacco curled up his cheek to sting
his eye and cause him to squint in discomfort.

"Le voilà," said Jean Paul over his shoulder. Here he is.

Around the corner walked a young woman who looked
to be in her early 20's. She was slim, well-tanned and wore no
makeup except light mascara and eyeliner. She was dressed
stylish-casual in a light colored, summer weight dress. On her
feet were sandals. Her hair was a shiny black helmet cut in a
pageboy that brushed the lower line of her jaw. She was not
beautiful. Instead, she possessed a quality that was slightly
exotic. When she saw Carter her look of expectancy changed to
one of mild surprise. Jean Paul stopped immediately and turned
his head slightly to the side. With fists on hips he regarded
Carter with a wry smile. Karine continued forward until she was
only a step away from the slumped Carter.

"Karine, je veux te présenter mon ami, Carter Martin.
Carter, Karine de Châtillon."

Karine's smile broadened and she held out her hand.
"Bon jour. Je suis vraiment contente d'enfin fair votre
connaisance."

When he did not offer to take her hand her smile began
to fade and confusion showed in her eyes. Carter waited, pausing
dramatically for effect. All the while he regarded her insolently
from head to toe. At last, in his best imitation of the amused and
smirking Jean Paul, he spoke. "Ah, mais quel BOUDIN!"

The words were hardly out of his mouth when lights
flashed in his head and his ears began to ring. The hand

proffered in friendship so shortly before struck with the speed of an adder. The cigarette flew from his mouth leaving a trail of sparks as his head bounced off the solid frame of the door. She prepared to slap him again when she heard the sounds of hilarity behind her. With eyes flashing and a determined set to her jaw, she whirled to face Jean Paul. She found him doubled over with laughter, as was Philippe behind him. Popi, who understood nothing stood some distance away, mouth open and hand to her cheek. A look of distinct alarm was on her face and she appeared ready to leap over the wall to the safety of her own backyard in a single bound. Karine regarded the two as if they were braying jackasses and then turned once more to face Carter. His eyes were wide in disbelief. How could this have happened? Who would ever guess he would be attacked in this manner for such a harmless comment?

Karine's rage turned to utter incomprehension. She looked from one to the other, wondering just what was happening. Carter wore an embarrassed lopsided grin to compliment the rapidly reddening handprint on his cheek. He searched for words to explain while the other two, tears streaming down their faces, pounded each other on the back. The realization began to dawn on her that perhaps there was more to this situation than met the eye.

Jean Paul was the first to act. He stepped forward to take Karine into his arms and hug her tightly to prevent any further attacks on Carter.

"Assez, assez les gamins! Ce n'était qu'une farce! A joke! What you don't realize, Karine, is that young Carter has been the recipient of a wonderfully liberal education that includes all of the best bon mots, jurons and other expressions. One can't be satisfied with just the classics and arts. To be considered complete, an education must be eclectic."

He turned from Karine to Carter and simply shook his head. "Well, you can't say we didn't try to warn you."

Karine turned toward Carter to find him holding his hand out to her. "Truce? No more hitting, please."

She looked at the hand and his contrite expression. In spite of herself she could no longer maintain her severity. A wide smile showed him an expanse of small white teeth and just the tip of her pink tongue.

"OK. No more hitting, if you promise me there will be no more insults."

"Bon, I'm glad that's over. What's that wonderful smell?" asked Jean Paul. "I saw the rotisserie when we got out of the taxi. Is that one of the neighborhood children you're roasting?"

Switching to English he turned to the dumbstruck Popi, still standing as if ready to flee. "Ah, the sweet Popi. Speaking of neighborhood children that need to be eaten... I didn't mean to ignore you. Ti Kánis?"

"Kalá efcharistó kyrie Zon Pawl." Her body language said otherwise, however.

Jean Paul turned back to Philippe and asked if he would show Karine the house and let her choose her own room. They knew each other from Paris and were congenial, if not close friends. He took her valise and quickly showed her the downstairs rooms, then led her to the second floor.

"So, le vieux, what news from the city of Katz?" asked Carter as he directed Jean Paul away from the villa and into the yard. "I take it your trip was a success. Come on. I'll pour you a glass of wine and you can tell me everything."

"Lamb, huh? I'm so hungry I'm trembling. Just looking at that aigneau makes me want to take if off ze fire and eat it right off ze rotisserie. I'd just hold one end in each hand and eat it like you Americans eat your épis de maïs. How do you call it: corns on ze cocks?"

Carter laughingly corrected him. "Non mon vieux. Corn on the cob!" He then pressed him for more information on his trip.

Jean Paul reached into his back pocket and pulled out a wad of hundred dollar bills, each one just as crisp and new as the first pile he brought back the last time. He recounted briefly his trip, exulting over the ease with which he passed customs in Athens.

"They didn't suspect a thing. Just stamped my passport like all the rest of the tourists. I'm planning the next trip already and I want to leave as soon as possible. We need to meet with

Deaf Yanni again soon. Hopefully he will have some new bric-à-brac for us by the end of this week."

The sounds of Karine and Philippe descending the stairs caused them to cut their conversation short. Carter announced it was time to eat and Philippe helped him remove the lamb from the fire and place it in the middle of the table. From the carcass they carved great slices and everyone ate with their hands. Dinner was a jovial affair with loud appreciation voiced for the sumptuousness of the fare. Karine, seated at the opposite end of the table, cast covert glances in Carter's direction throughout dinner.

That summer the cicadae were abundant and vociferous. Their arrival prompted the appearance of several small owls, which perched nightly on the lower limbs of the pines. Periodically they flitted from limb to limb, grasped one of the insects in their powerful talons and cut off its song in mid-shriek. Although only about the size of a fist, they were eating machines and competent hunters. Carter thought they were probably a species of screech owl. When one of them lit on the trunk of the tree it peered myopically at those at the table through the glare of the spotlights. On an impulse, Carter rose from the table and quickly caught one of the insects. As he stood in the middle of the courtyard he grasped it by its head and held it at arm's length. The little owl followed his every move with a wide-eyed stare. Carter remained motionless, his arm extended, the cicada protruding from his fingertips. For a long moment nothing happened. All conversation ceased as everyone looked on in anticipation. When the owl dropped from the trunk and flapped soundlessly toward the upraised morsel there was a gasp from those seated at the table. In a flash he plucked it from Carter's hand and soared up into one of the other trees, from where the sound of crunching could be heard. Everyone clapped and cheered.

Karine pushed her chair back and came to where Carter was standing. "If you'll catch one of those things for me I want to feed the owl, too."

He caught one and placed its wriggling body in her hands. She screamed and released it, but he caught it again and gently folded her fingers around its body. When she spied an owl sitting above her she faced it with her arm raised in the air. This one, too, dropped from its perch and plucked it neatly from her hand. By the time everyone took their turn the owls were so sated they would no longer respond.

This interaction served to break the ice between Carter and Karine and they conversed easily. He found her interesting, but that was all. Besides, according to Jean Paul she was not going to be there very long. He did not suspect that she might be considering plans of her own.

Chapter 29

"I see that look in her eyes and I know what it means. She's taken a real interest in this American who calls her a slut, or worse, upon meeting her for the first time," said Jean Paul laughingly

"She seems like a nice girl, but I don't want to get involved with one of your friends."

"Exactly. You don't need to get involved with her. There are too many other girls here for you to bother with Karine."

"Friends only," replied Carter raising his hands, palms outward. "Now, tell me more about Zürich. I want details."

In response Jean Paul reached into his shirt pocket, pulled out the wad of money and threw it on the bed. "I only have one thing to add to what I told you in the garden. Katz loves me like a son and he particularly loves the little things I bring to him."

Carter picked up the money, counted it quickly, and then counted it again. "Four thousand two hundred dollars! Is this about what you thought the statue and beads would bring?"

"Well, actually it was a little more, but between Zürich and here I spent about three hundred dollars on clothes and food and a little entertainment."

"Forty five hundred. That's even better. How soon can we see Yanni and go back?"

Jean Paul strutted and postured as he walked around the room, immensely pleased with himself. "I've already thought of that. Either tomorrow or the next day I'm going to see him to arrange another consignment. This is easy money. Easy money. Let's get everyone together and go down to the club to celebrate."

At the club they met Canif and Yves. Yves greeted them warmly and wanted to hear all about their activities since he last saw them. His real warmth was reserved for Philippe, however, and he arranged to sit next to the handsome author most of the evening.

Karine reacted to Carter as a moth to flame. Once or twice he noticed Jean Paul looking at him with that familiar wry smile upon his face. Carter tried his best not to respond to her or to give her any encouragement, but he could not ignore her completely. By the time they all piled into the car to return home she squeezed in beside him, complaining in a small voice that she was cold with the top down. Carter rubbed her chilly arms as he pulled her to him. With a coo of pleasure she snuggled down into the warmth of his side for the ride back to the villa.

The next day Carter only taught one morning class and returned to the villa before lunch. He found Jean Paul, Karine, and Philippe seated around the table in the courtyard drinking coffee. They all slept late and were just now eating breakfast. As he walked up he was met with a chorus of greetings. Karine insisted he take her seat and disappeared into the house.

"Glad you got back early. You and I have an appointment this afternoon."

Thinking he was talking of meeting with Yanni, Carter's face lit up in anticipation.

"It's not what you think. Today is Yves' last day. He and Pierre are flying out tonight and he asked us to come see him off. At first I was going to tell him we would be busy, but I thought this might be one last chance to talk to him about helping us. Besides, he insisted I bring you with me."

"Me!? Oh, no. O-o-o-h, no! I'm sorry, but you can go by yourself. Thanks, anyway."

"What do you mean? Of course you're going with me. He specifically requested your presence. Besides, why wouldn't you want to go?"

"Because I know exactly what'll happen. He's going to try to kiss me goodbye and I'm not going to have that. No! Uh-uh! You go. I'll just stay here. Tell him I was busy. Tell him I died. Tell him anything you want, just don't ask me to go see him off!"

"Now wait a minute. You don't have anything to worry about. Sure, he's going to kiss you. He'll kiss me, as well, but it'll just be a quick kiss on either cheek. It's what we French do. Come on, make up your mind that you're going to do it and let's get it over with. I promise you, it won't be painful or embarrassing."

Karine came out of the house carefully carrying a full cup of steaming coffee. As she set it down in front of Carter she asked why everyone was laughing. Jean Paul told her and she, too, began to laugh. "Bêta, what are you afraid of? It's just two little bisoux, one on each cheek. Like this." She leaned down to him and pressed her cheek against his, making a smacking noise close to his ear, then repeated it on the other cheek.

"See, now that's not so bad is it?" She stood back and looked at him, a mischievous smile playing on her lips.

"Assez de cette connerie! You're going and I don't want to hear any more argument. Compris?"

Carter shrugged and resigned himself. He knew further protest would accomplish nothing.

Later that afternoon, when they parked the car and walked to the bus stop near the port, they were welcomed effusively by the Count. Pierre stood a little behind Yves and to the side, beaming over his shoulder. Yves insisted they engage one of the photographers who set up shop in several of the squares during the tourist season. With their box and bellows cameras mounted on long-legged tripods they actively pursued clients. He posed the small group on one of the stone benches in front of an ancient grimy facade. With workmanlike competence he pulled a string from the front of the camera to the vicinity of their noses to assure himself of being at the proper distance. A photographic plate was slipped into the side of the box, a final sighting through a primitive viewfinder and, with a reminder not to move, he removed the lens cap with a flourish. His lips barely moved as he counted off the seconds before replacing the lens cap. Three minutes later he removed the photograph, swabbed it with a solution and proudly handed it to Yves, who admired the finished picture.

"I'll take it with me to remind me of this marvelous summer and friends old and new." He showed it to everyone and then placed it carefully in the side pocket of his shoulder bag just as the bus for the airport pulled up.

Carter glanced at Jean Paul, who shrugged and motioned for him to follow. This was the moment Carter dreaded. The two older gentlemen boarded through the double rear doors and immediately took possession of a pair of seats. They then turned to the two younger men. Pierre shook hands with Carter and Yves quickly bussed Jean Paul on each cheek. Carter watched the exchange of goodbyes, almost deciding his fears were unfounded. When Yves turned and placed both hands on his shoulders Carter reminded himself not to recoil and, with a kind of fascination, watched Yves approach his cheek. To his chagrin the kiss was slow and effeminate, the smacking sound thundering in his right ear. When it was repeated on his left cheek he glanced over the shoulder of the older man and saw Jean Paul standing, hands on hips, grinning hugely. He, at least, was enjoying Carter's discomfort. Carter arched his eyebrows and leveled a stony stare at him.

As he pulled away Yves looked into Carter's eyes. "Listen, you must make plans to come to Paris. I have many influential friends and, if you would like to live and work in Paris I can arrange it for you. If not, please plan to come spend at least a month. You will always be welcome in my flat. Besides, I'll introduce you to someone interesting every morning and someone famous every afternoon." Here he paused for effect, a smile flitting across his lips. "Every evening I will introduce you to someone sexy. But, and I emphasize that 'but', you must return to my house at night to sleep."

Carter was at a loss for words. He stammered out his thanks and told Yves he appreciated the offer. He thanked him again most sincerely for the introduction to Evgenia. Fortunately for Carter, the ticket-taker began to pass down the aisle, shooing everyone off the bus who was not a passenger. He and Jean Paul descended to the pavement once more and waved as the doors hissed shut and the bus made a U-turn in a cloud of diesel fumes.

"Well, mon vieux, it wasn't all that bad was it?"

Carter turned to reply, but when he saw the smirk on his friend's face he quickly changed his tone. "Putain de toi, de ta mère, et ta soeur! You knew that was going to happen, didn't you?"

"I don't understand why you're so upset. You got an invitation that most people would kill for. When he says someone famous or interesting he's talking about writers, artists, musicians, actors in the movies and on stage, or government figures. As for the sexy part, virtually all the women in Paris of any consequence are either personal friends of his or friends of friends. Maybe even Vadim's wife, Barbarella. They would do anything for him."

All the way back to Aghi Vasili Jean Paul told him of the types of women Yves knew. "What it comes down to is whether or not you would be willing to - how do you say - pay the piper."

"Oh, I agree, Jean Paul, it's a tempting offer. But that's just not me."

"No, I don't think you could, either. But, you know, in later years, when you are older, more secure with yourself, you'll look back on this and ask yourself what you missed by turning down his invitation."

"Maybe. I don't know. Look, there's Karine standing on the terrace," said Carter, anxious to change the subject. They nosed through the gates and as they rolled to a stop Jean Paul reached across and grasped his arm just as he was starting to open the door of the car.

"That one up there is more dangerous than Yves. You're starting with her, aren't you?"

"I'm not starting anything at all," Carter replied with a grin. "She's the one that's doing everything. I can't get her to leave me alone."

"I know. She's determined."

For the next several days things went smoothly. Carter met with his classes each day then hurried home. He would not admit he was becoming more and more taken by Karine's presence in the house, and they spent more time together than ever before. She seemed to always be waiting for him, seated upon the terrace outside his room, where she could see the street for a hundred feet or more. When he turned the corner she would be there, calling to him, waving. Upon seeing her his step took on a more lively bounce.

Andreas stopped by the club on Thursday to tell Jean Paul the news of Zakari. Zakari would be awaiting his arrival the next day to photograph the statue. Elated at this good news, Jean Paul rushed back to Aghi Vasili, where he arranged to borrow Stasso's motorbike. Friday morning he was up by the time Carter was on his second cup of coffee and left in time to give him a lift to the institute.

He was just finishing his last class of the afternoon when he heard the distinctive purring of the 'moto' as it pulled up outside. Carter suspected it was Jean Paul. A moment later he heard his voice coming from downstairs. By the time he dismissed the students Jean Paul was standing in the hall outside his doorway, hands in pockets, shoulders against the wall, head thrown back in an attitude of insouciance. A nearly silent tuneless whistle blew through loosely pursed lips.

Carter craned his neck around the doorframe. "Well?"

"Well what?"

"Was he there?"

"Ouais"

"Did you take the pictures?"

"Ouais"

"How many?"

"Two, maybe three rolls."

"Any problems?"

"Kathólou. Aucun. None at all."

"Is he going to give us more time to come up with the money?"

"Non."

"Merde."

"Well, I am leaving tomorrow morning for Zürich. Can't have these films developed in Greece. I'm just going to have to chance that most of the pictures are good. Philippe has an appointment at the French embassy in Athens tomorrow afternoon. Since he's flying out in the morning I'll go along with him, call Katz from Glyfada and, if he can see me, I'll fly on to Switzerland."

"Great! What are you taking other than the pictures? Have you talked to Yanni? He might have something for you."

"No. Not this time. I think it's important to take these pictures to Katz now. It'll give us an idea of what we can possibly get for the statue and will be a quick trip. I may even be back by tomorrow night."

"Good. I don't think you can be too careful. It would be bad enough to lose anything Deaf Yanni might give you, but if you were searched and they found something on you they might take the camera and film, as well. If we lost them we might as well forget the idea of the statue. Where are you going now?"

"Aghi Vasili."

"Got room for a passenger? I'm through here for the day."

"Sure, come on."

"Karine and I are going to the movies tonight. Want to come?"

"Uh, no thanks. I'd better get everything ready and get to bed early. Besides, my rear and legs are sore from riding this thing all day long. I'm out of practice. I think I'll just go spend a little while on the terrace with a friendly bottle of cognac."

Karine was standing at the terrace railing, her head thrown back to allow the evening breeze to blow through her still-wet hair. When she saw them she lifted a languid hand in greeting. Jean Paul stopped at the gate to let Carter off then continued down the cobbled lane to return the motorbike to Stasso. She looked down at Carter and gestured for him to come up with a jerk of her head. Carter grinned and hurried into the house.

Karine stood in the narrow doorway to the terrace, her arms raised and her hands pressing on either side of the doorframe. When he approached the door and tried to pass through to the terrace she blocked his way.

"Salut! And how was school today? I'm glad you're home. Are we still going to the movies tonight?" She continued asking questions until he raised his hand, cutting her short.

"Good. Thanks. Yes. There, I've answered all your questions. Tell me what you did today."

She moved closer to him and stood tracing the outline of his shirt pocket with her finger. In a move reminiscent of a child, she quickly raised her face to his and brushed her lips across his. Damn, he did not want to get involved. To change the subject he brought up dinner.

"There's a restaurant down at the port you might enjoy. Tourists don't go there. Mainly it's a fisherman's hangout. Why don't we go have a drink and eat dinner before going to the movies? The movie won't begin until it gets dark anyway. What do you say?"

"Oh, that sounds fantastique! Who else is going with us?"

"I invited Jean Paul, but he and Philippe are leaving tomorrow morning for Athens."

"Does that mean we'll be alone tonight?"

"Uh, yeah, it does. Is that all right with you?"

"All right? It's perfect." She kissed him once more fleetingly and brushed by him. "I need to get ready and I don't want to have to rush. I'll be down in an hour or so. OK?"

"Sure. Take your time. I'll be with Philippe."

They took the convertible and left it parked across from the club. The walk to the port through the soft early evening was delightful. Karine's hand slipped into his and he wrapped her smaller fingers in his. He came to the Kafe Miramare several times since coming to Iraklion and, as soon as they entered, the proprietor and his wife recognized him. They did not often get foreigners, particularly one who spoke Greek.

Because he was with a woman they did not know, Theodoro's wife, Rodula, came forward first. Carter introduced Karine and Rodula took her hand and patted it warmly before turning her attention back to him.

Carter's eyes swept the room and he recognized several faces from earlier visits. Those he remembered and spoke to seemed pleased he remembered them. As was their custom, they offered drinks and seats to the newly arrived couple, but since Karine would have been virtually excluded from the conversation, he declined. They smiled, winked and bobbed their heads in understanding as Theodoro set a table for them.

He ordered a bottle of retsina and, after pouring, raised his glass to the fishermen around them. Everyone raised their glasses in return before draining them. Throughout the meal they were entertained by the other patrons. Some sang, some danced, and one, an amateur magician, made Carter's ring disappear by seeming to pop it into his mouth and swallow it.

Carter called for the bill and was surprised to learn there would be none. Theodoro inclined his head toward the others, indicating they paid the tab. To thank them he called for a round of Greek cognac, toasted them all, and then thanked each personally with a handshake and a word. He would ask Jean Paul to pick up a bottle of whiskey from the Duty Free Shop when he came back from Switzerland to bring down to Theodoro and Rodula.

He looked forward to seeing Karine's reaction to the Kino. His first time in this particular movie theater he happened to lean back in his seat and look up at a panoply of palm trees, stars, a crescent moon and wispy clouds that moved across the ceiling. He marveled at the realism of the night sky depicted by skillful utilization of lights in the ceiling. It was not until the wall lights came up at intermission that he saw what he took for artifice was, in actuality, the real sky. The entire roof was open to the elements. This also provided perfect air conditioning in a country where summer rains were non-existent.

Throughout the movie they held hands. By the end her head rested on his shoulder and she caressed the inside of his bare arm with her nails. When the credits began to roll and the lights came up she reached over and touched his face tenderly with her free hand.

Any plans anyone may have projected about what was going to happen once they returned to the villa were dashed when they drove up and saw the lights ablaze in the courtyard. On one side of the table sat Philippe with Popi next to him. On the other sat strangers. From the way they dressed and carried themselves he guessed they were from northern Europe. From his seat at the head of the table Jean Paul held forth in fustian diatribe on the subject of de Gaulle.

In mid-oratory he stopped, raised his hand theatrically, a cigarette casually held between nicotine-stained fingers, blew a stream of smoke toward the stars and greeted them. "Les voilà! Salut les gamins! How was the film? I didn't expect you this early. Come join us. I have some friends here I want you to meet."

Karine swore under her breath.

The two newcomers, Luc and Bernard, were pilots for Francoptère, a French agricultural firm using specially fitted Alouette II helicopters to spray insecticides. They were hired by the government to spray in several areas affected by locusts blown from hard-hit North Africa, across the Libyan Sea, to the shores of Crete. They were gregarious, easy going, charming men. Bernard was married to an American woman, who remained at their home in Paris while he worked wherever his services were required. Most recently they were in Spain. Perhaps next month they would be somewhere in the Middle East. Carter fell into easy conversation with them, enjoying their banter and Gallic sense of humor. He barely took notice when Karine finally left the table and made her way upstairs.

By the time Luc and Bernard rose to leave it was well past midnight. Suddenly worried about getting enough sleep before having to make his flight, Jean Paul bid Carter a hasty goodnight and disappeared in the direction of his room. Philippe and Popi left the table two hours earlier and wandered off in the direction of the garden. Carter turned off the outside lights and mounted the stairs to his room. He undressed in the dark and climbed into bed, asleep almost before his head hit the pillow.

Sounds in the house brought him awake with a start and he was surprised to see the sun already shining through his open window. He looked at his alarm clock, chagrined to discover it stopped during the night. He hopped from bed, slipped on a pair of shorts and padded down the stairs. Jean Paul and Philippe were already up and dressed, the paraphernalia needed for each of their trips laid out on Jean Paul's bed.

"Bonjour. Vous êtes prêts?"

"Tiens, Carter, good morning. Want some coffee?" Without waiting for an answer Philippe went to the kitchen and soon reappeared with a mug in his hand. Carter thanked him and turned to Jean Paul.

"I'll drive you to the airport. I don't know how you were thinking of getting there, but don't you think it would be simpler to let me take you?"

Jean Paul gave an affirmative grunt and Carter grinned to himself. He knew his friend struggled with early mornings and did not pursue the idea of carrying on a coherent conversation with him. Instead he asked Philippe where he and Popi disappeared to last night.

"The underground bunker in the garden. It's perfect and very private. I'm even thinking of running electricity out to it."

"Just be careful her parents don't find out what you're doing. They'll latch onto you in a heartbeat. They would be delighted to marry their young daughter to the famous French writer, Philippe Moreau, more commonly known as o Morós."

"Don't you worry about Popi and me. You should be more worried about that one upstairs. Once she gets her claws into you she'll never let you go again." They both laughed at each other's jibes, a feeling of kinship growing between them.

Jean Paul walked back into the room, looked around, and picked up the camera from the table and a small valise from the bed. "OK, foutons le camp."

Philippe picked up his affairs and they went out to the car. Jean Paul insisted on driving and Carter leapt over the side and into the back. They would arrive with approximately an hour to spare, which suited Carter. He hated having to rush anywhere, even if it meant leaving an hour early.

As it turned out, they were fortunate to leave when they did. Carter walked with them across the waiting room of the small terminal, when two men approached them, one dressed in a business suit, the other in the uniform of some sort. The business suit intercepted Jean Paul, stepping between him and Philippe.

"Mr. Bonisseur?" he said in English.

"Yes?"

"My name is Zakovides. Airport security. You will please come with us." His manner left no doubt that he expected compliance. The customs official took the small valise from Jean Paul and led the way toward a door. Philippe and Carter followed along behind, but the man calling himself Zakovides turned and politely, but firmly, told them they should wait outside for their friend.

Twenty minutes later the sound of an approaching aircraft could be heard and they looked through the double doors in time to see the Olympic Airlines flight from Athens touch down with a squeal of tires and a puff of white smoke. Arriving passengers retrieved their luggage and left by available transportation. A half-hour later announcement came that the flight was ready for boarding. A grim-faced Jean Paul appeared with his hastily shut valise under his arm. Zakovides stood in the doorway of the office, watching Jean Paul's back.

"Come on, Philippe. We need to board right now. Carter, help me stuff these clothes back in this suitcase."

"What the hell..."

"Don't ask me any questions right now. I'll tell you as soon as I get back. Now, I may return tonight if Katz can't see me. If he can see me I may be gone for a day or two. Philippe, you'll be coming back tomorrow, won't you?"

"That's my plan."

"Carter, listen, don't worry. This was just routine, so they say. I wonder why they would do this to me. I wonder what they thought they would find. But, never mind. I'm just fine. We'll talk about it when I return."

By this time they reached the gate and Carter told them to hurry to board. No sooner did they mount the removable stairs than the ground crew pulled them away and the stewardess closed the door. Within seconds the props on the first engine began to rotate, and then roared to life. The other three followed, and within minutes they were airborne and out over the sea headed north.

Carter mulled over this turn of events, but was reassured by Jean Paul's release and subsequent departure. His drive through the mid-morning traffic took his mind off the problems at the airport, however, and he soon pulled into the gates of the villa. Karine was seated in a chair at one end of the table, her hair in charming disarray as if she just rolled out of bed. She held a cup of coffee in her lap. She began to talk even before he arrived at the table.

"When I woke up this morning no one was here. Then I remembered that Jean Paul and Philippe were leaving for Athens. I didn't even tell them goodbye last night before I went to bed. Also, I didn't thank you for dinner and for the movie. Bisoux!" she demanded. She set her coffee cup on the table and lifted her face to him expectantly, like a child, for a good morning kiss.

Wide, sensuous, delicious mouth, dark eyes, disheveled hair, a long cotton nightshirt with bare brown feet sticking out from under it, bare brown arms wrapped about her knees, hugging them to her chest. He leaned down obligingly, kissed her: left cheek, right cheek, forehead, drew back an instant, then kissed her quickly full on the mouth. She licked her lips and smiled up at him. He sat with his back to the open door so that when she stood up to pour a cup of coffee for him she stood between him and the sun. He glanced admiringly at her lithe body, evident through the material of her summer-weight sleeping shirt.

"Did they get off all right?"

"Problems at the airport. Right after we got there two men, one a customs official and the other security, accosted Jean Paul. They took him into an office and kept him there almost thirty minutes. I thought he was going to miss his flight. Just as the plane was getting ready to leave they released him."

"Non, mais ce n'est pas possible! Why do you think it happened?"

"I don't know and he didn't have time to say. He said he would tell me everything when he got back. He tried not to show it, but he was upset. Said something about a strip search in the office."

She asked him more questions about the incident, questions to which he either held no answers, or answers he did not feel free to give. The game was taking a new turn. New rules were being introduced that he really did not understand. He realized their significance, but was not sure how they would affect him. He felt that now it would be more and more difficult to take the artifacts out of the country, more difficult to get them into the hands of Katz, or people like him.

He recalled Jean Paul's talking of a Belgian antiquities dealer, Axel de Groux, who flew into Crete periodically for clandestine sales. He always came in by private floatplane. They flew low to avoid radar, coming in over the sea from either Tunisia or Malta and landed along a deserted stretch of south coast late at night. He was always in and quickly out again. Of course, he could not discuss things like this with Karine. Jean Paul reminded him often to keep his mouth shut, not to discuss any of the generalities - or particulars - of the game in which they were involved.

He was brought back from his reverie by her nearness. She got up from her seat and walked around his chair. She slowly massaged his shoulders with surprisingly strong fingers.

In response he rolled his head and arched his back. She leaned forward, fitting the back of his head between her breasts then reached down to rub his chest. Humming to herself, she shifted position slightly, dipped her head and touched the tip of her tongue to his right ear.

He asked her what her plans were for the day. In a dreamy voice she replied she planned nothing in particular, but since the others were gone she would like to spend the day with him.

"That's fine, but I have classes this afternoon. Two of them. Do you want to come into town with me and walk around? You might want to go visit Madame Daskaloyanni. Have you seen the Crozets since you arrived? Madame Crozet was telling me a few days before you got here how much she looked forward to seeing you."

"What time will you be through with your classes? Could I come sit in on them?"

With a laugh he told her he did not think that would be a good idea. If she wished, however, he would take her to the Institute and introduce her to Bunny. "Think about what you want to do. I've got to take a shower, shave and get ready to leave. It's getting late."

He gently removed her arms from around her neck and stood up. Looking a little put out, she crossed her arms and stuck out her bottom lip in a pout. He decided to ignore her behavior. Instead of trying to reason further with her he kissed her quickly on the cheek, patted her bottom as he passed and ran upstairs to his room. In a moment he returned wearing a towel wrapped around his waist and a pair of flip-flops. She was nowhere to be seen. Although the temperature was warmer than when he first got up that morning, he still found it difficult to take that first plunge under the cold water of the shower. He stepped into the stream of water and quickly lathered up, shaving quickly to save time.

Once finished he turned off the water and plucked his towel from the hook. He stepped into the open courtyard where the sun streamed down through the trees and toweled off. He felt invigorated, ready for anything, and headed once more for his room. There was still no sign of Karine. Her door was shut and he assumed she was inside still pouting. When he entered his room he removed the towel and flung it across the back of the chair in front of his makeshift desk. He was just reaching for a clean pair of underwear when he heard her voice behind him.

"Your back is still wet. Let me dry it for you."

He looked over his shoulder and saw her standing in the door leading to the terrace. "Sure. Thanks. I sometimes don't dry off completely because the air will do it and the evaporation cools me at the same time."

"Oh, but I don't want you to catch a cold. Here, stand still." She vigorously rubbed his back and shoulders with the rough, damp towel, but was gentler when she applied it lingeringly to his buttocks and the backs of his thighs. In spite of his attempts at self-control he now sported an erection.

"OK, mon grand, your back's dry. Turn around and let me do your front."

He shrugged mentally and turned to face her. Her eyes widened slightly when she looked down, and a ghost of a smile flickered across her lips.

"Bon, you seem to be dry everywhere else. If you need any more help just give me a call." With those parting words and a mischievous smile she dropped the towel over his erect penis, turned and walked out the door.

He looked down to see the towel hanging suspended in front of him, then looked up at the empty doorway through which she made her exit. For a moment he stood in disappointed silence. Then the humor of it hit him. She paid him back for what she took to be his earlier indifference.

She rode into town with him after all, went to the institute where she met Bunny, then walked down to the pension to visit with Madame D. After his two classes Carter left, intending to drive down and pick up Karine from the pension. As he passed through the gates and headed for the car he heard someone call his name.

"Carter Martin?"

He glanced over his shoulder and saw a man of medium height, a scruffy two to three day beard, wearing mirror glasses with wire frames, dressed in baggy khaki pants, a flowered shirt and sandals with white socks. Over his shoulder he carried one of the brightly colored wool bags that tourists, both men and women, affected. He leaned against the wall in front of the trees that grew in the forecourt and spread their limbs over the wrought iron gate and wall. He might have been just any other tourist, recently arrived on the quay in the harbor or the airport. Carter stopped and continued to appraise him before responding.

"Yeah, my name's Martin. What can I do for you?"

The man pushed himself erect and walked to where Carter waited. As he approached he held out his hand. "I thought I might find you here. I'm Matejowsky."

Carter took the proffered hand and applied brief pressure. "Glen Matejowsky? From Athens, right?" A brief nod was the only response. "Well, this is a surprise. What brings you down this way?"

"Is there somewhere we can talk?" From the tone of his voice Carter guessed this was more than a chance encounter.

"Sure, my car's just up the street."

Together they walked toward the bright yellow Ford. Only when Carter dropped the folders he was carrying into the back seat and turned around did Matejowsky speak again.

"I thought I'd better come down to see you in person. I've missed hearing from you. It's been over two weeks since you called Chania and over three days ago I sent you a little something through Horiatis. Thought I would hear from you immediately. Why do I get the impression I'm being ignored?"

"Ignored? No, not at all. I'm sorry I gave you that impression."

In reality he was not at all sorry. He almost gave up hearing from them again and was beginning to feel he was going in circles, waiting to tilt at windmills. He failed to report because he felt it futile to only be able to send 'Nothing to report.' In fact, almost two weeks earlier was the last time he checked the drop.

Matejowsky's expression hardened as Carter stared at his own reflection in the mirror lenses of the glasses. "Look, dickhead, I don't know what you think you're doing or who you think you're working for. I get the impression you think you're on some sort of vacation. When you're told to stay in touch that doesn't mean only at your convenience."

Carter resented his attitude, but bit back a retort. Instead, he began to explain why he failed to follow protocol. He realized his excuses sounded lame, so he stopped trying. "Well, obviously I made a mistake. Nothing seemed to be happening. I planned to go by there today..."

"Great, shit for brains! And who gave you the authority to make your own schedule and decide on priorities?" By this time he was spitting his words through a nearly lipless slit of a mouth and was almost nose to nose with Carter. "It's been three days. Three fucking days, for Christ sake! I just hope we haven't missed the window of opportunity. If we did, buddy boy, your ass is grass." Flecks of spume that glistened in the bright sunlight flew from his mouth.

"Window of opportunity? Do you mean..."

"I mean exactly what I said, asshole. Our sources tell us our raghead friend's on his way in. He may even be here by now. Athens is just about ready to send a search party out for you. Now's the time for you to get your little corn hole frog buddy and go to work. Playtime's over."

Carter's mind whirled with the news. Abu Bekr was probably already on the island. Time was of the essence and Jean Paul was probably in Zürich. It might be two more days until he returned and there was no way to get in touch with him.

"Look Matejowsky, I really am sorry about all this. I can go right away, but it's not going to do us any good. The Frenchman's not here."

Matejowsky looked ready to explode. "What the hell do you mean he's not here? Where the fuck is he? Go find the son of a bitch and drag him back here right now."

"I can't. He's out of the country and I have no way to get in touch with him. But look, he might be back tonight and certainly no later than day after tomorrow. I'm really looking for him tomorrow. Hopefully he'll be back on the evening flight from Athens. In the meantime, we're stuck." Before Matejowsky could interrupt he continued. "That doesn't mean I can't be getting everything ready for when he does get here. Where is our man supposed to be?"

The American started to speak, but stopped and waited for a passerby to saunter out of earshot. When he looked back at

Carter he seemed to be calmer. "Somewhere on the eastern end of the island. Near a place called Váï."

"Vai? That's right on the northeastern tip."

"Right. Sparsely populated with ready access to the sea and the sea-lanes going to Cyprus, Egypt, Lebanon - and the north coast of Israel. Once Bonisseur gets back how long would it take you to get him and drive down there?"

"Probably no more than five or six hours. He's anxious to see his old friend again."

"OK, good. I guess it's the best we can hope for. Here, I have some things for you." He reached into the shoulder bag and produced a standard travel guide of Greece. "Inside you'll find a very detailed topographical map of Crete. There are some notations on Vai and the area of Zakro. Open the book and act as if you are showing me how to get somewhere, then hand it back. As soon as you do that I'm going to thank you and start to walk away. Stop me and offer me a ride. I'll leave the bag in the car with you when you let me out. There's a little something inside that you may or may not need. I'd just as soon you have it...in case. Got it?"

"Sure," said Carter. "One question, though. Do we just wander through the countryside until we find him?"

"No, not this time. Let me know as soon as Bonisseur returns. Give me a call at the number penciled in on page 63 of the book as soon as you're ready to leave Iraklion. When you call I'll give you a rendezvous point. You're to go there and wait until you're contacted."

"Contacted? By whom?"

"Just hold your goddamn horses! I can't tell you who. I don't know myself, but I'll give you a way to recognize them. You're not going to be in this alone. We're providing you with support. Just be sure you uphold your end."

Carter shook his head in acknowledgment and Matejowsky turned and started to walk away. As instructed, Carter called after him and offered to give him a lift. Both men got into the car and Carter drove him to Knossos, where he let him out in the parking lot.

"I apologize again, Glen. I promise you we'll do everything we can to see this thing through to a successful end."

Matejowsky got out of the car and leaned across to tap Carter lightly on the shoulder. "Sure you will, kid. After this is over we'll get together and have dinner in Athens. Good luck. Giá xará. Keep in touch." He waved and turned toward the entrance of the palace as Carter made a U-turn back out onto the road.

On the way back into town he reached down to the floorboard of the front seat and picked up the shoulder bag. It was heavy. Too heavy to contain only the travel book. Carter reached inside and his fingers touched metal. He pushed back a corner of the bag and saw a 9-millimeter semi-automatic pistol. Taped together were four full clips. He smiled and pushed the bag under the front passenger's seat.

He drove quickly to the villa, where he took the bag and hid it and its contents, then went to the pension to pick up Karine. Rather than head straight back to the villa, they drove out to Tobrouk for lunch in the pavilion overlooking the beach. The crowds of summer were mostly the older tourists of September, those who were more wealthy and spent it without fretting over every penny, pfennig or centime.

On the ride back to the villa she became pensive, humming to herself while looking dreamily out at the dragon-shaped island of Dia riding several miles off the North coast on the calm, clear sea. When they made the sharp right-hand turn to mount the wall at the eastern entrance to the city she allowed herself to slide toward Carter and ended with her head resting on his shoulder. Before long she began to lightly brush the sun-bleached hair on his arm with her fingertips.

"Are you sleepy?" he asked.

"Hm-m-m-m."

"I asked if you were sleepy."

"Hm-m-m, I heard you. I was just trying to decide."

"To decide?"

"Uh-huh. Whether or not I wanted to take a little nap when we get back home."

"You've only been here a few days and already you're beginning to act like a little Greek. They close up their shops about this time each afternoon and take a siesta to avoid the hottest part of the day. About 4 they reopen and then go to dinner around 10. Does that sound good to you?"

"M-m-ouais. Perfect." After a pause of several seconds she continued, "Will you come lie down with me? Keep me company?"

"Do I have any choice?"

At that she lifted her head and craned her neck to look at him. "Do you want a choice?"

Carter pulled into the courtyard and parked the car under the trees. Karine got out and closed the door, but stood with her hand still resting on the side of the car. Carter pushed himself to a standing position behind the steering wheel, walked across the seat and vaulted over her closed door to alight beside her. "OK, enough of this. You're looking tired. Come on. Do you want to go to your room or mine? We have the house all to ourselves at least until tomorrow. Let's go upstairs and lie down...and talk."

"Well, all right. But only if we talk."

Without another word he swept her into his arms and began to climb the stairs.

Chapter 30

In the early dawn Carter slipped from Karine's bed. She lay on her side, her features relaxed, her breathing deep and rhythmic. She murmured briefly when he first eased himself from the bed, but did not awake. He stood above her now, looking at the contrast between the whiteness of the sheet and the deep tan of her skin. He repressed an urge to lean down and kiss her softly. Instead, he smiled to himself and tiptoed out of the room, being careful lest his steps set the old floorboards to creaking. He returned to his own room, threw on his clothes, wrote a brief note telling her he should be back by mid-morning, and stuck it on the inside of her door where she would see it as soon as she was up.

With light traffic he was outside the institute within fifteen minutes. There was a good chance Bunny would not yet be there, but he would leave a note requesting his forbearance. There was no way he could explain why he was asking for someone to cover for him for the next week. He just hoped the director would go along with him.

He scribbled out the note and took it into Bunny's office, where he left it on the desk. Just as he turned around to leave, however, the sound of someone's opening the front door and walking across the reception area came from below. Carter left the office and walked to the head of the stairs. Below was Bunny.

"Good morning, Carter. What are you doing in so early?"

"Just hoping to catch you before everyone else got in. Something has come up that I have no control over. I'm going to have to leave for four or five days."

"I see. When are you leaving?"

"I'm not sure. Maybe as early as today. If not today, maybe tomorrow. At any rate, by day after tomorrow. Look, Bunny, I really am sorry. I wish I could explain it to you, but..." He let his voice trail off, for he did not know what else to say.

Bunny now stood behind his desk and looked up pensively. When he finally did speak it was in a low voice devoid of any frivolity. "I was warned that something like this might happen and that I was not to ask questions or press you for an explanation. I've been asked to work with you. I, or someone else, will take your classes until you return."

"What do you mean you were warned this might happen?"

"My friend, I didn't ask you questions. I don't know what you're really doing, and I guess it's none of my business. I've just been asked by someone attached to my government to facilitate things for you in any way I can. That's all I'm doing now. I just ask you to let me know before you leave. If you can."

"I'll try. In the meantime, I'll take my first class this morning, but won't be there for the second. Depending on how things go this morning I should be here to take my afternoon group. Thanks, Bunny. I'll do my best to make it up to you."

Cruikshank nodded, gave him a thumbs up and Carter walked out of his office to have breakfast at a small café near the Knossos Restaurant. He would return afterwards for his first class. It would be over in time for him to meet the first flight from Athens.

All morning long he thought about Matejowsky and the confrontation the day before. He did not need to take that kind of abuse. The truth, he admitted to himself as he awaited the arrival of the plane, was that he never before experienced such happiness in his life. Here in Crete he found good friends, a stimulating atmosphere and the potential for making a great deal of money. What good was it going to do him, or anybody else, to chase halfway around the world to identify a terrorist? If Abu Bekr was caught or killed there would just be someone else to take his place. The killing and destruction would go on no matter what he did.

Neither his attitude nor his state of mind improved when the plane landed and all passengers disembarked without a sign of Jean Paul. Never mind, he thought to himself as he drove back into town. As soon as this is over I'm history. As far as I'm concerned the Israelis and Fedayeen can just fight it out amongst themselves. Leave me out of it!

Instead of returning to school he drove back to the villa, told Karine he was needed at the institute earlier than expected and took her to lunch in the suburb of Aghi Yanni. That afternoon he dropped her off at the beach, met with his class, spoke briefly with Andreas, picked up Karine and took her with him to meet the evening flight. Instead of Jean Paul, Philippe waved as he descended from the airplane and saw them standing at the gate.

Philippe finished his business in Athens and decided to return immediately. He knew nothing of Jean Paul since they parted company at the airport the morning before. In response to Carter's questions about the incident the previous morning with the two officials, he said Jean Paul refused to talk about it on the plane.

Almost as soon as they pulled into the courtyard Popi's head appeared over the wall. Philippe put his few things inside the entryway and disappeared next door.

Karine knew something was gnawing at Carter, but after trying unsuccessfully to cajole an answer from him she gave up. Carter finally decided there was no need to worry further about his friend's arrival. Whenever he came back they could move. Until then he would take advantage of his and Karine's alone time.

It was with a feeling of relief that Carter saw his friend emerge from the Olympic flight the next morning. As soon as they retrieved his luggage and got into the car both started to talk at once. Carter cut him off, however, and insisted he listen to the news of Abu Bekr.

Jean Paul proclaimed his readiness to leave immediately, and upon their arrival at the villa began to gather things he felt he would need. Carter slipped down to the kafeneion and called the number Matejowsky scribbled in the book. The phone at the other end was picked up after the first ring.

"Glad you called. I was starting to get worried. Did your friend get back?"

"Just picked him up at the airport and dropped him off at the villa."

"How soon are you leaving?"

"Within the hour."

"Good! Now listen. This is what I want you to do. Parked just down the street from the Youth Hostel is a dark green Opel. Under the left front fender is a small magnetized metal box with a key in it. It opens the doors and works the ignition. Don't take that yellow bomb you were driving the other day when I met you anywhere near there. Leave it at home. In the glove compartment you'll find another key. This one opens the trunk. Don't open it until you're well out of town. Inside you'll find two pairs of high-powered binoculars, two pairs of night vision goggles, an infrared flashlight and a Nikon with telephoto lens. It would be better to leave all that in the trunk until you get to where you're going.

"Take the car and drive directly to Palaiókastron. You have plenty of gas and it has an auxiliary tank. The toggle switch to change tanks is under the dash right by the steering column. You won't need to stop until you get there. Once in Palaiókastron you'll find a little sidewalk café called Kastronaíki's. Park your car near there and go sit at one of the outside tables. Dress like tourists. You don't have to worry about finding your contact. He'll find you. I don't care how goddamn long you have to wait, you're not to leave! Is that understood?"

"Got it, chief. One thing. How am I to know my contact?"

"Easy. When he approaches you he'll ask for a match. Tell him you'll trade a match for a cigarette. He'll offer you one from a box of Greek cigarettes, but there'll only be Lucky Strikes inside. That should cut down on the chances of going off with the wrong person by mistake. Once you meet you're to follow his instructions. Any other questions?"

"Yeah. What sort of action are we to take?"

"To the best of my knowledge, none. Take your cues from your contact. As soon as you've made a positive I.D. on Abu Bekr you're through. Get out of there and get back to me as soon as possible."

"That's cut and dried. Not much to it, is there?"

"Carter, I don't foresee any problems as long as you watch yourself and keep a tight rein on your Frog. No freelance shit and I mean that. Go in, do your job, and get out again. I'll look forward to hearing from you. Call me as soon as you get back to Sitía."

"What about the car? What am I supposed to do with it when we get through?"

"Good question. I almost forgot that. Just leave it where you found it. If, by any chance, you get stopped all the papers are in the glove compartment. They're in your name and state you bought the car in Athens and brought it to Crete on the ferry. Everything's in order. When you leave it in Iraklion take all the papers with you. I'll have it picked up. You don't need to worry about it."

"OK, well, I guess there's nothing more to ask. Thanks, Glen. I'll be talking to you soon, I hope. By the way, I took care of everything at the institute. The director was a big help. It seems as if someone's working behind the scenes to make things go smoothly."

"Yeah, the Blokes can be real sweethearts at times. Good luck."

Before Carter could respond the phone clicked and the connection was cut. He replaced the receiver and made his way back up the narrow lane to the villa.

Jean Paul was waiting for him in his room. He threw an extra pair of pants and two shirts in a battered gym bag laying on Carter's bed. When he heard Carter come in he stood up. "Ready to go?"

"Yeah, I'm ready. Did you say anything to Philippe?"

"I told him we were going away for a day or so and to take care of things here. I left him some money and he'll make sure Karine has everything she needs while we're gone."

"Good. Look, I'm going to run up and tell Karine good-bye."

"Bon, I'll wait for you in the car."

"No, not the car. Just wait for me outside. We'll take the bus. I'll explain it all to you while we walk down to the bus stop."

Jean Paul gave a Gallic shrug and picked up the bag from the bed. Carter left the room and ran upstairs to Karine's room. She was not there and he called her name. When she answered her voice came from the direction of his room.

"What are you doing in here?" he asked when he saw her lying on his bed.

"You're leaving, aren't you?"

"Oui, chérie, but I'll be back before you know it."

"Where are you going?"

"Jean Paul and I have some business to take care of. We won't be gone long. We should be back in a couple of days."

She started to ask him what kind of business, but he put his hand gently over her mouth and told her not to ask those kinds of questions. With his hand still over her mouth he kissed her lightly on the end of the nose and then rose to leave. Before he could move away and out the door she stood on the bed and threw her arms around his neck, squeezed him tightly, kissed him on the mouth and then released him.

"Hurry back," she said simply, as she let her arms fall to her sides.

He kissed her again and, without saying another word, walked out of the room. Jean Paul waited by the gate. When he saw Carter coming he opened the gate and they walked toward the paved road. Unnoticed on the upper terrace, Karine watched them until they turned the corner and were lost from view.

The car was where Matejowsky said it would be. No one paid any attention to them when they removed the key from its hiding place, opened the doors, threw the gym and shoulder bags into the back seat and drove away. In spite of its outward appearance the car was well-powered and moved easily on the almost deserted winding coastal road.

Carter asked about the incident at the airport. Jean Paul recounted how he was questioned thoroughly by Zakovides and two other men while customs officials tore his valise apart. They forced him to strip and even gave him a not-so-gentle rectal exam. At no time was he given an explanation of what they hoped to find or what they suspected he may have been carrying. To his relief they paid no attention to the camera around his neck. Before leaving for the airport he took the film from it and put the exposed rolls in empty film canisters. The anger and frustration of Zakovides and his men was evident as soon as they realized Jean Paul was carrying nothing that would incriminate him. Jean Paul knew they would not give up. In the future he would be well advised to exercise extreme caution.

Upon their arrival at the Athens airport, he saw Philippe off in a taxi and then placed a call to Katz. As soon as the old man came on the line the Frenchman identified himself and asked if he would be available the next day. During his last trip they discussed just such an eventuality so there was no misunderstanding the purpose of his call.

From the phone booth he went directly to the Swissair counter and purchased round trip tickets via Geneva. From Geneva he could easily arrange transportation to Zürich and back. This was one of the advantages of traveling in a small country. In case the Greek authorities were monitoring his comings and goings he felt it would be better to vary his itinerary. To make their job more difficult, the next time he would fly into Luxembourg, or someplace in northern Italy, like Milano, which offered the advantage of good roads and a straight shot up to Switzerland on the N2 through the St. Gotthard Tunnel.

He spent the night in Geneva and left early the next morning by express train for Zürich. Upon arriving he located a lab able to develop his film and make prints to his specifications. In a little over two hours after stepping off the train at the Bahnhof he picked up the photographs and was standing with his finger poised over Katz's doorbell.

Katz was incredulous when he saw the photos. Jean Paul elicited an estimate of one million US dollars from him for the statue and left his house in a state of euphoria. Katz made him promise he would have right of first refusal, to which Jean Paul readily agreed.

"Our first priority is to find the money for the statue. Zakari is unwilling to extend the deadline and I don't want to be so insistent he becomes unwilling to work with us at all. I broached the subject when I met him to take the pictures. He's adamant. Secondly, we must find a way to get our things out of the country without taking them ourselves. They suspect something and are going to check me no matter how innocent the trip may be. They've seen us together enough now that I think they might search you, as well.

"We need money and we need it fast. The money we've made on the first two trips is not going to last indefinitely and we must have liquid funds to be able to take a flight, or whatever else may be required. I'm going to make arrangements with Deaf Yanni to take another consignment. He trusts us and I know he must have a number of things we can choose from. What we need are things that are small with potentially high value."

"What about some more of the little ivory statues like you took the first time?"

"That would be ideal, but I'd rather take him something of a different nature."

"Why? The statuettes are small, easily concealed and command a high price. You proved that on the first trip."

"True, but if we provide the market with too many of the same type or style artifacts their value becomes diluted. See what I mean?"

Carter agreed reluctantly. They would need something else. Time was growing relatively short and now with the interference of security and customs things became more complicated.

By five they passed Sitía. They were now quite close to their goal and would arrive well before sundown. Palaiókastron appeared before them and within ten minutes they located their rendezvous site. Carter parked between a pair of bedraggled palms and they walked to the café.

By six thirty the sun was beginning to sink to the west and Carter continued to watch people come and go, but he saw no one who looked likely. At a quarter to seven he was startled by a voice from behind him and a light touch on the shoulder.

"Siggnómi, éshete spírto?" Excuse me. Do you have a match? The Cretan dialect was strong and Carter turned to see who spoke to him. Seated directly behind him was a man of indeterminate years, unshaven, black headband, and threadbare vest over a gray shirt and dusty and scuffed boots that came to right below his knees. An unlit cigarette was in his right hand and his left gripped a stout shepherd's staff worn smooth by years of use.

"Naí, éxo," responded Carter and reached into his shirt pocket for a small box of wooden matches. "I'll trade you a light for a cigarette."

The man took a red cigarette box from the sash at his waist, opened it and proffered it to Carter. Three slightly tattered Lucky Strikes, logo facing up, lay in the bottom. Carter took one and lit the man's and then his own. He inhaled deeply, muttered his thanks while regarding Carter with dark, intelligent eyes.

"Kyrie Dáskalos?" he asked in a low voice.

"Yes, I'm the teacher."

Continuing to speak quickly in a soft conversational tone he gave instructions. "When I leave you wait here for five minutes, understood? Take your car and drive to the north end of town. Exactly one and six tenths of a kilometer after you leave Palaiókastron you will see a dirt track leading off into an old olive grove. It is almost overgrown, so you must leave before dark. Drive onto the track. It will lead to an old abandoned house that cannot be seen from the road. Pull your car behind the house and wait there."

Carter nodded his understanding and turned back to his table. Jean Paul looked up, but when Carter said nothing he decided it was just a peasant asking for a match. A moment later the man left his seat and walked down the street. Carter seemed to pay no attention to his leaving. He waited the required five minutes then placed some coins on the table and got up.

"Foutons le camp, mon vieux." Let's get the hell out of here.

Within minutes they made their way out of town and soon found the turnoff and the abandoned house with no problem. Only after he turned off the motor did Jean Paul ask what they were doing. Carter told him the peasant was their contact and of his instructions. Jean Paul merely shrugged and lit a cigarette before getting out and walking a short distance from the car to relieve himself against one of the olive trees.

Carter felt a presence before he turned and actually saw the figure standing in the deepening dusk. In spite of himself he jumped. Jean Paul, further away among the trees, remained oblivious to the fact they were not alone.

"Kyrie Dáskalos?"

"Naí."

The man switched to correct, but heavily accented English. Carter could tell his accent was not Greek, but could not place the country. "So, you've finally arrived. Welcome."

Carter reached for the door handle, but the man placed his hand on the door to hold it closed. Without a word he reached in through the window and quickly found the dome light switch. There was a faint click and the man withdrew his arm.

"OK, the light won't come on when you open your door. You may step out now." He opened the door for him and stepped back.

The first thing Carter heard as he got out of the car was a muffled gasp from the direction Jean Paul took. Across the roof of the car he could see three figures advancing toward him.

"Ah, these are my friends. They have already introduced themselves to your French friend, I see."

Jean Paul appeared pale in the gloom as he struggled to zip up his pants. Carter turned to the man beside him. "Who is this?"

"Introductions are in order. I am Avram. This is my associate Ari and the other rather large gentleman holding onto the arm of your friend we call Golem."

"Well, I must say, with the exception of Ari, your names don't sound very Greek," said Carter.

Avram chuckled. "You are correct, my friend. We are working for a government friendly to yours. And you, I take it, are Martin."

"That's right. Carter Martin. Pleased to meet you. This is my friend, Jean Paul Bonisseur."

"Good to meet you both. Come with me and we will talk."

Avram turned and began to walk in the direction of the abandoned house. Carter and the three others followed closely behind. Through a door held tenuously in place by only one hinge they entered the deeper gloom of the interior. Avram paused an instant before Carter saw the thin beam of a penlight glow from his hand. He led them across the main room and stopped before a door in the back wall. They all passed through it and entered another room, which was considerably smaller.

Avram stopped again and Carter heard the door close almost silently behind them.

"Wait here a moment. I will give us some light." Avram moved away and lit an oil lamp on the wall. In the warm glow of the lamp Carter saw they were in a rather small room with no windows. Against one wall was a table sitting on the floor of packed earth. On the table were portable radio equipment and several paper tubes Carter supposed were maps.

"Now then, that's better," said Avram, as he turned back to the others with a smile.

Both of the men flanking Jean Paul appeared to be about his age. Avram looked to be in his early thirties. His face was darkened by a heavy growth of beard and he was dressed similar to any Cretan peasant. Ari was lean, about six feet tall, and peered through pale gray eyes. Wolf's eyes, thought Carter.

The one they called Golem towered above Jean Paul. He was at least six and a half feet tall and appeared to be constructed of fire hardened clay. The complexion of his cheeks was almost earthen and the onyx of his black eyes totally absorbed the flickering light of the oil lamp, reflecting none of it. His hands were massive with thick fingers that looked as if they were all broken and badly reset at some time or other.

Avram took two wooden boxes from against one wall and offered them to the newcomers. Once seated Carter and Jean Paul looked at him expectantly.

"As far as we know Abu Bekr is on the island. At least we think he is. We have fixed the position of a group of six Fedayeen between Váï and Erimoúpolis. We don't know for sure if one of them is Bekr." Turning his gaze to Jean Paul, Avram continued, "You probably do not know this man by the name of Abu Bekr. You will have known him as Belkacem Ben Boulaid. I understand you will be able to recognize him. It is for this reason we requested your assistance in identifying him. We do not want to act until we are sure he is actually with them. If we were to move too quickly, and he has not yet arrived, he would be warned and disappear again."

"How long have they been here?" asked Carter.

"We think no longer than four days. It was only a stroke of luck that we found them so quickly. Ari spotted two of them coming into Vái to buy supplies from a small store near the sea. He followed them north out of Vái and they led him almost directly to where they are hiding."

"Do you know why they're on Crete?"

"No. We have been following their activities as closely as possible for the past several months and suspected a move like this. Where they plan to go from here - or how - is unknown."

"So, where do we go from here? What's the procedure for trying to identify them?"

"We leave before dawn tomorrow. Are you hungry? We will eat something and then sleep for a while before leaving. I will wake you when it is time to go. We will not take the car, but will hike up the coast. I have some clothes for the both of you. Jean Paul will be easy to disguise, but we must do something about Carter's blonde hair and blue eyes." Smilingly he said, "You could not hide very easily in the souks."

Ari heated water for tea on a camp stove and they shared two kilos of peasant bread and cheese. Golem produced a bottle of wine from a knapsack and passed it around.

Avram soon rose and advised them to rest. Jean Paul stretched out the best he could in the back seat of the car and Carter took the front. They both left the doors open, for this not only allowed them to take advantage of whatever evening breeze presented itself, but they could also stretch their legs. Carter felt surprisingly calm. He laid back on the seat, his arms under his head and the steering wheel digging into his thigh.

Carter said to Jean Paul, "You certainly have been quiet. It's not like you. Are you sorry I talked you into coming along?"

"No, not at all. I've just been thinking."

"About what?"

"Boulaid. I would like to be the one who kills him. I would take great pleasure in pulling the trigger or slowly garroting him with a piano wire. Also, I've been thinking about you. Tell me again about this article you're writing."

"Yeah, well, I couldn't tell you everything in case you said no."

"Who do you work for? The CIA?"

"Something like that. Now, you tell me something: who do you think our three friends work for?"

"Mossad."

Carter nodded in agreement.

In spite of the thoughts churning in his brain Carter fell asleep shortly after Jean Paul began to snore softly. It seemed as if he just closed his eyes when he felt a hand on his shoulder. His eyes flew open and in the dim starlight he recognized Ari's profile. Carter unfolded himself from the seat and stood outside the car trying to work the kinks out of his muscles. Ari left two chipped mugs of strong black coffee on the hood of the car. As soon as they were able to move around without stumbling, they grasped the cups of coffee, relishing the steaming bitterness, and went into the house.

On top of some boxes were clothes that looked as if someone wore them for weeks in the fields. They were dirty and threadbare and gave off a strong smell of body odor, but once they put them on they knew they would blend in. The shoes provided them were old, but sturdy and, although a little large for Carter, two pairs of heavy socks made them fit more snugly. Ari sprayed black dye on Carter's hair and darkened his face, neck, ears and the backs of his hands. A cloth fisherman's cap with a short bill pulled far down on his forehead effectively hid the blue of his eyes. Carter looked at himself in a piece of mirror as he pulled a faded and worn brown suit coat on over his long-sleeved shirt.

He grinned at his reflection. Maybe not perfect, he thought to himself, but from a distance who would ever know. When they stepped outside they saw Ari coming through the orchard leading two Cretan donkeys. The little animals stood patiently while they were loaded with weapons and what appeared to be explosives. Carter took the night vision goggles from the back of the car, along with the maps, camera and telephoto lens. From its hiding place inside the car he retrieved the pistol and stuck it between his back and the waistband of his pants. The jacket fell loosely over it and hid any telltale bulge. He put the binoculars in a dirty canvas bag he found hanging from a nail inside the house and slung the ratty shoulder strap around his neck.

Ari took the car keys from Carter and drove the Opel away from the house without turning on the headlights. As soon as Ari drove off Avram and Golem motioned to Carter and Jean Paul and began to lead the donkeys away in a northeasterly direction.

They did not go far before Carter began to hear the dull sound of surf on rocks. They skirted fields that would soon have peasants working them and stayed to the sea side as much as possible. They traveled at least three kilometers before Carter saw Ari ahead among a jumble of rocks. His white teeth flashed quickly in the rising dawn. The sun was not yet above the horizon but the clouds to the east showed pinkish tints, which were reflected in the sea beyond the surf line. No one said anything as Ari fell in behind everyone else.

The only deviation from their route along the coast came when they neared Váï. Avram led them in a westerly direction inland in order to skirt the small seaside community. It was only after they were almost a kilometer beyond the palm tree-lined beach that they returned to the vicinity of the shore. There they paralleled the sea for another two to three kilometers before turning once more inland. Near a thick stand of cane they came to a halt and Avram called them together.

"Sit and relax. We will rest here for a moment."

Carter was pleased they stopped, for he could feel at least one place where a blister was forming. He thought the extra pair of socks would protect his feet, but the stiff shoes still chafed his left heel. He unlaced and started to take the brogan off when the wall of the canebrake parted and a peasant stepped into the open. Carter and Jean Paul were instantly alert, but the three Israelis simply looked up. Avram was the first to speak.

"Dov!"

"Shalom! Ari, Golem. Any problems?"

"None," responded Ari. "How about you? Are our little pigeons still in their roost, or have they flown off?"

"Still there. It's been very quiet." He looked at Carter and Jean Paul and grinned. "Shalom, my name's Dov. You must be Carter Martin." Without waiting for a reply he looked at Jean Paul. "And you, I take it, are Bonisseur. Welcome to both of you."

Avram explained that Dov was the fourth member of their party. He watched the Fedayeen while the three others went to meet Carter and Jean Paul. According to Dov, there was nothing new to report for the past 24 hours.

It was now close to 7:30 and the sun was well above the horizon. Avram gave instructions in Hebrew to finish unloading the donkeys before he turned once more to Carter.

"There is a vantage point from which it is possible to see the house where the terrorists are and most of the area around it. What we want to do is to put you and Jean Paul in a position that will allow you to see all of the men at the house and identify Bekr if he is there."

Carter nodded in agreement. He handed the binoculars to Jean Paul and slipped the camera's strap around his neck.

Jean Paul remained unusually quiet and Carter wondered what he was thinking. The week before Jean Paul told him of the incident in Algeria and, to Carter's surprise, even broken down and cried at the end of the recitation. Carter wondered how it must feel to lose someone close to you and then suddenly be presented with the possibility of meeting the one responsible face to face. He wondered how he would react in such a situation and a chill passed down his spine.

"Just remember, mon vieux, stay calm and follow our friend's lead. Just identify the son of a bitch and let them handle it. He won't get away this time."

Jean Paul maintained his grim expression. "I can tell you right now I don't really have to see Boulaid to identify him. He's here. I can feel him. I can almost smell him."

Avram approached them to give last words of instruction before they moved off together through a nearby olive orchard. They kept clear of paths or tracks that might be traveled, taking advantage of all natural cover, maintaining silence and constant watchfulness. Ari, Dov and Golem disappeared in different directions. Carter assumed they would position themselves at other points with different views of the house and its environs.

Fifteen minutes later they stopped in a brush-lined ditch that showed signs of recent occupation. Over the top of the bank, about 70 meters away, could be seen the wall of a common Cretan house. From their vantage point only one window was visible. Loose shutters hung forlornly from hinges that bled brown rust stains down the graying whitewash of the battered and pitted wall. This was one end of the house they were seeing. If it were constructed as most were, there would be more windows and a front entrance on the seaward side, and a back entrance, as well. Off to the side could be seen a well and a wisp of smoke rose from the chimney built into one corner.

No one was in sight, but Jean Paul took the protective caps from the lenses of the binoculars and started to raise them to his eyes. Gently yet firmly Avram reached out and pushed them down again.

"No, not yet. Remember, we are in a westerly direction from the house and it is still early in the morning. The sun is still not high enough not to reflect off the lenses and give away our position. Don't even bother looking through your glasses until someone can be seen with the naked eye."

"Merde, you're right. I didn't think. Sorry."

"No problem this time, but you must be more careful in the future."

Almost three-quarters of an hour passed before anyone came out of the house. When a man appeared Jean Paul glanced first at the sun and then at Avram. At a nod from the Israeli he put the binoculars to his eyes and studied the man across the distance.

"It's not Ben Boulaid."

Avram nodded and leaned back against the side of the ditch. Jean Paul continued to watch avidly, however, waiting for someone else to come into view. During the remainder of the morning they stayed in their positions. At one point four of them came outside and kicked a soccer ball around the barren area behind the house like children on an outing. None could be identified and the watchers surveyed them dispassionately while Carter took pictures through the telephoto lens.

The remaining two that were supposed to be there remained out of sight. The thing they knew for sure, at least from what Jean Paul told them, was that Abu Bekr was not among those that were outside. It was unknown whether he was in the house or left unseen by Dov during the night. The possibility existed that the missing two represented no one more important than the four already visible and that Abu Bekr might not even be on the island.

In the middle of the afternoon Ari arrived with a thermos of coffee, a half kilo of cheese, two dried sausages, a kilo of bread and four large lemons so sweet they tasted almost like oranges. Avram left in the direction of the sea to check with Dov. The entire house was covered. No one could slip in or out without being seen.

After eating, Jean Paul lay back and was soon asleep. Like Carter, he slept only fitfully the night before. He found the ground infinitely more comfortable than the back seat of the car.

While Ari and Carter maintained their vigil Carter took the opportunity to ask questions. Any attempt at discussion the night before and while on their trek northward was politely but firmly rebuffed. He never heard Golem utter more than one or two words at a time. Avram was obviously in charge and the others followed his directives. Both Dov and Ari, on the other hand, were young, probably the same age as Carter, and more gregarious. Ari relaxed visibly as soon as Avram disappeared from sight. Carter was pleased to be free of Avram's watchful eye, for there were a number of questions he wanted to ask.

They talked of education, sports, cars, girls, travel and experiences. They were two young men far from home. In other circumstances they might have this same discussion over drinks on the terrace of the villa or in the club.

"Ari, tell me what brought you to this place. I don't mean Crete exactly, I mean to this situation."

Ari sat with his eyes lowered, sifting the fine Cretan soil between his fingers. He sat that way for some time and Carter was not sure he was going to answer. He was preparing to either rephrase the question or try another tack when Ari looked up, brushed the dust from his hands and shrugged his shoulders.

"What brings us to any place in time? I mean, I'm here because there is a man who would take my country from me today, chase me from it tomorrow and kill me if he could. His forefathers set the precedence, I think. Others have tried this before and will continue to try as long as they are allowed this freedom. My government sends me here to make sure he will not succeed.

"You are here, at this place in time, because this same man threw explosives in the car of one of the officials of your government, killing him, his driver and bodyguard. I assume they want to ensure this man will never again succeed in such a mission."

Carter was instantly alert. "Where did this happen? The explosives? In Lebanon?"

Ari nodded.

"Sidon?"

Again the nod.

For a moment Carter could hardly breathe. This was too much to be mere coincidence. There could not possibly be another U.S. official killed in Sidon in this precise manner. Ari was talking of the murder of Carter's father! Carter was totally unaware until that very moment that for the past several months, in fact ever since he first found the reference to Abu Bekr in the communications from Cyprus, he was following the trail of his own father's killer. The Agency knew or suspected, probably from the very beginning who murdered his father. They knew and did not give any indication of the knowledge to Carter.

On one hand, Carter felt betrayed and incredulous. On the other he felt immense rage at what he viewed as his having been manipulated. He was lucid enough to know that it was certainly not Abu Bekr himself who dropped the explosives into his father's car, but he was the brains behind the act. Those that performed the actual deed were but extensions, marionettes that reacted to their strings being pulled from above. The master puppeteer was Abu Bekr. If anything happened to the puppets new ones were found and put to work by tying them to the same strings that controlled their predecessors. If something were to happen to the controller: ah, well, that was a different story entirely. Everything collapsed at that point. He was here to help bring down the curtain on this show.

What would happen once Jean Paul positively identified Abu Bekr? Would the Israeli's take him and his group? Would he ever pay for the chaos he perpetrated? Would he - Carter - ever know? The questions rankled him.

Ari talked on and on and did not seem to notice the change that came over Carter. He paid no further attention to what Ari was now saying and could not have cared less. When Carter no longer responded Ari ceased talking. He leaned back against the bank, still holding his Uzzi with silencer across his chest and closed his eyes.

By five o'clock there was still no activity around the house. Occasionally one or more of the men could be seen, but mostly there was nothing out of the ordinary. By six Carter began to give up hope of anything happening that day. Ari left and Avram took his place.

Through tedium, boredom and the monotony of the situation their attentiveness waned. Both Carter and Avram heard the sound of voices followed by a low masculine laugh. Avram turned to signal for silence. Someone was approaching from the direction of the canebrake. Whoever they were apparently thought they were alone, for they did nothing to hide their presence. The language was definitely not Greek and Carter thought it was perhaps Arabic. If they continued on their present course they would pass within twenty feet of Carter and the two others.

They came into view and Carter heard a gasp from Jean Paul. At the same moment the two men saw the three strangers against the bank. Both stopped suddenly and went into a defensive crouch. One with his coat over one shoulder threw the coat aside. Hidden beneath it, hanging by a strap from his shoulder, was a deadly looking automatic weapon. The man clawed at the strap trying to bring its muzzle to bear on any of the three facing him across the short distance. Before he could succeed, however, there came a series of low coughing detonations from Avram's Uzzi. With a look of utter astonishment the man's weapon flew from his grasp and landed five feet in front of his companion.

A series of short violent actions followed. To Carter they were dreamlike.

From his right came the voice of Jean Paul, a bellow of rage and triumph. "Boulaid!" Then a blur of motion as the Frenchman launched himself from his crouched position in the direction of the man facing him.

At the same time Jean Paul threw himself across the narrow expanse separating him from his old enemy, Belkacem Ben Boulaid leapt forward for the gun lying in the dust, just as Avram's Uzzi began to cough again. Pieces of bark exploded from the trees directly behind where his target crouched, leaving stark white wounds on the trunks of the trees. As the bullets passed harmlessly over his back Abu Bekr snatched his fallen companion's machine gun from the ground, clutched it to his chest as he executed a roll to one side, and came up on one knee, firing a sustained burst to Carter's left. Of the ten bullets he fired five found their mark, producing devastating results as they stitched five blood-red blossoms across Avram's upper chest. He was dead before he hit the ground.

More would have hit their target and he would have certainly then turned the gun on Carter had not Jean Paul's hurtling body impacted him, spoiling his aim and slamming him to the ground. The Arab still held onto the gun, but was unable to aim it at his attacker. He tried to club Jean Paul with the butt, but in his position his attempts were totally ineffectual. Their fight was bitter, hand to hand, life or death. Both strained to gain the advantage. Legs kicked and arms swung as they rolled about in the dust.

Off to one side the terrorist wounded by Avram screamed and flopped like a fish thrown on a riverbank. To Carter's left blood from Avram's wounds seeped into and nourished the thirsty Cretan soil. As a spectator Carter saw everything. It all happened quickly. In less than five seconds one man was wounded, one died and now two were engaged in mortal combat. He wanted to help, to go to the aid of his friend. His brain was aware of that desire, but it seemed incapable of communicating the message to his muscles.

Out of nowhere Golem arrived at a dead run. His appearance finally galvanized Carter. With jerky strides he moved toward his friend and the terrorist who still struggled on the ground. Golem waded into the fray as if he were merely separating two scrapping dogs. He pinned the arm still holding the machine pistol to the ground with his foot and clubbed the Arab across the temple with the barrel of his gun. He then peeled the two combatants apart, one limp, and the other unaware the fight was over. Golem dropped the unconscious Abu Bekr and moved to the side of the one who was wounded in the upper thighs by Avram's opening burst. An artery in the groin area was obviously severed by one of the rounds and blood gushed unchecked from the wound. Golem looked at the man for a moment, weighing his chances for survival, and then decided they were slim at best. Having come to that conclusion, he quickly and expertly broke his neck. With no apparent effort he lifted the corpse and carried it to the thick stand of cane. There he hid it before returning to Abu Bekr.

Although Carter held him tightly from behind, Jean Paul continued to struggle. Carter wrapped his arms tightly around his friend's upper arms and torso and pulled him away from Golem's grasp. Sobbing for breath, covered in dust and blood from an eyebrow split by a head-butt, the Frenchman's rage finally subsided and he slumped to the ground

Only then did he become aware of activity from the direction of the house. Alerted by the sound of firing from the burst loosed by Abu Bekr, the Fedayeen rushed into the house for their own weapons. Ari and Dov, also alerted, were well-positioned. They allowed all but one of the terrorists to get into the open before opening fire. A deadly crossfire cut down those in the open as they foolishly tried to run to the aid of their comrades. The one still in the house was quickly captured when two stun grenades were lobbed through a window. The explosion left him reeling and bleeding from both ears.

By the time Ari and Dov arrived with their prisoner, Golem trussed Abu Bekr and tied him to a tree. They tied theirs to the other side of the tree and rushed away to dispose of the bodies as quickly as possible. There was a chance no one heard the firing, but the detonation of the two stun grenades would likely bring curious peasants from the surrounding area. Dov stayed with the prisoners and Ari and Golem disappeared over the lip of the bank.

Carter pulled the camera from his shoulder bag and asked Jean Paul to hold up Bekr's head. Jean Paul complied with savage pleasure. He grasped a handful of the man's hair and slammed his head back against the trunk of the tree. Carter took pictures from several different angles, including full-face and profile shots.

By the time he finished ,Ari and Golem were back. Dov produced two donkeys and lashed the body of Avram onto the back of one of them after wrapping it tightly in a poncho. The two Fedayeen, now fully conscious, were gagged, blindfolded, wrapped in separate ponchos and thrown over the back of a sturdy mule Dov found to complement the donkeys. They packed all of their remaining gear on the back of the last donkey before heading west. Once darkness fell they turned south southeast and trekked in the direction of Palaiókastron.

Few words were spoken during the entire return trip. Each kept his thoughts to himself and shared them with no one. The Israelis were all business, even though the body of their commander was strapped across the back of one of the pack animals. The hulking Golem walked beside the mule. Neither prisoner made a sound the entire way.

It was after eleven when they arrived at the house. Carter and Jean Paul helped unload Avram's body and the prisoners while Ari left to retrieve the car. The two Arabs were taken into the house and tied back to back. Dov put them in the corner of the front room and went through the door into the back. Golem remained outside.

For the first time Carter and Jean Paul were alone with the man they came to find. Jean Paul took the flashlight left him by Ari and approached the two captives. He knelt close to the head of his old enemy and shone the light in eyes ablaze with fury. Jean Paul looked closely at him a moment before beginning to speak in a low, hoarse voice.

"Ben Boulaid, on se rencontre de nouveau, hein. Tu me reconnais?"

For the first time Belkacem Ben Boulaid, nom de guerre Abu Bekr, spoke. His voice was gravelly with guttural intonations. "Non. Pas du tout."

Still speaking in a low voice Jean Paul told him who he was and where they met before. A glimmer of recognition came into his eyes and the corners of his mouth twitched as if wanting to turn up into a smile or sneer. "Ah, oui! Bonisseur. I remember you. That was a terrible night. I lost some very good men. But then, if I remember correctly, and please tell me if I'm wrong, you did, too."

Jean Paul flinched inwardly at the memory of the carnage in the hallway. Of course, it was the result of stupid carelessness, but he always felt partly at fault.

"I just have one regret about that night, mon pote. Are you interested in knowing what it is?"

When Jean Paul did not respond, Ben Boulaid continued, "Never mind. I'll tell you anyway. I only regret I was unable to assist you in joining that garbage in the hallway in the same fate!" This time the sneer was evident. It was followed by a gob of spittle that Jean Paul was unable to dodge.

Carter removed his jacket and left it draped over a limb outside the door. He listened to the conversation between Bekr and Jean Paul, thinking of his own loss at the hands of this man. Now the assassin was in his power. At this moment he held the choice of life and death over this animal. The fate of this miserable excuse of a man rested in his hands. Could he cold-bloodedly pull the trigger that would end his existence? He struggled with the thought, weighed the choices. He knew he could, but the choice was no longer his when he heard the sound of the car nearing the front of the house. He was leaning against the wall, but pushed himself away from it and stood in the doorway, his back to the room. He was unaware of silent footsteps behind him.

As soon as Jean Paul stood to wipe the spit from his face the beam from his flashlight swept across Carter's back. Before his eyes, was the answer. As swiftly and silently as a wraith he reached for the butt of the 9mm pistol, jerked it from Carter's waistband, flicked off the safety, placed it alongside the flashlight he held pointed at Abu Bekr, and increased the pressure of his finger on the trigger.

From the rear doorway Dov shouted, but it was too late. The first bullet found its mark, quickly followed by six more. All hit their target, all inflicted maximum damage. Each by itself would have served to violently end the violent life of Abu Bekr.

Dov slammed into Jean Paul and propelled him head first into the stone wall to his right. Golem burst through the front door and bowled over Carter. It was as if he were run over by a truck. The force of the crunching impact sent him flying through the air into the wall on the far side of the room. Both Carter and Jean Paul sprawled unconscious on the floor.

The pain in his head was not severe, but his entire crown felt swollen and distended. Carter raised his hand without opening his eyes and gingerly probed his scalp with tentative fingers. A knot the size of a chicken egg caused him to wince and jerk his hand away.

From nearby came the sound of movement and Carter barely opened one eye. The light of early dawn was faint, but provided enough illumination through the door hanging askew on its hinge to see Jean Paul seated several feet away, his back against the wall. His face rested on drawn up knees.

"Jean Paul?"

When he did not answer Carter rolled over onto his stomach and pushed himself to his hands and knees. At first nausea almost overcame him and his head began to throb with a dull cadence. He lifted himself to his knees and, when he realized the throbbing was less painful in that position, came to his feet. Erect he was not totally steady, but at least the nausea passed.

Jean Paul still did not acknowledge Carter's presence. It was only when he touched him on the arm that the Frenchman finally raised his head. The entire left side of his face was scraped and swollen from where it impacted with the wall. The left eye was purple and barely open. He looked at Carter as if not really recognizing him.

For the first time Carter realized they were alone. The body of Abu Bekr and the other terrorist were gone. A quick search outside also proved fruitless, although their car was there. Carter got in and turned the key, which was still in the ignition. It started immediately and he checked the gauges. Over a half tank remained. He shut off the motor, pocketed the key, returned to the house and went straight to the room to which Avram took them the first night. The door was closed and he tapped lightly on the scarred and discolored wood. When there was no response he put his shoulder to the door, thinking it was probably locked. It offered no resistance and swung inward easily, almost causing him to fall.

The room seemed empty, but it was too dark to be certain. Carter struck a match and held it high. Gone were the maps, the generator, the lantern, the camp stove - any signs of recent habitation. He moved back out into the main room and went to the corner where Abu Bekr lay after being shot. No trace of blood could be seen on the dusty floor. There was not even any sign of the body, or bodies, having been dragged. Nothing.

He began to wonder if it was all a dream He was sure that if he went to the house near the beach there would be no sign of anything out of the ordinary. It was spooky and he felt ill at ease.

Jean Paul raised his head and rested it against the wall. He addressed Carter through cracked lips. "They're gone, huh?"

"Yeah. I find no trace of them whatsoever. It's as if they were never here."

"Ben Boulaid?"

"Gone. So is the other one. I'm sure you killed Abu Bekr. I don't know if you shot both of them or not."

Jean Paul gave a laughed mirthlessly. "All I asked is to be the one that sent him to hell where he belongs."

"Yeah, well it's done. Did you by any chance hear what Dov told me yesterday when we were watching the house? He said it was Abu Bekr's group that assassinated my father in Lebanon last year."

"Your father? Dieu! No, I'm sorry..." At a loss for words, Jean Paul's voice trailed off.

"I admire your courage, old friend. When you shot him you did something I should have done myself. Thanks. I owe you one." He reached out and helped him to his feet. "Let's go home. There's nothing more we can do here."

Together they walked out into the brightening morning.

♈ ♈ ♈

The voice at the other end of the line rose to such a scream of fury that, in spite of the poor telephone service on the island, Carter held the receiver away from his ear.

"You're sent out to do a simple job and you allow that bastard who's supposed to be under your control to destroy months of work! Not only does he blow away a prisoner who might have given the Israelis - and us - a handle on what's going on in Syria and the Lebanese cesspool, but then, you little shithead, you have the nerve to accuse me of using you and that you're going to quit?! Fuck you, asshole! You can't quit! I'm going to burn your ass and take out your Frog friend myself. Do you realize just how many months are down the tubes because both of you lost your heads?" Matejowsky was on a tear.

Immediately upon their arrival in Iraklion they returned the car to where they picked it up two days earlier. Jean Paul hailed a passing taxi to take him back to the villa and Carter went to find a phone.

When Matejowsky learned it was Carter on the line he exploded into a monumental rage. It was apparent from the extent of his knowledge of events the Agency was contacted and briefed within the past five hours. Whoever reported the incident did not mince words. The old adage, 'shit flows downhill' was never more true. What began at the top was an avalanche by the time it reached Carter.

He did not even attempt to reply. He merely listened until the moment Matejowsky appeared to run out of gas. When the man on the other end of the line paused to take a breath Carter cut him off in a low, icy tone of voice.

"My answer to you is 'yes' and 'no.' Yes, I am going to quit. In fact, whether you approve or not, I already have. And no, there is nothing you can do about it."

"The hell I...." he began, but Carter cut him off again.

"You can go to hell, my friend, and take the Agency with you. Enough of it and you. Stay out of my life; stay out of my friend's and family's lives. Oh, and one last thing: be particularly careful who you threaten. Someone gave excellent advice with the warning, 'know your enemy.' Believe me when I tell you, my friend, you don't know yours." Before Matejowsky could reply the line went dead.

Carter stood reflecting on his decision. There were no regrets. In spite of all Matejowsky said, he felt in no danger. He would stay on Crete. Here he enjoyed wonderful friends, a lifestyle anyone would envy, with the possibility of making untold sums of money. Why should he leave? Here he possessed the best of all worlds.

Suddenly very tired, he left the phone cabinet and stepped out onto the dusty sidewalk. The rumble of the canary yellow Ford's mufflers could be heard even before it pulled into view from around the corner.

Chapter 31

For the next few days Carter found himself looking over his shoulder and around corners. He was not sure just how seriously to take Matejowsky's threats. For that matter, he was not comfortable with the uncertainty of how the Agency might regard what amounted to his defection. In addition to being furious, he felt betrayed and totally justified in his actions.

On Carter's third day back at work Bunny called him into his office to tell him someone from the British embassy in Athens notified him that Carter's employment at the institute was no longer imperative.

"I told the pillock I appreciated his concern, but that you were doing important work for us and that your presence was imperative to me. They didn't press me. If they insisted I would have simply told them to bugger off."

Carter heard, or read, that the Agency, and whoever represented the powers that be in the UK, cooperated willingly only in times of direst need. Other times they went out of their way to be contrary to one another. He appreciated Bunny's sticking up for him and wondered once again just how much he knew or suspected.

Jean Paul wasted no time. By noon of the day following their return he contacted Deaf Yanni. Yanni told him to come by in two days. At that time he would bring several finds from which they could choose. When he and Carter went to his atelier for the meeting Carter noticed the absence of the butcher, but said nothing. He was more interested in the seven boxes sitting on a dust covered table. Each box contained a different example of Minoan artifacts. Some of them came from as close as the area around Knossos, while others from as far away as Gournia, Zakros and a place called Apodoulou.

They looked over the offerings and chose four miniature faience plaques from Knossos, each constructed to resemble a multi-story townhouse. Had they not known better, one would have easily guessed they were representations of the modern Cretan houses. Some architecture changed remarkably little since the 15th century BC.

Carter insisted upon the second item chosen, a baked clay tablet the size of a man's hand. Yanni said it was discovered near Kato Zakro, the oasis village with its banana groves and the ever-present olive trees, located at the far eastern end of the island. Scratched into its surface were well delineated lines of script and pictographs known as Linear A. Other baked clay plaques found in other locations contained Linear B, the successor to Linear A. Linear B was thought to be little more than bookkeeping lists of inventories and statistics. Linear A remained to be successfully deciphered.

Items in the five other boxes were left for another time. Jean Paul and Yanni negotiated a price by scratching alternate amounts on the smudged page of a lined tablet.

For almost a week they kept their new treasures hidden at the villa while searching for a way to get them safely out of the country to Switzerland. They agonized over each lost moment, wondering if they were ever going to be able to meet their deadline with Zakari. They even approached Crozet the day before he and his wife left to return to Paris. They knew he was a successful businessman with extensive investments in the European art world. They finally decided to take a chance and approach him. When they told him of their quandary he listened politely. In the end he simply gave a rueful smile and wished them luck.

He told them of an icon he purchased through an antiques dealer, much like Manoli, three years before when he first began to vacation on Crete. Once the money exchanged hands and Crozet innocently tried to return to France with the icon, he found himself detained in customs. Fortunately for him he was able to convince them he was ignorant of the icon's age or historical value. The police confiscated it. A Byzantine treasure they said and he left the country empty-handed. Although unable to prove it, Crozet was certain the dealer alerted the police following the transaction. When he returned the following summer he immediately went looking for the dealer, but he was nowhere to be found.

"Non, non, mes amis," he said shaking his head and finger at them simultaneously. "I was burned badly trying to deal in antiquités from Crete and I won't take that chance again."

They thanked him for at least hearing them out and assured him they understood his position.

They accompanied Crozet and Marie-Claire to the airport the next day to see them off. Just as the Crozet's flight was starting its engines Jean Paul noticed an olive colored, twin engine aircraft making its final approach from the east. From the markings on the wings and fuselage he recognized it as a French military transport. He quickly forgot about the departing Olympic flight and focused his attention on the arriving one, watching intently as it touched down, reversed its engines and taxied up to the recently vacated gate. A number of men in the uniform of the French Army disembarked.

Jean Paul acknowledged them as they filed by and two of the men stopped to talk with him. They said theirs was a flight in transit from Tunisia to the French Army base in Trier, Germany. They were forced to make an unscheduled stop in Crete in order to repair their engine. The flight crew nursed their aircraft across the Mediterranean, but did not want to chance crossing the remaining expanse of water between Crete and continental Europe.

They were a congenial group and became very friendly with Jean Paul when he alluded to his military service in Algeria. A captain named Gardy was in charge. Raised in Blida, his family lost everything in '62. In spite of the climate of the times, his father absolutely forbade him to leave France and the army to return to Algeria. He soon found that he and Jean Paul had a great deal in common.

Gardy kept his men together while the flight engineer and a mechanic worked to repair the engine. Within thirty minutes it became apparent to them they would need more time than originally estimated to complete the job. Apprised of the situation, Gardy called his men together and instructed them to remain at the airport. At Jean Paul's urging he accompanied him and Carter back into town, where they treated him to lunch at Adoni's restaurant. They eventually ended up back at the villa after dropping Carter off at the institute for his afternoon class, promising they would pick him up again on their way back to the airport.

At 4:30 Carter walked out of the institute to find a smug Jean Paul leaning against the side of the car. Carter knew that look, like the cat that swallowed the canary, and laughed as he approached.

"OK, what've you done now? I recognize that smirk. What's her name great poker face?"

"Nothing like that, I assure you. It's just that I've spoken with Gardy and he's agreed to take the things from Deaf Yanni when they leave. They're flying directly from here to Trier. I'll leave tomorrow on Lufthansa from Athens to Hamburg, rent a car there and drive over to the French caserne where our little shipment will be waiting for us – safe and secure. They don't have to pass through customs and..."

"Sans blague! This is too good to be true. Wait. You know what you ought to do? We should run over to Yanni's right now to pick up...."

"If you'd let me finish, I'll tell you the rest of it. That's exactly what I did. As soon as I let Gardy off in town to do a little shopping I ran over to pick up the other five boxes. This is the break we've needed. I'm hoping with this one shipment we'll be able to come up with most of the funds we need to cover the cost of Zakari's statue."

"Where's everything now?"

"In the trunk of the car. Come on. We need to go find Gardy and run him back to the airport."

Without opening the door, Carter vaulted into the car. Jean Paul strutted around the hood of the car to the driver's side. He was proud of himself. As far as he was concerned, all their problems were solved by one fabulous and unforeseen turn of events. They wended their way through the narrow streets until they eventually turned into one of the main thoroughfares. Gardy sat on the edge of the fountain across from the Knossos Restaurant waiting for them. He waved as soon as he saw them and strode to the car. Carter opened the door and moved to the back seat, allowing him to sit in front with Jean Paul. He carried one of the net shopping bags full of items he found in the shops. On their way back to the airport they turned off onto a side road and stopped under some trees of a deserted olive orchard. The wrapped artifacts were taken out of the car's trunk and put in the shopping bag among the things Gardy purchased during the afternoon.

When they reached the airport they saw the group of soldiers seated out of the sun under the plane's wings. Gardy got out and immediately walked to the plane, disappearing through the open cargo door just forward of the wing. He was gone for some time, talking to the flight engineer and pilot about how soon they could leave. The mechanic advised him that he was able to make the repairs necessary for them to continue their flight. He assured Gardy they would be able to leave before dark. With this in mind, Jean Paul and Carter settled down with the soldiers to await the departure of their investment.

The evening flight from Athens arrived and left again before the French contingent received the news from the mechanic and flight engineer that everyone could reboard. Gardy herded his men back onto the plane before turning to Jean Paul.

"Bon, ben, à bientôt alors." He repeated the instructions on how they could find him in Trier and expressed his desire to repay some of the kindness he received during his forced stay on Crete.

"Thanks, it was nothing. It's we who are indebted to you for taking these things out of the country for us. Bon voyage! I'll see you no later than day after tomorrow."

"Bon, les gars. T'à l'heure." With a final brief wave he climbed aboard. The flight engineer pulled the door shut behind him, the pilot revved the engines and the plane pulled onto the tarmac. Jean Paul and Carter watched it taxi away into the failing light, heading for the far end of the runway. The wind was now out of the east and they would be taking off toward the rising moon. The breeze off the sea was freshening and pleasantly cool. Jean Paul and Carter stood watching while the pilot ran through his final checklist before taking off. It seemed to Jean Paul the aircraft remained in takeoff position for an unusually long time and the engines were revved up several times. The plane finally began to move before they heard its motors. When the sound reached them it was a steadily rising roar. Its propellers clawed at the air and pulled it down the runway with increasing speed. Halfway down the airfield's length its nose tilted into the air and the entire fuselage began to rise. As it drew parallel with them it was already 250-300 feet in the air, but the engines seemed to be laboring. Carter turned to Jean Paul to comment on this when they heard a loud, metallic bang. He looked back in time to see a streak of fire from the port engine, the very one the mechanics spent the greater part of the afternoon repairing. The plane banked sharply to the left and began to drop rapidly. The pitch of the engines rose to a shriek, but the plane remained in its dive. They watched in stunned silence as the struggling machine fell from the sky and disappeared from view, looking as if it were going to fall directly into the sea on the far side of the runway. An instant after they lost sight of it a geyser of flame rose toward the first stars, which twinkled to life only a short time earlier.

Horrified at the sight, the two began to sprint across the wide expanse of the airport. They were almost to the main runway when the first fire and rescue vehicle careened through the gates behind them. They were nearing the edge of the airfield when a fire truck screamed past and skidded to a stop several hundred feet further on. By the time the firemen pulled the hoses from the truck and began to pump water onto the burning craft Jean Paul and Carter arrived on the scene.

Below was total confusion. Fire boiled from the left wing, which was torn from the fuselage as it rolled to the left in its final plunge. The fuselage lay crumpled on the rocks two hundred or more feet from the flaming wing. In the glare of the truck's lights and the lurid pyre of the burning wing they could see a figure stumble from the rear of the fuselage and stagger up into the rocks. In a moment another figure emerged, his shoulder obviously broken or badly dislocated. More vehicles arrived and men ran down the rocky slope to where the plane lay. Soon the entire top of the hill above the wreck was lined with curious onlookers.

Ambulances with sirens screaming added to the general confusion. The wing blazed furiously and the remaining engine was shrouded in smoke. There was a strong smell of aviation fuel in the air, but responders could be seen entering what remained of the plane and re-emerging with limp bodies. Some were laid on the ground and immediately covered with blankets. Only two of those carried from the wreckage seemed to have survived. In the confusion Jean Paul and Carter made their way down the slope. They surveyed the living, and then went from body to body, lifting the blankets covering the faces of those who perished. Under the sixth blanket they discovered Gardy's still form. He was almost unrecognizable. Carter noticed the broken nametag still clinging to his bloody military blouse, confirming his identity.

Jean Paul tried to slip onto the plane, hoping to find the treasures stowed by Gardy. He was met at the twisted doorway by a large Greek airman from the base located adjacent to the airport, who pushed him back out the door and told him succinctly to keep his distance. Realizing there was nothing more they could do or learn they resigned themselves to the fact they would never recover the treasures consigned with such great expectations not more than an hour before. They trudged back across the field to the car and drove home with heavy hearts.

Carter regarded the events of the evening with a certain degree of fatalism. Jean Paul, on the other hand, was devastated. Their hopes, which grew with each passing hour, ultimately perished in the flames of the French aircraft. He attempted to impart his philosophy to Jean Paul that 'all things happen for a good reason.' The Frenchman found the credo to be naive and trite.

"I can understand why you'd have a hard time coming to grips with what's happened, and I really don't blame you for not subscribing to what I believe," said Carter to the distraught Jean Paul. "There is a solution out there somewhere, though, and we just have to resolve to find it."

"Noble sentiments," retorted Jean Paul into his hands covering his face. When he received no response he lifted his head and looked at Carter. The American was standing at the window looking out at the courtyard. He finally pushed himself off the bed and walked over to where his friend stood with one foot on the wide windowsill. Draping his arm across Carter's shoulder he remarked with a tone of resignation, "You're right. There is an answer out there. A setback, even of this magnitude is not going to make us throw up our hands in defeat."

Carter turned his head to look at him, expressionless at first and then a twinkle appeared in his blue eyes. He straightened up, put his left arm around Jean Paul and clapped him on the shoulder with his right hand. His only reply was in English.

"Fuckin' aye! Let's find that money!"

♈ ♈ ♈

For the next two weeks they explored every possibility they could think of. Carter again wrote an impassioned letter to his uncle asking to borrow the money needed for a period not to exceed thirty days, at an interest rate of ten percent. Jean Paul flew to Luxembourg and slipped into France before taking the train to Paris. A week later he returned to Crete with Roger de la Pierre, ex-heavyweight boxing champion of France in tow. De la Pierre, a man of about 40, parlayed his successes in the ring into a comfortable lifestyle through astute investments in real estate and was always open to looking into new investment possibilities. The silver tongue of Jean Paul, weaving its familiar magic of Minoan treasures virtually laying exposed on the open ground, was too much for de la Pierre to resist.

It was Jean Paul's intention to have him lend them the money without telling him specifically for what it would be used. They would tempt him with some of the less valuable items they could get from Deaf Yanni, including some of the things taken from the tomb on the south coast. Barba Yorgi failed in his attempt to extort all he hoped for and some of the artifacts were even recovered intact from the ruins of the talcum mill.

The first night de la Pierre went with them to the club. Canif was there with two American girls on a tour of the islands and who stopped on Crete for three days. The older of the two spoke enough French to get by, but the younger was strictly monolingual. Canif and the older sister were getting along famously and he was looking for someone who could take the younger off his hands for a time. In spite of his boxing career, de la Pierre was still a big, handsome man who stood six-two.

Canif invited de la Pierre to sit with them. De la Pierre spoke a little English and set his sights immediately upon the younger sister. Things went well for an hour or more. Wine, the normal Cretan red, flowed freely. The macho de la Pierre mocked its strength, called it grape juice and drank copious amounts.

"C'est comme de l'eau," he hooted as he poured himself another.

Near midnight his companion insisted they dance. De la Pierre slurred that he was game and rose to follow her onto the dance floor. He took two steps, stopped, looked around blankly and collapsed across a table occupied by a German couple. At first Carter thought he merely tripped, but when he did not move they realized he passed out. The young Mavis boogied alone among the tables, totally oblivious to her partner's condition.

The next day, showing no outward effects of his experience the night before, de la Pierre encountered a dealer of antiques and souvenirs. He was shown a selection of 'Byzantine treasures,' icons of such obvious newness they defied all imagination. He told de la Pierre they were restored to their original pristine state by artisans from a museum in Athens who did this sort of work on the side. Ostensibly they came on the market because one of the monasteries in the mountains was in dire need of funds.

De la Pierre took the bait. In spite of all protestations from Jean Paul and Carter he bought two of the icons, paying an enormous sum, and left Crete immediately. He flew back to Athens with his purchases, passed them easily through customs in Pireaus and took the next boat for Brindisi, Italy. From there he flew back to Paris. The day after his arrival he called upon a friend, a curator of religious art at the Louvre, made an appointment to see him that day and proudly and carefully laid the two icons on his desk. His immediate thought was to sell one of them to the museum and recoup his entire investment. The curator took one look at them and told de la Pierre he regretted to tell him, but he was duped. At first he refused to believe the news, preferring to think instead his friend was mistaken. Finally convinced, he flew into a monumental rage, picked up one of the icons, threw it to the floor and stomped it to pieces before his startled friend could restrain him.

Back on Crete, Carter and Jean Paul, in spite of their failures, were still convinced there was a solution. The solution, when it appeared, was simple and totally unexpected.

Tired of either taking the bus back and forth to town from Aghi Vasili or of borrowing Jean Paul's car, Carter withdrew money from his bank account the day after de la Pierre's departure. Cretans rode motorbikes everywhere, buzzing here and there with a freedom of movement Carter envied. He went to a local dealer to pick one out, paid for it in cash and proudly rode it home. One afternoon a few days later he packed a liter of wine, bread, cheese and fruit from the garden in one of the saddlebags that hung on either side of the rear wheel and headed east along the coast in the direction of Aghios Nikolaos. Karine held on tightly behind him. Near Mallia they turned inland onto a dirt road that wandered through the olive groves into the mountains.

A curious flock of sheep tended by a young shepherd lifted their heads nervously as the motor bike passed in a cloud of dust. A small white chapel high atop a rocky hill caught their attention and they looked for access to it. They eventually found a narrow, little used path, which seemed to lead in the direction they wanted to go. Bouncing from side to side and up and down they proceeded slowly up the hill.

When eventually they reached the chapel they were thrilled with the sight awaiting them. Looking out to sea it seemed they could see all the way to the mainland. To the east and west mountains stretched endlessly. To the south towered rugged peaks reaching with jagged fingers for the clouds floating silently overhead. Inside the deserted chapel they walked around looking at the various icons stacked against the walls and the tin representations of limbs, hearts, heads and bodies hung to one side of the altar. The name of the chapel was unknown, although it was sure to be named after one of the pantheon of saints and used only once a year on that holy person's Name Day.

After poking around for several minutes they walked back outside into the sunlight and ate their lunch on the nearby boulders. Carter took off his shirt to take full advantage of the sun. Karine complained that it was unfair, but he convinced her no one was within miles of them. Off came her shirt in a flash and she leaned back on the broad expanse of rock, letting the sun soak into and cook flesh that rarely saw the light of day.

Carter found it wonderful to be sitting on the boulders almost at the top of the world sharing a bottle of wine and breaking bread with this wonderful French girl/woman. He watched a trickle of sweat run down between her breasts and puddle in the reservoir of her navel.

When they finished eating she lay flat on her back with her hands clasped behind her head and her eyes closed. He sat with legs crossed, gazing out at Dragon Island. From the direction of the sea he followed the flight of a bird coming toward them. He watched until it changed direction and disappeared behind one of the craggy peaks further to the east. When he let his eyes drop he thought at first he was seeing things. He rose to his feet and discovered an opening among the rocks not much higher up.

Without bothering the dozing Karine he jumped down from his perch and headed up toward the opening. As he drew nearer he realized it was quite large. He increased his pace until he found himself on the threshold of what appeared to be the entrance to an enormous cave. Below him was a field of boulders disappearing into the darkness. He retraced his steps excitedly, woke up Karine to tell her of his discovery, took a flashlight from the other saddlebag where he kept a small tool kit, and returned to the opening with her.

Out of the sun it was moister and greener than the sunny area just a few paces away. From the dark depths came a cool, almost primeval current of air, instantly cooling the sweat that formed on their bodies while sitting in the sun. Carter and Karine were not the first visitors here as evidenced by names scratched into the limestone walls. There were even dates. The earliest they noticed was 1763. They halted their downward progress to look about them, taking in the prolific graffiti that appeared as high as a person could reach without climbing. As soon as they reached the point where natural light no longer illuminated the interior, the graffiti diminished. From that point on the walls, stalactites, stalagmites and columns were almost pristine. It was as if theirs were the first voices ever to echo in these majestic corridors.

They walked soundlessly on spongy ground. When he shone his light upward the ceiling was covered with bats. The winged mammals hung with heads down, some sleeping, others watching the progress of the two intruders below. Through the centuries their excrement dropped from the heights and collected on the floor of the chamber. Where they walked the rich deposit of guano was many feet thick, muffling their footsteps.

Carter led Karine by the hand, shining his light first ahead then behind him so she could see where she was walking. The natural formations were fascinating and gave him the urge to climb, explore and discover. He amused himself by hooting loudly then sitting quietly while he waited for the resonating echoes to die out. When she tired of his games, he led her back to the opening and left her there while he returned to explore niches, nooks and crannies. He followed a rocky passageway down into the earth until he came to the spot where a rock fall blocked further progress. He climbed up onto a rocky ledge, wedged himself in and turned out his light.

The stygian blackness engulfed him entirely. He might as well have been stone blind. The only sound was that of his breathing and the soft rustling of his clothes. When he held his breath he imagined he could hear the beating of his heart and the blood rushing through his veins and arteries. In the total solitude he became one with the mountain. It was if he returned to the womb and found his body unconsciously assumed a fetal position. At the same time his mind seemed to open up and become receptive to input he heretofore totally blocked out. His thoughts turned to the Minoans and their civilization and the known fact that many of their rituals were performed in caves and other underground sites. He wondered about Minos. Was he just one person named Minos, or was this a title, such as Pharaoh, given to each new ruler who ascended the throne. How long did each Minos rule? Was his a seven year reign as was suggested by a noted author? Did that reign end underground, in a "labyrinth," or a cave, put to death symbolically, or in actuality, by a priest wearing a bull's headdress, the Minotaur of mythology?

The questions inundated his thoughts. As they flowed faster and faster they were followed by the answers, a trickle that quickly grew into a torrent. His mind was replete with answers: answers to all the questions concerning the Minoan civilization. He wanted to leap up and run back up the winding, twisting, rocky passageway. He wanted to rush back out into the sunlight, stand on the top of this mountain, right at the entrance to this cave, and shout at the top of his lungs the information that was his alone. And...

Then it was gone.

He no longer possessed the knowledge.

That world of knowledge he momentarily possessed, that filled his being to the bursting point, was no longer there. All the answers that belonged to him for a microsecond - a nanosecond - flew away, disappeared in a flash. He knew the answers were his because he remembered having them, remembered the power of the knowledge. But he could not remember the specifics. The realization that he was no longer the repository of all the answers so many sought so unceasingly was a deflating experience. It was as if his soul deserted him, leaving an empty husk.

With this crushing realization he relaxed completely, his mind and body limp. As he lay there, still in the fetal position, the flashlight slipped from his grasp. Before he could reach out to grab it it fell from the rocky shelf on which he lay and clattered on the stones below him.

Without a light he was not sure he would ever be able to find his way back. He remembered one branching of the path. Suppose he missed it and, in the darkness, took the wrong one? It was at that moment that the darkest thought of all occurred to him. Suppose, just suppose, that suddenly the earth should hiccup. Even the slightest tremble could cause rocks to fall, effectively sealing him forever in its bowels. Karine did not know where he was and would be totally unable to tell prospective rescuers where to begin looking. For a moment he panicked. He would have fallen prey to the labyrinth.

Rational thought returned to replace incipient panic. With great care he swung his legs over the ledge and reached out with his feet for places to put them. He moved slowly, not wanting to fall, even though he knew he would not fall far. He moved his hands cautiously back and forth in front of him, then held onto the rock as he let himself slide to the area below. When he felt comfortably situated he began a braille search for the flashlight. With a sigh of relief his fingers closed over the cold metal cylinder. He was even more relieved when he flicked the switch and a strong beam of light replaced the darkness. He almost hyperventilated in his excitement. At least he would not have to make his way back out to the light of day in total darkness.

While catching his breath he played the beam in front of him. Because he was below the level of the shelf upon which he rested earlier, the area beneath was illuminated. The first thing he noticed was a small movement. Craning forward, he flashed the beam from side to side until the movement was repeated. To his surprise he saw an insect, a cricket-like creature with long antennae and legs. But this cricket was totally white, an albino. Another moved into his line of sight and it, too, was white. He watched them moving about and wondered if they ever experienced light, any kind of light, before. One of them moved across some pebbles and Carter noticed what seemed to be a design on one of the rocks. He reached out to pick it up and saw that it was a piece of pottery. What would pottery be doing at this depth? He sifted through the dirt in front of him and came up with other pieces of what looked to be the same type of pottery.

Leaning still further forward he poked his flashlight under the stone shelf. At first he thought he was seeing things. It looked like a bull lying down. His eyes widened in surprise, for there was not just one, but five in all. Each was of terra cotta and depicted a bull in repose. Each lay on a base the approximate size of a brick. Best of all, each was completely intact. Carter's breathing now came in short gasps. He laid the flashlight to the side and reached for one of the statues. He held it in the light as he turned it over and saw that the bulls and their bases were hollow. He lifted each in turn, checking their condition.

To ensure he missed nothing he stuck his head into the space beneath the shelf. Standing up in a corner was what at first appeared to be a black bar. He reached for it and held it up to the light. It was a statue of a woman, probably a priestess judging from her posture and attitude, about 8 inches tall, carved from dark material he could not identify.

He laid it alongside the statues of the bulls and wondered how he was going to get them all out of the cave in one trip. He took off his shirt and carefully placed each of the bull statues in it, then twisted the open end, making a sack that permitted him to carry the bundle in one hand. The statue of the priestess fit into the pocket of his shorts. Satisfied that nothing else remained, he picked up the flashlight and began to wend his way back to where Karine awaited him.

As soon as he saw her he called out to get her attention. She jumped to her feet, glad to see him. She said she was worried about him and did not know what she would do if anything happened to him. He laughed at her concern, and gently set his bundle on the ground. He was gratified by her gasps of surprise upon seeing the statues of the bulls. He was relieved to see they made the trip to the surface in good condition. When he showed her the statue of the woman she gushed over it as if it were a priceless jewel. She rubbed the smooth stone against her cheek, exclaiming over and over at the simplicity of its fine lines. She visited the archaeological museum in Iraklion more than once and was well aware of the beauty of Minoan artifacts.

She helped him pack the bulls in the saddlebags, picking dry grass and placing it between and around each to cushion them. Tying a length of cord from the tool kit around the black statue's narrow waist and then attaching the cord around his neck solved the problem of carrying the black priestess. He slipped her inside his shirt before kicking the motorbike to life and starting back toward Iraklion. Karine sat as far forward on the seat as she could, her thighs tight on either side of his hips, her arms gripped securely around his waist, taking great care not to press the insides of her calves against the saddlebags.

Jean Paul was inside the villa when they wheeled through the iron gates. Carter nosed the motorbike through the double doors of the ballroom, then sat revving its motor, listening to the echoes within the confines of the plastered stone walls and high ceiling.

"Eh, oh! Dis donc! Assez de ce putain de bruit. Tu me casses la tête!" Jean Paul put his hands over his ears and screamed to make himself heard.

Carter hit the kill switch and turned to Karine who still sat behind him. "You see what happens when someone drinks too much the night before? Gueule de bois. When was the last time you saw such a malignant hangover? Tell me, mon vieux," he said, tilting his head back and looking down his nose at the pained expression on the face of his friend, "do you think it's terminal?" This, at least, elicited a wry smile from Jean Paul.

"Calm yourself. We have something here we think might cure you in an instant." Karine slid from her perch in back of Carter and began to unbuckle the straps on the saddlebag.

"If you're looking for something to eat or drink in there forget it! I'm not going to do either ever again."

"No, no. Don't worry. This is not something you put in your mouth, although from the looks of you I might suggest you try your thumb. Petulance, my dear boy, will never endear you to anyone. Ah! Here we are. Voilà. Ta-da!!"

With a flourish he pulled out one of the bulls still wrapped in grass and placed it carefully into Jean Paul's hand. He looked at it with a puzzled expression for an instant before beginning to unwrap the grass.

A look of wide-eyed, open-mouthed amazement suffused his face when he finally saw what he held. He turned it over in his hands, examining it closely, putting his fingers into the hollow insides. All signs of his hangover disappeared, replaced by avid interest. While Jean Paul studied the one in his hand Carter pulled the others from the saddlebags, released them from their protective wrapping and set each carefully on the round wooden table.

If the bulls impressed him, he almost fainted when Carter lifted the coarse string from around his neck with the black priestess attached. Tears welled up in his eyes from the rush of emotion. Carter told him of the discovery of the cave and Jean Paul wanted to return immediately to see with his own eyes if they missed anything, to find something of his own. Carter was adamant, however, insisting instead they find a way to get their treasures out of the country to Switzerland.

"This could be the answer we've been looking for, Jean Paul. This way, if Katz gives us a good price for them, we'll have most, if not all of the money we need to give Zakari...." He stopped in mid-sentence, realizing he spoke of things only the two of them knew about. They both turned to look at Karine. She followed the conversation closely and now sat wide-eyed.

"Who's Zakari?"

"Nobody. Uh, well, just a man we know that...."

"Who's Katz? What's this about Switzerland?"

In the end they told her everything. They were like two little boys who became so excited in the simple telling of their exploits they were almost babbling. They made her swear on her life, on the grave of her (stillliving and well inParis) mother, a cross my heart and hope to die kind of promise she would tell no one. She became so caught up in the excitement she could hardly contain herself by the time they finished explaining everything to her.

That night Carter awoke to find Jean Paul standing over him, trying to shake him awake. Karine opened one eye, saw who it was, then pulled the sheet over her head. Carter dragged himself from the bed after disentangling his legs from Karine's and followed his friend out onto the terrace.

"Francoptère!" said Jean Paul.

"What do you mean 'Francoptère'?"

"Francoptère! You remember. Luc and Bernard. The pilots I introduced you to. The ones doing the agricultural spraying with the Alouettes. You remember! They were here the night you and Karine came back from the cinema."

"OK, I remember now. Bernard is married to an American. Why in the hell did you drag me out of bed to tell me this? Come to the point and let me go back to sleep."

"This is the point. Francoptère finished spraying today and tomorrow they'll be loading the helicopters onto a ship that's already in port. They'll leave tomorrow night and sail directly from here to Genoa."

When Carter still did not show any evidence of understanding Jean Paul lost his patience and hissed through gritted teeth. "Espèce de con! The statues. Do you remember the statues? The ship. Their ship doesn't pass through customs and sails directly to Italy. To Genoa. You know, Genoa? It's just a little south of Milano? Milano is just a little south of the St.

Gotthard? The St. Gotthard is the tunnel leading from Italy into Switzerland, and Zürich, and Katz - and money?"

Carter was now totally awake. Now he understood why Jean Paul awakened him so rudely in the middle of the night. Jean Paul would contact the two pilots early the next morning and ask them take the artifacts on board their ship. Carter would be the one to deliver the relics to Bernard's ship at the port. There would be less chance of the authorities suspecting Carter than Jean Paul, and less of a chance he would be stopped.

At dawn, after only a few restless hours of sleep, Jean Paul went to Bernard's hotel. Bernard was only too happy to do the favor for Jean Paul. At first Luc and Bernard rejected the idea of receiving $100.00 apiece for their help, but when Jean Paul insisted they reluctantly accepted the offer of compensation.

The transfer went without a hitch and four days later Jean Paul was standing on the dock in Genoa when the Nicéphore Niepce pulled into port. As soon as the statues were once more safely in his hands he pointed the nose of his rented Fiat north on the A7 in the direction of Milan.

The meeting with Katz far exceeded their wildest expectations and Jean Paul returned with $62,000.00. Upon seeing the newest finds, Katz was unable to hide his obvious excitement and negotiations concluded quickly. Jean Paul wondered at the time whether or not Katz would be able to extract that amount of money from his wall safe, but without a pause he counted it out to the dollar. Jean Paul recounted it once it was in his hands, not because he did not trust Katz, but rather for the thrill of feeling so much money pass through his fingers. He then stacked it carefully into a new briefcase he purchased that very day in Zug, just south of Zürich. He closed the briefcase and placed it on the floor beside his chair, then leaned forward with an earnest expression on his face.

"Herr Katz, one last thing I would like to discuss with you before I leave. There is a statue which is now in our possession. Unfortunately I do not have pictures of it with me to show you, but I would like to make you aware of this very special and exceptional artifact." Jean Paul continued to speak of the statue, describing it in minute detail, leaving an indelible mental picture for the old Schweizer to ponder. When he finished speaking he sat back in his chair and remained silent for a long moment.

"Would you have any interest in such a singular piece?"

When Katz softly replied that indeed he would be interested Jean Paul concluded his ploy. "In that case I'll leave you to do what you must to find either the money or the buyers for this statue. I plan to be back within a few months with this statue in my possession. We, meaning my partner and me, anticipate realizing $1,125,000.00 for it. Quite frankly, we would like to do business with you, but we are adamant about the amount of money we expect for it and are not disposed to negotiate. If you feel this is too much and don't want to work with us I feel sure we can find other buyers."

Katz looked at him a moment, weighing the statement. The Frenchman most assuredly was now in a position to dictate terms. It was definitely a seller's market, particularly with what was being offered.

"Understood, Monsieur Bonisseur. You have only supplied quality. I will do everything I can to meet your expectations."

Upon leaving Katz's house Jean Paul went directly to the airport and purchased a ticket to return to Athens on the first available flight.

Carter was speechless from the shock of seeing so much money laying in the briefcase Jean Paul dropped in his lap when they returned to the villa and relished each bit of information concerning Jean Paul's meeting with Katz. Immediately they began to make plans to claim the statue.

Their first priority was to exchange the money into a form immediately negotiable and acceptable to Zakari. To accomplish this without arousing suspicion was not as easy as expected. They visited banks in Athens, Rhodes, Mikonos, Limnos and Khios. In each place they exchanged several thousand dollars at a time for drachmas in the largest available bills. By the end of the week they held the required number of drachmas in hand to cover Zakari's asking price. Through Andreas, who took specified amounts to banks in Iraklion, Chania, Rethymnon and Aghios Nikolaos, the bills were exchanged for gold coins. This done, Andreas contacted Zakari and set up an appointment to finalize the transaction.

Two days later Carter and Jean Paul rode south on the back of Carter's motorbike to meet with Zakari. The exchange went smoothly and by late afternoon on a fine Cretan day in late September the two sat in Carter's room. The statue rested on Carter's desk, spotlighted by a ray of setting sun coming in the westward facing window. They admired the craftsmanship and beauty of the gold, wondering aloud about the mind that conceived it and the hands that fashioned it millennia before. They hid it in what they considered to be a most illogical place, should anyone (Zakovides and his men?) ever come to Aghi Vasili looking for contraband: among the thick ivy atop the high wall between the courtyard and Popi's house.

With the acquisition of the statue their major goal was achieved. The next step would be to devise a foolproof method of taking it safely out of the country. For this to happen they were in no hurry. With the sale of the pieces Carter found in the cave, even after paying Zakari, there still remained over $30,000.00. Carter took half the amount and gave the rest to Jean Paul.

Two weeks later Karine returned to Paris. With her she carried two-thirds of Carter's portion of the money. There could be no thought of putting such an amount into his account in the bank on Crete and no way would he consider wiring it out of the country without arousing suspicions. They made plans for Carter to come to Paris in December, at which time he would open an account for himself in Switzerland. He would keep the remaining $5,000, putting it a little at a time into his account in Iraklion.

If life seemed good before, it now seemed perfect. There were no money worries and a sense of infallibility. They walked through their days with a spring in their steps and a cockiness they could not hide.

There was a feeling of change in the air, as well. The days were shorter and much cooler and the nights longer. A long-sleeved shirt or light jacket felt good. They lived extravagantly, eating and drinking what they wanted, never having to count drachmas. They were sure this prosperity would never end, particularly with the key to their financial future hidden in their ivy-covered safety deposit box behind the house.

Chapter 32

With Karine's departure Carter found himself with much more free time on his hands. From the beginning he was fond of her. The fondness quickly turned to affection and the affection to love. He resisted falling in love with her. He did not want to fall in love with anyone, but with each day and night they spent together his attraction to her grew.

A few days after their fortunate picnic, and the discovery of the bulls and the black statue, he and Karine saw a small house between the road and the sea on the coastal road between Chersonisos and Iraklion. Although some furniture could be seen through the spaces between the boards of the shutters, it appeared to be uninhabited. Its setting, with a view of the sea across fields containing white-sailed windmills and a small whitewashed stone chapel located on a coral promontory, was perfect. The house, although small, was immensely charming with a covered verandah on the front and another facing the sea in the back. At each end were enormous bushes protecting the back of the house from the late afternoon sun without blocking the view. Through a window they could see a small kitchen containing shelves and a niche in the wall for placing a water jug. The floor looked to be made of terrazzo.

They fantasized about living there together and even went so far as to make inquiries at a nearby kafeneion to find out if anyone lived there and, if not, who owned it. As it turned out, it belonged to a dentist from Ierapetra. Originally from the nearby village of Gournes, his family built the house when he was just a boy on the parcel of land belonging to his grandfather. Because of its proximity to the sea and its cooling breezes, they used it most often in the summertime. Now that both parents were dead and his sister was married to a lawyer in Athens, the dentist never went there anymore. There were no children and he and his wife were not interested in spending time among the peasants, even though he came from peasant stock himself.

The proprietor of the kafeneion was obliging, even going so far as to contact the owner to advise him of their interest. He told the dentist that a young couple was perhaps interested in renting his house. He agreed to meet them later in the week.

Once inside they knew this was their dream house. It did not matter to them there was neither running water nor electricity. Neither were they bothered by the fact that there were no shower or bath facilities. Carter would carry water in five liter clay jugs to bathe in and drink from a nearby irrigation tap near the house. Heated on the wood cook stove or on a gas hot plate it could be used to take sink baths or wash dishes. Carter knew that leaving the jugs out in the sun all day long was sufficient to heat the water to an almost scalding temperature.

It was decided Carter should take the house. He wanted a place of his own and this one, hard by the sea, was ideal. There were certain repairs to be made and a great deal of general cleaning to be done, but they both decided they would be foolish to pass up this opportunity. He would not be as close to the institute here as in Aghi Vasili, but the trip into town would be less of a problem. At Karine's urging he agreed to negotiate a lease with the dentist, who seemed all too anxious to oblige. For him, leasing the house would provide yet another source of income.

They finally agreed on the sum of 750 drachmas per month, a mere $25.00. Dr. Themides agreed to have electricity installed before Carter took possession. At some time in the future he would bring in running water. It was all relative to Carter. He could certainly afford the rent and, in actuality, would not have hesitated to pay twice that much. The dentist agreed to have it ready for him by the first of December and was given a month's rent in advance. Carter would continue to live in the villa with Jean Paul until everything was ready.

Karine was already making plans to return to the island as soon as she could arrange it. If at all possible, she would come back in early spring and stay for at least six months. According to her plans, if things continued to progress like this summer there was a good chance she would never again leave his side. In the meantime, he would see that the house was put into order. In November he would meet her in Paris. There they could discuss the future at leisure.

That night they were all seated around the table in the courtyard when Carter told Jean Paul of the house. "Karine and I have found a little place out toward Chersonisos. I rented it and it'll be ready by December. When she comes back next spring it will be ready for her."

Jean Paul seemed genuinely surprised by the announcement. Philippe wanted to know all the details. He was looking for a place of his own and was delighted to know that such houses were available.

During the rest of the meal Jean Paul was unusually subdued. By the next day, however, he seemingly accepted the idea of Carter's taking a place of his own. He even thought it a good idea. Because of the cloud of suspicion which hung over him, he rationalized it would be best that Carter not be associated with him in the eyes of the authorities. This way, too, they could secrete their treasures away from the villa. Carter was pleased Jean Paul seemed to no longer view the decision as a personal rebuff.

The night before Karine's departure everyone went out to a restaurant specializing in chickens roasted on a spit. Located west of town it was commonly referred to as 'Chicken Beach'. Philippe invited Popi to go with them. Canif, with his most recent companion, invited himself. They stuffed themselves almost to the point of pain with the succulent chicken and then danced to the music of Theodorakis and Hadzidakis on the jukebox.

After dinner the others decided to go back to the Club Fez. Carter and Karine begged off, deciding instead to return to Aghi Vasili. They wanted time completely to themselves and this would be the perfect opportunity. The others would not return for hours.

They took the mattress from his bed and dragged it through the narrow double doors to the rooftop terrace. Under the stars they undressed one another. He loved her body, knew her small breasts jutting proud and firm from her chest, the sensuous curve of her hip and the silky, tanned skin of her stomach and thighs. He delighted in her scent, the scent of healthy youth, of sunshine and sea breeze. When he kissed her breasts and stroked the length of her fine, supple body, she came alive. The scent of youth was transformed, giving way to a muskier aroma of womanhood: the rich, dark scent of sun-ripened figs and kumquats.

Her fingers traced his skin from shoulders to chest, along his ribs to his hips, where they gripped him, demanding that he enter her. Her lips whispered hotly and urgently against his cheek of her need for him. "Je te veux...je te veux. J'ai besoin de toi"

Guided by her hand, he slipped slowly and deeply into her close fitting, marvelously warm and velvety sheath. Warm butter and honey, tightly gripped and caressed by muscles indescribably delightful, held in place by legs wrapped around his to exert maximum leverage. A fine sheen of sweat enveloped them in spite of the coolness of the night and he felt as if he were drowning in her; wanted to be enveloped, pulled entirely, bodily into her. Her hands roamed his back and she cooed mindlessly in the intensity of the moment. Toward the end she thrashed her head back and forth on the mattress, groaned and dug her nails into his back. As her paroxysms of pleasure subsided his began and he was no longer able to hold back. She moved her hands to his buttocks, gripped them tightly, arched her back and crooned his name, exulting in the feeling of his spasming inside of her. She greeted his release with a deep, earthy chuckle. For long moments he dared not open his tightly closed eyes for fear they would fall from their sockets.

Without getting up, without pulling out, he drew the light quilt up over them and they nestled down. Before they slept, she whispered, "I'm not going to be able to stand being away from you. Tu me manques déjà." I miss you already.

"Don't think about it," he replied softly. "Think only of this moment. This is all that exists for right now."

They awoke to a lovely, cool early autumn morning. She lay cradled in his arms, her back against his chest, and his warm breath against the nape of her neck. They arose, showered together, vigorously soaping each other trying to warm flesh now chilled by the cold water gushing from the pipe. Afterwards they dressed, packed her belongings, told everyone goodbye, drove into town for breakfast and then to the airport where he put her on the first flight for Athens.

♈ ♈ ♈

In early November, with Bunny's approval, Carter took a three-week's sabbatical. He flew directly to Paris for a joyous reunion with Karine. Her living with her parents and two younger brothers did not afford them the complete freedom they enjoyed at the villa. Her parent's apartment, reached by private elevator from the ground floor, was on the top floor of a building in the 16th Arrondissement.

The first week they attended the ballet, a comedy revue and the opera. They dined in quaint out-of-the-way places known only to true Parisians. The second week they took the train from Paris to Basel, where he opened a numbered account with the remaining ten thousand dollars. They stayed in Switzerland for three days. Away from her parents for the first time since his arrival, they passed almost the entire first day in bed.

Once back in Paris Yves gave a cocktail party at his apartment on the Boulevard St. Germain. They lunched with Hervé and Marie-Claire Crozet and drove to Louviers to visit Karines' grandparents.

Their time together passed swiftly and it was soon time to say goodbye. His stay in France with her was wonderful, but by the time he boarded the plane to return to Athens he could hardly wait to once more be in Aghi Vasili.

Following his return from Paris he rode his motorbike out the coastal road each day after classes to assess the progress. Much to his surprise, the house was ready only two days later than originally promised. It was wired, but until the electric company sent someone out to hook it up he would have to make do with kerosene lamps. This posed no problem for him. He was happy with his return to basics. Andreas took him to a ramshackle warehouse he owned and let him pick out a double bed and mattress, tables, chairs, an old armoire and various kitchen utensils. Additionally, he bought a kerosene space heater and several kerosene lamps.

The day he moved, both Jean Paul and Philippe helped. There was not much, but he could not possibly transport it all on the back of the motorbike. They put the top down on the convertible, stacked everything in and roared out of town with the radio blaring out the beat of bazouki. Carter supplied bread, hunks of roasted lamb, cheese, fruit and a demijohn of peasant red.

They secreted the gold statue in the trunk and took it with them. There were numerous places in and around the new house where it would be safe. They discussed such a move at great length and both agreed it would be the wisest thing to do until they could pass it safely out of the country. Philippe was still unaware of their activities. He remained so engrossed in the two loves of his life, writing and Popi, that he never questioned their sudden wealth.

With the approaching holidays Jean Paul decided to return to France. He pined for some of the finer things in life, one of which was a Paris Christmas. Years before, while a first year student in Montpellier, he experienced the lights and other decorations and the holiday festivities. The second week of December he flew to Basel and slipped across the border into France. Once in Paris he stayed two days and nights with Karine and her parents, then accepted an invitation to stay with a friend from the 50's.

Canif's plans for the holidays involved a trip to Athens, where the French community always enjoyed a round of parties during the week preceding Christmas. The day of his departure Carter invited him to have dinner with him before sailing. They met at Theodoro and Rodula's café, The Miramare, where he and Karine were entertained by the fishermen the past summer.

After dinner Carter left his motorbike parked beside the steps leading into the café and they walked across to the quay to the Keftiu. Passengers were already beginning to board and Maurice insisted he come to the first class lounge for a drink before the ship sailed. When the whistle sounded for all those not sailing to go ashore, Maurice told him not to worry, assuring him there was plenty of time. They ordered another drink and then one more. Carter thought he detected movement and drained his glass, wished Canif a Merry Christmas and hurried out onto the deck. To his surprise he could see the lights of Iraklion across almost a mile of dark water. Maurice followed him out onto the deck, laughing uproariously. Carter's pockets contained perhaps five dollars worth of drachmas. There was no way he could pay for this voyage on which he found himself to be a reluctant passenger.

Canif insisted Carter take a first class cabin of his own. He could pay him back upon their return. Carter was obliged to agree. After all, his students were on their thirty-day Christmas break and he planned nothing of any importance.

He remained in Athens for four days, during which time he attended a party given for the upper echelon of the French embassy staff at a restaurant owned by a French chef near the airport. A gala ball followed a sumptuous dinner. To the amusement of all those who knew him, Canif made a play for the ambassador's young wife. Diplomat to the end, the ambassador quietly called for his car and ushered his wife into the back seat long before the last guest departed.

Friends from his student days in Athens lent him the necessary clothes for all eventualities. Together with them he revisited old haunts in the back streets of the city. In the Plaka they dined and danced until the early morning hours. Afterwards they sat drinking and catching up in a small sidewalk café, watching the sun rise on the Parthenon. They took him to dives in Piraeus and upper class lounges in Athens. By the end of the third day he was ready to return to Crete. The next evening Canif accompanied him back to Piraeus, where he reboarded the Keftiu.

During the night a storm blew up. He lay in his cabin listening to the sounds of the wind and stormy sea. By the time they arrived off the coast of Crete the first light of day was beginning to brighten the sky. As they sailed into the lee of the island the waters calmed. Passengers who suffered the entire night with horrendous bouts of seasickness came creeping onto deck, peering through blinking bloodshot eyes set in greenish faces. He stood on the bow of the ship watching his beloved island loom higher and higher as they drew closer to shore.

As soon as the ship docked he walked across the cobbles of the port to find Theodoro already in his kitchen preparing food for early customers. Over Turkish coffee he told him about his unexpected trip to Athens. Rodula entered just as he finished his account. She gave a little squeal of delight and crossed the room to pat his cheek. Words tumbled out of her mouth as she rushed to tell him how worried they were when they found his motorbike sitting beside the steps when they left to go home the night he and his French friend ate dinner there.

"But, don't worry. My Thodora locked it safely away for you," said Rodula with a moue in the direction of her amused husband.

At the Daskaloyanni house, over hot coffee and fresh rolls, they laughed with him at the antics of Canif. He accepted their invitation to celebrate Christmas en famille and wondered what he could do for them that would be special.

He missed Karine, but his time was fully occupied. On Christmas Eve Madame Daskaloyanni's brother came to the house. The whole family sat around the living room illuminated only by candles and the lights of the tree and sang Greek Christmas and holiday songs. Carter was deeply moved by the occasion, as well as by the music. Madame D's rich contralto blended exquisitely and harmoniously with her brother's full baritone. Carter knew most of the music, but not the words and simply hummed along with them. The old gentleman sitting in his armchair, legs crossed, nodded his head in time with the music and used his cigarette holder as a conductor's baton. In the other hand he gripped yet another glass of the pink champagne Carter bought for the occasion.

The day after Christmas Carter sat on his back verandah looking out to sea. He felt as if he were being watched, but when he looked around he saw no one. When the feeling persisted he moved into the yard. As soon as he did he caught a movement of something among the dormant grapevines surrounding the back of his house. A medium sized female dog was seated, watching him intently. He spoke to her, even offered a piece of the bread he carried in his hand. She just watched him warily, her pink tongue extended from her smiling mouth. He tried calling, even tried approaching her, but she would allow him no closer than twenty feet before getting to her feet and moving off a short distance.

He understood her caution. Too often he saw the cruelty of the peasants toward dogs. It always surprised him that it extended to all animals, even their beasts of burden, which many times represented a large part of their livelihood. He finally tossed the bread in her direction and walked back to the porch. Once he took his seat the dog approached the morsel cautiously, sniffed it for a moment and then wolfed it down.

"Why, you're hungry, aren't you?"

He went into the kitchen and reappeared with rinds from cheese he cut earlier. He seated himself on the bottom step and this time threw them one at a time. He tossed each piece a little closer to where he sat, enticing her to come nearer to him. At the same time he talked softly to her, letting her become accustomed to hearing the sound of his voice, trying to gain her confidence.

When he went out the next morning she was still there. His greeting eliciting a small wag of her tail, but she still would not allow him to come near her. By the end of a week of feeding and cajoling she inched nearer to him as he squatted on the ground, finally touching her outstretched nose to the back of his hand. This small success pleased him.

Evenings, when she would hear the sound of his motor coming down the path bisecting the fields between his house and the road, she would rush to greet him, dancing and leaping around him, just out of reach. He continued to feed her, even went to a butcher shop in town to buy bones and scraps to bring home to her. Over succeeding days she danced ever closer to him and finally allowed him to touch her. The red-letter day was when she allowed him to sweep her into his arms. In his almost daily letters to Karine he told her of Skilí, as he named her. The literal meaning was Dog.

"I must tell you, my love, just how wonderful it is to come home to happy cries of delight and warm, wet kisses. Skilí won't come into the house at night, although I've tried to entice her inside. Instead, she sleeps just in front of the door. None of the peasants can come closer than the edge of the property before she sets up a racket to warn them off and to let me know someone is coming our way. When I'm at home she follows me everywhere. When I stop, so does she. She just sits, watching me with adoring eyes. There are lessons to be learned there, I'm sure. Hope you're taking notes!"

New Year came and went. School reopened and Carter went back to teaching his two to three classes a day, five days a week. Jean Paul returned from France full of himself with tales of his exploits. His pockets were virtually empty, having blown his nest egg in a month of riotous living. No expense was spared in his search for the apex of hedonism.

They saw each other almost every day and Carter often went to the villa for a drink after work or out to dinner with him. It was not at all unusual for Jean Paul to show up at his house by the sea either.

Almost every weekend they went to either Amnisos or one of the other sites. With regularity they discovered pottery, much of it intact, or at least with all the fragments present. One of the most fascinating sites was one upon which the Germans constructed a beach fortification during the Second World War. After the war the Greeks dug up most of the mines sown along the north coast. Those they did not use for explosives to fish with they planted under fortifications and blew them to pieces. When Carter and Jean Paul began digging there they were amazed at the number of examples of pottery they recovered. Many, such as cups, were discovered nested one inside the other. One day while digging Carter discovered a large portion of a lens-shaped round piece made of baked clay. Unable to discern its purpose, Carter simply tossed it aside.

Three weeks later while reading a book on the Myceneans and recent discoveries he found that a European archaeologist came across just such a piece. Unable to decipher its use he put it aside, but came back to it from time to time. He finally realized it was an ancient potter's wheel. Carter rushed back to that particular site to look for the shard. It was gone, perhaps one of the pieces he tossed into the sea. The stacking of the pottery and the numerous pieces found lent credence to his belief that they too, stumbled upon the remains of a potter's workshop.

Whatever they found they carried back to the villa. There they cleaned, glued broken pieces back together and displayed their finds in cupboards built into the walls of several of the rooms. Their collection grew steadily, augmented from time to time by articles bought from Deaf Yanni. They simply waited for the time when they would be able to remove the best of them from the country and sell them to Katz or whoever would pay the highest price.

Carter was financing the operation almost entirely now. Jean Paul never seemed to have any money at all. Carter failed to understand why, for the club appeared to do well under the direction of Jean Paul's partner. He seemed to be always borrowing from someone. Philippe brought this to Carter's attention, for Jean Paul attempted to touch him for a 'loan', as well.

In February, trying to put Jean Paul back on an even financial footing, Carter agreed to make the journey to Zürich. They chose three objects, which could be easily hidden, and took the Saturday morning flight to Athens. The customs official stamped his passport with hardly a glance at either him or his small valise and he passed onto the Swissair flight unchallenged. His arrival in Zürich and subsequent meeting with Katz he viewed as anticlimactic. Jean Paul placed a call to Switzerland before Carter's departure to pave the way. To Carter it all seemed routine. He listened spellbound to Jean Paul's accounts of his trips so many times that this trip was almost like déjà vu. Katz greeted him cordially, eager to do business with him. Within an hour of their meeting he was once more on the street with almost four thousand dollars in his pocket.

He was back in Crete by the next evening. From the airport he took a taxi to his house, changed clothes, deducted his expenses from the money, and took the rest to Jean Paul.

"This is not a bad day's work, but I think there are more possibilities we are overlooking. On the flight back I started thinking about how we could come up with some very nice things for only a little money. You remember the things taken from the tomb by Zakari and his friends? Well, Barba Yorgi was unable to get all of them. Some pieces are still out there, just waiting for two enterprising individuals to come along."

"What are you suggesting?"

"Simply this: I'm going to make a little visit to Zakari. I'll offer him the chance to act as middleman between his friends and us. If he could arrange for us to buy them.... Look, we know they're good quality, if for no other reason than they came from the same place as our statue. Even giving a fair price for the things we take, we still only pay a small fraction of their actual worth. If he and his friends agree, we can just add them to our collection until such time as we can dispose of them. What do you think?"

Jean Paul only reflected upon Carter's logic for a moment before he agreed. He insisted, however, that he accompany him to see Zakari. In the end Carter was glad he did.

The following Saturday they roared off in a cloud of blue exhaust smoke with the rising sun at their backs, Carter astride his motorbike and Jean Paul riding Stasso's. The sun was already high in the sky when they reached the top of the path and pulled onto Zakari's property. Due to the difficulty of getting in touch with him they arrived unannounced. In case they missed him today they would simply return another time. They knew these treasures were going nowhere and they were no longer under time constraints.

They pulled up in front of the house, the door of which was slightly ajar, turned off their motors and got off to stretch the kinks from backs and arms. It was peaceful on the mountaintop, particularly after the constant din of the bike motors and the wind rushing in their ears. The sound of their bikes brought no one to the door and they wondered if maybe he were somewhere else on the property. When they rapped on the door they were greeted only by silence.

"Where do you think he could be?" wondered Carter aloud.

"He can't be too far away. I don't think he would go off and leave his door open like this."

"Let's look around. He's got to be fairly close."

The only sign of life was the chickens strutting among the olive trees, scratching for morsels in the dirt. They paid little heed to Carter as he strode toward the well and beyond. He was surprised to see the headless body of Zakari's goat draped over the lower branches of one of the trees. She was butchered but not gutted. He could not imagine Zakari killing his milk goat for meat, but then he was no farm boy. He knew enough to realize that the meat would spoil if left hanging too long in the tree in the still warm weather. Swarms of flies covered the stump of the neck and the blood that dripped onto the ground. If the goat was slaughtered recently he must be around somewhere. He called Zakari's name several times, but the only response was the echo of his voice bouncing off the higher rocks.

Carter was thirsty from the wind blowing into his teeth on the ride and a dipper of water sounded inviting. As he walked to get a drink he noticed the bucket was not sitting on the rim of the well as usual. The rope trailed down into the black interior and he assumed it fell and was in the water below. He looked back toward the house as he began to crank the handle to bring the bucket up. He saw Jean Paul again knock at the door, then push it open tentatively and step into the dark interior.

Once inside Jean Paul softly called Zakari's name while waiting for his eyes to adjust to the gloom. A sweetish odor permeated the interior. In an effort to let in as much light as possible he pulled the door all the way open and for the first time noticed the bed against the wall. Under the covers he made out the form of a body and was sure he found Zakari. He could not understand why he failed to awake either when they knocked or called his name.

"Kyrie Zakari. O Zon Pawl énai." It's me. Jean Paul.

When there was still no response Jean Paul walked to the bed, gently prodded the form under the covers, then stepped back and waited for him to roll over. There was no answering movement, not even a sound. An arm and hand lay on top of the covers and Jean Paul knew it could only be Zakari, although the face was hidden behind a pillow with no pillowcase. Once more he called Zakari's name, while touching the visible arm. Still unable to elicit a response, he gently pulled the pillow away from the face.

The body belonged to Zakari, of that he was sure. Without a doubt it was Zakari from the shoulders down. From the neck up, however, it was something else. A long tongue hung out the side of a partially open mouth and glazed eyes stared sightlessly at the ceiling. From the top of the head pointed black horns curved up and back. It took him a moment to comprehend what he was seeing.

And then he screamed.

Carter cranked the bucket upward with some difficulty. He could not recall it's being this heavy the last time they were there with Andreas and he drew a drink. When at last the bucket began to become visible rising through the gloom, he heard a strangled cry from the direction of the house and turned his attention away from the well.

When he saw Jean Paul appear in the doorway he could see something was wrong. Without even a glance at the bucket, which was now wedged against the drum of the crank, he grasped it and set it down upon the flat stones forming the rim of the well.

"Come quick!"

Carter started across the yard toward his friend. "What the.... What's the matter? Jesus, you look awful! Are you sick?"

Jean Paul breathed raggedly through his open mouth, gasping for breath, as if he had run all the way up the mountain. His eyes, too, gaped as Carter came up to him. "Water! I need some water!"

"Come on out to the well. I just drew a bucket."

Jean Paul glanced back toward the house and Carter looked at him with concern. He turned to get him some water and pulled up short, all his attention now focused on the bucket and its contents. The liquid inside did not look clear and refreshing. It was red. As red as blood.

His gasp made Jean Paul look up. He saw Carter staring at the bucket and its contents. Carter reached out, grasped the side of the bucket and pulled it off the ledge to the ground. Red liquid splattered in all directions and from inside the bucket Zakari's head rolled out onto the ground.

They ran to their motorbikes and leapt astride, both kicking madly to start them. Carter's roared to life first, followed shortly by Jean Paul's. In tandem they sped away from the house, both fishtailing, almost out of control. They both felt as if they were being pursued by demons. More than once they looked back over their shoulders, not knowing what they expected to see behind them.

What neither noticed when the bucket fell and its contents spilled out was the bloody water coursing over the dust of the ground, ground marked by a series of curious footprints. One of the prints looked normal. The other looked as if it were being dragged. Parallel to the footprints were a series of round indentations in the dust; indentations that looked as if they were made by someone walking with the aid of a staff.

Chapter 33

As soon as those who were sent to the talcum mill returned to town they searched out Andreas. Their babbled account left him highly agitated and anxious. At first they thought he was going to have a heart attack. He promised to handle everything and begged them to tell no one and to simply forget what they found.

This was easier said than done. It was difficult for them to put behind them events of this magnitude. There were many evenings they relived the horror of their discovery, although they rarely spoke of it. They asked Andreas weeks later what he had done, but the older man made it perfectly clear to them the subject was closed and would discuss it no further. They never brought it up again.

♈   ♈   ♈

Winter finally turned into spring and the entire island was verdant and lush from the winter rains. When Jean Paul began to run low on funds once more Carter volunteered to make another trip to Zürich. He timed his departure to coincide with the spring break at the institute and Karine's spring vacation.

Following his meeting with Katz, he took the train from Switzerland through Germany to Liège in Belgium, where she met him. They wandered the narrow streets of the ancient, fortified town, visited museums, the observatory and cathedrals. Carter reveled in the town, the countryside and the descendants of the subjects of Bruegel, Van Eyck, Bosch, Rubens and Laerman's paintings. He found it charming, a perfect place to renew their love. Karine wanted to know all about the house, the dog, and everything he did. He laughed and told her it sounded as if she never received any of his letters.

"*Non, non, mon grand,* I did. It's just that I want to hear it now from your own lips."

All too soon their idyllic interlude came to an end. They regretfully departed Liège for Luxembourg, where they caught a flight for Athens. Because of the short time she would be with him before returning to Paris to finish her last semester at the Sorbonne, they planned to spend most of their time together. The first night, since they knew it was expected of them, they ate dinner with Jean Paul and Philippe. The rest of the time, other than incidental meetings in town or when the others came to their house, they spent their time alone.

She was enamored of the house, the dog, the sea and the view. Each morning she slipped out of bed, made coffee and sat with Carter and the dog on the back verandah watching the sun rise from the sea. They took long walks with Skilí along miles of deserted beaches, across fields and through orchards during the day.

One evening, local peasants who knew Carter, invited them to accompany them while they fished the shallows. Shortly after sundown they all walked to a rocky beach where the waves washed and rattled across the round pebbles with which the shoreline was covered. Three of the peasants waded into the water. One carried a lighted propane lantern that hissed and threw out a bright, white light. The second carried a bucket of sand into which he emptied a liter bottle of used olive oil. The third carried a trident.

They watched fascinated from shore as the three men waded in thigh deep water. The man with the lantern held it high to attract fish to the light. The man with the bucket took handfuls of oily sand and cast it upon the water. The sand sank and the residue of oil on the surface formed a perfect window into which the third man peered, spied the prey below the surface and wielded his spear with unerring accuracy.

They were fascinated at the number and variety of fish caught that evening. A scorpion fish, called a *skorpídi* by the peasants, fell from the trident and flopped toward the sea. Carter rushed to pick it up, but a shout from Thanassi warned him not to touch it. Thanassi explained afterwards that close to the dorsal fin was a spine containing a poison that, although not deadly, could inflict an extremely painful and slow to-heal wound.

At the end of five short days Karine left once more for home. Carter came to realize that he loved her with a deep, abiding affection. Furthermore, theirs was also a friendship even deeper than their love for one another. He respected her and appreciated each day they were together. When apart he looked forward to her letters, reading and re-reading them. Their separation would not be as long this time. With her studies ending she would return to him, for at least the whole summer, maybe longer. He kissed her goodbye, tenderly, wanting to hold onto her and not let her climb aboard the airplane. In the end he stood almost alone at the gate as her plane sped down the runway, lifted into the sky and turned north.

He deviated little from his normal routine during the next two months. He and Jean Paul continued to explore and, in many instances, discover. They developed what Carter referred to as "The Eye". More than once, while riding through the countryside they spied rocks in a field or on a beach that did not look quite natural. When they stopped to investigate they found that what they saw were indeed ruins of one type or another. In most instances they could not risk doing more than just walking around the area, scouting the surface terrain for clues. Other times they explored more leisurely and, if the site was in a truly deserted area, would dig below the surface. These excursions sometimes resulted in surprising finds.

The shelves in the cupboards were given entirely to artifacts and began to look like a small museum. The really extraordinary things, as they judged them, were not entrusted to the villa, but were instead consigned to Carter's care. In addition to the golden statue, he carefully hid two or three other treasures, including a terra cotta shrine containing three figures in almost perfect condition.

In mid-June Karine returned, this time with one of her brothers, Didier, a year younger than Karine, and his girlfriend, Thérèse, a model from one of the well-known Parisian salons. Didier and Thérèse went directly to Aghi Vasili with Jean Paul and, without wasting a moment, Carter and Karine disappeared in the opposite direction. Almost two full days passed before they deigned to acknowledge the existence of anyone else, even though Didier and Thérèse came to the house and banged on the door. Skilí seemed to sense they somehow belonged and let them approach with a minimum of grumbling.

The next two months became a time of carefree existence. Carter and Karine learned more and more about each other. He only taught two classes a day, three days a week, which gave them considerable time together. They went from one end of the island to the other, from the palm-fringed beaches of Váï in the east to Palaiokhóra in the west. Often she would go digging with him on days when Jean Paul was otherwise occupied. Her forte, however, was the reconstruction of the broken pottery and oil lamps they found. The results of many of the projects she undertook rivaled anything he found in the museums.

Their peace of mind came to an abrupt end late one afternoon the third week of August. They rode up to Aghi Vasili to take a bottle of wine to Jean Paul to celebrate his birthday. They had not seen him for over a week, which was a rare occurrence, and both looked forward to spending a few hours with him. He was a delightful raconteur and his stories could leave them enthralled or in stitches. When they arrived no one was there. As usual the doors and windows were wide open and they walked in and began to make themselves at home.

Carter was the first to sense that something was different, although he was unable to put his finger upon anything specific. Each time he walked through Jean Paul's bedroom or the ballroom, he felt as if something was wrong. What finally caught his eye was the door of one of the cupboards built into the wall. Although usually closed tight, this time it was slightly ajar. Idly curious, he approached and pulled it open. His shock was immense and immediate. Other than terra cotta dust, the shelves were bare. He rushed to each of the cupboards in turn and found each of them empty. Without saying anything to Karine he strolled outside and, with seeming nonchalance, inspected the various hiding places along the ivy-covered wall. He could scarcely believe what he was seeing, for everything they kept at the villa was gone. He wracked his brain trying to come up with a good reason why Jean Paul might have taken all of the artifacts and put them elsewhere, but he could find no logical solution.

Karine wandered outdoors and when she saw the look on his face she knew something was amiss. They sat talking in hushed tones on the upstairs terrace when, with roaring motor and a flash of bright yellow, the convertible pulled into the courtyard, careened around the corner of the house and screeched to a halt near the well. Carter descended the stairs three at a time and was there to open the car door for him as soon as Jean Paul shut off the motor. One look at his face told him all was not well.

"*Dis-donc,* I was just in the house and...."

Before Carter could finish his thought Jean Paul cut him off in mid-sentence. "And I'm sure you brought something for us to drink and you put it in the kitchen, *hein?*"

Carter immediately realized there was something behind his friend's brusque manner. "*Ben, ouais,* as a matter of fact we did. Happy Birthday, *vieux con*! Come on, Karine's up on the terrace. Let's go join her and we'll open your birthday gift. You look as if you could stand for us to drink to your health."

Once everyone was seated on the terrace with drinks in their hands Jean Paul told them of the visit the previous day. He was in bed, although awake, when he heard a vehicle pull into the courtyard. It hardly stopped before several doors slammed and heavy footsteps sounded on the paving stones. An instant later someone struck the panels of the door causing it to tremble and the hallway to resonate. He leapt from the bed, slipped on a pair of jeans and pulled a knit shirt over his head. In bare feet he padded out of his bedroom to the door. No sooner did he draw the deadbolt than the door burst inward and five men pushed into the house. He was knocked back against the wall but quickly recovered. He followed one of them into his bedroom when he found his way blocked by a man of medium build. He put his hand in the middle of Jean Paul's chest to restrain him from following the men who preceded him into the house.

"You will stop there and go no further," he said to him in English.

In the same language Jean Paul responded, using some of the invective Carter so carefully taught him.

"Just what in ze 'ell do you sink you are doing? Where do you sons of beetches sink you are? You can't come in 'ere like zis. Get your grissy asses out of my 'ouse!"

His verbal attack produced no apparent effect on the man confronting him. In different rooms of the house he could hear the others moving around and the unmistakable sounds of search. He looked over the shoulder of the shorter man standing in front of him and recognized the smirking face of Zakovides. He has no further need to question who these men were. He was standing face to face with the Secret Police.

A shout from the direction of his bedroom told him they probably found what they came for. In confirmation, one of the men who rushed inside with the first five stepped into the hallway with a statue in one hand and a piece of pottery in the other. A rapid exchange between the two men and a shouted directive from Zakovides to the others told Jean Paul everything was lost.

They left him standing in the courtyard and returned to their search. He walked across the courtyard and sat disconsolately on the low wall, watching the men remove piece after piece to their Land Rover. Soon two of the men came out and began to wander around the property. They both descended the steps into the underground room and were out of view for several minutes. When they reappeared empty handed, Jean Paul experienced a moment's satisfaction at their lack of success.

In the end they even discovered the 'wall repository'. To both his and Jean Paul's relief the few things they considered to be of supreme value, such as the golden statue, were well hidden in the vicinity of Carter's house. Since no interest was ever shown in Carter's comings and goings they felt there was little danger of his house ever being searched.

"So, *mon vieux,* what happens now?"

"I've just returned from town, where I met with Andreas and a lawyer friend of his. Andreas laughed and told me I need not worry. The lawyer told me the same thing."

"Is there going to be a trial, a hearing, anything? Or do they simply put you under the jail?"

"The lawyer told Andreas the authorities want to conclude this as quickly as possible. I read a book about an American court case where they wanted to rush it through. What do you call it? Railroading? Yes, I think that's what they want to do: railroad me."

"What's the lawyer going to do?"

"He's going to try to delay as long as possible."

"One thing you can count on is that I will be there when it comes to trial."

"No! That's the one thing we don't want. Andreas told me to tell you to act as if you never met me. Whatever you do, don't go to the trial, if it comes to that. We don't want the authorities to think there is even the remotest possibility of collusion between us. Understood?"

"Yeah, but...."

"No buts! You are to stay away from the proceedings. We'll keep you informed. Andreas even told me not to go to your house. Look, Carter, I'm going to do whatever they tell me. This lawyer knows about the idiosyncrasies of the Greek court system. I don't and neither do you. So, let's do as they tell us. Please do as they suggest."

Carter thought a moment before replying. "I just want to be sure you don't think I'm abandoning you when there's a little trouble."

"A little!? No, seriously, don't worry about that. I know you're behind me. Just take care no one ever finds the statue. That would be a loss we would never recover from. As for the other things they've taken, remember, most of it we found and it never cost us a penny. The other things we paid only a small percentage of their actual value. Also, you have to figure we paid for all of the other things we've gotten from Deaf Yanni with the proceeds of the sale of the statues I took to Katz on that first trip."

Carter nodded in reluctant agreement.

"Now, get out of here. I'll send you word as soon as I know something." Jean Paul hugged them both before ushering them out the door.

♈ ♈ ♈

From the opening day of the hearing, which took place the second week of September, Jean Paul's lawyer was able to obtain one continuance after another. It wasn't until the first week of October that the prosecution got their chance. They attacked with ferocity and evinced an air of personal affront at the Frenchman's actions. Then, almost as soon as it actually began, the trial was over.

Jean Paul came by the institute immediately afterwards to tell Carter the news. There was nothing much to tell. His attorney quite simply made the prosecution's case look ridiculous, for there was no proof he was either taking the artifacts out of the country, intended to do so, or that he was making a profit from them. He was acquitted on all counts, but it was a pyrrhic victory.

In spite of the lack of evidence, the judge apparently was under considerable pressure to get Jean Paul out of the country at the very least. Acquittal meant he would not be sent to prison, but the judge would not let it rest. He gave a long dissertation on the evils of trafficking of artifacts, warning all who might attempt it they risked much. His final word, which was not to be questioned by anyone, declared Jean Paul declared *persona non grata* and banned him from Crete and the Kingdom of Greece. All his personal effects, with the exception of his clothes, would be forfeited. Within an hour of the closing of the trial the car was impounded and everything in the villa inspected to determine its value. His portion of the club was handed over to his partner, Stefano, who smiled with satisfaction and turned his back on him.

"To tell the truth, Carter, I feel lucky not to be sitting in some stinking cell in one of their prisons, wondering whether or not I'll ever get out. I certainly couldn't expect any help from the French government. They want nothing to do with my case or me. Maybe this is best."

"You seem to be taking all of this philosophically. Why?"

"I'm tired. I'm going to take what I have and go to France. I can lose myself in Paris. Who knows? I may even go back to Montpelier. At any rate, I need to be some place where there's city life. You know what I mean?"

"When do you have to be out of the country?"

"Four days."

During the next four days they avoided Jean Paul. They did not venture to Aghi Vasili or the club and were careful not to be seen with him. Everyone suspected he would be under almost constant surveillance until he was out of the country and they did not want to be included in the web of suspicion surrounding him.

Every evening they managed to meet in secret, however, planning their next move, the ultimate move, designed to make both of them independently wealthy, able to go anywhere, do anything their hearts desired.

Jean Paul changed his immediate destination to Switzerland. Carter gave Karine money to buy a ticket for herself on the *Keftiu*. She would leave the same evening as Jean Paul. From Athens they would both fly directly to Zürich, the statue in Karine's possession, and pay a visit to Herr Katz. From Zürich Karine would return to Paris with Carter's portion of the money, and await his arrival at her parent's house.

Jean Paul was not sure exactly where he would go from Switzerland. He said he would make that decision in due time.

Their plan seemed so simple and foolproof. Both of them were convinced it would work. Neither could see how it could go wrong.

The day of their departure dawned unusually warm for that time of year with uncomfortably high humidity making clothing stick to sweating bodies. Carter and Karine left together, taking a valise containing a few clothes and the statue. They felt the only danger would be in passing through customs in the Athens airport. As an added precaution, they went shopping the previous day in one of the tourist oriented souvenir shops. There they bought a cheap copy of one of the Mycenaean treasures, removed the wire from it containing the lead seal denoting the piece was only a copy and attached it to the statue. If by chance she were stopped, this little artifice might serve to completely allay any suspicions. In their estimation no precaution was too trivial to exercise.

The last afternoon Karine and Carter stopped off at the Miramare Cafe to have a drink before the *Keftiu* sailed. As always, Rodula rushed to greet them while Theodoro smiled from behind the glass fronted display cases where he busily prepared fish. When they learned Karine was leaving they insisted on her eating something. The more she tried to refuse the more the older couple ignored her protestations. Rodula busied herself preparing little treats, which she brought to their table one at a time. Each time she stood beside them until they both tasted and expressed suitable satisfaction over the new offering.

When they finally left Rodula followed them to the door and slipped a small package into Karine's knit shoulder bag. "Don't even open it until you get on the boat. It's just a little something for tonight before you go to bed. Now, get out of here! You don't want to miss your boat!" They both laughed, hugged her, waved to Theodoro and walked out the door.

As they went aboard the *Keftiu* he looked around trying to spot Jean Paul, but did not see him anywhere. Carter went with her to her cabin in First Class to make sure everything was in order and that she would be comfortable. They knew Jean Paul purchased Second Class accommodations and would avoid making contact with Karine until their Swissair flight left Greek airspace. After that, they would be free to do as they wished.

The announcement for all non passengers to disembark sounded over the public address system and Carter took Karine in his arms one last time. This was not really a goodbye, for she would be returning within a week at the most. It was more of a bon voyage, a wish for a good trip, and a final word of caution. He kissed her one more time before turning to make his way down the deck.

He took only a few steps when he stopped and turned to face her. There was an expression on his face she could not fully read and it puzzled her. What puzzled her even more was when he walked back toward her.

"Cheri, qu'est-ce qui se passe?"

"I've been thinking. After we get all these affairs taken care of and meet in Paris, what would you think of...uh, maybe, uh....?"

She looked at him, trying to anticipate his words. When they did not come she reached out and took his hands in hers, trying to will him to finish his thought.

"Quoi? What in the world are you trying to say?"

"It's really very simple. I think I may follow you directly to Zürich and meet you there. I was thinking. If you agree, we could rent a car and drive from Zürich to Vienna."

"That sounds wonderful! Oh, yes, Vienna! And what would we do in Vienna?"

"Well, we might get married. We could go to the American Embassy and...."

She squealed and threw herself into his arms, cutting off the rest of his statement. She kissed his neck, his cheeks, his nose, his eyes, chin and finally his lips, giving resounding affirmation to his suggestion. The final call for all non passengers to go ashore sounded and he held her away from him and looked into her eyes.

"Does this mean you'll think about it?"

"No, it means yes! Yes! Yes! YES!!"

"I can't tell you how happy this makes me. I've got to run, but I'll call you tomorrow afternoon at the hotel. I just want to know you've arrived safely. If I don't get off now this *sacré* barge is going to leave with me on it. Have a good trip. *Je t'aime de tout mon coeur.*"

With these final words he rushed from the First Class deck. He passed through the hold, where the crew was tying down the last of several large trucks loaded with tons and tons of oranges and then proceeded down the gangplank to the quay. As soon as he was ashore he looked up for Karine and found her immediately. They waved to one another while the huge side door in the hull was closed and the gangplank removed.

Even from this distance he could see tears glistening on her cheeks. Out of the corner of his eye he saw the figure of Jean Paul leaning on the railing of the Second Class deck. He glanced at him, nodded his head and received a slight nod in return. The boat's screws began to turn and it moved slowly away from the quay. Carter waved to Karine as long as he could see her. When he could no longer make out her form he returned to the Miramare, mounted his motorbike and headed for home.

In spite of the day's unseasonable warmth the weather was the harbinger of long-awaited change. Endless dry days of summer gave way to clouds building over the mountains. There were already hints of rain, with an occasional mist blowing onto land off the sea to the north. The water, almost body temperature in July and August, now took on a chill. It was not unpleasant, just refreshing. The dusty brown of the land itself was relieved only by the eternal green of the olive orchards, vineyards and citrus trees.

Riding out of the city he noticed again the unusual humidity and oppressive - almost uneasy - atmosphere. Even riding on his motorbike the air blowing across the handlebars and into his face did not refresh. Sweat glued his shirt to his back and stained his armpits.

As he rode along the road above the sea he noticed the color of the water. Close to shore it was normally clear blue above the sandy bottom, changing to a dark blue-green as it dropped off into the depths. Now it was roiled and gray with none of the sparkling highlights tourists associated with the summer season. Out over Dia and Paximadi and all along the northern horizon clouds intensified and darkened. The wind was fitful, blowing first this way and then that. It was not blowing hard. Rather, it was uncertain, like an animal of prey searching for a scent, looking for a path to follow.

Turning off the pavement toward his house he carefully crossed the shallow ditch between the road and the edge of the fields and then, giving the throttle a small nudge, rode along the top of the narrow dike separating the sere remains of fields of rye and tomatoes. He had taken this path along the dike so many times he could even negotiate it in the dark, merely following the faint luminescence of the eight inch wide strip of bare earth.

As he approached the house a sudden flurry of activity erupted from the front verandah. A black and white bundle of energy rushed up the dike to greet his arrival as she always did. Still half-wild, Skilí threw herself up the path towards him, her tail streaming behind her as she advanced, each bound punctuated by her song of excitement. He and Karine were the only ones she permitted to touch her or to gain her confidence. He befriended her, protected her from stone throwing peasants and sometimes gained their enmity in the process.

He acknowledged her greeting, but only perfunctorily. His lack of enthusiasm did nothing to dampen her wildly ecstatic dance. She continued to follow him insistently as he dismounted in front of the house and put his motorbike up onto the verandah. Finally kneeling and allowing the dog to leap up onto his leg, he swept her into a tight embrace. This was what she awaited since he and Karine left earlier in the day.

He walked with her to the back of the house and sat on the veranda. Their attention was drawn to the sea where, from miles away came the low ominous rumbling of thunder. Clouds continued to build fed by the moisture of the sea and sparked away to the north. There was no immediate sound. Moments later there was yet another spark, this time longer and more well-defined. After what seemed an interminable wait, came the bass undertone that could be felt more than heard. At the same instant the dark green leaves of the olive trees standing between his house and the sea began to show their undersides in flashes of silver as the wind suddenly increased.

Fields, which shortly before were devoid of human life, now began to show signs of activity. Graceful, picturesque windmills, cloth sails attached to each of the eight arms, began to pick up speed. The fitful wind became more intense and directed, no longer variable. It finally determined its course and blew with increasing authority from the sea. Of the thirty or more windmills Carter could see from his seaward facing verandah, only four or five still turned. Sails of the others were tightly wrapped around individual spokes and the spokes immobilized by tying one of them to the base of the windmill. Of the ones that still turned, he could see peasants hurrying to batten down for the coming blow.

Several hundred feet from his house, near a line of olive and lemon trees, grazed a small flock of sheep. One ray of late afternoon sunlight pierced the clouds spotlighting them. Against the dark of the trees and the dark of the building storm they stood out marvelously white. It was apparent, however, that the impending tempest made them nervous. They began to mill, their movements fraught with indecision.

At that very moment a blast came from the heavens, stunning the universe. As if by magic, two old women, dressed in black from head to toe, hurried from the lee of his house. They scurried as fast as they could toward the flock of sheep, threading their way through the low grapevines, the wind striking and pulling at them. Their voices, high pitched and carrying a note of hysteria were snatched up by the wind and carried back to where Carter stood. Long black dresses and shawls blowing in the wind made them appear as two coal black crows with broken wings running along the uneven ground. Their ululations grew fainter and fainter, but were still audible in spite of the steadily increasing wind.

And then they were gone: the crows and the sheep and the peasants furling the sails of their windmills like sailors on the deck of a ship. There was no one except him, and the wind, and the clouds, and the lightning.

Great jagged bolts of lightning linked the clouds and the sea. Waves rose and threatened the little Orthodox church of Aghios Stephanos, situated right at the edge of the sea on a rocky promontory, with inundation. The one room chapel looked particularly tiny and vulnerable. On three sides waves smashed into rocks, spouting and thundering high above the curved roof.

For the first time he experienced the sea in this mood. He lived beside her for over a year, but never dreamed she could be so angry. He recalled Homer writing of the 'wine dark sea'. Who could imagine a sea the color of rich, dark Greek wine? But it was true. Today it resembled the dark red tones of Mavro Daphne.

The storm built in fury. Lightning struck all about. Trees closest to the beach were whipped to and fro, brushing the luring sky with frenetic strokes. Carter's house, built of whitewashed stuccoed cinder blocks, trembled before its violence. Although the shutters were tightly fastened and the windows locked, the fury of the storm blew rainwater through the minutest cracks, forming puddles under the windows on the floor tiles.

The tempest continued for almost two hours. Then, as suddenly as it began, it was over. The balance of the night was relatively calm. Carter's feeling of unease remained, however, and did not ease. Nothing seemed able to dispel the disturbing aura that pervaded his subconscious.

Early the next morning, in the watery light of dawn that often follows a tempest of such magnitude, he left his house. As he often did, he rode into town to Theodoro and Rodula's cafe for morning coffee. A group of fishermen gathered around one of the tables discussed the previous evening in hushed, almost reverent tones. As he joined them he became aware of the cause for his feelings of dread.

According to the fishermen, during the night at the height of the *meltemi,* one of these fabled and dreaded storms that sweep periodically across the Mediterranean from the north; storms of such ferocity that, when they strike, ships are warned not to sail from the great port of Piraeus. The previous evening's gigantic seas besieged the ferryboat Keftiu, fully loaded with passengers and cargo. Enormous trucks, loaded with produce, such as oranges destined for the markets of Athens and other European cities, broke loose in the cargo deck of the ship. At least one battered repeatedly against the giant loading door before finally succeeding in smashing it open. As the bottom of the opening was only a meter above the water line, the raging sea poured in unchecked. Within minutes the vessel foundered and went down, taking with it an undetermined number of passengers and crew to watery graves. Optimistic guesses put the number lost at approximately 450 persons. Those fortunate enough to be rescued told of stark terror on the dark and stormy sea. One of the first to be pulled to safety was the ship's captain, Thallasos Kastronis.

Upon hearing the news Carter felt as if someone punched him in the stomach with a giant fist. He found it difficult to breathe and struggled to control himself. When Theodoro passed his table Carter reached out and laid his hand on his arm, stopped him and asked him to sit down for a moment. He plied him with questions about the news, but was unable to learn any more than the other men already told him. Disconsolate, but with the faint hope that Karine and Jean Paul would be among those who swam or floated to safety, he stood and walked away as if in a dream.

All day he tried to stay abreast of the latest developments by listening to the radio and going to the office of the ferry lines. He placed a call to the Chargé d'Affaires at the French Embassy in Athens, whom he met at the embassy Christmas party the previous year, trying to find out what he knew of any survivors. Embassies would be informed of any survivors or bodies from among their countrymen and the Chargé promised he would call him at the institute as soon as he heard anything at all.

He next called Karine's mother. She was not aware her daughter sailed on the *Keftiu,* not even aware she was making a trip to Zürich. Everything happened so quickly between the time of the trial and the final resolution that Karine did not take the time to advise her mother of her plans. Madame de Châtillon was devastated and wanted to leave immediately for Greece. Carter persuaded her to remain in Paris, telling her he would let her know as soon as he found out something.

Three days later the government suspended search by air and sea. This final blow was almost more than Carter could stand. In an instant he lost the love of his life and his closest friend.

The loss of the statue was incidental. Since taking possession of it he always regarded it as the equivalent of 'found money'. If it were lost or confiscated, he rationalized, he would not really be out anything as it came into his possession by chance.

One week to the day following the accident he met the Olympic flight from Athens. Madame de Châtillon, who insisted she come collect Karine's affairs, hugged him as if he were her own son and sobbed on his shoulder. He tried to comfort her as best he could, but his own pain was too acute. During her two days with him they talked endless hours, long into the night, of his and Karine's plans. Her mother was not even aware of their marriage plans, for they talked of it too late for Karine to call before her departure.

He accompanied her to the airport the day she left. Before boarding her flight she turned to him and placed her palm tenderly on his cheek. "Please remember, *mon cher* Carter, you will always be welcome in our home. It would have been your home too, had things not gone awry."

Her eyes filled with tears and, unable to say more, she squeezed his hand and turned to walk to the plane.

Epilogue

Carter's world lay crumbled and strewn across the rocky soil of Crete like the shards of Minos' kingdom. A future of enormous promise was reduced to ashes in a flash. Days passed, perceived dimly through a film of deep, personal, inconsolable pain. Nothing could lift him from the dark pit of depression and self-pity in which he wallowed.

Friends came to convey their empathy, offering the inane words of all who profess understanding of such catastrophic events. But, he would not be consoled. He found himself wandering his old haunts, often at night when others were long since at home in bed. He walked the cobbled lanes of Aghi Vasili, stopping in the shadows to gaze forlornly at the dark outline of the villa. Several times, when wandering the worn historic stones of the harbor, he got as far as the steps of the Miramare only to turn around and walk away again. For him the sounds from the Club Fez, now called the Club Kritikós, were a mockery to the memory of Jean Paul. Everywhere he went, everything he saw or touched reminded him of Karine or Jean Paul and all he lost. He was unable to concentrate enough to conduct his classes. When Bunny insisted he take time away from the institute, he agreed. After a week he knew he could never return.

An evening spent with Andreas and a bottle of cognac, although meant to console, only deepened his depression. After several hours of drinking and talking Andreas finally told him everything that happened with Barba Yorgi and the men from the tomb. He told of the telltale footprints found outside Zakari's house and of his and Deaf Yanni's fear that an ominous fate awaited them as well.

Carter rode to Amnisos and stared for hours out to sea from the hilltop. Sitting amid the low ruins covering its crown he began to realize the meaning of the legacy of the golden statue and the rest of the objects found in the tomb.

The discovery of the tomb was indeed the opening of Pandora's Box. The real legacy consisted of greed and pain and heartache - and death.

He felt his bitterness could never be assuaged. His only recourse, as he saw it, would be to leave Crete, remove himself as far away as possible. The island had been both home and crucible. He was not the same person who arrived sixteen months earlier. In truth, he arrived as an innocent abroad. He would survive this tragedy, but what would be the nature of the survivor.

Closing the house entailed sending a month's rent to Dr. Themides and making arrangements to have Andreas' furniture returned to the warehouse. The artifacts that remained in his possession he buried at the edge of a field in an area that did not risk being disturbed by cultivation.

To protect his faithful little Skilí from unnecessary suffering, he visited a veterinarian who put her down. She would not have understood his leaving and would have waited forever at the house for his return, protecting it as she always did. The peasants would have eventually killed her, probably by stoning her to death. After much deliberation he felt his decision was the only humane solution. He buried her on a cool, blustery day in the same location as the artifacts with a final, tearful admonition to keep perpetual watch.

His final two days on Crete were spent anonymously in a hotel in town, avoiding contact with everyone he knew.

The day he left, Carter traveled one last time from Crete to Athens. As he flew over the blue waters of the Mediterranean, the airplane passed over the grave of the *Keftiu*. The epitaph to the night of the storm was an oil slick visible on the calm water. In the middle of the lengthy slick, bright against its rainbow-hued background, floated a long line of bobbing oranges.

ΤΕΛΟΣ

www.ingramcontent.com/pod-product-compliance
Lightning Source LLC
Chambersburg PA
CBHW071151250626
47159CB00001B/58